God's Love Most Gentle

God's Love Most Gentle

When a pregnant widow returns from the mission field she harbors a secret that may lead to her spiritual downfall.

ISBN-13: 978-1515284802 (CreateSpace-Assigned)
ISBN-10: 1515284808

Catalog: 1. Christian Fiction 2. Grief – fiction 3. Second chances – fiction 4. Family – fiction 5. Relationships – fiction.

God's Love Most Gentle is entirely a work of fiction. The names, characters and incidents portrayed in it are the work of the author's imagination. Any resemblance to actual persons, living or dead, events or localities is entirely coincidental.

Cover - Danielle Thorp of Virtual Felicity

Acknowledgments

Thanks Janene Grace, Tari Britton, and Joanna Politano for your valuable suggestions and to Danielle Thorp for helping me polish the final copy, develop the cover, and for giving me a tremendous boost of confidence to finish the project by being so enthusiastic about the story.

For those who believed in me when my heart was tattered and to Jesus, who never casts me aside, but creates in me a clean heart and renews a right spirit in me, each time I ask.

God's Love Most Gentle

Mary Marie Allen

Mary Marie Allen
2016

You can't heal a wound by denying it exists. Jeremiah 6:14

Chapter One - Kim

February 14, 1995

Kim Macomb jostled and bounced around the back seat of the jeep. The African sun, like a ton weight, threatened to press her as flat as the grassland. Wind whipped dark silky strands from her thick braid. She tucked them behind her ear, but it only took a moment for them to whip free again.

In the front seat, her husband gestured as he discussed the future of Zaire with the driver. Kim was grateful that most of their discussion was drowned out by the engine's drone. She was too miserable to care about anyone else's future. It was all they'd talked about since leaving the airport moments before the militia shut it down. Like a surreal scene from a 3-D hero movie there'd been people screaming, scrambling, gunfire, yet the three of them escaped unscathed. How did she get here, anyway?

Kurt turned to her and grinned. Her heart leaped in her chest and she smiled back. Beneath the brim of a khaki hat his blue eyes twinkled with excitement. His pale skin, the blight of red-haired people, already showed signs of sunburn. "Hang on. Things are about to get interesting," he shouted. They slowed and veered off the highway, bumping along deep ruts that sliced through dense jungle.

Every jolt felt like the start of a new bruise. Occasionally Kurt glanced back to check on her, his excitement at realizing his dream never dimming. She closed her eyes and lapsed into a weary stupor until the jeep lurched to a stop. The engine's drone was replaced by the buzzing of a fat fly circling her head. She swatted at it and sat up. "What's wrong?"

"There's a tree blocking the path." Kurt pointed. The dirt lane looked like a thin brown belt cinching tall grasses that spread right and left into a full garment of brush and trees. One large tree with leaves dried and brown lie directly across the road.

"I've got a chain we can use to move it," Uzachi said. His Bostonian accent surprising her again. In a loose white shirt and shorts, Uzachi looked as if he belonged to the land, yet he was decidedly American. "Reverend Macomb, would you give me a hand?" Kurt jumped out the passenger side while Uzachi unfolded his frame from behind the steering wheel and went to rummage through the luggage in the back of the jeep. He said, "Wouldn't you know? It's on the bottom of the heap. This'll take a while. You may as well get out and stretch, Mrs. Macomb, but stay close."

Kim hunched her shoulders and threw her hands out, palms up. "Where would I go?"

Uzachi flashed a brilliantly white smile and offered her a hand the color and softness of a well-used baseball glove. Once she was on the ground, he towered over her. He was maybe eight inches taller, while she and Kurt both stood five-five. He returned to the rear, handing bags and boxes to Kurt to stack on the ground.

Kim stretched stiffness away and rubbed at the sore spots on her lean body. Clutching for a hold during the rough ride hadn't doing her manicure any good. She picked at a chip in the red lacquer on her left thumbnail. She smoothed wrinkles from her pretty pink shirt and tan trousers. Perhaps not the most practical of outfits, but just because she was going to the jungle didn't mean she had to dress ugly. Kurt glanced her way, grinned and winked. She smiled back, knowing he appreciated how she looked.

She wandered toward the obstruction. A path of beaten grass skirted the downed tree and some branches had been stripped away. She scrambled on top of the horizontal trunk, wobbling a bit before balance beam training took over. Everything looked better from up there. She stepped the length of it and back, performing a routine she'd used years before in high school competition.

"Kim," Kurt said. His low tone held a warning.

"Don't worry. I won't fall." One foot poised in midair, she leaned back and held the position so he could marvel at her dexterity. Kim tipped her head back in triumph and looked to him for admiration. His face was tight. Beside him, Uzachi stood motionless, whitened knuckles clutching the winching chain. Each man's gaze was not quite on her, but a few feet to the front.

A thick brown vine hung strangely. She righted herself for a better view. A snake, rising vertically from the tree trunk, was almost as tall as she was. Beady eyes fixed on her. Its smooth, ear-less head flattened. Its mouth stretched wide baring fangs, hissing. Kim flipped backward and landed on the ground. *Thwack!* The chain rattled and slid off the tree. The snake dropped and was a blur of dark brown escaping through the yellow sun-burnt grass.

She stumbled forward. Kurt caught her and dragged her by the armpits to the jeep. He crushed her to his chest. He was speaking, but Kim couldn't understand between the pounding of blood in her ears and the thumping of his heart. The jelly in her legs became bone again as she pushed away from him like a chick popping out of a nest. "Let me breathe."

Kurt's normally ruddy face was ashen and his hands trembled. "Don't ever do that again. Ever…"

She stammered, "What was that thing?"

Uzachi had collapsed against the hood of the jeep. Large beads of sweat glistened over the strained grimace lines of his black face as both hands cradled his shaven head. "That was a black mamba."

"It was huge—"

"Nine feet or more." Uzachi dropped his hands.

"—and fast."

"Faster than a man can run and deadly. Thank God you're safe."

Kurt squeezed her arms and shook her, claiming her attention. "Princess, you can't go climbing about the trees without checking for snakes. Didn't you read the book I gave you?"

Kim squinted at the chain that lay in the grass. She'd been meaning to read that book. With college finals, bridal showers, the wedding, the honeymoon, the trip across the ocean, language training, and the excitement of finally arriving, she hadn't found time. "God sure guided your aim, Uzachi. It was perfect."

Uzachi's laughter boomed. "How about you? What a gymnast. I'd give that dismount a ten."

Kurt hugged her and his grip felt less like he wanted to shake sense into her and more like he was proud and happy she was alive. "That's my wife."

"Mrs. Macomb, you must always watch for snakes. The village would never forgive me if I lost you before you even get there," Uzachi said.

Kim shivered despite the oppressive heat. "I'll be more careful."

After moving the tree, they reloaded the jeep and drove until nearly dark. Right beside the dirt road, Uzachi started the fire while Kurt pitched two tents. Kim unpacked the food, eyeing every movement real or imagined in the nearby bushes.

With supper and cleanup completed the men stretched out on opposite sides of the fire and stared into the snapping, crackling flames. Orange sparks danced upward before winking out. Kim stood nearby gazing heavenward. "It's stunning. It's like sparkling diamonds on a black velvet canvas."

"Yes. I never saw a sky like this in Boston," Uzachi said.

"How did you get from here to there and back again, Uzachi?"

"My family moved away from the village when I was a small boy. My father became a merchant in the capital, saved money, and with the help of his brother who already lived in Boston, we went there. He was a very successful businessman. His dream was that I become a doctor. When my father died during my second year of medical school my mother told me to do what I felt I should do, so I came back to the village to help."

Kim sat on the ground beside Kurt. "And your mother?"

"My mother stayed with my uncle and aunt. She didn't think she'd adjust to the harsh village life after years of ease in America. When I see so much poverty, ignorance, and political trouble, the need compels me to teach. When I see the ailments and struggles of the people, I think I should become a doctor like my father wanted.

I'm torn, but even more necessary is spiritual healing. That's why I asked for a missionary."

"What about a family for yourself?"

Uzachi's wide grin gleamed across the flames. "That's a question every aunt, mother, and single woman would like me to answer. Of course I'd like a family someday. For now, I'll keep doing what I'm doing and leave that in God's hands."

Kurt rose, dusted his pants and picked up a lantern. "Good plan. It's been a long day. I'm positive God's plan for me right this moment is to go to bed. Good night."

"I'll watch the fire die down," Uzachi said. "Good night, Pastor and Mrs. Macomb."

Kurt said, "Coming, Kim?"

She'd dozed during the day and didn't want to go to bed, but she couldn't very well stay alone by the fire with a strange man. Kim sighed and followed.

The lantern caused crazy shadows to dance against the tent walls as Kurt removed his boots, long sleeve shirt and pants. Despite the sunscreen he'd used, his neck and chin and hands were bright red. "Uzachi is a great guy. You know how sometimes you simply connect with someone? It's like we always knew each other. I think we're going to make a great team. Don't you?"

"Mm-hm."

His square face softened and he fumbled with one of the bags and extracted a red envelope. "For you. I know it's been crazy, but I'd never forget my beautiful, brown-eyed girl on our special day."

Kim sliced the envelope open with a well-shaped nail and read the valentine. She said, "Oh Kurt, it's beautiful. I'm so lucky to have you for a husband."

"I know."

She tapped him with the card. "I don't know if your smugness is endearing or exasperating."

"Endearing, of course."

"Yes, it is." She ran her fingers through his reddish-blond hair, just one of the many things she loved about him. All day they'd been separated by the noise of travel. It'd be good to simply chat for a bit. She fluffed her pillow and lay on her side.

He lowered the flame and the kerosene lantern hissed softly as its light faded. Kurt kissed her and lay on his back. "Good night. Isn't Zaire wonderful?"

Kim pressed his valentine to her chest and envisioned the mamba rising like an armless alien. Ominous sounds like the breathing of evil Darth Vader oozed from the black jungle. It didn't help to think the noises were tree frogs, huge insects, and shrieking nocturnal monkeys. "Wonderful," she said. There was no reply to her sarcasm. Kurt was already asleep. Kim's tears flowed until exhaustion claimed her.

In the morning, they broke camp and after two more grueling days similar to the first, the village came into view. It was much larger than the villages they'd passed. Children swarmed in noisy welcome. Women in printed cotton dresses with scarves about their heads and men in pants or shorts left their activities to stand behind the chief, a spindly man in a grass skirt, feathers, beads, and suit coat. He brandished a large intricately carved stick as he issued a formal greeting.

Uzachi said, "The chief welcomes you. There will be a feast tonight in your honor. For now, he wants me to show you to your home where you can wash up and rest." He led them down a hard-packed dirt path. The villagers followed.

In a quarter of a mile they came to a clearing. A huge banana tree shaded a faded gray wood structure with a small generator Further back sat a privy. Several men jabbered and pointed out the house's features. Three rooms with wood flooring. A propane stove, hand-worked pump, some shelves and a table made up the main room. A ham radio and a bed occupied another tiny room to the rear while a bed, chest of drawers and a chest were in another.

Kim tried to pay attention, but she longed to wash away the filth of the road and collapse on a normal bed. Kurt talked on and on. Finally the people headed back toward the village. Only Uzachi and a young girl remained.

He smiled with obvious affection at the child. "This is Nsia, a cousin to my mother's sister-in-law. It would be a great favor to me if you would let her cook and clean for you. She speaks French and wants to improve her English. She's very smart and may one day go to university. She, can help you learn the local language and the culture."

Kim replied, "She's what, nine? Isn't that a little young?"

"Nsia is fifteen."

"I work very hard." The stick-thin girl cast shy yet hopeful glances at her.

"I don't know." Kim touched her lips doubtfully.

"I help much. Learn much. You will see, Mrs. Kim. Yes?" One hand clutched the fabric of her orange flowered dress in an anxious gesture.

Kim took in the intelligent eyes, confident exuberance and was charmed. "Yes."

Nsia clapped her hands with pleasure. "That is good."

Uzachi said, "Come, Nsia. We'll let Pastor and Mrs. Macomb rest. After dinner, we'll bring your belongings here."

"Bye. Bye. See you later." Nsia waved until she was out of sight.

Kurt jabbered about the men he'd met and plans for his new congregation as he worked the kitchen pump. He handed her the basin of water. "This should be enough to take a sponge bath."

Kim clutched the pan to her chest. "Thank you."

"This is home for the next three years."

"Hmm."

A frown quashed excitement from his face. "What's the matter?"

Kim bit back her annoyance and crammed down the shrewish scream that she wanted to go home. She set down the pan of water. "Everything is so different. It's scary and so blasted hot."

"Come here." He tucked her close against him. The solid strength of him comforted her and worries slipped away as he put a positive, even funny, spin on their adventures. He said, "I'll wash the dirt off you, if you'll wash the dirt off me." Kim giggled.

She ached all over. Weariness caused even her eyelids to hurt. In a sleep fog, her mouth felt cotton-thick. She licked her lips without moistening them. "Kurt? You left the TV on again." When there was no reply, she listened harder for the steady breath, breath, wuffle that had marked his sleeping presence during the few weeks of married life.

The TV voices of a French program laughed, making comments about her as if she'd said something funny. Unwilling to part from sleep, she let her hand wander over the mattress. "Honey, turn the light out and come back to bed." Voices again laughed softly, talking about her.

"Good morning, Mrs. Kim," came a chipper voice. A chorus of odd sounding "good mornings" echoed.

Kim cracked one eye open. An assortment of village women and children stood around while others sat cross-legged on the floor or peered through the open window. Kim blinked, rubbed her temple, and propped herself on one elbow, careful to hold the sheet against her nakedness. Africa. She was in Zaire, Africa somewhere in the jungle.

There had been a welcoming feast in the thatched pavilion the night before. Some of these same ladies had served her bananas and rice and palm wine and encouraged her to eat from bowls of mixtures that included peanuts, yams, cassava. She remembered sitting stiffly on the ground, smiling, thanking them even as she sniffed everything before tasting it. The festivities went late into the night with children singing and each of the important men giving a speech. She wondered if the palm wine from the feast contributed to her fuzzy state.

Kim focused on the child who spoke. Nsia. She shook her head to clear the cobwebs from her brain and pushed into a seated position. Her voice cracked. "Nsia, why is everyone in my bedroom?"

Nsia spoke in both French and her native language, evidently relaying Kim's words to the others before answering the questions.

"We never had a princess in our village before. We wish to welcome you on your first morning."

"What princess?"

Nsia giggled. "You."

Kim shook her head again and blinked, rubbing the nighttime crust off her eyelashes. "You're mistaken. I'm not a princess."

Nsia conveyed her words and the others all nodded, smiled, and nudged each other. Several spoke in soothing tones. "We will keep your secret."

"What secret?"

"That you are a princess."

"I'm not a princess." Kim struggled to stay civil despite a definite grumpiness at this nonsensical conversation so early in the morning before coffee.

Nsia spoke in halting English without conferring with the others. "Your husband told me. I fixed breakfast for Pastor Kurt. He said, 'Let the princess sleep. Be sure the coffee is ready when she wakes."

Kim fell back on the bed and laughed. Finally, she sat up and said, "I am not a real princess. It's my husband's special name for me, like *ma cherie*."

Nsia relayed this and the ladies covered their mouths in amusement, while the small children laughed out loud. A lady came through the doorway carrying a tray. Nsia said, "This is Mrs. Thema. She is important lady here. She is honored to bring you first coffee."

Kim smiled at the woman and thanked her. The woman gestured that Kim should drink up. Everyone seemed unnervingly interested as she swallowed so she said, "Ahh! That's good." Chattering broke out among the visitors and Mrs. Thema grinned broadly, exposing several gaps among her teeth. Kim set the cup down and moved the tray beside her. She gestured to Nsia, "Could you please ask everybody to leave? I need to get dressed."

It took a bit of doing, before Nsia could herd them out the door. Kim kept gesturing to those peering in at the window, asking them to leave as she struggled to stay covered while drawing on a

9

thin cotton housecoat. Finally, she swung her feet to the floor and made a dash for the door, dodging between stragglers on the porch.

Mrs. Thema announced in French, "Even a princess must make water." Everyone hooted with laughter as she ran.

When she returned, the women and children crowded back through the door after her. Nsia was busy cutting a melon and the toothless old woman had set the coffee on the old table and gestured for Kim to sit.

"Thank you, but I'll dress first." Kim darted into the bedroom and closed the door with a sigh. Choosing a pink sun dress from her duffle, she went to a corner where someone would have to poke their head far through the window to see her. Perspiration beaded her upper lip. Her long dark mane was like a fur stole on her shoulders. She twisted it up and secured it with a band before returning to the kitchen. "Where's Pastor Kurt?"

"He went with Mr. Uzachi to the village."

"When will he return?"

"He will be back for lunch soon. You sleep a long time."

"I feel like a truck hit me. I'm bruised and sore all over from that ride."

Every time she spoke Nsia repeated everything in the local language like a confused echo.

One woman plucked at the ruffled eyelet on her sundress. Another fingered its material while a third murmured as she stroked her pony tail. Children stretched fingers to touch her fingernail polish. Kim gulped coffee and prayed for God to help her be polite when what she wanted was to tell them all to go away and leave her alone.

Who were her people? Where did she come from? How did she meet Pastor Kurt? She didn't stop answering questions until Kurt burst in the door. "Well look at you. Aren't you popular? Hello, ladies."

The women rose, greeted him, and left giggling. Kim dropped her face in her hands and massaged sore smile muscles.

"It's great that you're getting on with the village women," Kurt said.

"They're nice, but thanks to you, they think I'm royalty. I tried to explain, but going to college and feeding enough wedding guests to populate three large villages only proved it to them."

"Well, it can't hurt our status any." Kurt laughed and put his arm lightly over her shoulders. Monkeys chattered in the banana tree and the smell of hot dust wafted in with a breeze as he said, "Come on, Princess. I've got loads to tell you."

Kim listened with interest as they walked along the path toward the village. He was so happy, so excited. She didn't like roughing it, but overall, she'd been silly to worry. Kurt was here. What could go wrong?

Chapter Two - Carol

Carol glanced up from Kim's letter as her best friend, Trudy, plopped into the chair beside her. "Kim said to tell you hi."

"How is she?" Trudy's smooth, caramel-courtesy-of- the-tanning-bed skin appeared washed out in the fluorescent lights of the drugstore.

Carol shook the bulky missive before cramming it into the depths of her cavernous purse. "How would I know? This is so old, anything could happen and I wouldn't know for half a year."

"I'll interpret that to mean Kim is fine, but you miss your daughter."

"I don't think she likes it there. I think she wants to come home."

"And leave Kurt? That'll never happen. You're just cranky."

Carol scratched her left hip and muttered, "I'd give anything if I could unzip my skin and hang it up until this poison ivy runs its course."

Trudy's ginger-brown curls bounced as she laughed. "Wouldn't that be something? I can see it hanging on the clothes line, flapping in the wind, scaring little kids in the neighborhood. If you figure out how to do that, I want in on the patent."

"At least I have ready access to medication. I don't know how Kim stands it. Three days to drive to town. No phone. No TV. Only a ham radio for emergencies."

"It'll be good for her. She'll grow up. She's been spoiled."

"I suppose you're right. Her father did treat her like a princess. Evidently, Kurt does too." Carol pulled the letter out and read. "The villagers think I ran away with the servant boy because he treats me so well. Yesterday before he left for a nearby village, he ran back to kiss me. The men laughed at him, but he didn't care and it made me feel very special. They act like children who groan when their parents kiss, yet are secretly pleased. Half the village women are in love with him and the other half want him as a son-in-law. As usual, everybody loves Kurt."

Trudy laughed. "Yep. That's Kurt."

Smiling, Carol continued reading. "Kurt acts like he's lived in the village all his life while I lack basic understanding of ordinary chores, customs, and survival. They insist I was raised in a palace. Compared to the way they live, it's close to the truth. They have equal parts contempt for my abilities and awe for my clothes, mannerisms, and speech. They were fascinated by my nail polish. I only brought one bottle. We finished it in short order when I painted all the ladies' nails one day. It was fun."

Carol paused as they pictured that scene. Trudy said, "Spoiled, but generous. What else does she say?"

"She's become a morning person because the afternoon heat is so terrible."

"That I'd like to see."

"Uzachi's young relative, Nsia, pampers her by insisting on fixing breakfast while she and Kurt pray and have devotions."

"I bet she loves that." Trudy leaned over and read aloud. "Nsia reminds me of cousin Jasmine, always asking a million questions. I'm less homesick with her around. Every morning Nsia and I do lessons on the porch where the breeze is cooler and there's extra shade from the banana tree. There's an old iron chain buried beneath the tree. They say it makes the tree bear lots of fruit. Who knew? Other ladies have joined us, eager to learn. We can't all fit on the porch anymore for lessons, so they cluster under the banana tree while the children play nearby. The classes have cemented my usefulness in their eyes. They do their lessons in the dirt with sticks and don't think anything about it."

"Hey." Carol folded the letter up. "If you read it, then I can't share it with you."

"Then share already."

"She's teaching Sunday school to the children, but is fascinated by the teens like Nsia who seem older and wiser than she."

Trudy shrugged and her curls bounced. "It's a different world. They grow up fast."

Carol nodded. "Kurt led the chief's son to the Lord so more men are interested. They have to build a bigger meeting place."

Trudy's brows shot up. "Wow. They are growing fast."

Carol touched Trudy's arm. "Listen to this written the end of April. Today during lessons I saw a green snake near a baby under the banana tree. There weren't any men around, so I grabbed a shovel and chopped it in two just like Dad did to that garter when I was ten. The women shrieked and carried on for quite a while before I learned it was a black mamba, not a garter. It's the inside of the mouth that gives a mamba its name, not its skin. I nearly fainted. Now, I'm the local hero. I'm not sure I'd have been brave enough to save the baby if I'd known. I must have been out of my mind to come to this wild, infested place."

Trudy and Carol both shivered. Carol said, "She adds 'Just joking', but she isn't."

Trudy patted Carol's arm. "She's okay."

"Really? Because I have this nagging feeling. The last entry was May 3rd. The men were headed for the capital for supplies, that's when this was mailed. Kurt wouldn't let her go because of the conflict. How can war be safe?"

A professional-sounding voice announced, "Carol Streeter."

Carol gave her arm a quick scratch and stepped to the counter. A tall man, about her age, in the pharmacist's coat had a pleasant smile. "Carol Streeter? Identification, please."

"Dr. Blair didn't say this was a restricted drug."

"Not restricted. Updating info. New computer."

"Oh. Uh, sure." She dug through her purse and produced a driver's license.

He scrutinized it and her. "Blonde hair. Nice blue eyes. Five one. Husband's name?"

"A.J.—Andrew Jacob, but he's deceased."

"Address correct?"

"Yes.

Other medications?"

"No."

"Wonderful." He leaned over the counter toward her in a friendly manner and winked. "Keefer Farraday. Single. From Ohio. How about dinner?"

Carol's eyes widened and her mouth opened, shut, and opened again. "What?"

Trudy's hand was hot on the small of her back, shoving her forward. "She'd love to, Keefer. What did you have in mind?"

"A Taste of Thai. Tonight. Six?"

"Make it At Home in Italy and you've got yourself a date," Trudy said. Her brownish-green eyes gleamed. Carol's head swung back and forth as they made plans for her.

"At Home in Italy. Great. Pick you up. Quarter to six." He winked.

Carol stuffed the I.D. into her purse with the change. The bag crinkled as she twisted it. She shook her head. Before she could get the word 'no' out, Trudy shoved her through the perfume department and out the automatic doors into a brilliant, warm fall day.

"Stop manhandling me Trudy, and I can make my own dates."

"Sure you can, but you don't."

"I itch like crazy."

"Exactly why you should get out and think about something else."

"I don't want to go."

The car lock clicked as Trudy punched the code into the door pad. "Think of it as a practice run. You don't want to go so it doesn't matter if he doesn't like you."

Carol straightened and stared at Trudy. "What do you mean? Why wouldn't he like me?"

"I mean if it doesn't work out. You'll have fun and you love Italian food."

"He winks."

"Nobody's perfect. If you don't like him you don't have to see him again, but he's a nice-looking guy. He's carrying a little excess weight high in front, but not a deal breaker. Give him a chance."

"Why are you being so pushy?"

Trudy sighed and leaned over the hood. "Look, Carol, you aren't going to meet anyone if you sit at home every night."

"What are you talking about? I travel all the time."

Trudy crossed her arms in a no-nonsense way. "You speak at women's grief seminars. Come on, that's not the same as going on a singles cruise or touring Rome. I'm tired of seeing you live a half-life."

"You're like the Queen of Singles, Trudy. Your mantra is 'Women don't need men to have a full and happy life.'"

"Absolutely. Happy to be one. That's me. But, you aren't living a full life, single or otherwise."

Carol shoved sunglasses on her face to cut the glare of the September sun. She wrinkled her nose at her friend. "I hate it when you're right."

"When I'm right? I'm always right."

Chapter Three - Kim

Kim sat cross-legged on the bedroom floor with a basin of tepid water nestled in her lap. She dipped a wash cloth and without wringing it plastered it to her neck. Water drenched her blue cotton dress and pooled about her waist and hips. She prayed for rain. Secretly, of course, for Kurt counted each dry dawn as a gift from God and devoted most of each day to construction of the new church.

Nsia entered the room with the laundry basket on her hip.

Kim plunged the cloth again and raised it over her head. She lifted her face. Clumps of wet hair clung to her cheeks and neck. "They said September was the start of the cool rainy season, but this humidity is more oppressive than any Midwest-summer day I remember. I hate the heat."

Beneath a red headscarf, round dark eyes studied Kim. "I do not think it is the weather that causes your problem, Mrs. Kim. I will ask Mrs. Thema about a drink to help with baby sickness."

"Are you saying I'm pregnant? I'm not pregnant." Kim gave a dismissive wave of her hand letting droplets from the soggy washcloth fling about the room. Nsia knelt and set about sponging Kim with the water. Kim sighed. "That feels so good. You're a blessing, Nsia, and a good friend."

Nsia said, "You cry. Yesterday you cry over a watermelon."

"I was thinking of my father. We won a prize for our watermelons one year. He died five years ago. I miss him terribly."

"You get sick every morning. Eat or not, you get sick."

Kim bolted upright. Her mouth gaped.

Nsia laughed and covered her smile with her fingers, but her luminous eyes were big with mirth. "You should see your face. You will give Pastor Kurt a fine, fat baby."

"But, I don't know what to do. There weren't any babies around when I was growing up."

Nsia patted her hand. "Do not worry. I care for you and the baby. I am the oldest of six."

She smiled at Nsia. "You are like a little mother."

"Thank you."

"I miss my mother." Tears burned in Kim's eyes. She pushed homesickness away and pressed her stomach through the thin cotton material of her dress. "I don't feel pregnant."

Nsia rolled her eyes. "That comes later."

Kim stood and hugged herself. She giggled. "I'm going to be a mommy. Kurt'll be thrilled." She twirled around then nausea overwhelmed her. She grabbed a bucket near the bed and groaned.

Nsia laughed. "Maybe you should rest a bit. Will you tell Pastor Kurt tonight?"

"No. I can't wait that long."

"Mrs. Macomb! Mrs. Macomb! " Uzachi's urgent voice blasted through the open window. His face appeared and he saw her. "Kim!"

Nsia scurried to fling open the front door. Men carried Kurt into the room and Kim ran to him. "Kurt! Take him to the bed. What happened?"

Uzachi's face twisted. "Heat stroke. He never complained. None of us noticed anything until he collapsed and fell off the roof."

A short man with a scarred face snatched up a braided palm frond beside the bed and fanned Kurt. "He fell on his head."

Kim whimpered at Kurt's still form. Nsia pressed the dripping cloth into her hand. "Wet him." She moistened Kurt's head and worked down his flushed frame.

His body was hot and dry. His breathing rasped in and expelled with a ragged sigh as his chest rose and fell unevenly. Her own lungs seemed frozen and she gulped for air. Kim re-moistened the cloth and gripped Kurt's wrist. His pulse surged against her fingers. She swallowed back the bile that rose in her throat as the stench of hard-working bodies thickened the air in the small room.

More men, speaking in low, worried tones gathered outside the open window. Soon their voices rose in a clamor of supplication to God.

"Bring the pills from the desk drawer, Nsia," Uzachi ordered. Nsia hurried off and trotted back, her hand extended as if to get help to Pastor Kurt more quickly. He placed two salt tablets under Kurt's tongue. "Keep doing what you're doing, Kim. I'll call for help on the ham radio."

A short time later he returned. His face was grim. "The helicopter can't come. It's on a call up in the mountains. That's the other direction entirely. We'll have to do the best we can and let God do the rest."

Fear stole words from her mind; a coherent sentence wouldn't come together. Kim sank onto the edge of the bed and stared at Kurt's still, pale form. Nsia bustled about, fanning the air, whispering urgent instructions. "Dribble water in his mouth. Now, wet him."

The unfamiliar scents of spices and herbs accompanied the large-boned Mrs. Thema as she hobbled in and surveyed the proceedings with a grunt. Other women arrived and stayed for a few hours in rotation, but Kim wouldn't leave Kurt's side for more than a few moments.

Her head bobbed and she jerked awake. Long shadows were creeping in the window. Nsia handed her a cup of strong-smelling tea. "Mrs. Thema said you good nurse."

"No. I don't know what I'm—"

Nsia shushed Kim's denial with a warning shake of the head. "Yes. Good nurse. Drink Mrs. Thema's baby herbs." Kim took a sip and forced down the bad tasting stuff without making a face. The cup clinked against the saucer.

"Here." Nsia said, "Fresh water for Pastor Kurt."

He jabbered in a mixture of languages, but this time heat didn't radiate off his body. Kim said, "He feels cooler."

Uzachi bent to check Kurt's pulse.

Kim gripped Uzachi's arm. "Will he ever come around?"

Uzachi didn't answer. Worry clouded his brown eyes and she found no comfort in them. "He should've responded by now, Kim."

"Don't say that." Kim put her hand against his lips to stop the words.

"Wa-ter."

"Kurt. Kurt. You're awake. Nsia bring a glass of water." Kim bent forward and kissed Kurt's forehead. "We were so worried."

Uzachi, pressing palms against his lifted head, praised God. The women in the room chattered amongst themselves. One of them left to spread the news. Uzachi supported Kurt's back and Kim helped him drink.

"Good. Keep him cool and have him drink often. If he makes it through the night he should be okay. I'm going out with the men to pray," Uzachi said. He squeezed Kim's shoulder. "He's not out of the woods yet, but I think he'll be all right."

Kim wept with relief. One of the ladies held Kim's hand. "We will stay with you all night."

"You're so kind."

Evening became night and the prayers of the villagers were as unrelenting as the humidity. Kim toyed with the food Nsia insisted she eat. "How can they pray for so long? I haven't been able to say more than 'Please, God, please.'"

Nsia replied, "Pastor Kurt always say God hears your heart, Mrs. Kim."

Close to morning Uzachi returned. He moved the lantern closer to the bed while Kim watched. Kurt opened his eyes and licked cracked lips. "Don't forget to keep doing the work, my friend. We must be finished before the rains come."

Uzachi beamed. "The men will see to it, Pastor Kurt."

"They better, or I'll take a switch to them," Kurt said.

Kim frowned, but Uzachi hooted as if it were the funniest joke his gentle pastor had ever told. He hurried out the door. Soon all the men were laughing.

"The men are happy Pastor Kurt will be strong again. He will lead them in the work," Nsia said.

Through the flickering lamplight, Kim peered at the girl's face then at the man who tossed and turned on the bed while vowing with foul language to beat them all within an inch of their lives if they didn't get the job done. "He threatened them."

"Do not worry. It is the way men talk."

"Not Kurt. Kurt doesn't talk like that."

Nsia shrugged and patted Kim's shaking hand.

The next day work on the church resumed with renewed vigor as the men wished to show their new pastor how much they cared. Kim said a prayer of thanks for them because despite complaints of a horrible headache, the staccato music of the hammers was the only thing that kept Kurt in bed. For three days Kurt rested willingly.

On the fourth day, Kim sat at the kitchen table trying to choke down a dry piece of toast and tea. She grimaced as she sipped Mrs. Thema's foul tasting concoction.

"Why the frown? Aren't you glad to see me, Kim?"

The sharp edge in his voice caught her by surprise. He stood in the doorway dressed in pants and shirt as on any normal day. "Kurt. You're up." She rushed to him, stroking his brow to clear the scowl from it and to check for fever. "Do you think it's wise to be up already? Maybe you should rest today yet. Is your headache very bad?"

His mouth smoothed and he leaned forward to kiss her. "I'm fine."

She ran her fingertips down his face in a loving gesture. "You do look much better. Even so, you may have a concussion. Uzachi said—"

Kurt's smile turned upside down. He pulled her fingers from his face and squeezed them. "He doesn't know everything. You shouldn't hang on his every word."

"You're hurting me," she gasped.

Kurt's eyes darted to their hands. He kissed her knuckles. "I'm sorry. I guess I didn't realize my own strength."

Doubt snatched the smile as he kissed her hand again and released it. She sat, tucking her hand into her lap and rubbing the throbbing fingers.

"Pastor Kurt, good morning." Nsia greeted him with a huge smile as she entered.

"It is a good morning. I feel as if I haven't eaten in a week. Fix me two eggs, please." Kurt dropped into the other chair with a squeak. "What are you drinking, Kim? It stinks."

"Thema gave me this tea the day you fell. It tastes as nasty as it smells, but I wouldn't offend her for the world."

Kurt beamed at her. "You have a heart of gold, Kim."

Kim's body went weak at the praise and she giggled. Over the cup of awful tea, she studied him as he wolfed down breakfast. How she'd missed his assurances, his approval. She needed him so badly. The fear that he would die had been horrible. God had truly answered. She flexed the last of the soreness from her fingers and couldn't explain why she didn't tell him about the baby.

After breakfast Kim walked with Kurt to the new church building. The men crowded around Kurt, welcoming him with wide smiles and friendly banter.

"The thatching is almost finished, Pastor Kurt. The men have been working very hard," Uzachi said.

"I see that, Uzachi. It's a good job." He smiled at the men and the men nodded with pleasure. "But it must all come down."

The black faces around them took on a mixture of confusion and disbelief that reflected Kim's feelings. Uzachi spoke with a half-smile as if waiting for a punch line. "Why?"

"We're going to put up sheet metal instead."

There was a rumbling of uncertain voices. Uzachi moved in close and spoke low. "Pastor Kurt. You know the village can't afford sheet metal. Thatch roofs are cool and efficient. The work is almost done."

Kurt clapped a hand on Uzachi's muscular arm. "Don't worry. I've already taken care of it."

Kim gaped at her husband who had always been sensible, if not predictable. "What do you mean, Kurt?"

"I radioed the order yesterday morning. It should be here in a week."

"But, how?" A cold fear snaked up Kim's spine. "How did you pay for it?"

"I used our fund money."

"But that was our support for the next three years. You need to cancel it—" Pain flared across her cheek, her neck snapped backward at his slap. Tears stung her eyes.

Kurt scowled. "Don't tell me no. Go home."

Her shock was reflected in the faces of the men. With hand still plastered to the hot, stinging cheek, Kim turned and fled. Behind her Kurt's angry voice mingled with Uzachi's outraged one. She rushed into the house, and came face to face with Nsia. Kim spun away quickly, but Nsia grabbed Kim by the shoulders and sat her on a chair. "What happened Mrs. Kim?"

Kim flung herself across the table weeping. "Kurt slapped me."

There was a sharp intake of breath from Nsia, then hands covered Kim's outstretched ones. Eventually, Kim raised her head. "It's that head injury. I've got to call the Mission Council. They'll send help. Go tell Uzachi what I'm doing. Don't tell Pastor Kurt."

Nsia left quickly and Kim looked over the knobs and dials. Why hadn't she paid more attention to the instructor? In her panic, they all seemed to blur. At last, she remembered and made the call. "Kurt's been hurt. He needs a doctor. He fell off the roof. Please send help."

Kurt's hand peeled her fingers off of the microphone. "This is Pastor Kurt. I'm fine. It was a good crack on the head, but I'm fine…My wife is overreacting. No need to send help." He carried on enough conversation to convince them. When he signed off, he turned to her. "Why did you do that?"

"You aren't yourself. You need help, Kurt."

"Do you want me to call them back and tell them to send a doctor?"

Kim breathed a sigh of relief. "Oh yes. Please. You know, just to be sure. I really think it's the best thing."

Kurt nodded. He grabbed the wires and ripped them out of the radio. She screamed, "Stop. Stop it. What are you doing?" She followed as he carried the machine outside and threw it to the ground. With a mallet, he smashed the ham radio. "What have you done? Are you crazy?"

Kurt dropped the mallet and grabbed her by the wrist and pulled her into the house. The first punch to the gut came as a total surprise. She felt a tearing inside and bent over. After that, shock numbed her as more blows fell on her back.

"Now there'll be no more of that," the monster who used to be Kurt said.

She stayed hunched long after he left. When at last she straightened, slowly and painfully, a damp stickiness trickled down her legs, pooling on the floor. Blood. The dishes on the open shelf were still in order. The cheery flowered table cloth still covered the table. How could it all look the same when everything was different?

The voices of Nsia and the ladies rang out as they came down the path for writing lessons. What would they think? They couldn't see her like this. She shut the door, bolted it and pulled the shutters over the windows. Panic like a trapped bird fluttered in Kim's chest as she huddled in a corner in the darkened room and barely breathed while they knocked and called her name. Finally they left. She stayed on the floor trembling, her mind and body feeling hot and cold at the same time.

Days later, Kim followed the sound of two hammers pounding on metal. She hurried up the muddy path, hoping she didn't meet anyone. Embarrassment heated her face to think they might know what Kurt had done even though the bruises were almost gone.

As she neared the church clearing, another of Kurt's tirades pierced the air. Kim stopped, fled a few steps the way she'd come, stopped again. Teardrops plopped on the covers of the tin plates she carried. Kurt often didn't eat anymore. He might not notice if she didn't bring lunch, but if he did notice, he'd be furious. A sigh, akin to a sob, escaped. Rain again pattered against the dense foliage and hid her tears. She brushed past dripping leaves and entered the clearing.

Kurt looked like a madman with an angry face and wet hair plastered to his forehead like horror movie axe gashes. Mid-sentence he stopped his harangue and pointed at her. "What're you doing here?"

She cringed. "I brought food." She lifted the two plates as proof.

"We'll never finish if we keep stopping to eat."

Uzachi crawled down the ladder and rested on the floor out of the rain. As he accepted a plate from her, he spoke in a low voice. "He's very bad today. I told him I was going to Mobutu."

"For a doctor?"

"Yes. My medical books said Closed Head Trauma can cause aggression and uncontrollable emotions, but I didn't find treatment or recovery information. I wish he'd go with me. He needs to go to the hospital."

"He won't. I've tried." Kim covered her mouth with her hand and closed her eyes for a moment. "I wrote a letter to the Mission Council. Will you post it?"

Uzachi nodded. He tucked the letter she slipped him into his pants pocket. "I'll take care of it. And I'll call them from Mobutu."

"Hey! Leave her alone!" Kurt stepped from the ladder and strutted forward—a banty rooster ready to fight.

"Kurt, dear, Uzachi was thanking me for the food." Kim opened his fist and placed a plate in it.

Kurt's eyes narrowed and then dropped to the warm plate he held. His voice softened, "Yes. It's good of you to bring us something to eat, Kim. Thank you."

Glimpsing the old Kurt flooded her with giddy relief. "You're welcome."

Kurt bowed his head. "O Lord, we're so grateful for all you've given us, food for strength and energy to do the work. The load is heavy. More should be here to help, but they've turned away." The tin plate clattered to the porch floor. With his head in his hands he moaned and rocked back and forth. Then, Kurt lifted a fist to the sky. "They won't listen to me. Bring judgment on these evil men who came to you and then turned away." He sank to the floor.

Uzachi set his plate down. He whispered, "It'd be safer if you came with me. I've got to grab my overnight bag. If you want to go, meet me at the jeep in fifteen minutes."

Kim closed her eyes, but hot tears leaked anyway. She shook her head. Uzachi slipped away.

Kurt continued rocking. "Why, Kim? Why have they all left?"

She bent over him, stroking his head. How she loved him, in sickness and in health. "Perhaps if you didn't yell at them so much."

He stilled and she gathered courage. "Once you're better, they'll all come back."

He reared. "Are you saying this is my fault? It was you. You drove them away because you hate it here. And now you're carrying on with Uzachi."

A sour taste filled her throat. "No, Kurt."

The plate toppled into the mud as Kurt leapt to his feet. He grabbed her arm and shook her. "I saw you. I saw you fondling his face when you thought I was sick. I heard you making plans to run away together just now. I know what to do with you, you unfaithful whore and I know what to do with him."

Chapter Four – Kim

Kim lay in a fetal position on the bare floor in hot dark silence. The rusty iron shackles Kurt had dug up clanked as she rolled to a sitting position. She grabbed the chain and threw her weight backward. Fortified by shiny new screws and metal plates, it remained fast to the floor near her bed.

Kim paced the six-foot circle that had become the extent of her world. Her ankles, raw from the bands, burned like iodine on an open wound. Her empty stomach pinched and her tongue felt swollen.

For days she hadn't seen any of the villagers although she sometimes heard chopping in the forest or children playing. If they heard her calls for help, they deemed it best not to interfere. She cradled her empty womb and sank to the floor, longing for the safe arms of her mother.

The outer door creaked on its hinges. Footsteps stole through the house. She held her breath as the knob turned and light outlined the doorway. A small form peered in. Kim rattled to a sitting position. "Nsia," she croaked. "Help me."

"Mrs. Kim, oh, Mrs. Kim." The door flung wide. Nsia, face creased with concern and eyes wide in horror, hurried forward and knelt. She pushed dirty hair from Kim's face with comforting strokes. A few seconds later, those eyes surveyed the room. "Where is your husband?"

Kim shook her head and shrugged. She stroked her throat.

Muttering in her native language, Nsia sprang to her feet, and left.

Kim wept, but no tears came. Her lips formed the words, "Don't leave me" but her throat was too dry to grind them out. Nsia reappeared with water and helped Kim drink. The girl hugged her.

"I run fast to the village. The men will free you."

Kim slumped against the bed. Minutes passed like hours before she heard the sound of a crowd. Nsia entered followed by women bringing bananas and that thick paste of cassava and yams they called fufu. Nsia scooped bits of it into Kim's mouth with two fingers. Children peeked in the window and were ordered away in urgent hushed tones by the mothers. Grim-faced men arrived with hacksaws and hammers. The rasping of metal on metal filled the little room as they labored to free her.

When Kim pushed the bowl away, the women brought more water and Nsia washed her face, neck, and arms while two women cleaned the filthy floor. Others watched with pained expressions and distressed silence. Everyone moved with gentleness and a sense of shame.

The unmistakable growl of the mission's jeep filtered through the jungle. With hope rising, Kim said, "Uzachi's brought help back."

A murmuring burst among the people. One man ran to the window. "Pastor Kurt."

The group sucked in a collective breath. The men rose from their task and the women clustered together. Kim whimpered. She quaked and leaned into the protective arms Nsia placed about her.

"Princess, I'm home," came Kurt's lighthearted voice. Boots pounded across the porch and through the main room to the kitchen and back. He laughed. "Where are you?" He halted at the door of the bedroom. "Why is everyone here? Is Kim all right?"

Kim peeked through the legs of the men forming a barrier in front of her. The clear blue eyes she so dearly loved roved from one face to another. Fear streaked across his face. "What happened?"

The men moved aside and Kurt's jaw went slack. He dropped to his knees. Involuntarily she drew back. "Oh, Kim. Who did this? Did the militia come?"

The group exchanged perplexed glances. Kwame, the chief's son said, "No, Pastor Kurt. It was you."

Kurt stood and turned from one person to the other. Confusion and hurt rang in his voice. "I'd never hurt my wife. Besides, I was with Uzachi." He winced, pressed both palms to his temples, lurched through the main room, and clamored down the steps.

Kim jerked at the unrelenting chains. "Don't let him hurt me again. His head. La tete. The pain in his head. He'll strike. Like the mamba."

The rumbling of another big vehicle grew louder. Kim stiffened. Was Kurt going to bulldoze the building with everyone in it? The villagers looked at each other trying to understand what was happening.

Footfalls pounded on floorboards. Kurt reappeared, his handsome face marred by a snarl and an automatic rifle in his hands. Just then, Kwame pointed out the window and yelled, "Soldiers."

Kurt swayed for a moment in the doorway. "Don't worry my friends. I'll handle it." He rushed to the window, raised the gun and opened fire. With his back to them, the villagers scattered. Kim squealed and covered her ears. Nsia's tight grasp nearly cut her in two. Kwame tore Nsia away, carrying her kicking and screaming out the door.

The ping, ping, ping of the pin hitting empty chambers filled the room. Kurt stopped firing, set the gun against the wall, and shuttered the window. He turned toward her. Before she could move, he was beside her. He pressed kisses on the top of her head and cradled her in the security of his strong arms. He swabbed tears from her face with cool water and spoke scripture verses of comfort. Through the ringing of her ears she heard him soothe. "They're gone. They're all gone. Those soldiers won't be harming or stealing from this village. No one will hurt you now, Princess. I'm here. I'll keep you safe. I'll protect you."

Relief. Confusion. Hope. Fear. The room whirled and went black.

Chapter Five - Carol

Carol tapped her foot impatiently as Trudy unlocked the frosted glass door and led the way through the reception area of the elaborate office. A towering Christmas tree decorated in silver and burgundy filled an entire section of the room. She set the bag of lunch leftovers next to her purse on the edge of Trudy's glass-topped desk and sank into its cushy leather chair. She swiveled to look out the window. "What's going on? What's the big mystery?"

"Carol, I think you should go skiing with Peter in Montana."

Carol slowly spun the chair to stare at her best friend.

Trudy looked the other way as she busied herself combing shoulder-length hair before an enormous ornate mirror. "Oh, don't look so shocked."

"Don't you think it's a tad bit deceptive given the fact I'm not remotely interested in him?"

Trudy shrugged. "Peter knows that already. You've been telling him for two years. You're a client. Look at it as a simple perk of working with Faulkinroy Publicists."

"I don't know."

"The way I see it, you aren't romantically involved so you'll be safe. It'll put you into the dating mode without really dating. When you come back, you'll feel more comfortable about real dating." Trudy smoothed color around her lips and smacked them.

Carol slumped a little in the chair and propped her chin in her hand. "I don't ski and hardly exercise. It'd be hard work going up those huge mountains."

"You ride the lift up. Gravity takes over and you ski down. It's a piece of cake. Besides, you start out on the easy slopes. They're almost flat."

"I don't know, look what happened the last time you set me up."

Trudy pointed a finger at Carol. "Hey, I didn't set you up. Keefer approached you directly."

"And you accepted for me."

Trudy tilted her head. "I was helping you take advantage when an opportunity presented itself."

"And now he won't allow me in his store. He says I'm a fire hazard. I miss shopping there. I've got to go all the way over to Welly's Value World now."

Trudy shrugged. "Quit complaining. It's only two extra miles. Besides, it was your first date. You were nervous. It could happen to anyone."

"With that logic I'm surprised more restaurants don't catch fire."

"Think of the publicity. You made front page news and your local book sales rose fifteen percent. I bet his store sales boomed, too. That was a great shot of Keefer with his chest on fire. I clipped it for my album."

"It was his napkin. His napkin. And the newspaper people thought it was a publicity stunt for the new restaurant."

Trudy returned the brush and lipstick to her purse. It snapped shut with a gentle click. "Anyway, this is better. You already know Peter and there's no reason to be nervous."

"Peter is capable, energetic, and personable, but—."

"But what?"

"I can't put my finger on it. He'll never be anything more than a friend."

"You've made that clear, but that doesn't mean he doesn't like being with you. Who knows, you may meet someone wonderful in Montana. Even if you don't, all those handsome ski instructors are bound to perk up the spirits."

"If it's about friends having fun, why don't you vacation with him, Trudy?"

Trudy tossed her purse into the bottom desk drawer and motioned for her to vacate the chair. "Are you kidding? Getting rid of the Everything-Must-Be-Perfect boss for a week is my idea of a vacation."

Carol let Trudy have the seat and moved around to the front of the large, cherry desk. She glanced around to be sure no one could hear, leaned forward and lowered her voice. "I can't believe you've worked with him for this long."

"He pays well and I like what I do. Besides, I'm the Mary Poppins of personal assistants. I'm practically perfect in every way and frequently work magic."

"Trudy, are you getting a bonus if I agree to go?"

"Yes and I want to take a trip to Bermuda so badly. Please, Carol. Please. Please. Please." Trudy lifted her face and clutched her fists to her chest in supplication.

Carol closed her eyes. This wasn't a good idea, but how could she deny the request? Trudy had repeatedly proved herself the best of friends, including keeping vigil at the hospital with Kim after a car accident when Carol had been speaking at a grief conference two states away.

"Oh. All right."

Trudy faced her computer and tapped the keys with her fingertips. "You won't regret it."

Carol gathered her belongings and the doggie bag. "I already regret it. I can't believe I'm doing this after the last fiasco."

"Old history. Here's your itinerary. Your speaking engagement ends on Sunday. You'll fly straight to Montana. He'll meet you at the airport. I've sent a copy to your email box and here's a copy now, because you're a hard-copy kind of girl. Have you heard from Kim?"

Carol took the paper and fiddled with it. "Not for a couple months. I called the Mission Council, but they hadn't heard anything. Communications are poor at best and the country is so volatile, I can't help worrying."

Trudy patted her hand. "Your daughter is fine. If there was any danger, Kurt would get her out of there. He loves her too much to let anything happen to her."

"I suppose so."

"You're praying for them aren't you?"

Carol nodded. "Of course."

"So leave it in God's hands." Trudy pointed to a snowy scene on her computer monitor. "Montana. Isn't it gorgeous?"

"It's probably photo shopped."

A few weeks later Carol was in that snowy scene and it definitely wasn't photo shopped. The blue Montana sky shone with such brilliance she thought it might shatter like glass if she poked it with her ski pole. Instead, she contemplated poking Peter for the simple pleasure of hearing him yelp.

It wasn't fair that Peter looked like an Olympic ski champ as he forged ahead, suave and confident. He made the climb appear effortless while she panted with exertion and each labored step reminded her of the bruises on her hips and the fact she hadn't wanted to ski. Her spine tingled every time she glanced toward the bottom of Skeleton Run so she kept her eyes heavenward.

Peter halted, pulled his goggles from his eyes and turned his rakish smile on her. "Come on, Carol. You're going to love this."

"I'm coming. I'm coming." She grumbled, "A.J. never dragged me against my will. He made new things fun and easy."

"What did you say?"

"Nothing." She paused long enough to rub the cramp in her leg. A tiny rivulet of perspiration tickled down her back. Skiing belonged to the category of Insane-Things-Never-To-Do-Again. In the future she'd prefer to appreciate the mountain, deep in fresh powder, from the window in her suite and the sharp, clean air would be far more enjoyable from the hot tub on the deck of the ski lodge.

"Don't stop now. It's only a bit more," Peter called.

"Right." Carol jabbed her pole into the snow pretending it was Peter's backside. When she reached him, he extended a hand to steady her. She sidestepped the last few feet to the edge of a precipice.

He waved toward a panoramic view of the valley. "What did I tell you?"

What little breath she had caught in her throat. "Peter, this is stunning."

"It's the most perfect place on earth."

"Okay. I forgive you for dragging me up here. It was worth it. I admit it."

Peter's handsome face was exultant. "I told you to trust me."

"'The mountains declare the glory of God and the firmament shows his handiwork'. How can anyone look at something like this and say God doesn't exist? It's beautiful."

"You're beautiful."

Afraid to move her body, even a little, she turned only her head at the tone of his voice. His gaze dropped to something in his hand. Nestled in a velvet box, a diamond ring sparkled in the sun. She gasped. His finger lifted her chin until their eyes met. Peter's face was tender and sincere. "Carol, will you marry me?"

"No."

His face hardened a tiny bit, but his voice remained cajoling. "Why not? Andy's been gone for five years. It's time to put the proverbial widow's garb in storage."

"I'm not clinging to the past. It's about me. I enjoy being single."

"Nobody enjoys being single." Peter's lip curled with derision.

"Well, I do. I like to come and go whenever I want. I like to make a decision without having to check with someone else first." This was true. She was able to think more clearly when her emotions weren't screened through what A.J. wanted.

"I understand. You're scared to love again. But, we've worked together four years and we get along perfectly. Marry me and everything will be fine, like coming here. You were scared, but it turned out well. Trust me."

He wrapped his arms around her and tried to draw her close. The skis slid from beneath her. Fear rocketed up her spine and burst in her brain in a trillion tingles. She squealed. He grabbed her and backed her several feet from the edge to a level place near a big rock. Her breath came in short bursts. Her chest heaved and her lungs ached from the crisp air. Carol pushed away his supporting hands. "You almost got me killed!"

"Don't be hysterical. You're in no danger of falling over the edge. I'm here. Trust me."

"Why should I trust someone who bullies me into doing what I don't want to do? Peter, I am not now, nor am I ever, going to marry you."

"You need me." Peter's face darkened. His eyes sparked with fury. He seemed to grow larger like the Green Hulk. Surely he wouldn't hit her. The ring case snapped shut with the crack of a gunshot. She jumped.

"You're a great publicist. But I don't need any man in my personal life. I thought I'd made it clear before. That's final. Please, don't ask me again."

Peter stuffed the case into the little pocket over his heart and tugged the zipper closed. "Very well. You're wrong, but if that's the way you think—"

"It is. You want to lead me around like a pet on a leash. I've been around the block and I don't need you to show me the way home."

"Fine, Carol. You can find your own your way home." Peter adjusted his goggles over his eyes, settled his cap more securely on his head, and worked his fingers into his gloves. He kneaded the poles with his fingers. His skis slid back and forth.

"Not funny, Peter."

"It's a straight shot down."

Her heart pounded. "I can't ski that on my own."

He lifted his chin and his words were cold and clipped. "As you said, you don't need me."

A fresh set of tingles ran the circuit of her spine. "Don't you dare leave me here."

"You can backtrack. After all, you excel at looking back." Peter turned from her, pushed along the ledge away from the sheer drop. He moved to where the steep slope called Skeleton's Run lie

35

past an outcropping. He launched off, sailed through the air, landing firmly. The cloud of snow that rose around him momentarily obscured him from view.

"Peter!" She clung to the rock wall, calling until he was only a tiny speck schussing the slope. Sobs shook her. "God. Help me." After a several moments she gulped deep chill breaths. "I can do this. I can do all things in Christ who strengthens me. I buried a husband. I can do this."

Carol adjusted her goggles and bumbled along the ledge, retracing their path. She held a steady stream of imaginary angry conversations to keep from crumpling in fear. "I'll never trust you again, Peter Faulkinroy. Bully. Coward. See? I'm making it without you."

As she entered a dip in the mountain floor, Carol let loose a shriek, long and shrill. Some of the tension, fear, anger, and frustration flew away with the sound like the trailing tail of a kite. She shrieked again. "When I get back, I'll fire you." The yell echoed and faded to silence. Tears pooled inside her goggles as she dug her poles with renewed vigor.

A low rumbling vibrated through the air. A glance upward proved the sky over head was clear and cloudless. Carol glanced over her shoulder to where only moments before snow had covered a crest. The mountain beneath shook as hundreds of pounds of weak ice and snow rushed toward her. Avalanche.

She forgot about the trail. She dug in her poles to speed ahead of the white wave. Down the slope she flew. She didn't know how she stayed on her skis, but she didn't dare look behind or she'd lose her balance. She whizzed past trees and boulders and reached a flat expanse.

Snow crystals filled the air. The white tide hit like a linebacker tackling an opponent, yanking her off her skis. Carol rolled head-over-heels and up again, jolting to a stop with a wrench of the ankle as the blue sky was blotted from view.

Carol couldn't breathe. Her left arm was packed tight against her waist but she worked the right until she could touch her face. Flailing, she broke through the snow above and gulped big breaths. She beat a bowl shape and tilted her head back as far as it would go and stared at the same sharp blue sky that had made the day perfect only an hour before. "Lord God, help me!"

Her cheeks tingled from cold. She wiggled. She couldn't move much, as one foot was pinched at an odd angle, yet there was no pain, only an overall soreness. She squirmed, wriggled, and struggled with no effect. How long would it be before help arrived? Forever. No one knew where she was. She whipped her arm in frenzied effort. "Help! Help!"

Tears burned her cheeks as they crystallized to ice. Eventually, she forced herself to stop crying and think. The first thing to do was pray. "God, please send someone to help me."

She remembered reading the biggest heat loss came from the head so Carol worked her cap on more tightly with her free hand and butted her head backward to get the snow away. Would that make a difference when she was encased in ice?

Wind whistled across the hole and dipped into her little bowl of breathing space. She was so close to the surface. Why couldn't she get free? She had to keep warm until help came. Impossible, because no help was coming. A sob escaped. She choked back others. She simply couldn't give up. Carol kicked her free leg as if swimming upwards from the bottom of a deep pool. Her muscles screamed and sweat soaked her armpits and back. She rested her forehead on her bent arm. Cold seeped into her body.

The sky turned a menacing gray as Carol tensed her toes and released, tensed her legs and released and worked the muscles in order until she flexed her upraised hand. She sang worship songs and started the routine again, keeping at it even as stiffness settled into her fingers and time became irrelevant. "How Great Thou Art" turned into "Frosty the Snowman" in mid-verse and she was seized with a fit of giggles.

Her words slurred like drunken ramblings. "I'm sorry God." Should she apologize for drinking too much? That didn't make sense. She didn't drink. She sure was thirsty. A great shaking twisted her insides like a severe case of flu. A fevered heat flooded her. Too hot. Too hot. She clamped her mitten with her teeth and yanked it off. She clawed at her clothes and fumbled to grip the zipper. It was frozen shut. Anyway her fingers wouldn't work. They were blue. Well, what could one expect from blue Smurf fingers?

Chapter Six - Jack

Jack picked his way along the rocky stream bed. Despite the rubber chest waders which kept him dry, the near-freezing cold from the running mountain water seeped into his calves. Overhead the sky was still clear, but dark, angry clouds gusting from the northern peak promised a blizzard.

He loved the harsh, beautiful Montana winters and all the hunting, trapping, and snowshoeing that went with it. Even so, he much preferred riding out a storm in the warmth of his crude but well-stocked cabin to some makeshift shelter along the way. If he hurried, he should be able to finish this part of the line in three hours and still reach the cabin's safety before the storm.

Jack found one of his traps and reached into the stream. Black rubber gloves stretching from fingers to shoulders protected his hands. He released a dead muskrat, flung it into his backpack and reset the trap. He continued along, being rewarded a few more times for all his hard labor. Finally, he pulled himself up the bank and paused to catch his breath.

Across the river a lone coyote nosed a spot in the snow. It spooked, leapt back, returned. He'd noticed that same coyote worrying the same spot when he'd first arrived. "Better make quick work of your dinner, sport. When that storm hits we'll all be denned up for a few days."

Jack took his own advice. He trudged to the snowmobile, hefted his loaded backpack into the trailer and set about emptying its contents, laying the catch out on the floor, and readying to move on.

The coyote continued its antics. Snatching and tugging, it brought up an odd bit of bright blue.

Jack exchanged the cumbersome rubber gloves for leather ones and reached for binoculars. He sighted along the rough edge of a fresh avalanche and found the animal. A blue cap came into view. He strained to see. Could someone be out there? A sense of urgency stirred.

He traced a possible route from the spot to the stream. With top snow hiding areas of honeycombed ice from a recent thaw, every step would need to be tested. Travel time might be doubled or even tripled. He peered at the clouds roiling about the mountaintop.

Jack threw a thermos, rope, a small pick and shovel, and some stakes to use as pitons into the large woven pack basket and wrestled into the shoulder straps. He checked the pistol at his waist, grabbed a walking stick, and splashed across the stream.

Boulders were piled haphazardly here. He scrambled up and across and surged into the drifts on the other side, all the while lambasting himself for leaving the snow shoes at the entrance to the cabin. Jack waded on through knee-deep snow, sometimes sinking up to his thigh.

As he approached the spot, Jack bellowed, "Get. Get." He waved his arms and whistled. The coyote trotted off a few hundred yards and paused before disappearing.

The blue stocking cap sat in a hollow in the ground. Jack plucked it up. The pale, unnaturally blue-tinged face of a woman appeared underneath. What a grim way to die. The "corpse" moaned.

"Hang on! Help's here!" Jack yanked his thermos out and tried to dribble a few drops of lukewarm coffee into her mouth. Her eyes opened. Her tongue worked at the moisture then her head fell slack.

He dug with the pick and shovel until he had cleared snow down to her chest. From behind, he gripped beneath her armpits and pulled. She didn't budge. "You're caught on something. Don't worry. I'll free you."

Unconscious, she didn't reply and offered neither resistance nor help. He wiped sweat from his eyes as the storm clouds that had been moving restlessly around the peaks stampeded toward them.

Jack dug wider and deeper and reached her waist. He gagged. The stomach spasms from hypothermia had done their work. He labored with the shovel and pick, grateful for the occasional blast of fresh air that dipped into the deepening pit, showering them with misty swirls of snow.

With savage thrusts he shoveled until he found her left boot wedged into the crevice. He twisted her foot, one way then the other. She never woke to protest. He chipped at the rock. The foot popped free.

As Jack climbed out of the hole, sharp crystals of blowing snow bit his face. Every muscle screamed for a break that he had no time to take. He looped the rope beneath her armpits and yanked. Once she cleared the edge, he flipped her face-down and threaded her arms through his pack straps.

"Give me strength, God." With a groan, he shuffled her onto his back and secured her to him with the rope. He straightened, ready for the return trip, and stared into white nothingness that hid the waterway and his snowmobile. He turned 300 degrees. There. Footprints. Thank God he didn't have his snowshoes. Those impressions would've been obliterated by now. Even these deep marks were filling fast.

He took a step and tottered beneath the unwieldy weight. "Please, God. Don't let us fall through." He stepped and stepped again, saying a prayer of thanksgiving with each. After much effort, he reached the boulders. Jack carefully forded the river and with difficulty mounted the opposite bank.

There he released the ropes and slid the still form to the ground. Without her weight, Jack moved easily, too easily. He crashed into the trailer, righted himself and pulled along its length until he reached his bedroll.

He returned and dropped to his knees beside the woman. The bedroll billowed violently like a cantankerous magic carpet straining to escape. He secured it with his knees while he ripped the foul, sodden ski suit from her with his hunting knife and rolled her in the dry downy sleeping bag. Grunting, he placed her in the trailer beside his other catch and lashed a tarp over the top.

The storm muffled the roar of the engine as it sprang to life. Jack pulled goggles over his eyes and throttled forward while snow like BBs pelted him. The next hour felt like forever before the cabin loomed out of the white. He parked at the door and carried the frozen form to the bed shelf that ran along the wall of the single room.

He yanked his gloves off. Her pulse was slow. Too slow. But at least it was there. Jack tucked the bedroll about her and said, "Come on, lady. Hang on. I'm heating the water bottles. We'll soon get you warm."

The blue lips didn't move. The eyelids didn't flutter. Yet, he couldn't, he wouldn't, give up.

Jack primed and lit the Coleman stove. He slammed a pot of snow on it to melt. Next he nursed a fire to a roaring stage. Only then, did he take time to remove his gear and warm himself.

Once the water was ready, he tended to her. Her still, chilled body was painfully cold to touch. He shuddered as he lay beside her and pulled her close. "Not another death, Lord, please."

The storm raged all through the night. Jack periodically rose to encourage the fire to blaze. He paced the room, flapping his arms to limber up and restore the body heat she'd drained from him before reheating the water bottles.

It became a routine over the next twenty-four hours. Each time he'd dribble lukewarm broth down her throat. Each time he'd hoped for a sign that she would make it. "I walk by faith, not by sight, Lord. Keep showing me what to do to help her live."

***

Jack awoke with a start. Light from the dying flames swayed across the ceiling. He lit a lantern and brought it close to the sleeping form. The woman's body temperature was still below normal, but her coloring held a hint of pink. She stirred, groaning incomprehensibly. Hearing it was like winning the grand prize. He offered thanks, then turned to tend the fire and cringed. The wood pile was used up.

Jack bundled into coats, boots, gloves, and hat. As he did so, he spoke to her because he believed doing so would encourage her to live. "I'm going to bring in more wood from the shed. It's still storming out there, but there's no remedy for it, but to do it. Besides, my daddy always said he who chops wood, warms himself twice. I'd sure like to get warm. You've chilled me to the bone. Be back as soon as I can."

As days went by, the woman's body temperature was noticeably warmer. Her bouts of delirium subsided into long periods of deep sleep. Jack kept watch, but no longer feared for her life. Besides caring for her, his daily routine included thawing his catch, stretching the pelts and hanging the stretcher frames from bent nails in the ceiling. The fire he kept roaring for her had the benefit of helping dry the pelts. The excessive use of wood was a luxury he'd never allowed before.

The bright sunshine was dazzling after the prolonged mountain storm. He prayed his patient would be well enough to travel before the next storm hit. He set to work chopping.

With arms loaded with firewood, he walked the path worn between the snow banks. As the sun set, it brushed a rose color on the peaks of the mountains deep with snow. He paused as a peculiar ache tightened like a lariat around his chest. Karen had loved the way the sun stained different shades on the earth. He could almost hear her husky voice say, "Big J, look at God's handiwork, look at it." He always replied it was grand. In truth, he hadn't paid much attention. It would've been such a simple thing to share the moment with her, yet now it was impossible to do it. He regretted every moment he had given only a part of himself to his wife. He'd been too busy with work, with the trap line, with his various wood-working projects.

Jack sharply inhaled the fresh air. That time was gone. He had a different task to do. The raw, gamey smell met him when he entered the cabin. If his guest noticed the stink, she was in no position to complain. He dropped the load he carried beside the hearth and shed his coat. His eyes grew accustomed to the gloomy interior. The woman was lying on the floor.

She felt limp and shaky as he helped her back to the bed. "Look, lady, I'm sure you're anxious to get well, but take it easy and ask for help. Be patient. Another day or two and you'll be much stronger. Don't rush it. You realize you had a brush with death, don't you?"

She nodded and her eyes stayed focused, following him as he applied fresh hot water bottles for good measure. He said, "You might lose some skin in a few places, but not the fingers and toes."

Jack rubbed his eyes and turned to the table to work. His knife made solid thwacks against the cutting board as he chopped meat into bite size pieces. Despite his reassurances to her, he was anxious to get back to the ranch where he could call into Free Dance for medical help. She was improving, but he'd heard far too many stories of the complications of hypothermia to be complacent.

Chapter Seven - Carol

Carol was in a cave. A fire roared in the grate with violent cold. She quivered and every part of her body was pierced by needles. A bare-chested bearded giant in Hawaiian swim trunks poured a magical potion into bags and hid them in flannel cases.

"I must be alive. This sure isn't heaven," she said.

The giant chuckled. "Hey, you're talking. That's a good sign."

He came close. Heat radiated from him and beads of sweat dotted his face and forehead as if the room wasn't freezing cold. He folded the covers back and placed the magic bags on her stomach and along her sides. Pain like knives cut her. "Stop. Stop," she cried soundlessly as the cold closed in around her.

Carol awoke in the gray of the room with an unutterable weariness tugging at her as if she had completed some horrendously physical task or had the flu. Then she recalled the argument and the claustrophobic panic as the white powder covered her head. She squirmed to be free from its confines and stilled. She was not alone.

Dreamy images of a waterfall, of being spoon fed, and welcome warmth trickled back. Whoever it was had helped her. Jack or Jake or Jock. What was he doing in her bed?

"Sorry for the lack of privacy. You needed my body's warmth or you wouldn't have survived."

She jerked at the sound of his voice. The man slipped from the covers. This was the friendly giant wearing yellow and blue Hawaiian bathing trunks in her hallucinations. Carol struggled against yards and yards of cloth in an effort to sit. He reached forward and strong warm arms moved her into an upright position. They felt familiar.

He said, "Are you feeling a little more like yourself today?"

"Some," she squeaked.

"I know the thermal underwear is too big, but it's all I had."

"You live here?"

When he smiled his whole face softened. "No. And if I ever get the notion I want to, I'll remember this adventure. I'm sure I can find you better things to wear when we get back to the ranch." He produced a flannel shirt from a back pack and handed it to her.

Carol stared at the garment. It was long and large, like the man who towered over her.

"Let me give you a hand. You're still pretty weak." He slipped her arms into the sleeves as one would dress a small child. She wanted to protest, but her head was spinning with the upright position. Before she could get the words out the job was done. He folded the sleeves back so that they didn't flop about her hands. "There you go. I wouldn't recommend it for 'Sunday go-to-meeting' clothes, but it'll keep you warm. I'll get breakfast."

She stood, wavered, and fell back exhausted. Nestled into the blankets she watched unthinkingly as he prepared the meal. This world was moving slowly, which was far better than when it had been whirling and weird. Carol giggled, remembering her hallucinations of the brown-haired giant with the red beard. He glanced up and smiled.

When the meal was ready he helped her to a chair and sat across from her, folded his hands and spoke clearly. "Father, thank you for bringing Carol safely through this ordeal and for the food on this table. Provide the strength we need for what lies ahead. Amen."

"Amen." Carol sent a look of approval his way, but he wasn't looking. "Where are we?"

"This is one of my trapping cabins. I have a place not far as the crow flies. It's pretty rough terrain and will take us a couple hours to get there. We'll risk it as soon as you're strong enough. We'll have to take care to keep you warm and not tax your energy. You could relapse easily."

"How long have we been here?" She frowned with the effort to hold her spoon, but her fingers didn't seem to want to obey her command. She managed to close them around the handle by gripping it in a fist like a baby.

"Six days. Were you staying at the lodge?"

She rubbed her head and considered what to tell him. "Peter is a much better skier than I am. He persuaded me to visit an overlook to the valley near Skeleton Run."

"I know the place."

"We had an argument and he went on from there. I backtracked because the skiing was too difficult. Then suddenly I was trying to flee the avalanche."

"You can't outrun one. You go sideways to get out of its path."

"That would've been good to know. I didn't think it possible to be so scared. I'm sorry, I've forgotten your name."

He told her and then explained how he'd been in a position to find her. "God had his hand on you. No one else is around for miles. If I hadn't been trapping, I wouldn't have seen you."

"My husband used to trap."

"Peter?"

She bowed her head suddenly shy. "No. Andy. My husband died of a heart attack years ago. It didn't seem fair."

"Death never does. I lost my wife last year after a three year struggle with cancer."

"I'm sorry is so inadequate, yet I am sorry for your loss. Do you have children?"

"One son, Mitchell. He didn't take her death well. He dropped out his senior year of seminary. Of course, he didn't want my advice. We quarreled. I haven't seen him since. He's eaten up with anger and bitterness. I'm afraid he's getting into some bad stuff."

"It's hard to watch someone you love turn their back on God."

Jack nodded. "My father and grandfather were ministers. I was so proud of Mitch following the tradition. In some ways it's harder to watch him struggle with his faith than it was to let Karen go. Do you have children?"

"Yes. My son, Nick, builds churches and schools for missionaries. He's in Guatemala. My daughter, Kim, and her new husband are first year missionaries in Zaire."

"You must be proud."

"Don't give up on your son. It's hard to lose a parent and the world is a very wicked place."

He turned from her under the pretense of cleaning the supper dishes, but Carol was sure she'd seen tears glisten in his eyes. He dipped water into a pan from a kettle he kept simmering over the fire. It made the little room more like a sauna than a cabin, but still she was never warm enough. She pulled the flannel shirt more tightly about her.

To move the topic into less emotional territory she said, "I think Andy had a book by you."

"It's possible. I write about trapping, give a few private lessons, and travel to conventions to teach about it and animal conservation."

With the cheery fire crackling, they talked about this until shakes and nausea overcame her. Jack heaped more blankets on her and brought hot water bottles. After several minutes, the episode passed and Carol turned her face to the wall and slept.

Chapter Eight - Mitch

Mitch scowled at the gospel tract and a five-dollar tip left under the coffee cup. The words 'God is for you' were written in a blank space on the back side. "Freak," he grumbled. Did the guy honestly think his attention could be bought? He most likely could out-quote the man verse for verse and it didn't change the facts. He swept the offending message into the garbage. The cup and saucer clattered as he deposited them on the rack of the ancient dishwasher.

A swatch of stringy hair escaped the food service net and he hooked it behind his ears. He checked both ways and pulled a flat half-pint bottle from the back of a low shelf of plates. He sipped a quick nip and returned his liquid stash to its hiding place.

A thin trail of smoke rose from a greasy burger spitting and sputtering on the grill. He'd left it on too long. Again. He pried the meat off the griddle with a metal spatula and flipped it over. The bottom was crisp and black, a sure sign it had transitioned from edible to something with the taste of a used tire. He slathered margarine on it in hopes it would soften the charred part and flopped it onto a bun. He added a squirt of mustard, ketchup, mayo and a few skimpy slices of pickle before delivering it to a large Mexican at the counter.

"It took you long enough," the man growled as he snatched the burger and bit into it. He grunted, spewed it out and flung the rest of the sandwich at Mitch. The heavy accent kept Mitch from understanding exactly what the man said, but he gathered everything from his origin of birth to his brain capacity came into question. Without paying, the customer stormed out, past a balding man with a cleft lip.

Mitch tried to sound nonchalant as he swabbed the ketchup and mustard from his apron. "Hi, Barry, how's it going?"

Barry, the owner of the dismal diner, understood the scenario at a single glance and Mitch had no trouble understanding Barry's 'invitation' to leave. His ex-boss assisted him to the door with a strong grip and threw his dirty blue-jean jacket after him.

Mitch yanked the hairnet free and threw it to the concrete. He dug into his pocket and fingered the five-dollar bill. He had enough to forget he'd lost another job on the seedy side of Helena, Montana.

He picked his way along the icy sidewalk and inched around a man hunched against the wall. He hated these hopeless homeless. How could they live like this? A vagrant stumbled against Mitch. He shoved the man away, saying, "Get a job."

Mitch turned into a nondescript liquor store. At the checkout line the queue of buyers was reflected in the security mirror. Among them a scruffy, bearded man fidgeted. Dirty dishwater-blond hair hung about his face. He looked in pretty bad shape. What a loser.

Mitch shook his head in derision. A long spike dangled from one ear lobe, catching the florescent light as the man also moved his head. The reject must like the Australian rock band G'Nailed as much as he did.

A bag rustled as a woman grabbed her purchase and headed for the door. The full image of "the loser" remained. Mitch flinched with recognition and dropped his gaze to the counter where the words "It's Not Too Late" peeked from under a box of breath mints. Tract-man had been here, too. He hesitated. Maybe he should—

The store clerk snatched the money from his hand and replaced it with the usual bottle of whiskey. Mitch dragged leaden feet out the door. The impression of himself burned like a brand in his brain. He retraced his steps past the men.

Had they, like him, merely been working through their grief? Mitch no longer knew exactly how long he'd been here. Had they, like him, only planned to be there temporarily? Was this how it happened?

The thought depressed him, but was he ready to give up his anger at the God who had betrayed him? No. He cranked the cap and chugged a bit. "Amen. So be it."

50

Sometime later a semi-truck thundered past. A crash followed by heavy clanging and banging threatened to split Mitch's head apart. He pressed his head between his hands and blinked awake. Someone jostled him. "Leave me alone," he said and sank back into his stupor.

Shouts, curses, bustling activity roused him fully. He was on his back on top of a trash bag. His breath formed fountains of cold mist. If the air was cold, why was he warm? Someone grunted. He was sandwiched between two bodies. A new low. Mitch raised up on one elbow.

A huge pig twisted its head and pressed its snout to his nose.

Mitch hollered. Pawed his face. Scrambled to an upright position. A white light seared his brain. Nausea overtook him. He clutched his head, fell forward, bumping it against the wall. He bellowed again.

Two sows lumbered to their feet, squealing as if displeased that he had disturbed them. The first one trotted down the street, the second snuffled Mitch's belly, knocking the whiskey bottle from his belt. It smashed against the concrete forming a puddle at his feet. The smell of spirits invaded the air. He waved his hands at the beast. "Get! Go on!"

A man in cowboy boots and a quilted flannel shirt prodded the creature with a long staff, driving it toward a slatted, flatbed truck where the first sow lumbered up the ramp under the guidance of two men.

Mitch staggered forward. Police cars sat at odd angles in the intersection with lights flashing. A wrecker pulled a yellow Volkswagen Rabbit off of the truck's front bumper with a shrieking of metal. Water spewed from the engine. The tow truck hoisted the VW and left.

A tiny woman in a high-pitched tirade was being calmed by two policemen as they helped her into their cruiser.

At the flatbed, the sow that had cornered Mitch was near the ramp when it charged again and pinned him against a parked car. It squealed and squealed. Mitch yelled. The two truckers cursed as they circled it, but the pig raced ahead and shot straight up the ramp. One man said, "I've never seen anything like it. Have you?"

51

The other sneered at Mitch. "She must have recognized you as one of her own, buddy, and came to say goodbye. Maybe she's got a crush on you." Their coarse jokes and taunting guffaws rang through the chilly night air while they secured the flatbed and rumbled away.

The street was quiet. Those along the sidewalk shuffled back to their own little worlds in the quiet shadows of the night. A late night snow began to fall. Across the street, the red-neon cross of The Mission House lit the sidewalk. The store front windows emitted a cheery, inviting glow that promised a hot meal, a warm bed, and help.

Mitch pushed himself to full height on rubbery legs. He stomped to get the circulation going and stroked his whiskered face. Long ago, another prodigal came to his senses among pigs. As his father would say, God sure has a sense of humor. He grunted and like a window shopper stood outside The Mission House looking in.

A lounge area with decrepit red-and-white tiled floor and faded orange walls was visible. Beneath an industrial-size wall clock reading 2:45, two old men, as still as wax figures, sat on red plastic couches studying a chess board.

A lean, wiry man, absorbed in a magazine, leaned over the check-in desk. His weathered face glowed with an inner joy. Many times this man had presented the Gospel on the street corners in a booming voice that had seemed to chase Mitch as he hurried past.

Mitch swallowed his pride and pushed opened the heavy door. Warm humidity swept over him. A bell jangled above him.

The man lifted his head. Piercing blue eyes were made bluer by a blue flannel shirt. The open neck revealed a clean white round-neck T-shirt. How wonderful it'd be to wear a clean, white shirt again. Still—Mitch glanced back toward the door.

As if anticipating escape, the preacher man sped forward as fast as a pronounced limp allowed. His hand extended for a handshake. Reluctantly, Mitch took it. The grip was strong, his hands rough like a cowboy's, but his greeting was soft as new leather. "Welcome, friend. I'm Pastor Jim."

"Mitch."

Pastor Jim took a few steps into the room, drawing Mitch with him before he released the hand. "What can I do for you, Mitch?"

Wasn't it obvious? Maybe not. Some men and women he had met had been on the street for years and weren't interested in leaving it. After all, even Jesus asked the blind man what he wanted. Mitch sighed with deep resignation. "I'm ready to get off the street. Will you help me?"

Pastor Jim nodded and slapped his blue jeans. "Of course. I'd be honored. Come along. You can pick out fresh clothes and get a shower while I rustle you up a hot meal. Then we'll talk." He led Mitch past the desk where a copy of *Rodeo World* lay open.

Before long, Mitch was clean, dressed and seated opposite Pastor Jim. He shoveled in macaroni and cheese, hot dogs, pork and beans, and buttered bread. The meal had come from boxes and cans, nothing like Maggie used to make at the ranch, but it tasted mighty fine.

Pastor Jim gestured to photos lining the cafeteria walls. "I'm retired from rodeo. I posted those pictures to give people something ordinary to talk to me about and to remind me of where I once was. I was at the top of the heap until drink, sex, and drugs brought me to the dust. That's how I did this, busted my leg in several places. I was drunk and let the bull ram me against the wall."

Mitch ran a bit of bread around the plate to soak the juice and shoved it into his mouth. He chewed, swallowed, and said. "I watched you compete at Twin Bridges. You hung on until the very end even though the bull was shaking you all over the place."

Pastor Jim grinned wide. "Yeah. I remember that ride. First Class Male. Man, he was an ornery buzzard. It was one of my last rides before I hit it big. I thought I was hot stuff and indestructible – 'til this. The rehab was awful. It took years. Thankfully I had a doctor who was able to show me how to heal my spirit as well as my body." Pastor Jim refilled Mitch's coffee cup. The steam curled upward in a friendly way and smelled great. "What's your story, Mitch?"

The man's eyes were bright with empathy and somehow Mitch's dreams and plans of ministry gushed out. He told how his prayers, spoken with such assurance, had not stopped his mother's death. The betrayal he felt and how her death had been the death of his faith.

"Yet, you're here at the Mission House instead of going to Social Services."

"Yeah." Mitch didn't share about the pig, but answered the unasked why. "I'm tired of living like this. Can you help me find a job?"

Pastor Jim wore a thoughtful look as he massaged his damaged leg for several moments. Mitch braced for the refusal.

"Yeah, I could put the word out tomorrow, but getting clean and straight can be hard work, too. Let's get you through detox before you head into the workforce. Are you willing?"

"Yeah. Sure. Yes, I'm ready."

Week after week Mitch expressed his gratitude for Pastor Jim's kindness by sweeping, serving meals, and doing light construction around the mission. The only thing he wouldn't do was go to the church meetings. It was bad enough having to listen to the familiar songs ring through the building. Sometimes those stayed with him all night.

Soon, Pastor Jim arranged an early morning interview for a position as clerk at the Big Banana Split. It didn't pay much, but was better than nothing. Mitch played a hand over his shaven jaw and nodded to the trimmed, clear-eyed fellow in the mirror. "Good luck."

He slid his arms into his clean denim jacket and absentmindedly hummed, "His Eye is On the Sparrow." He felt more like himself except for that one large sore place in his soul. Even if complete happiness and peace were the price, he couldn't forget past disappointments in God.

Chapter Nine - Jack

Jack took stock of the food supply. Even though he'd supplemented with some of his catch, a good portion of the canned food had been used during the days they were there. He didn't want to strip the cupboards bare in case someone else in an emergency needed to use the cabin. It was another reason added to the growing sense that it was time to leave. He roused the patient and helped her to the table.

"What is it?" she asked after tasting the chunks of meat.

"Maybe you shouldn't ask."

"I'm not squeamish, just curious."

"Muskrat."

"Well you make it tasty. I could take a turn cooking, too."

"I'm not taking the chance you'll collapse into the fire. You just concentrate on getting well."

She looked relieved. "Okay."

When supper tasks were done, she pointed to the Bible on the shelf, "Would you mind reading aloud?"

This was something he and Karen had shared at the end. She had always said how comforting his deep, rich voice was. With only a brief hesitation, Jack complied. Reading brought up painful memories, yet there were good memories too. By the time he finished, Carol was asleep. He turned down the lantern, prepared for bed, and lie on his side next to her.

Carol was pleasant and positive, short, like his late wife, but where Karen had been dark-haired, olive-skinned and robust, fair Carol reminded him of a newborn fawn. Their discussions had moved past general topics, religion, faith, and the Bible to deeper issues about family and dreams, regrets and reservations. After their talks he no longer saw her merely as a creature in need, but as an interesting woman.

She was different from Karen. Even though she didn't trap, Carol had ridden with her husband on his trap line. Karen hadn't shared his love of trapping or hunting, but was always there with arms outstretched and a welcoming heart when he returned. How he missed her. Subconsciously, Jack drew Carol close.

Carol sighed in her sleep and mumbled something that sounded like "Love you, Big J."

Jack scrambled up and paced the confining area. Since Karen's death it had been impossible to go to town without being accosted by females who batted their eyelashes and giggled, while shoving phone numbers or brownies into his hands. He'd taken to locking his house after the night he had returned from a conference to find a young woman in his bed. One had even staged a flat tire and almost drowned when her car tipped over into a flood-filled ravine. Carol couldn't have faked the avalanche or her physical condition, but like that other woman had she been out there as a ploy and nearly gotten herself killed?

He was sick of being the donkey in a single woman's pin-the-tail-on-the-donkey game. The sooner they reached Free Dance, the sooner this woman would be out of this life. They would leave after breakfast. Too agitated to be near her, he slept on the bed shelf on the other wall.

When daylight came, Jack stood over her. Carol was balled into a fetal position and wore a frown in her sleep. He grabbed her shoulder and felt the chilled trembling in her body. He shook her until she awoke with a start. "What's wrong?"

"We're leaving. I'm going out to finish packing the snowmobile. Layer these over the clothes you're wearing. We'll leave as soon as you've eaten." He slung an extra flannel shirt and a pair of pants at her.

Carol wiped sleep from big blue eyes that still appeared so innocent. "Okay."

Jack spun on his heel and left. When he returned she was dressed and fumbling with the buttons. He let her struggle and moved to the fireplace to serve up the oatmeal. The brisk *tink* of metal spoon against tin bowl seemed as brusque as he was feeling, but he wouldn't apologize. People should be honest. They both remained quiet throughout the meal and the cleanup.

Once everything was ready, he bundled her in the blankets and carried her out, the snow crunching beneath his boots. He plunked her into the trailer and packed her in among the fur.

The muskrat pelts were inside out, ugly and stiff, but he'd covered their rawness with rounds of plush beaver hides and soft coyote and fox fur. Being warm and comfortable as possible in the furry nest with a couple of hot water bottles for good measure, she would have nothing to complain about. Not that he'd known her to complain, even when she was in pain.

She gave him a tentative smile as he strapped the tarpaulin to cover her completely. "It's a pity I'll miss the view. I bet it's spectacular, but I'm glad the tarp will block the cold."

"Yeah," he said. After that the engine's roar made further conversation impossible on the long, bumpy ride.

At the ranch, Jack whipped the tarp back. Carol shivered involuntarily and squinted, raising her hand against the dazzling sun. She cried out when he wrenched her from her temporary lair and carried her up snow-laden steps, through an open door, and set her, none too gently, into a chair in Karen's bright and spacious kitchen.

Carol tightened the blanket around her shoulders, confusion showing on her face. Jack reined his emotions in a bit. She'd be gone soon and it wouldn't matter. "Can you walk on your own?"

She nodded uncertainly. "Where do I go?"

"Go through the dining room and down the hallway to the blue bedroom. Shower and use the whirlpool to get the chill off. I've got things to take care of outside. I should be back in a half hour. Then I'll lay some clothes on the bed and get you something to eat."

"Okay." She took a step and nearly toppled. He caught her and held her upright until she regained her balance. She didn't lean on him as he'd expected. She merely said, "Thanks. I think I can make it."

As Jack moved the snowmobile to the shed and unloaded the fur, he puzzled over the disturbing incident of the previous night. After refueling the snowmobile, he re-entered the house through the mud room. It had a full bath where he normally showered and changed before going into the house proper. He'd told Carol he would lay out clean clothes and he'd already been gone a half hour. He removed his boots and coat and moved in stocking feet to the master bedroom, a room he rarely entered anymore.

At the door, he held his breath and listened. No sound came from within. He tapped. No answer. His stomach churned as he opened the door, but the bed and the bedroom were empty. The bathroom door was completely closed, as anyone with an ounce of discretion would do. Behind it the whirlpool hummed.

His shoulders relaxed. He hadn't realized how tense he'd been. Maybe he'd misunderstood what she'd said. Maybe it was his own imaginings he had to worry about.

He picked through Karen's clothes closet. Somebody should use these things. Maybe this year for the November fundraiser he'd finally be able to sort them, but that was months away. He didn't have to worry about it now. He tossed a flannel nightgown, slippers and housecoat on the bed. He knocked on the bathroom door. "Carol, I've laid some clothes out here for you. I'm going to go shower. Are you okay?"

"Thanks. Yes."

A long hot shower, a close shave and fresh clothes did much to restore Jack's mood. He whistled as he grilled cheese sandwiches and stirred tomato soup. When it was almost ready, he knocked on the bedroom door and announced. "Lunch is served."

He ladled soup into bowls, placed the hot sandwiches on each plate and carried a few condiments to the table. She still hadn't come. He knocked again at the bedroom door. "Are you dressed?"

"Yes," her oddly muffled voice answered.

"Are you all right?"

There was a slight pause. "I'm okay. I'll be out in a bit."

He entered. The door of the bathroom was ajar revealing that she was on her knees wiping the floor. He peered over her shoulder.

A bright red puddle marred the pale blue-green tiling. More blood was splattered up the wall. Placing his hands on either side of her arms he lifted her to her feet.

"What happened?" His spoke sharply, but turned her around gently. A red slash on her forehead below the hairline oozed blood and was swelling.

"I'm sorry. I messed up your lovely bath—"

"What happened?"

"I got dizzy. I was afraid I'd pass out and slip under the water. I lost my balance getting out." She swallowed a sob and clamped her teeth shut. He felt her tremble.

Jack settled her on the edge of the bed. "Let me see it. It's looks nasty, but it's actually not that deep. A bit of salve and gauze and you'll be good. You'll have a knot there for a few days. We'd better put ice on it."

"No. No ice."

"All right." Jack treated the gash, cleaned the mess and brought lunch. He stayed, talking with the same ease they'd shared at the cabin. Afterward, she slept.

At the doorway, Jack turned the lights off in the bedroom. All the memories he'd locked away assaulted him. His helplessness as his lovely wife shrank to skin and bones. After surgery failed, she had become too weak to leave the bed. He'd fed her and cared for her in this very room, when she could no longer hold a spoon. It was why he'd known how to care for Carol at the cabin. This woman dredged up everything he wanted to forget. Why did Karen have to die?

He escaped into the living room to ponder this and other questions he'd tried to avoid. He stood by the window watching amber and lilac hues of evening steal over the snowy fields and succumb to gray. That was his life these days. Gray. Bleak. Filled with the pain of failing Karen when she needed him most. He, who handled every situation with ease, made quick, accurate decisions, and kept everything under control, could do nothing to save her. Salvation and healing were not his to give, but God's. One thing he knew, God was good, even in this.

He fell on his knees by the large bay window and wept into his hands. "Almighty Father, I haven't accepted your will in this matter. Karen is with you, happy and healed. Forgive me for not wanting to let her go. I fooled myself, thinking I was doing well by going through the motions. Forgive and heal me." Outside thick darkness had settled when he finally rose, but his heart and his step were lighter.

Chapter Ten - Carol

The next morning Carol curled up to read on the couch under two throws and a comforter. Jack entered and went to the phone. He waved the receiver. "Still no phone service."

"I know. It's frustrating. I've checked it myself ten times today."

"What I can't figure is why there are no missing person reports on the radio. I'd think your friends and family would be frantic."

Carol imagined Peter waiting for her at the hotel. She wanted to make him sweat and worry about her. It was childish, but she wanted it anyway. "Yes, but maybe Peter didn't report me missing."

"Why wouldn't he?"

She shrugged. "Only my best friend Trudy knew I was here. She's a mother-hen type, so Peter must have explained it in some way or she'd have the National Guard combing the area."

"You look chilled. Are you strong enough to make the trip to town? You ought to see a doctor."

"That ride yesterday really taxed me. Besides, you've done a good job medically. The rest is simply going to take time. As soon as I get back to Indiana, I'll visit my doctor."

"If that's the case, are you strong enough to stay by yourself? I should finish checking my trap line. I'll pull what's there without re-setting. I'll be back late tomorrow."

"I'm sure I can manage."

Carol filled the hours after Jack left with prayer, reading, and writing letters to her children even though she couldn't mail them. She explored the huge house. Behind one door she found stairs leading to a chilly second story filled with bedrooms and bathrooms. Most looked never used. All were decorated with Karen's stitchery, comforters and pillows, and had a general homey feel. She shivered.

Back on the main floor, she picked up the phone and cheered when she heard a dial tone. The hotel informed her Peter had left the same disastrous day he proposed, taking the luggage they'd already packed in the rental car with him. Only her overnight bag and her purse were held in safe keeping.

For a few moments, Carol indulged in a pleasant fantasy of pushing Peter off that scenic overlook near Skeleton Run. Gingerly she punched his office number. She had no desire to talk with him, but it's where she'd find Trudy. "It's Carol. Did you think I'd dropped off the face of the earth?"

"Carol, where are you? I've been so worried. It's not like you not to call me and the hotel said you'd checked out."

"That was Peter's doing. I got caught in a snow storm, trapped in an avalanche, and rescued by a handsome wealthy rancher who was on his trap line. I'm recovering in his fantastic house deep in the mountains where we're snowed in, except for snowmobile or airlift."

"Sounds like a great story. I always said you should write fiction. You still should've called me. Where are you really?"

"I'm not joking, Trudy. It happened. The phone was reconnected only today. How's Minnie?"

"That beagle is getting fat. She eats Trixie's food as well as her own, but I can't seem to catch her at it. She misses you. She's taken to watching the door. When're you coming back?"

"I really don't know. I'm snowed in and I've had a slow recuperation from hypothermia."

There was no reply. "Hello? Hello? Trudy? Is this thing dead again?"

"You mean you really were caught in an avalanche? Why didn't Peter tell me?"

"It was after he proposed and deserted me on the mountain."

"He didn't."

"Oh, yes, he did. Let's talk about it when I get back. I don't have anything pressing on the calendar, do I?

"Nothing until February 20. The hospital called your house umpteen times the first few days wondering when you're getting back. Transcriptions are piled to the sky. I told them you were delayed and suggested they hire a temp."

"Good. Thanks. I'm still recuperating. I'll be back in a few days. I'll let you know."

"You received a letter from Nick and two from Zaire."

"Read them and call me with an update. I'll give you my phone number; only don't give Peter this number no matter what," Carol said.

"Peter's not here. He's in Florida. He was in a real foul mood when he returned from skiing. He had me change his schedule and left the same day. He said you were staying out there awhile on vacation."

"Only if you call a near-death experience a vacation. I'm sick and I'm hurt and I'm angry. At this point, I don't even count Peter as a friend. I think I need a new publicist."

"Okay, you have got to give me the details. Only I've got a meeting in five minutes. Give me your number then I've got to go."

Carol recited the number and disconnected the phone before it could ignite in the heat of her renewed fury at Peter. He was so self-absorbed he had never even checked to see if she had returned safely. Had he dumped her luggage at the Butte airport or checked the bags onto the plane so that they were in the no man's land of baggage claim in Indianapolis?

Carol wandered back to the kitchen looking for comfort food. Ice cream held no attraction. She longed for a cup of herbal tea. Jack only drank coffee and regular tea, both strong enough to straighten hair. Carol rummaged through a cupboard, opening tins and peeking in canisters as she ruminated on Peter's betrayal. Even though she admitted she was relieved to be rid of his constant attentions and incessant demands, it still hurt. "How dare he?" she demanded out loud as she wrestled open a canister lid. It was empty and she shoved it back into the cabinet.

In the far corner, behind a canister of cookies, she found a vanilla café instant coffee mix. Almost as good as Earl Grey! She clasped it to her breast and broke into tears feeling she had found a treasure.

She nursed the coffee while soaking in a tub of hot water. Trudy was onto something. Why not write about her experience? Would it be better as a biography or fiction? Carol patted dry and snuggled into Karen's plush red terrycloth robe. She picked up the empty cup and headed for the kitchen for a refill.

The turn table twirled as the microwave whirred softly. How many times did it rotate in the ninety seconds it took to heat water? She noticed an odd reflection in the microwave window. Carol yelped and pivoted.

A man in faded jeans and flannel shirt scowled at her fiercely. He brushed back thin hair from his shoulders causing an earring like a long spike to dangle. "No wonder the old man likes to spend so much time here."

The microwave beeped, returning the world to normal. She turned her back on him to retrieve her tea. "You scared me half to death. Jack is out on his trap line."

"I figured as much when I saw the snowmobile gone. I didn't figure to find another woman."

"I am not 'another woman'. I'd been caught in an avalanche. Your father dug me out of the snow just as the last storm hit. I'd have died if he hadn't come along."

"Sounds about right," he said icily. "Big J to the rescue."

"Excuse me. I'll be back." When she returned, fully dressed, the new arrival was still in the kitchen staring out the window over the sink.

"Can I make you a cup of coffee, Mitchell? It is Mitchell, isn't it?"

He turned toward her, the scowl in place. "So he told you about me. I worried the old man was doing okay only to find he's made himself a love nest in my own mother's house."

"Stop it! We were at the cabin for over a week before I was well enough to travel and I still needed a lot of invalid care once we were back here. It wasn't easy to be reminded of his death vigil with your mother."

Mitchell snorted, but failed to hold the hard edge in his voice, "Yep. That's dad. He'll always do what is right."

Carol sipped her drink. "He left today to check his traps. As soon as he gets back, he'll take me to town so I can go home to Indiana. The phone was out until today, too."

"I know. I've been trying to call."

"Since you're here I guess the road must be clear."

"No. I jumped in."

"Jumped in?"

He waved his hand as if it were an ordinary everyday occurrence. "Yeah. Jumped. With a parachute. I have a friend with a plane and he dropped me."

"Well, I'm impressed. I like to keep my feet on the ground or at least have a big old plane under me. I didn't even know people did that sort of thing in winter."

He sneered. "I've jumped lots of time. In winter you just wear winter gear, like for skiing."

"Oh. It was nice of you to check on your dad."

"I don't know why I bothered, really." Mitchell stomped away.

Carol wrapped in a quilt and curled on the couch with her mug. That man had attitude problems. No wonder Jack was concerned. She picked up her book, read three paragraphs and fell sound asleep.

A violent shiver woke her. The room was dark except for a bright shaft of light from the kitchen which formed a yellow parallelogram on the floor. The gentle clinking of metal and the aroma of cooked chicken told her dinner was underway. Cautiously she rose. Holding on to furniture and the wall to ease the dizziness, she made her way to the kitchen. Mitchell worked over the stove.

"Are you a good cook?"

A sour expression darkened his face. "Didn't my father tell you?"

"Tell me what?"

"I'm a bona fide chef. I worked the mid-night grill at one of the grubbier burger joints in our fair capital."

She ignored the sarcasm and asked, "Do you like cooking, Mitchell?"

"It beats the streets." Mitchell forked a chicken breast onto each plate and spooned green beans and canned pork and beans next to it. He carried the plates to the table. "I didn't ask your name before."

Carol introduced herself. "This looks good." She bowed her head briefly and reached for her napkin.

"You can give thanks aloud. Actually, it helps when someone says grace, keeps me from choking on my food. You know it was law around here when I was a kid. It's just right now, I can't say it myself."

Carol bowed her head again and prayed aloud, including a request for Mitchell.

The scowl returned. "How much do you know? Did he tell you what a disappointment I am? How I'm not following in the family's sainted footsteps?"

"He said you took your mother's death hard. I know how that feels."

"Do you? You didn't see how she suffered."

Carol spoke quietly, evenly, "I have an idea. I lost both my mom and dad when I was sixteen. My dad had both legs and an arm amputated due to advanced diabetes before he found release from the suffering. My mom had a heart attack two months after he died. I've lost two children. One drowned when he was seven and a baby girl died of sudden infant death syndrome. Five years ago my husband died. I think I'm qualified to understand a bit about loss."

Mitchell stopped chewing as empathy then disbelief swept his face. Before he could speak, she said, "Let me know if I'm close. You're angry. Angry at your dad, who all your life was able to fix things but wasn't able to fix the most important thing - your mom.

"You're angry with yourself because it was out of your control to help her. Deep down you fear maybe her death was punishment for something you did or didn't do.

"You're angry at God for not healing your mom the way you thought he should even though he was able. If you are anything at all like I was, you told God you don't like the way he runs things and you don't think he's qualified to be in control of your life."

Mitchell's fork had halted halfway to his mouth. His eyes bored into hers and his face drew tight. He looked ready to explode. He lay his fork on his plate. The chair squeaked as he pushed himself away from the table and stood stiff and tall.

She spoke rapidly, softly, tenderly. "Meanwhile your pain is killing you and you'd rather it did than submit to God's will."

Mitchell whirled and stalked out of the room. Carol let him go. He needed to think through her words. No, those weren't her words. She'd never be so bold in herself. As she stored the leftovers and washed the dishes, Carol prayed the words would find their target.

The next morning, Carol wrapped her hands around a mug and inhaled the aroma of freshly-brewed coffee as she took in the view of snowy mountains from the warmth of the kitchen.

"You don't pull any punches, do you?"

Mitchell stood in the door way, his hair a rumpled mess and his clothes wrinkled as if he'd slept in them. He didn't look particularly pleased to see her.

"I just came back from a women's seminar. The topic was 'Life after Death - Beginning again after the loss of a loved one.' It never fails to minister to me."

Mitchell snorted. "What do you do? Attend the same seminar all over the country?"

"Yes, as a matter of fact, I do. I'm the speaker." Carol laughed.

Mitchell grinned, then, too. He padded across the kitchen floor in bare feet and took a cup from the mug tree on the counter and filled it. "I hope you're gentler on those women than you were on me."

"Do you forgive me for being so blunt, Mitchell?"

"I needed to hear it. I've been feeling pretty sorry for myself. And I go by Mitch."

"Okay. Did you get your thoughts sorted out last night?"

"Truthfully, I guess that's why I'm here. I wanted to talk with Dad. I don't know how he did it. He was so accepting. He never questioned God at all." Mitch settled himself at the table.

Carol took the seat opposite and waited as he swigged coffee.

"I had fasted and prayed so hard for mom to be healed. I truly believed she would get well. When she died, I thought, who needs a God who doesn't care or won't listen. I thought I was making an intellectual decision. Growing up. Getting Smart. Moving away from worship of a non-existent being. Instead, I was—" Mitch searched for words.

"—throwing a temper tantrum?"

He frowned. "I was going to say acting crazy, but, yes, I guess I was throwing a temper tantrum. Now, I see how the poor choices I made have hurt me and others, especially my dad. I used drugs, you know. I've stayed drunk for days on end. I've stole and—" He broke off the litany, too embarrassed to continue.

"All of us seek to escape pain in different ways."

"Dad would be so disappointed to know this. I can't believe I'm telling you."

"Sometimes it's easier to talk to strangers, someone whom we can't disappoint, who has no stake in our lives. Maybe even someone we'll never see again. It's not always a wise choice to be so candid with a stranger, but I promise I won't betray your confidence."

They sipped coffee to fill the silence. Soon Carol said, "I handled my hurt and anger over my parents' deaths differently than that. I went to live with my aunt in another city and got busy. I was in everything in school, working hard to find a way to fit in at a new place. I was very involved at my aunt's church, choir, Bible memorization team, youth group."

"A good girl. You found comfort and relief."

"No. Not at all. I filled every waking moment so full I didn't have time to think and was too exhausted to feel. I was using that as a substitute for God. Running away never brings resolution no matter what form it takes. Did you find relief?"

Mitch said, "It felt like it at first, not having to face what was too painful to face, but it only made things worse. Why didn't I see it sooner? Why didn't I give God my pain?"

"Oh, Mitch, you've known it all along. Perhaps your pride was pricked. After all, you were an enthusiastic preacher, doing God's will, full of faith, praying for a miracle, which you fully believed would happen and you told everybody she would get well. Then it didn't turn out the way you had said it would."

"Why wasn't she healed?"

Carol shrugged to indicate she couldn't answer. "The year after my mom died, I was at the park studying. A mother and a toddler were walking along the hedge which grew around the edge of the park. The little girl's balloon got away from her and the wind bounced it along the grass and into the street. The child chased after it, ignoring her mother's order to stop. Because of the hedge, the child couldn't see what the mother, being taller, could see. There was a truck barreling down the street. The woman couldn't reach the girl in time, but the child tripped and fell flat. Thank God the truck went right over the top of her and she was unhurt.

"Suddenly I knew. I was that child. I was running into the path of danger and didn't know it. I couldn't see all the perils but God was aware of them and was trying to help me before I got hit. He loved me, even when I wasn't doing it his way."

"A temper tantrum."

"Yes. When I made the decision to accept Christ's will for my parents and for me, comfort came. I quit struggling. I started to live again and my life had meaning once more."

"I miss my mother."

"I still miss my mom, too, and my dad, A.J. and our children. I can't explain why things happened in a certain way, why one person is healed on earth and another is healed by being taken in death. I do know I love my Lord and want to be with him. I certainly don't want to be separated for eternity from him or my family."

Mitch grunted. Carol let the silence stretch and then she went to the refrigerator. "Do you want some eggs?"

"Sure." As Carol broke eggs into a skillet, Mitch poured a second cup. "So you speak at conferences?"

"Yes. I wrote a book on grief. I travel to promote it."

"My dad travels and teaches, too. Did he tell you? He's got some trapping books, videos and has developed a couple of lures. They used to sell pretty well. I don't know if they still do. He's a real sportsman, not to mention conservation management and all that stuff. Maybe it's not as important as helping people with grief, but he likes it."

"We all have our purpose."

Mitch pursed lips in a begrudging smile. He poured orange juice and set the glasses on the table before sitting again. "I suppose so. Is it full-time ministry?"

Carol placed buttered toast beside the eggs and set one of the full plates in front of him. "No, but it feels full time. My day job gives me a break from the pressure of dealing with people. How about you? Are you going into street ministry or becoming a musician?" She flicked his dangly earring and froze at her forwardness with someone she didn't really know. "I'm so sorry. I shouldn't have said that."

Mitch took a few moments before his face relaxed again. He waved at her. "Aw, forget it. No to both questions."

"What do you see yourself doing?"

"I'm not sure. It's one of those things I hope to sort out while I'm here. Do you mind? I think I'd like to give the blessing."

Chapter Eleven – Mitch

Mitch finished clean-up in an introspective mood. He missed his mother. They'd always enjoyed a comfortable relationship. He'd surprised himself when he told Carol details of his rebellion he never would have shared even with his mother. As they talked, he realized he'd been longing for God, even more than for his mom or his dad.

He wandered the house, noting small signs of Carol's presence such as a loose blanket on the sofa, his mother's recipe cards spread out on the dining room table and the closed door to the master bedroom where she stayed. Knowing she was in his mother's room bothered him a little. However, he was certain his mother would have welcomed Carol with open arms.

His father had moved into the guest room before Karen's death and evidently never left it. The bedside table held his big study Bible and a notebook. The room felt calm and orderly right down to the change on the dresser arranged in neat stacks. Mitch settled on the bed to capture the sense of his father's presence. Unlike himself, his father never had doubts about God. What a failure he was compared to his father.

Mitch's gaze fell on the open notebook to an entry dated two days earlier.

My dearest Karen,

Last night I realized how desperately I've been holding on to you. I'd buried the pain of your absence and been going through the motions because I didn't want to go on living without you. Perhaps if I'd let go sooner Mitchell wouldn't be struggling as he is. I wasn't much of an example. But, how could I help him when I needed so much help myself? It's odd to think God has a plan for me that doesn't include you. Of course, nothing could ever replace the part of you I carry in my heart. But, if I am to be a faithful servant, than I must go on alone. I'm not sure how to do that. As a start, I think this will be my final letter to you.

Love, Big J.

Mitch flipped through the notebook. What did he really know about his father? Page after page the pain, fears, and burdens of the past years were spelled out. He was shocked at his dad's loneliness and even more at the obvious love for his son.

Mitch placed the book back on the nightstand. He hadn't meant to intrude but he was glad he had glimpsed this very human side of his dad. If his father still had questions about God and life, maybe everyone did.

He stretched out on his father's bed to think, but soon fell asleep. When Mitch awoke, the sun had moved to the other side of the house and the room was soft with evening shadows. A darker shadow filled a nearby chair. Mitch propped himself on his elbows. His voice was hoarse from sleep. "Dad, when did you get back?"

"An hour ago. I hope you don't mind. I've been sitting, watching you sleep. I missed you, son."

"Hey, it's your room. How'd the line go?"

"I pulled everything so I wouldn't have to go out again until after I get Carol to a doctor. You've met Carol?"

"Yeah. She makes a big impression in a short time, doesn't she?"

Jack gave a short laugh. "Yes. In no time at all it's like I've known her for years."

"She told me you found her buried alive."

"She was near our fishing hole close to the Bear Park Trails, so cold and blue I thought she was dead. She almost was." Jack shook his head at the memory.

"Pretty scary."

"Yeah." Jack's face softened. "It's good to see you, Mitchell."

Mitch stood for a welcome-back embrace. "It's good to be home. Can I stay for a while until I get a few things straightened out?"

"Take all the time you need, son." The acceptance in those words was a healing balm.

The phone rang and both men moved to answer it. The answering machine recorded an urgent, breathless voice. "Carol it's Trudy. Call me ASAP."

Before Mitch even knew Carol was behind them, she pushed past and snatched the phone. "Trudy? What's wrong?"

The message was still recording so they all heard Trudy's response reverberate through the room. "Kurt is dead."

Carol's face grew ashen. Her voice came out in a thin squeak. "No. What happened? What about Kim?"

"I don't know. Kim left a message on the phone and didn't say. I called the Head Office of the Missions Council. She's in the States, but they didn't have a contact number. She'd already left the Council and is headed home. She'll arrive tomorrow afternoon."

Determination crossed Carol's face. "I don't know how, but I'm coming home today. I'll call you with the time."

"I'll be there, no matter when you come in."

Tears leaked from Carol's tightly shut lids as she pressed the phone to her closed mouth. Her neck muscles worked up and down. She weaved and Mitch thought she was going to collapse.

Jack started toward her, but stopped when she suddenly straightened and rummaged through the desk for a phone book. Her fingers trembled as she punched in the numbers for the airline. She slammed the receiver down. "Circuits are busy. I can't get through. I have to get my credit cards and ID from the lodge. Maybe I can call the airline from there."

Jack said, "Let's go. I'll rig the trailer with blankets and bring the snowmobile to the back door."

Mitch said, "Right. I'll get Mom's ski outfit and a warm coat."

Within the hour they were bouncing through drifts sparkling in the sun, but the air still nipped at any exposed flesh.

At the lodge, they pulled off their ski masks before casting off the tarp to free Carol. Jack lifted her out of the furry nest of the trailer. Her red face and puffy eyes were reminders of her grief. She said, "Thanks for bringing me here. I'll mail these clothes to you."

"Don't. I have no use for them. We'll wait here to take you to the airport," Jack said.

"I'll take the shuttle. Thanks again for everything, Jack. If there's ever anything I can do for you, please don't hesitate to call." Carol extended her hand.

Jack pulled off his glove and shook her hand. "Seems we both benefited. I hope you'll come for a visit."

Mitch caught her up in a bear hug. "Thanks for helping me find my way home."

"You were already there. I'll be praying." With a final wave Carol quick-stepped up the broad concrete stairs past a noisy group in ski jackets and disappeared into the lodge.

Jack turned away from the lodge slowly before pulling his glove on, but his voice sounded normal enough. "We may as well pick up supplies. Who knows when we'll next have a chance? I need a dozen more #2's to thin out a pack of coyotes near Bender's Pass or come spring they'll be killing calves for fun."

Chapter Twelve - Carol

The next morning, Carol dragged herself out of bed and appeared at the office of Faulkinroy Publicity, coffee in hand. There, standing before Trudy's desk as distinguished as ever and distinctly displeased to see her was Peter still in his overcoat. A very beautiful, very young woman was at his side.

"Carol," Trudy greeted. "Will surprises never cease? Come meet Peter's new wife, Cynthia. She was Miss Belle of the South two years ago."

Carol's jaw dropped. "That was fast."

Peter's face colored and his voice was brittle as he turned to Cynthia, "I represent many corporate clients and some authors and artists. Carol Streeter is one of the authors."

"How exciting," Cynthia enthused in a southern drawl. "I'm thrilled to meet a famous author."

"I'm not famous. Now, you on the other hand, Miss Belle of the South and a new bride, too. Congratulations, Mrs. Faulkinroy. How did it happen?"

"It was one of those whirlwind romances. We met in Florida at the beach and Peter swept me off my feet." She giggled and fluttered her lashes at her husband.

"I've had that experience myself. It's memorable," Carol said. Trudy's mouth quirked up at the corners as she appreciated the sarcasm.

Peter patted Cynthia's hand. "Well, my love, I have work to do. You need to go home and settle in."

Cynthia looked disappointed. "Oh. I guess there is so much to do."

"We'll have lunch sometime," Carol offered.

"Thank you. You're so sweet. I sure hope I can remember the way back." She tittered nervously as she headed for the door.

"Don't you worry. It's easy," Trudy reassured her. She plucked a business card from the holder on her desk and drew a map on the back of it. "If you should get lost, call me. I'll be right here."

"Thank you so much. Y'all are so kind. I don't think you Yankees are rude and stand-offish at all. Bye." With a bright smile and a practiced wave she left the office.

Carol clucked her tongue. "My, my, Peter, when you said you were ready to get married, you really meant it, didn't you?"

Peter glowered. "I don't believe you are on my calendar of appointments today."

"No, I brought my friend a thank-you latte." She set the cup on Trudy's desk. "I didn't think there was a chance I'd see you. Don't worry, I'm not interested in rocking the boat today. However, you may be hearing from my attorney."

"Your attorney?"

"You left me on the mountain. I nearly died."

Peter's lip curled. "Yet, here you stand supremely self-sufficient."

"The resort director insisted I file a complaint with the sheriff for insurance purposes. He even gave me a ride there. I think they were afraid of bad publicity. You know all about that. They gave me a complimentary weekend and airfare and said you aren't welcome there anymore."

"You exaggerate."

"No. Actually, I don't."

"If you have business to discuss, Trudy can schedule you next week. I don't have time for you today."

"I don't have time for you either. I'm picking up Kim at the airport. Congratulations Peter. Your wife is sweet, very young, but very sweet."

"And beautiful," he retorted in a tone to imply Carol was not.

"I'm glad I had the sense to say no to you, since your declarations of love and devotion can so easily be diverted."

She caught only a glimpse of his eyes sparking with anger before Trudy stepped in front of her and gently shoved her toward the door. "Thanks for the latte. I'll be by tonight to see Kim. Better get going. You don't want to miss her."

In the elevator, Carol put a hand on the hall wall to steady her wobbly knees. She couldn't care a fig who Peter married, but it made her ordeal so much more unnecessary. He was detestable.

At the Indianapolis International Airport, Carol parked in the short-term lot. With the engine running and the heater cranked high, she gripped the top of the steering wheel with both hands and rested her forehead on them. The gray wool of the mittens was soft against her skin and she breathed a sigh of thanksgiving that she'd arrived early enough to catch her breath. She added a prayer for the strength to walk to the terminal.

She pulled off the mittens, dug through her purse for lipstick, and tilted the rearview mirror. Make-up hid the unnatural pallor of her skin and the circles under her blue eyes were hopefully no more than what any mother might experience from a sleepless night upon hearing her son-in-law was dead and her daughter was arriving that day.

Carol applied fresh lipstick, reassured that concern for her well-being would not be added to Kim's grief. There would be plenty of time later to talk about her recent near-death experience. Right now, Kim was all that mattered. With one last look, she tucked a few stray wisps of blonde hair under her cap, shut off the engine, and grabbed her purse.

The airport was busier than when she'd arrived from Montana the night before. Carol anxiously surveyed the new arrivals. An elderly woman with a cane, accompanied by an equally aged man was the first to appear. The rest of the travelers were men except for a disheveled female of an age hard to identify who shuffled as if carrying a heavy burden. Her stark face was so sunburnt it was almost black. Underweight like a terminally ill patient, a thin skirt hung to the floor beneath a brown oversized coat.

As the woman drew near, Carol sent a quick prayer asking God to help her. The woman stopped in front of her. "Mom."

With a cry, Carol lunged forward enfolding Kim. Weeping, they rocked back and forth, clinging to each other. "You're home. You're safe. It's so terrible about Kurt. I'm so sorry you have to go through this."

"It's been awful, Mom. Just awful." Kim wiped tears with her hand. "I can't talk about it here. Let's go home."

"What about your luggage?"

"I don't have any."

"What?"

"We had stored some boxes of clothes and things at Kurt's parents. I stopped on the way to the airport to tell them about Kurt, but they weren't home. So I came as I was."

"I'd have thought the Missionary Council would've had some clothes for you."

"They offered. I didn't want to wait. It doesn't really matter anyway."

"It doesn't matter," Carol repeated softly in surprise. Since when did clothes not matter to Kim?

Kim turned her back and shuffled away. Carol hurried to catch up.

All the way home, Kim was too quiet as if she were only an empty shell. Carol kept talking, needing to fill the painful silence.

Minnie greeted them with crazy excitement, baying and turning circles. Kim burst into tears and dropped to the floor. She hugged the wiggling dog to her chest.

Carol choked back a sob. "You relax, honey. I'll make hot chocolate and be right back."

A little later, as they wrapped in a downy quilt and nestled on the couch with steaming mugs of hot chocolate, Kim rested her head on Carol's shoulder as she had many times growing up. With a big sigh and without prompting, Kim told her about Kurt's heat stroke and concussion. "He was a miserable patient, complaining and demanding."

"That doesn't sound like Kurt. He must have been in pain."

"He insisted he was well and went back to work, but nothing was the same. It was as if someone had taken his place. He had nothing good to say and denounced people for every little thing. The congregation shrank. Then they quit working on the building. I tried to talk to him. He got very angry—"

Kim sobbed and pressed one hand to her lips as if to silence herself. Her mug shook and Carol pulled it from Kim's fingers and set it on the end table. "Go on."

Kim twisted the blanket in her hands until it was a tightly compressed tail. Her face contorted as tears flowed unrestrained. Sobs wracked her. "I lost a baby. Kurt got worse. He was so—mean. Uzachi tried to go for help—but died. He kept getting worse and worse and worse…I was all alone and then the rebels came."

The garbled tale made little sense. Carol patted and soothed and crooned, "I'm so sorry. I'm so sorry, my dear, sweet girl."

Kim wailed, "I'm pregnant again."

"Oh, Kim." Carol squeezed her. Was this good or bad news? Kim was holding something back.

"Mom, I know I should forgive, but I don't know if I can."

"Of course it's hard to process this. Take it one moment at a time. Forgive one memory at a time. God understands and loves you. You know he does."

Kim nodded, but the furrow on her brow hinted at doubts. Carol crooned hymns, one after another until during *A Cleft in the Rock*, Kim joined in. Minnie jumped on the couch, howling. Kim gathered the dog into her arms. "I don't want anyone to know I'm here. I don't want sympathy. I don't want questions. I don't want to see anyone."

"Just rest. You don't have to see anybody you don't want to see."

Kim fell asleep hugging Minnie. Carol patted the faithful dog and tucked the blue and white quilt around Kim as if she were still a little girl. Her breathe caught. White marks encircled Kim's wrists where the skin was still healing. Carol squeezed her eyes shut and then pulled back Kim's socks. Deeper scars, still blotchy-red and angry-looking marred one ankle. What, oh what had her girl endured?

Carol kept watch from a nearby rocker until she couldn't fight her strained body any longer. Drifting asleep, she thought, "I can't do this, Lord. You're going to have to take care of her."

"I am."

The ringing phone jarred Carol awake. She hurried to answer it before it woke her daughter. "Hello."

A high-pitched quavering voice pierced the air. "We got back from visiting my sister and found Kim's note on the door. We were still reading it when that Brother Bryan from the Mission Council arrived to tell us about Kurt."

"Mrs. Macomb, it's tragic. We all loved Kurt. He was a wonderful man."

"Yes, he was. I can't believe Kim didn't stay until she talked with us. She let us find out in that impersonal way."

"She wanted you to hear it from her, but she's very ill. She shouldn't have stopped, but she did because she was thinking about you."

"Is she in the hospital?"

"No, but—"

"Put her on the phone now."

"I'll have her call you when she wakes." After many more refusals, Kurt's mother relented.

Kim was still asleep on the couch that evening when Trudy arrived. "She looks awful," Trudy whispered as they stood over her.

"I know. She hasn't moved from that spot since she got home." Carol turned toward the hall as the phone rang. "That's probably Kurt's mother again. She's called six times in as many hours. I told her Kim would call her back when she woke up."

Trudy's face took on a staunch nothing-gets-past-me look. "I'll handle it." She marched into the hall and snatched up the phone. "Streeter residence. How may I help you?"

The unmistakable reedy rambling of Kim's mother-in-law issued from the receiver. Fifteen minutes became a half hour as the woman poured out her pain and Trudy remained calm and caring. "Really Mrs. Macomb, at this time, a grief counselor or your pastor would be a better choice to talk with instead of Kim. Like you, she's in shock and devastated. You know how much she loves your son. We haven't been able to talk with her ourselves."

Carol gave Trudy a thumbs-up and murmured a prayer that the woman would accept this.

The determined voice raised an octave, but the words weren't clear.

"A memorial service is extremely important, but it'll be a week or more before she can deal with that. After all, Kurt has been gone for a month already even though the news is fresh to us." Trudy closed her eyes in concentration and moved the phone away from direct contact with her ear. At a pause in the verbal torrent, she said, "If you feel that strongly, have a memorial service without her."

Carol grabbed Trudy's arm as she continued, "How will it look? It'll look as if Kim is heartsick and physically ill. If anybody is so cruel-hearted as to not understand, then you simply say that you lost your son and you have to think of what is best for his wife and baby. That's right. A baby. We only found out this morning. Please, don't call back. She'll call you within the next twenty-four hours as soon as she is able. I knew you'd understand. Good-bye."

"You handled that so well."

"Ow." Trudy rubbed her ear. "I'm glad to be able to do something to help Kim."

"Thank you, Trudy," Kim held onto the wall with one hand. "I can't make those plans. I'm happy to let them do the memorial service."

"She intends to have a viewing for two days and a funeral at the church, a short internment, and a dinner afterward."

Kim stared at Trudy in bewilderment. "But there's no body."

"She wants the closed casket on display. She expects a large turnout."

Kim sighed. "She's right about that. Kurt never met anyone who didn't become a friend. How will I manage, meeting all those people?"

Carol put an arm around her. "Do what you can and no more."

"At least they're footing the funeral bill," Trudy said. "That has to be a relief."

"Yes. I have nothing." Kim yawned wide and rubbed her eyes. She reached for the phone. "I have to call her back."

"Tomorrow," Carol said with authority. "Call tomorrow."

Kim pulled her hand back as if the phone were hot. "Yes, Mom," she said meekly and went into the kitchen. Trudy and Carol stared at each other unable to verbalize what disturbed them.

Carol remained unsettled. At the funeral, Kim stood before the filled church gripping the podium, speaking haltingly. "Africa was Kurt's second home. He wanted to grow old and die there. Part of his wish came true when he tried to save the church from rebels."

"It was just like him," Kurt's mother sobbed while the face of Kurt's father twisted in an effort to hold back emotion. Kim swayed and collapsed. The minister assisted her past the flowers and the casket into her seat.

Carol recalled the moment in a thank you letter to Jack. "Even her in-laws didn't fault her for leaving early, treating her condition as a sign of her love for their son. I feel there's much more than grief involved. Something's eating Kim and I don't know what. She seems so distant."

Carol poured out other concerns in frequent letters to Jack and knew that he was praying. His return letters comforted and encouraged her as days flowed into weeks and the weeks into months. She wrote, "It's been four months. If the house is messy, Kim picks it up. When someone speaks to her, she answers. She eats when urged to. Her skin is still dark, but no longer looks charred. The average person would think she's improving, but she's stuck. She rarely leaves the house and refuses visitors. Something radical must be done." Carol paused and bit her pen. She was about to ask a huge favor.

Chapter Thirteen - Jack

Jack paused outside the barber shop and brushed the last few strands of loose hair from his shoulders. They glistened reddish-brown as a summer breeze swept them away. Since Karen died white streaked the hair at his temples. He could probably thank Mitchell for most of that. His son, mischief lighting his face, strode from the post office, flipping a letter back and forth.

"Hey, Dad! It's another letter from Carol. I wonder what this one says."

Jack reached for it. Mitchell moved it behind his back.

Jack frowned. He couldn't quietly enjoy the view from the porch or plan a woodworking project without Mitchell thinking he was pining for Carol. It was especially irksome since he often was thinking of her. "When I said I was glad to have you back home, son, I didn't know you'd turn out to be such a pain in the neck. If you want to know what she has to say, open it and read it yourself." He stepped off the sidewalk and yanked open the truck door.

"Testy. Testy." Mitchell laughed, but he wrenched the passenger door open and jumped in quickly enough as Jack revved the engine and pulled away from the curb.

At the sound of paper shredding, Jack said, "Hey, what're doing?"

"You said I should open it."

"Do you have to rip it to pieces? It is my mail, you know."

Mitchell held up the long, jagged shreds he had produced and gave a grin that was so like his mother's it pinched Jack's heart. "Forgive me. I should've used my pocket knife."

"Yes, you should've."

Mitchell drew the letter out and a photograph of a beautiful brunette with smiling eyes fell into his lap. He turned the photo so Jack could see it. "Wow. She's a looker. Did you ask Carol to find you a mail-order bride?"

"Cut it out. What's it say?"

"Dear Jack, I've enclosed a picture of my daughter, Kim. The psychiatrist recommends a change of scenery. I remembered how restful and calm your house in the hills is and your many invitations. Would you let Kim and my niece, Jasmine, stay for the summer? I realize this is a huge imposition, but Kim doesn't require special care. She merely needs a quiet place to mend. I'll pay whatever you feel is reasonable and I must tell you, she is seven months pregnant. Whatever your answer, I'll never forget all you did for me. Your friend, Carol."

Mitchell folded the letter and reinserted it in the envelope, tucking in the ragged edges that flapped in the wind. He gazed at the photo. "It must be rough to be having a baby on top of everything else. What do you think?"

Jack didn't have to think about it. He may have pulled Carol from her death in the snow, but she'd rescued him too by helping face Karen's death and rebuilding a relationship with Mitchell. "Well, we'll ask Maggie to keep house and cook so Kim won't have the burden of doing anything but healing. We'll bring home the boarded horses in case she or the young girl wants to ride. If you don't want the responsibility of caring for them, I'll hire a man, maybe Morgan. Yes, it'll all work out. I think I'll call Carol as soon as we get home."

"Good idea, Dad. Get the daughter here and the mother will be sure to follow."

"Sheesh. You need a woman of your own, Mitchell, so you'll stop pestering me." Jack turned up the volume on a country western station and ignored his son's impish grin.

When he called her, Carol heaved a huge sigh. "I can't tell you how much this means to me. It's a bonus she's so eager to leave here. Jack, I didn't want to influence you before, but when I send you an email with her itinerary, I'll attach a current photo. She's improved much since she's been home, but I'm not sure you'd recognize her from the photo I sent."

This sounded ominous, so he simply said, "I'll be expecting it."

A week later when he and Mitchell drove to the airport in Bozeman to fetch their guests, he was glad for the current photo for he'd never have been able to hide his surprise. The first photo and the tales Carol had told in the cabin of her unmarried daughter didn't match with the withdrawn widow that de-planed. Her companion made up for her reticence.

Jasmine was tall and gangly for thirteen, with freckles scattered across her face and arms. Copper colored hair was tamed by two braids. She fired a million questions throughout lunch and didn't stop there. By the time they arrived at the ranch, Jack was sure there wasn't much about them Jasmine didn't know. "So Maggie has lived on the ranch since your son was a baby?"

"That's right. She helped care for Mitchell, and cooked for us."

"She's the best cook," Mitchell added. "And, there's not much on the ranch she doesn't know how to do."

"Cool," Jasmine said. "Does her family stay with her?"

"She lost her husband and child before she came to us. She's never remarried," Jack said. In the rearview mirror, dark-haired Kim continued to stare out the window. Was she listening? She showed no reaction to hearing about someone who had experienced the same losses she had. He added, "We are her family. After my wife died, Maggie moved to town."

"How come?"

"I was gone most of the time and the ranch is too isolated to for her to stay by herself."

"Where were you, Mitch?"

"Oh, uh, well, I was having a temper tantrum."

Jasmine wrinkled her freckled nose. "That's a funny thing to say. What do you mean?"

Mitchell met his father's gaze and then turned to face Jasmine. "I was going to be a preacher and I thought I understood everything about how God worked. I knew he was able to heal my mom. I figured all I had to do was pray and God would do it, like that." The sharp snap of fingers shot through the air-conditioned Blazer. Kim flinched. So she was listening. Mitchell smiled at her, but Kim turned her face to the side window again.

"What happened?"

"Well, Jasmine, I was so angry that I told God I didn't want to do things his way anymore. I ran away. I wouldn't talk to my dad. I stayed drunk until pretty soon I couldn't hold a job and was sleeping on the streets. I was cold and hungry, but through all that, God still loved me. He sent something as a reminder of his love, something to call me back."

Jasmine held the back of the Mitchell's seat and pulled herself forward as far as the seatbelt would stretch. "What was it?"

"A pig."

Jasmine laughed a light happy sound. "A pig?"

"Yes. I'll tell you all about it sometime. Here we are and that's Maggie."

Jack stopped near the front porch. "We're not formal here. She'll want you to call her Maggie."

The sturdy woman descended the stairs with quick, spry steps. Her wrinkled, kindly face glowed. She welcomed both young women as if they were dearest family members. At first, Kim drew back at the hearty greeting then leaned into the hug. Jack sent a thank-you heavenward for the inspiration to have Maggie stay at the ranch.

The men hauled the luggage to the master bedroom and returned in time to hear Kim decline a snack. "If you don't mind, I think I want to rest a bit on the porch rocker."

"You go right ahead," The older woman assured her. "This house is your home for the summer. Do whatever makes you comfortable."

Jasmine piped in a sweet voice, "Well, I want some cookies and milk. I hear you're a terrific cook. Who taught you how to cook? How old were you? What is your favorite thing to bake?"

Jack leaned toward Mitchell as Jasmine followed Maggie into the kitchen. "Even you weren't that talkative. Maggie is going to have to step up her game to keep up with Jasmine."

Mitchell clapped him on the back. "I have a feeling we all will, Dad."

They trailed along unable to resist the promise of Maggie's huge, warm sugar cookies. Jack paused in case Kim should decide to follow, but her focus was on the distant mountains as she pushed through the screen door.

After a goodly number of cookies had been eaten, Jasmine quieted and Mitchell said, "Would you like to see the horses?"

The girl's eyes glowed. "You bet."

Jack said, "You two go on ahead. I'll see if Kim wants to come."

Mitchell and Jasmine banged out the screen door. Maggie raised her eyebrows when Jack snagged a couple more cookies. He said, "These are for Kim."

"Good idea. That girl needs fattening."

Jack lowered himself into the rocker next to Kim's chair. She was nestled deep into the pillows with her legs curled under her. Before them the green land rolled away to where the hills mounded into the sky.

"My great-grandfather settled this area, built a sod house over where the smoke house is."

"It's so beautiful and peaceful."

"It's always been beautiful, but not always so peaceful. They fought Indians, weather, and disease. Took them a few years, but they built a house and kept adding on. It burned to the ground a few years before my dad died."

"Was anyone hurt?"

"No. My grandparents had died already and my parents were away at the time. After that, my mom and dad moved to town. It was easier for them since they traveled as interim preachers. My elderly uncle didn't want to run the ranch by himself and I was at college. I inherited the ranch when my parents died. My wife Karen and I built this big house with the idea we'd have six or eight kids, maybe a dozen. The whole top floor is bedrooms. It didn't work out, except for Mitchell."

Kim placed both open palms over her belly, a tiny, protective gesture.

"We've kept it closed for years for heating and cooling purposes. I put you and Jasmine in the same room on the main floor. It's got a king-size bed. If you want your own room, I could easily open the second floor."

Fear flashed across Kim's face. "No! I mean, don't bother. I believe Jasmine would be much more comfortable sharing a room. We don't often get to see each other. She'll think that it's fun, like one long pajama party. Young girls love that kind of thing."

Jack nodded and rocked back and forth. What fears haunted Kim? "I brought you a couple of Maggie's sugar cookies."

Kim nibbled one. Her face smoothed with pleasure. Her eyes met his directly for the first time. "This is superb."

"Yup." When she finished eating, he said, "Mitchell took Jasmine to meet the horses. Do you want to walk to the corral with me?"

"Sure."

Jack escorted her down the steps. Her hand on his arm was firm and comfortable. "Tell me more about the original farm."

"Not a farm, a ranch. A farmer may grow livestock, but his basic purpose is produce and grain while a rancher might grow crops to support his livestock, but his main livelihood is cattle, horses, or in some cases buffalo or elk."

"Oh. You said you'd closed the ranch down. Are the horses yours?"

They rounded the corner of the barn. "I still own three, but boarded them for several years. I rented another two for the summer in case we need—ow." Kim's fingernails dug into his bare arm like the talons of a falcon. A terrifying, blood curdling shriek pierced his ears.

Chapter Fourteen – Kim

Shrieking, heart pounding, Kim hurtled forward. She pummeled the bronze-skinned man in feathers, buckskins, and painted face who gripped Jasmine by the waist, pulling her from a horse. "Leave her alone! Let her go!"

The Indian straight-armed her to fend off her attack. Yelling, Mitch raced across the paddock. Her arms were pinned against her and Jasmine's calm voice in her ear repeated, "I'm fine. He wasn't hurting me. He was helping me. He's a friend."

Kim blinked. Jasmine, not Nsia. Montana, not Zaire. She quit struggling and sank a little. Jasmine's restraining hold now supported her.

The Indian dropped his hands. Mitch teetered on the top fence rail before jumping to the ground. Puffs of dust rolled over his boots. Jack wiped a stream of blood from his arm. He was the first to speak. "This is my good friend, Myron Yellowtail. He's a Crow Indian and was practicing the ceremonial dances not too far from here in preparation for the big August powwow. He thought Jasmine would get a kick out of the authentic ceremonial garb."

Ice and fire flooded Kim's veins. She pulled away from Jasmine and straightened. She gestured toward the feathered headdress, but couldn't bear to look at the painted face. "I'm sorry," she mumbled, "for a moment you looked like the witch doctor."

Myron's voice was deep and soothing. He patted the horse. "Don't worry about it."

"People died. I'm so sorry." Her bones were melting like wax, her legs buckling, the corral and the blue sky swirling into blackness.

***

The persistent creak of the porch rocker filtered through the open window. Billowing curtains reminded her of laundry on Nsia's clothesline. Kim recalled the incident with the Indian and wished she could slip away and get lost in the hills. Let it all be over with. She would, too, except there was the baby to think about.

That little person was even now using her ribs for a StepMaster and her bladder for a beanbag. Kim shoved into a sitting position and came eye-to-eye with Jasmine who was draped sideways over an easy chair, standing guard, just as Nsia had done. Jasmine closed the book she was reading and swung her long skinny legs to the floor. "Feeling better?"

"I'm embarrassed."

"Don't be. It's understandable. Anyway, I sure feel safe knowing you're around to kick anybody's backside that might give me trouble. From the look on your face, I thought you could've tossed Mr. Yellowtail to the ground like a toothpick."

"He must think I belong in the nut house. The Bronners are probably sorry they agreed to let me come."

Jasmine stretched overhead, pulling a coppery pigtail in each of her hands. "Nope. They all said they were glad you came here to recuperate since it's obvious you had some pretty scary experiences. They feel honored you'd trust them. I think these people are some of the nicest on earth. I'm glad we're here."

Kim agreed.

At supper, Kim again apologized to Myron and to show that she liked him—and was sane—engaged him in conversation about his tribe, their history, his life, and the upcoming powwow. The others watched her as she had watched Kurt those last months, studying every movement, every word, to gauge moods and be forewarned of erratic behavior. She wished they'd leave her alone. "The powwow sounds like fun. I look forward to seeing you in your traditional dress. Don't worry I won't attack you again now that I know what's what."

90

Jack laid his knife across the top of his plate. "Weren't you seeing a doctor in Indiana?"

"Yes. The Mission Council referred me to a psychiatrist who specializes in trauma."

"Perhaps you should think about calling him and telling him what happened today. He may be able to offer some insight or helpful suggestions."

"Maybe," she said. The adults seemed to accept her statement as an agreement, but Jasmine narrowed her eyes. Kim turned to Maggie. "Your rolls are so tender. I think I'll have another. Could you please pass the butter?"

That night Kim slept like a rock and woke the next morning in the position she'd fallen asleep. She stretched to release some of the stiffness and turned on her side. Jasmine's eyes were wide open, staring at her. "Oh, Jasmine, I didn't know you were still in bed."

"I didn't want to leave you alone."

"I'm fine. Really."

"I think you should call the doctor."

"Yes, well, if it's necessary, I will." Kim went into the blue tile bathroom, locked the door and turned the tub faucet on full. When she came out, the bed was made, the bags unpacked, and Jasmine sat in a chair reading a book. Kim dressed and went to breakfast with her cousin at her side like a puppy scenting a treat.

By the next afternoon, when she hadn't had more than a moment away from Jasmine, Kim placed the call from the privacy of the bedroom. The conversation lasted about an hour. When she came out she announced to all of them. "You can all relax. He gave me the name of a psychiatrist in Bozeman in case I need one."

"What did he say about your reaction to Myron?"

"He said that was a one-time thing. There's nothing to worry about." It wasn't exactly what he had said, but she knew it was true, and therefore wasn't really lying. Besides, ranch life was slow and quiet and exactly what she needed to get her bearings. The vistas went on forever. Nothing could sneak up and surprise her.

Once everyone quit surveilling her Kim felt as carefree as a young girl. She spent hours walking or watching Jasmine ride. She slept often and long. So that no one would treat her with kid gloves, she took care to fit into the flow of the household, helping Maggie clean, cook, and tend garden.

From the bean row next to Kim, Maggie hummed as she weeded. Jack and Mitch were fixing some string to poles for the beans to climb. Doofus, Maggie's dog, rose from the spot where he was sunning himself and barked.

About twenty men on horseback approached at a slow, steady pace. Maggie said, "Jack, Mitch, you go meet them. I'll mix up more ice tea."

"Yes. Ma'am."

Kim wiped her brow and moved into the shade of the porch. It amused her no end how the Bronner men deferred to the plump woman. Mitch treated her like a grandmother and Jack said Maggie's common sense was one of the most valuable assets a person could possess.

"Hello," Jack called to the riders. "Where are you headed?"

"We're on a three-day ride from the Triple K Dude Ranch."

"Can you stop and visit?"

"We were hoping you'd ask." The men dismounted and slapped hats against their legs, just like cowboys did in movies.

Jack led them to the watering trough. By the time everyone had settled in the shade of the porch, introductions made, and a few stories related, Maggie was bringing out plates of food as if she cooked every day for twenty extra cowboys. Kim hurried to the kitchen to help bring out the iced tea.

Maggie was a piece of cork floating. If she could copy Maggie's exterior calm and unruffled manner no one would suspect the contradiction of raging thoughts and swirling emotions. Maybe, if she kept it up long enough, she would become sensible and capable and calm. Then, she wouldn't feel so lost.

Chapter Fifteen – Carol

Carol left the ranch house and followed the sharp whine of a power saw to a nearby outbuilding. Jack was bent over a sheet of plywood. The saw moaned to a stop and he tossed rectangular pieces onto a pile on the floor where they landed with a wooden *clop. clop. clop.*

"Hi."

Jack pulled the protective glasses from his eyes and broke into a smile. "Hello. This is a surprise. Did you appear out of thin air?"

She fanned herself. "I used Mitch's method and parachuted in."

His grin broadened and she quickened the speed of her fanning hand. "Actually, I parked the rental car out front. I was flying back from a conference in California and couldn't resist stopping. I hope I'm not intruding."

"You know you're welcome." Jack took her hand in both of his and gently shook it.

Carol felt heat rise to her face. What should she do? She nodded toward the wood. "I see you're keeping busy. How are you, Jack?"

"I'm fine, but I'm sure it's Kim you're really interested in. She's doing well. She's less strained and more energetic these days."

"Where is she? I was at the house and no one was there."

"Kim and Mitchell are on the reservation. Maggie and Jasmine are in town buying groceries."

"The girls haven't been any trouble this last month, have they?"

"No. They fit right in, always willing to lend a hand."

Her eyes wandered to the hand he still held. He released it. Free and at sudden odds, she gestured toward the woodpile. "What are you working on?"

"The kids, I mean, Mitchell and Kim, are cooking up Christmas plans already. I'm making some wood wagons as gifts for reservation children."

"Is she really doing fine?"

"She seems to be coming out of her shell. Those two get real excited about what they're doing out there. The number of teens has tripled since they took over the meetings. Say, I could use some iced tea, how about you?"

They sipped their drinks and rocked on the porch swing. Jack gave details of the summer that Carol had not heard from Kim. She laughed at some anecdotes about Jasmine and a mishap he'd had at one of the trapper's conventions where he was a featured demonstrator. In turn, Carol shared some of the more interesting moments in her own speaking schedule and added, "I've decided to quit speaking."

"Why? I thought things were going well. You've had engagements every weekend all summer."

"Yes, and then a couple of mid-week conferences like this one. Between that and work, I'm worn out. Anyway, I have fewer engagements next year. I think Peter is turning down requests. One woman told me their group was disappointed I was booked for September of next year yet I only had one event on the schedule. He rarely will see me in the office and I can never get him on the phone."

"After what happened, I'm surprised you haven't hired someone else."

"I meant to, but Kim came home and I was involved with her. Besides, since he married, it didn't seem as important. And of course, my best friend, Trudy works there. Now, I find with Kim's baby on the way, I'm not as interested in traveling."

Jack shifted in his chair. "Peter married?"

"Didn't I tell you? He married Miss Belle of the South a week after he proposed to me on the slopes. I don't think he treats her very well. Anyway, Kim is my first concern."

"Would you like to pray together?"

"Yes." Carol extended her hand and Jack clasped it. His pressure varied as Jack petitioned God. This was what they'd shared in the cabin. She'd missed praying with him.

Beep! Beep! A faded red Chevy tore up the road, a cloud of dust billowing behind. It had barely stopped when Kim bounced out of the cab as fast as her big belly allowed. "Mom, you didn't tell me you were coming."

"Oh, Kim, look at you." Kim had much of her old glow back. Her face was rounder and softer and had lost that cracked-leather look. Her arms no longer showed her bones.

Carol released her and turned to Mitch who moved in for a hug. "You're looking good, Mitch. What happened to your long hair and earring?"

He laughed. "I'm a clean-shaven conservative dude these days."

"You look great."

"I'm doing great. I'm planning on going back to school."

"Good for you."

Kim stepped closer. "Mom, I've been helping Mitch get the hall ready for a youth rally Sunday night."

"It sounds like you're keeping busy."

"Yes. You're staying aren't you?"

"Well—"

From his place on the porch, Jack said, "You can't come all this way and then leave after a few hours. There's plenty of room."

"I guess I could stay overnight, but only one night."

"You can sleep with Jasmine and me. The bed is huge. We'll have lots of room. Then, we can talk. Mom, so much has been happening. Come on in and I'll tell you all about it." Kim dragged her into the house with a steady pressure.

"I'll get the luggage, Dad. You take care of our guest." Mitch moved to the rental car.

Carol glanced backwards. "Are you coming, Jack?"

"No. You go on. I won't intrude on your mother-daughter moment." He headed back to his woodworking.

Carol looked around the spacious living room with its orderly bookshelves and warm colors. She often thought about the conversations she had shared with Jack here. She gave Kim another squeeze as they settled against the back of the couch. "I can't believe how much better you look. Being here agrees with you. Tell me, what's it like living with those two?"

"Mitch and Jack are as different as night and day and it makes for some interesting conversations. Mitch discusses everything. His dad can be a bit abrupt. It takes a little more to draw him into a conversation, but then he always says something of value. Mom, I don't think there's a kinder man or a better one."

"I wouldn't have asked him to let you stay here if I wasn't sure of his integrity."

Kim shot her a look of exasperation. "I'm not talking about me, Mom. I'm talking about you. You've been lonely. Daddy's been gone a long time. Jack's perfect for you."

"Don't match-make. Those kinds of antics are rarely appreciated and frequently backfire. For now, I'm happy being single. Promise me, you'll leave this alone." She fired the no-nonsense look she'd always used to warn her children of impending the doom that follow disobedience.

Kim screwed up her face. "He likes you."

"Then let him tell me. I'm serious, Kim."

"Oh, all right."

"Mitch entered with the overnight bag and plopped into a chair. "What's up?"

"I'm thinking Kim shouldn't fly back alone with Jasmine since she'll be so close to term. I'm coming back to fly along."

"Dad's got a convention in Indiana the third week of August. Maybe he can escort the two of them to you."

"Mitch, that's a great idea." Kim said. "We'll ask him at supper."

"Good. I suppose I've got to clear out of here and leave you ladies to discuss the Bronners and our peculiarities." He gave an exaggerated wink.

Carol felt the warmth of a blush, but Kim didn't bat an eye. "We'll do that later. I'm sure she wants to know about the youth work. Mitch does a super job with the kids. Tell her, Mitch."

Carol settled back as Mitch talked about the teens and the ministry. Kim kept interrupting to run commentary. She was so much like her old self that for the first time since Kim's return, the tightness left Carol's chest.

Later, amid the sweet smell of sawdust in the work area, Carol watched Jack and said. "Kim is like her old self. She's so lively."

"She's more animated with you here, but we have seen a big difference since her first reaction to Myron. Of course, she might never have an episode like that again. The doctor seemed to think it was a one-time event. Tomorrow will be a test. We're all going to a rodeo. Jasmine didn't think she could leave Montana without seeing a rodeo. Say, you're changing your flight anyway, take one later in the evening and go with us."

One half dozen reasons why she shouldn't popped into Carol's mind, but what came out of her mouth was, "Okay."

The next day at the rodeo, Carol held her new Stetson in one hand as she stood with Jasmine to cheer when a rider made eight seconds on a bucking bronc. They reclaimed their seats in the crowded bleachers. She said, "I never expected to have so much fun. This is really something. Since Jack explained the history of the animals and the competitors, it all seems very personal."

Jasmine cracked a grin at her and the metal from her braces flashed in the sun. "What's not to like? Horses. Heat. Horses. Clowns. Did I mention horses?"

"I don't think I've seen you have this much fun since Daddy died," Kim said.

"The Bronners can make anything feel like a good time," Jasmine added.

Carol laughed, thinking of the recuperation time in the cabin after the blizzard. "Well, I must admit, I've found that to be true."

Kim stood, waved her hat, and called, "Myron. Here we are." A man taller than Jack turned and waved, before making his way up the bleachers. "Mom, this is Myron Yellowtail, a good friend of the Bronner's. Myron, this is my mom, Carol. Come sit with us. There's room beside me."

Kim scooted over and chatted in a friendly manner, trying a little too hard to join in as Myron and Jasmine discussed horses, riding techniques, and history. Still it was one more point of her progress Carol ticked off the list.

Jack and Mitch appeared through the stream of spectators, carrying cold drinks for all of them. A big bear of a man followed close behind. He had wild curly black hair and bushy brows that formed a straight line over his eyes. After introductions, Brewster squeezed into the seat behind them and regaled them with ever more elaborate stories of a young Jack Bronner.

Jasmine whispered, "Aunt Carol, they're looking you over to see if you're worthy of Jack."

Kim leaned in from the other side. "Oh, yeah. That's for sure."

Carol denied it, but the heat of a blush bloomed from somewhere in her tummy and rose to her cheeks. It might be true. Jack's friends spent the rest of the day giving her gossip and assessment of the rides and riders in equal portions as fillers between stories about Jack.

Over barbecues and pops at one of the stands, Brewster related how seventeen-year-old Jack taught his show horse to tiptoe around the ring to the total amazement of the judges.

Carol gave Brewster the most wide-eyed look of innocence she could muster and nodded her head. She leaned forward with a conspiratorial air and Brewster bent toward her. "I couldn't tell anybody else this, but I bet that is the same horse he used to pull me out of the avalanche. Of course, that horse has grown wings now and simply hovered over me while he slipped a rope under my arms and airlifted me out. It was amazing."

Brewster swatted away the ridiculous story. Jasmine clapped her hands while Myron exclaimed, "She's on to you, Brew."

Jack was beaming as he pushed his chair back. "I hate to end the party, but Carol's got a plane to catch."

Everyone cleared the table, draining their drinks and gathering hats. Brewster said good-bye and sauntered off.

"I'm so glad you stayed Mom. It was like a real family day." Kim's kiss was a tickle on her cheek.

Feeling mellow, Carol turned to her host. "It was a terrific day. Jack, you have some fine friends."

Jack chuckled. "I was beginning to wonder how gullible you were. You really strung old Brewster along. He went down, hook, line, and sinker."

"How far back do you and Brewster go?"

"I've known him since first grade. Karen and I square-danced with him and his wife when we were first married until Vera developed ALS. He cared for her at home as long as he could. Big Bear Brewster can be as tender as thistledown. When Karen got sick, he was my mentor. Whenever he wasn't driving truck he'd come play chess or just sit with me through the night."

"That's some kind of friend."

Jack nodded and had a faraway look in his eye. She didn't want him lingering there with Karen so she said, "And Myron?"

"Have you ever read about the confrontation of Robin Hood and Little John? We were kind of like that tussling over a section of river we both wanted to trap, except neither of us could best the other, so we became best friends instead and trapped it together. We still do that."

Myron stepped closer and clapped his hand on Jack's shoulder. "Actually, I could've won, but I was afraid his ego was so fragile he'd cry like a baby. I didn't want to be embarrassed by his tears. As it was I had to carry him over two miles on my back one time, bawling like a newly branded calf because he got a scratch."

Jack said, "I was twelve. I slipped while climbing a boulder and drove a ten-inch spike entirely through my foot. I was on crutches for six weeks."

"See? He's still whining about it." Myron said.

Chapter Sixteen – Kim

Kim felt Mitch's attention on her as she fiddled with a bag of chips on the refreshment table. The gym was still empty. Light from a line of windows that ran near the ceiling lent a smoky impression as they waited for teens to arrive. She playfully punched his middle. He was firm, muscular. "I promised her I wouldn't match-make. You, on the other hand, made no such promise."

Grinning, Mitch massaged his stomach. "What do you think I've been trying to do? Dad's not cooperating, either. I carried her luggage yesterday so he could be with her and he wandered off to the workshop."

"Did you see them on the porch when we first got there? It was like they'd always been there." She peered into his face trying to read him. "It doesn't bother you to see them together, does it?"

"Nah. Once it would have but I'm as keen as you are about this. My dad really likes your mom. His mood improves if anyone even mentions her. I like her too. She's one of the easiest persons to be around."

"Unless you're one of her children and you don't do what she wants. Did you see the look she gave me yesterday when you came into the room? When we were little, my brother and I called it the Evil Eye. I miss him so much. We used to have such fun together. You've been like a brother to me, Mitch. It's been so much fun being with you. You've made this summer a good one and I really needed it, you know?"

Mitch stared at his boots, taking forever to reply.

Kim rubbed her eyes before tears could form and jumped to a safer topic. "I don't know what Mom was getting all bent out of shape about. She likes your dad. Have you seen the way her eyes linger on him when she thinks no one is looking?"

"Yes, I saw. Listen, Kim. Maybe we should back off. If he likes her and she likes him and God wants them together, then it'll happen in its own timing."

The door burst open with a hollow popping. Three boys entered. Mitch called, "Hey" and hurried over to them.

That Mitch. He was smart and fun and always checking to make sure that what he was doing was in God's will. He was right. Their parents had as much right to heal on their own and seek companionship when they were ready as she had. But, she liked the Bronners. She liked the ranch. She liked not being reminded of the past every place she went. She didn't want to leave and if their parents were together that made everything easier.

The familiar popping filled the gym as a group of girls entered and waved to her. Kim returned the wave and headed toward them.

By midnight, the empty gym had a cavernous echo when Mitch darkened the lights and locked the door. With leaden legs, Kim followed him to the truck certain her feet were swollen enough to make removing her boots a tricky business.

She twisted, searching for a comfortable position against the jostling of the truck on the bumpy dirt road. Her head and back throbbed. Worse, Mitch hadn't said two words since they'd left. Her heart fluttered like a moth trapped in a jar. The dash lights were too dim to make out more than the outline of his face. She bit her lip. "I think it went very well."

"Yes."

"The kids enjoyed it. I saw Fred Red Shoes. I wasn't sure we'd ever see him grace our door. He really was paying attention when you did the devotional."

"I talked with him quite a bit. He said he'd be at the regular meeting on Tuesday, too," Mitch said.

"That's great. I prayed with Margaret tonight about her grandmother's surgery."

Finally, he'd looked at her. She relayed parts of every conversation she'd had with the teens and Mitch emerged from his uncustomary silence to ask questions. Kim exhaled slowly and deliberately. He was fine. Nothing had changed. He was simply tired. They were both tired.

He parked the old Chevy near the back door where a single yellow porch light shone. They eased out of the cab and trudged up the steps. A June bug buzzed past. "You want something to eat? I'd be glad to fix it."

"No, thank you. I'm turning in. I'll see you tomorrow." There it was again, that indefinable something. Mitch disappeared down the hall into his room. The door closed, shutting her out. Had she displeased him? His words sounded normal, but—.

She forgot to tell him she'd let their parents to do their own matchmaking. She paused at his door with raised hand. Thinking better of it, she lowered her knuckles and went to her room. There, as expected, was her cousin asleep in the big bed.

Kim worked her boots off and set them quietly on the floor. She slipped a cool cotton nightgown over her head and didn't bother to brush her hair. A huge yawn and a growing numbness dispelled any fear of a long night of worry. Her eyelids fluttered heavily as her body settled into the mattress. Tomorrow everything would be back to normal. God wouldn't let anything bad happen again, would he?

Kim awoke and moaned as she struggled into a sitting position. She groaned as she pushed herself off the bed and tottered to the window to pull the curtain. A high sun filled the room with light. Jasmine was long gone, probably in the barn with the horses. Again. Some companion. Always riding. Or brushing those stupid horses. Kim shrugged into her robe and found her way to the kitchen.

Maggie bustled about in a far too cheerful manner preparing lunch. "Well, don't you look like something the cat dragged in?"

"I hope the coffee is strong," Kim grumbled.

Maggie handed Kim a steaming mug. "Jack made the second pot. It'll be strong enough to make your baby do cartwheels."

"What else is new? The other day a bump appeared right through my top and moved clear across to the other side of my stomach. I think he's practicing Tae Bo."

They grinned at each other and her bad mood dissolved.

Maggie said, "How'd the youth night go?"

"It was great. Fifty-two kids showed. Didn't Mitch tell you at breakfast?"

"I haven't seen him. His truck was gone when I got up."

"Funny. He didn't say anything about leaving early."

"Men. Get something in their brains and they're gone. He'll get back and insist we've been talking about it for a week. My Elmer was that way. If he thought it, he figured I knew it. I always had to tell him that I wasn't a mind reader. You want some breakfast?"

Her comments dulled the edge of Kim's panic. "No, I'll wait for lunch. I'm going to dress."

"Don't go starving that baby."

"I'll take a couple of your famous oatmeal cookies to tide us over." In the bedroom, Kim used the back of her hand to brush dust off the top of her Bible. She set the coffee and cookies on it and plopped onto the bed.

Why hadn't Mitch said anything about where he was going? Of course, he had no obligation to tell her what he was doing, except he always had. He probably remembered something he'd told his dad he'd do. She had to quit expecting bad things to happen all the time. Even Jesus said not to worry. She couldn't recall how the verse went, something about sparrows and hair, but she didn't feel like looking it up either. Where was Mitch?

Chapter Seventeen – Mitch

Mitch cast the fly onto the surface of the stream and jerked it back. He continued this rhythm, until a fish swallowed it. He reeled the trout in, worked it off the hook and added its weight to the others in the basket at his waist.

He moved through the cold, running water, feeling each step for safety. Pressure from the swift moving stream buoyed against the waders giving the sensation of walking on a big balloon. He selected a new position and repeated the whole casting procedure.

When he tired of fishing, Mitch shucked his gear and crawled onto a big boulder and just sat. The stream lapped and gurgled. The sun beat down, warming him. This spot, where he'd come as a boy with his dad, was his favorite. Later he'd spent a lot of time alone here while his mother was sick. He'd never shared it with his friends, not because he wanted the best fishing spot for himself, but because it was a sanctuary, as if God were particularly close here. It was where his dad explained about Christ taking his place and punishment so he could stand clean before the heavenly Father. It was where he'd first heard the call to ministry. "Am I wrong to have feelings for Kim? What should I do, Lord?"

Mitch lay back, watched the whitish-green aspen leaves flicker in the breeze, and listened with all his being. There was no spoken word, no divine revelation. He didn't know yet what he was going to do, but God was at work. When the sun reached its zenith, he headed back to the ranch with a feeling of quiet peace.

Mitch placed the basket of cleaned fish on the sink and Maggie shouted, "Bless you. I've been hankering for fresh fish for a week now."

"You should've said something. I'd have gone sooner."

"You were busy with the youth rally. I didn't want to bother you."

"Please bother me more often. There's nothing like getting out there and fishing."

"I'll fry this right now and save this ham for supper." Maggie stowed the meat in the refrigerator and pulled out seasonings and crackers to mix a dredging.

Jack entered the kitchen and handed him the phone. "It's Pastor Ralph."

The elderly pastor spoke slowly and deliberately in English. "Mitch, you and Kim did a great job last night. We'd like you to continue working with the teens. Start a new class in the fall. We are most in need of a program to address purity in today's culture. You choose the curriculum and present it to the board for approval. However, we were thinking of the first book of Timothy, Chapter 5. 'Treat younger women as sisters, with absolute purity.' Do you think you'd be interested?"

Mitch's spiritual ears perked. He straightened to attention. "That's a terrific verse, Pastor Ralph, but I don't know if I'm the man for the job. I may be starting school in September instead of January."

"We can't fault you for wanting to finish seminary. Let us know."

Mitch agreed and took the phone to its cradle. "Treat them like sisters," he said softly.

His father nodded toward the phone. "What did Pastor Ralph want?"

"He suggested a ministry opportunity."

Jack waited and Maggie swung around with an expectant face. Mitch said, "I'll tell you later. I'm going to wash for lunch."

Passing Kim in the hall, he said. "Pastor Ralph called to say thanks."

"How thoughtful. I just got out of bed. What have you been doing?"

"Fishing."

A goofy grin crossed her face. Then she made a little gurgling noise. Pain creased her face as she grabbed her midsection and rubbed furiously. He touched her shoulder. "Are you all right?"

She turned red, smiled and straightened. "I'm fine. Everything's fine."

The smell of hot grease wafted down the hall accompanied by a sizzling. Mitch said, "Good. I better hurry to clean up. Lunch will be ready soon."

He continued down the hall, but when he turned to go into his room, she was still in the same place watching him with a funny look on her face.

Chapter Eighteen – Jack

Later that afternoon, Jack threw the last of the woodchips into an old crate of scraps for the fireplace and put the tools away. The sweet smell of fresh wood shavings hung in the air. Behind him, Jasmine swept sawdust.

The child was a sweet-tempered delight. He enjoyed answering her questions for she listened well and catalogued information like a librarian. This day she'd been quiet, not even humming or singing.

He latched the toolbox and perched on the edge of a sawhorse. "What's on your mind, Jazz? Are you getting homesick?"

"A little, but I think I'll miss Molly and Gruber and Hodges when I go. You have such nice horses. Do you think I can come back next year?"

"You're always welcome at my house, but you'll probably have a boyfriend and won't want to come back."

Jasmine grimaced and shook her head. "I don't think so."

"You sound pretty sure of yourself."

"The way I see it, relationships take a lot of work. Frankly, I've got too much to do."

Jack rubbed his chin to hide his mirth. "Such as?"

Jasmine dumped the contents of the dustpan into a bag, put it in the wood box, and dusted her hands with sharp smacking sounds. "When I get home, I'm going to see if Mom and Dad will find a stable so I can keep working with horses. Then I'll know more when I come back next summer. And I've decided I'm going to learn the guitar. I really like it when Mitch plays and a guitar can go practically anywhere. He's helped me pick out a few chords and I caught on pretty fast. Then, with school and choir and volleyball, well, there just isn't time for a relationship. Maybe after college, I'll have more time."

"You amaze me. How did you work all that out?"

Jasmine sat beside him. "Relationships seem like work. I've been watching Kim and Mitch. I could tell right away Kim likes him. I think it scares her. I don't know what happened, but Kim still has nightmares about her husband – before he died. She whimpers in her sleep and wakes crying. I pretend to be asleep or she gets even more upset. She won't talk about it. When I asked if she thought Mitch was cute, she got all red and said she hadn't noticed. When I asked if she thought he would make a good boyfriend, she said I was a little young for him."

Jasmine rolled her eyes and added, "Mitch isn't much better. He can't take his eyes off Kim. When she walks into the room it's as if he can't think of anything else. She came out on the porch the other night when we were playing rummy and I took four turns in a row before he even thought to ask if it was his turn. I told him no and I played again. He never knew the difference."

Jack roared with laughter. Jasmine eyed him to see if he was making fun of her. He reined in his response a bit and drew her to his side. "You little card shark. I'll remember to pay attention whenever I'm playing with you. I'm going to miss you when you're gone. You've been a breath of fresh air in this stuffy old place."

Jasmine leaned against him for a moment. "Both my grandfathers are dead. Do you think it would be okay if I called you Grampa Jack?"

Jack pressed a quick kiss on the top of her head. "I'd be honored. And, Jazz, you're right about relationships. They do take work and it's best to let people work things out on their own. Kim's been hurt badly and the loss of her husband is very fresh. It's good that Mitchell cares enough to give her time to heal. God has a way of making everything come out right."

"I suppose so."

Together they left the workroom. Mitchell was coming down the steps as they approached the house. "Where are you heading, son? Maggie has ham ready for supper."

"Frank Bedlowe is on leave for a few days. I'm meeting him at the diner to shoot the breeze."

"Tell him I said hey."

Mitchell flipped the brim of his hat with his fingers. "I will."

Jasmine said, "Mitch, you're my honorary cousin now 'cause your dad agreed to be my Grampa Jack."

Mitchell tugged gently at one of Jasmine's braids. "Does that mean you're going to go easier on me when we're playing cards? I'm getting tired of losing."

Jack exchanged a look with Jasmine and burst out laughing. She said, "Not a chance."

"Didn't think so. Well, it's cool anyway."

Chapter Nineteen - Mitch

Briefly Mitch wondered what the two found so hilarious, but thoughts of the future at seminary or with the reservation youth ministry interspersed with longings for Kim distracted him. He was at the turn to the main road before he knew it. A dark mood settled over him as iron-gray clouds prepared to dump a ton of water. Determined to gain a more cheerful frame of mind before meeting his friends, he turned on the radio. The regular country-western station faded in and out as it tended to do on stormy days.

Mitch tried to conjure negative aspects of Kim's personality, but thought more about the way the corners of her mouth turned upwards when she smiled. How kissable her lips seemed.

"...we are commanded to treat the younger women as sisters."

Mitch stared at the radio as the voice of a radio preacher continued. "Guard your thoughts. Don't give in to emotions for self-gratification. Fill your time with service to the Lord, family, and community. Respect and honor will prepare the way for true love. Treat a young woman so she has nothing to be ashamed of when she goes into marriage... Jesus Christ calls us to a higher standard so we'll be known by our love and the Father will be glorified..." A gust of wind rocked the truck. Rain pounded, drowning out further words. Mitch silenced the radio and prayed the rest of the way to the diner.

Inside, Frank was already seated at a table near the rear. He called out as Mitch stomped through the door, shaking water from his hat and jacket like a wet retriever. Frank was only five six in height and lithe, but Mitch would rather meet Brewster in a back alley than him. Frank threw a few pretend punches. Mitch feinted and danced forward on his toes before they clasped hands for a hearty shake. They settled at the table.

Mitch said, "What are you doing back here, Frank? You swore never to come back."

Frank ran a hand over his stark military-cut hair. "I was over in Butte to visit the folks and thought I'd see you one last time."

How are the folks?"

Frank shook his head. "Mom doesn't know anybody. She sits in the nursing home and stares at the wall. I'm not going back. Mom doesn't know the difference and Dad never cared. Anyway, my new post is in Georgia."

"Jaw-ja," Mitch exclaimed. "What's happening in Jaw-ja?"

"You're looking at the newly promoted Sergeant Bedlowe."

"Congratulations. We always knew you'd fast-track the ladder."

They ordered and Frank related stories about his experiences in the Army all through supper. Afterward, Mitch chalked his pool cue while Frank made the break shot. "Have you thought anymore about your relationship to God, Frank?"

"I knew you'd bring that up. I want to show you exactly why I'd never be a Christian. I've been carrying this around since it happened." Frank laid his cue across the green felt table and drew something from his back pocket. He unfolded a piece of newsprint and smoothed it out on the tabletop. He stabbed at the article with his index finger.

Mitch bent over the piece and raised his eyes to meet Frank's. "This is French. I don't read French."

"It's about a missionary in Zaire. The militia there regularly loot, rape, and burn. This guy was trying to stop them from tearing down the church he'd built. They shot him and hacked him in little pieces and burned him."

"He was willing to sacrifice his life for what he believed."

"So what? I'm willing to sacrifice my life for what I believe. It's his wife I'm talking about. Militia didn't do this. The man did it

112

to his own wife. The rebels found her chained to the foot of her bed, half-dead. That's your godly preacher man."

Mitch stared at the picture of soldiers leading a woman out of a building. Revulsion, rage, and fear raced through him.

"Glory be the silver tongue is speechless," Frank said.

"This man was clearly sick. Don't base your own eternal destiny on another's actions."

As they played pool, Mitch told Frank what he'd been through the previous two years and his recent return of faith. He concluded, "The relationship is between you and God. You're using this an excuse."

Frank shot the nine-ball and it clacked against the final two balls on the table. They split apart and all three balls found a pocket. "I don't want hear it. I've got to go. It's been good to see you again, Mitch. I don't believe this stuff you're selling, but you've been a good friend and I respect you. I don't expect to be back here again."

"You said that before."

"I mean it this time."

"Whenever you're ready, wherever you're at, God's waiting." Mitch held out his hand.

Frank grasped it. "So you've been telling me for the last six years."

When Frank left the diner, Mitch scooted down in his seat. He stared at the article and the barely recognizable photo of Kim. He folded the clipping and tucked it into his wallet. What had she been through? How could she possibly receive a proclamation of love from him so soon after that experience? "God, you know best. Help me and heal her heart."

Chapter Twenty – Kim

Kim rocked, rubbed her belly, and brooded as the whole outdoors, sympathizing with her mood, pelted rain like pebbles against the living room window. Even if Mitch was visiting with friends in town, which was a perfectly natural thing to do, his absence disturbed the comfortable balance of the evening. No one noticed, except for her.

Jack and Jasmine were glued to the side table playing a stupid game of rummy while Maggie, encased like a saintly statue in a yellow pool of bright light, embroidered. Kim wanted to scream, "Why does everything have to change?"

She bit her tongue. They'd think she was nuts, but soon summer would end. Jasmine would go home. Jack would leave to trap. Maggie would move back to Free Dance. Mitch would be busy on the reservation or attending school in Bozeman and she and her new baby would be forced to leave. Kim burst into tears.

Jack blinked like a surprised owl. Jasmine spun around concern etched on her freckled face. Maggie rushed to place a worn hand on her shoulder. "What's wrong, honey?"

Kim wailed, "I don't want to go home. I don't want to face everybody. I don't want to be near my in-laws. I want to be left alone. Why am I so weepy?"

Maggie patted her hand. "It's the hormones. You're getting close to your due date. Don't let it worry you. If you don't want to go back, stay in Free Dance."

"Stay in Free Dance?"

"Why sure. Everybody here loves you and didn't you say you hit it off with Marta Eidy? Find a job. Get an apartment. Hire a babysitter."

114

"Stay in Free Dance?"

"Is there any reason why you couldn't? You're an adult. You can do whatever you have a mind to do." Maggie handed her a box of tissues.

Kim wiped her eyes. "I never thought of it."

"Well, honey, you've sure had your share of things to think about. Then, the baby's been bothering you and I'd bet you've been having contractions, too. Haven't you?"

Startled, she studied Maggie and said, "I guess I have, from time to time."

"It's nothing to worry about. It's God's way of helping that baby get into position. How about we go into the kitchen and I'll make you a nice cup of herbal tea and we'll talk."

"Okay." She pretended not to notice Jack's eyebrows were still lifted and Jasmine's mouth remained an 'O' as wide as her eyes.

Maggie helped Kim to her feet. "What are you two staring at? Haven't you ever seen a pregnant woman before?"

They were already out of the room when Jasmine softly said, "Grampa Jack, do you think it is hormones or the bad stuff that happened?"

She couldn't make out Jack's low response, but Jasmine's higher tone was clear. "But what about the baby? Will she be able to take care of the baby?"

Fear clutched Kim's heart. Would she? She had to make sure she would.

***

In Bozeman, the pretty, pleasant-faced psychiatrist waved Kim into the office. Kim lowered her baby bulk onto a flowered sofa. More like a sitting room than an office, copious plants, a few knickknacks, even a tatted lace doily under a bowl of fresh flowers on a long low coffee table evinced a homey-ness.

Dr. Annalee Bradley positioned herself across from Kim next to a winged-back chair. She tilted her head to the right and dangly

115

turquoise earrings swished at her ears. The face of the square-jawed woman was kind. Brown hair streaked with blonde highlights was brushed straight back into a barrette and cascaded over her shoulders. Bangs wisped over a wide forehead and brushed the tips of arched eyebrows.

Lovely. Professional. Carrying the evidence of one who had overcome. Yes, it was possible this woman would understand her brokenness. Relief flooded Kim.

"What can I do for you?"

Kim said, "I thought the Mission Council would have given you all the details, Dr. Bradley."

Dr. Bradley's smile made her cheeks chub a bit on either side of a cute nose. She fingered a single strand of turquoise beads above the modest scoop neck of the dress. "Of course they did. I have copies of your evaluations, before and after your time in Zaire, plus transcripts of your debriefing. However, I want to know in your own words what you hope to gain from our visits."

Sun poured through the slats of the blinds, but the rays were deflected toward the ceiling where they gleamed like strange ceiling lights. The air conditioner kicked on and the beams of sunlight danced as cool air fluttered the window blinds.

Kim twisted the hem of her red maternity top in her fingers and finally met the doctor's gaze. "Peace. I want peace."

Dr. Bradley nodded to indicate she accepted this statement. Kim waited for a comment. Silence grew uncomfortable. "My mind won't quit spinning. I worry over any little change in routine. Sometimes, I'm emotional for no reason, like it's raining or I want a piece of pie and it's all gone. Other times, I feel removed from everything as if I'm not even there and I don't care what I do or what happens to me."

"Are you sleeping?"

"Yes. I sleep fine."

Dr. Bradley smoothed her brown and turquoise print dress over her knees. She folded her hands together and rested them in her lap and looked at Kim.

Kim bobbed her head back and forth with the admission, "Okay. I fall asleep fine, but I don't rest well and sometimes I have nightmares."

"Are these new dreams or reliving the past?"

"Both, mostly reliving the past."

"You've been in Montana for several weeks. It's almost time for you to go back home and see your regular doctor. Why did you decide to come to me now?"

"I've decided to live in Free Dance." Kim put a positive spin on answers to every one of Dr. Bradley's questions. She carried on about how much she liked the town and what the job opportunities were. They chatted about her pregnancy and particulars about the Bronners, Maggie, Jasmine, and ranch life. The time passed and the initial consult—which felt more like the start of a friendship—was concluded.

"I've enjoyed our visit, Kim. I think we should meet once a week." Dr. Bradley called her assistant, Angela, into the room. "Kim will need an hour next week."

Kim shook her head. "I don't think I can get here that often."

The doctor didn't blink. "Can you do two hours every other week?"

Kim frowned and was about to argue that once a month would be plenty when she remembered the fears Jasmine had expressed that rainy night. She needed this. She needed to be well enough to care for the baby. She bit the inside of her lower lip and nodded.

Kim left the cozy office by a door that opened onto an outside deck and ramped to a grassy yard bordered with flowering bushes. A picnic table sat under dense shade of a cottonwood. She rested there, reviewing her session until Mitch arrived. She waved and waddled to the curb. She said, "How did registration go?"

"Everything is set. I start classes on Monday, but I move in this Friday."

"Will you be back for the Fall Festival?"

"I'm afraid not. I really wanted to go to the dance with you, but you'll be busy helping Marta, anyway." He put the truck in gear.

"You looked quite comfortable sitting there in the shade. How did you like the doctor?"

Dr. Bradley had such a gentle, calming spirit that she'd felt—safe. Kim smiled. "I did. I really did. I'll see her again in two weeks."

"Terrific. Hey, whenever you come for a session you can visit me, too. Let's drive around and scope out all the good places to eat."

"Sounds like a plan. I'm starved," she replied.

Kim was floating on a cloud. She was going to be fine. Dr. Bradley was going to get her back to the way she was before she went to Africa. She'd be herself again and all the bad stuff would be over and gone, like it had never, ever happened. She and the baby would have a new life, a happy life in Free Dance with good friends and family. It wouldn't be long before Grandma Carol would move out here to be with them and Jack and everything, yes everything, was going to be great.

Chapter Twenty-one - Carol

Carol's thighs burned hot like torches as she climbed the steps to Kim's new apartment for probably the twentieth time that day. At the top she squawked at the sight of a bulky Kim balancing on a kitchen chair. "What are you doing? Are you trying to kill yourself?"

Kim had the face of an imp. She spoke over her shoulder and continued hanging a cheery blue-flowered curtain. "I'm safe, Mom. If I fall, Dora will catch me, won't you?"

Dora Rheinhardt, a round-faced, very large German landlady in her late thirties nodded emphatically and a broad grin lit her entire face. "Yah. I catch. Kim is good to do. Make strong baby."

The end table scraped on the floor as Carol set it down then collapsed onto the second-hand couch. "I'm bushed. I'll probably sleep all the way back to Indiana tonight."

Kim stepped to the floor to appraise her work. Carol had to admit it made the two room apartment a bit cheerier. Dora bustled over to the ancient Hot Point refrigerator and produced a pitcher of iced tea.

"Dora, you don't have to do that. I'll get something for my mother in a minute."

"I help," Dora insisted. "Look." From the recesses of a brown paper bag Dora produced a decorated tin and opened it to reveal strudel.

"Oohh, Dora," Kim moaned. "You know, Mom, I almost took a first floor apartment a few blocks away, but Mrs. Eidy doesn't bake."

Dora clucked in disapproval. "Her family, no get goods. She buy. Always buy. No bake."

"The family likes it that way. I was over there talking with Marta about the plans for the Fall Festival and she invited me to stay for dinner. The roast beef was so tough I could hardly cut it. Thank goodness I had an empty candy bag in my purse. I slipped the roast beef in there."

Dora clapped her hand over her mouth in delighted horror.

"Oh Kim, you didn't." Carol appraised her daughter. Kim's eyes sparkled with mischief.

"I did indeed. Marta was trying to get me to take hers, but the bag was full. She dropped her piece on the floor for the dog. He snatched it and trotted into the living room. A few minutes later he brought it back and laid it in Marta's lap."

Dora hooted with laughter. Kim took two glasses and delivered one to her mother. "Dora and I have a deal. I make her laugh and in exchange she invites me to dinner with her and Mr. Rheinhardt three times a week."

"Dora, that's positively wonderful."

"Ach! Dinner taste good with company. Your Kim she like my cooking. I watch out for her. She too skinny."

"Of course, this little tale is between the three of us. I wouldn't want to hurt Mrs. Eidy's feelings," Kim said.

"'Course. 'Course," Dora agreed in her heavy German accent. "Mrs. Eidy good Christian lady."

Carol sipped her tea. "How are the plans coming for the Fall Festival dance, Kim?"

"Oh, I forgot to tell you. Marta was admitted for an emergency appendectomy yesterday. I've been helping her, so I'll keep things running and take everything to the hospital for her to make the final decisions. You are coming back for it aren't you?"

"I wouldn't miss it. I bought a new dress and everything."

"Good." Kim visibly relaxed. "Mitch will be at school and I don't think I could stand it if you couldn't make it either. Marta wants me to oversee the dance that night, but she'll be there to help and I want you to meet her. She's a lot of fun."

"I'll be back Friday after next. I hope this couch is decent to sleep on."

"If not, we'll get one of those air mattresses." Kim said.

Dora distributed slices of strudel. Carol bit into it, "Mm. I'm in love."

Kim nodded knowingly, "What'd I tell you?"

Dora waved her hand as if to brush away the compliment she so plainly enjoyed, "I go now. Harry fix that leaky faucet when he get home."

"That's fine. Thanks for your help," Kim said.

Her departure was delayed as Jack and Mitch carried a twin size bed through the doorway. Mitch said, "Mrs. Eidy sent roast beef sandwiches so you wouldn't have to worry about fixing food tonight."

Dora's short laugh boomed as she descended the creaking steps. The men stared after her. Kim only said, "She shouldn't have. She already gave me the bed and mattress and a bunch of old towels. I think the nicest people live here in Free Dance. I'm really glad I decided to stay.

"I like my job, too. At the vet's yesterday, a Pekingese had been bitten by a German shepherd and whined and thrashed until I held it. Dr. Mullins gave it shots and cleaned and dressed the wound. It only needed a couple stitches and since it lay so quietly in my arms, he didn't even put it to sleep. It was amazing. I felt so useful."

Kim looked like a kid at Christmas, excited and happy, as she talked about the job while plating more strudel and pouring two more glasses of ice tea.

"I thought you hired as a receptionist." Jack accepted a glass beaded with cold.

"Oh, I am. I also have to feed and clean out the cages week days. Sometimes, like yesterday, I get to help doctor with the animals, too. He's a real nice man, very gentle."

Mitch said, "That's terrific. I know Forrest Mullins has been looking for help for a long time because Tammy wanted to leave. He hung with Rudy's older brother, Lewis, while I hung around with Rudy and Frank Bedlowe." Mitch fingered his wallet suddenly looking uncomfortable. Carol wondered if he was going to offer cash to Kim.

Kim snorted, "I suppose you have stories about how he mutilated animals as a kid."

Mitch dropped his hand and shook his head. "No. Forrest was always kind and gentle. I wasn't thinking that at all."

Kim narrowed her eyes at him.

Carol said, "You know, Kim, I'd hate to carry everything back down those stairs again, but, maybe you should've taken someplace better. I could help you with rent and a phone."

"I don't want help. I want to live on what I can do myself. I like this place. It's cozy. I like Dora, too."

Carol sighed with resignation. "It is a sweet little place, Kim."

"Oh, right. You don't believe that for one moment, Mom. It's dark and small, the paint is faded, the linoleum floor is chipped, somebody's dog scratched the door and ate the couch legs, and the bathroom door is a dollar store sheet I hung myself. But I don't care. It's the first place I've had on my own and I like it."

Carol lifted her hands. "Okay."

Mitch turned a thumb toward the door. "I've got to go. I'll take these empty boxes to the trash on my way."

Jack grabbed a wrench protruding from his back pocket and fished in a front pocket for a rubber gasket. "Meantime, I'll fix the kitchen faucet."

Carol said, "My plane leaves at five o'clock."

"This'll only take a minute," he said.

Kim peered over Jack's shoulder. "You really don't have to do that. Dora said Mr. Rheinhardt is coming to fix it when he gets home."

Arms loaded with boxes, Mitch leaned back inside the door long enough to say, "I wouldn't count on it."

"Now what does that mean?" Kim asked.

"Finished," Jack said. He rose and washed his hands. He waved the towel playfully at her. "Carol, that jet won't wait on you, you know. Kiss your daughter and let's go."

In spite of her bravado, Kim's grip seemed suddenly clingy. "Give everyone at home my love."

Carol squeezed Kim tighter. "Call me if you need anything and let me know how your next visit in Bozeman goes."

"It'll be fine, a piece of cake, as Trudy says."

Carol smiled reassuringly and sincerely hoped it would.

Chapter Twenty-two – Kim

Kim inspected the tropical fish in the tank at one side of Dr. Bradley's office. They were so tiny compared to some of the fish in the Congo River. The door opened and Dr. Bradley glided smoothly across the room. "Good morning, Kim. I'm glad to see you could make it."

"Jack Bronner drove me over. Nobody wants me making that trip alone in this condition." Kim rubbed the round, hard belly filling out her navy smock top and shuffled toward the comfortable couch.

"Very wise. How are you today?"

"Fine, except the baby is kicking hard. I'm a little sore."

"Yes, I've heard the last month can seem long." They talked about expectations and practicalities of babies and motherhood, her job, and the new apartment. Dr. Bradley said, "Are you afraid of being a single mother?"

Kim hunched her shoulders and crossed her arms over her chest. "A little, but that's normal for any first-time mother. Right?"

"Certainly. Of course, not every first-time mother has experienced the loss of her husband."

"I don't want to talk about that."

"Okay, for now. How did you feel when Kurt was offered the missionary post in Zaire?"

"Fine. What a beautiful pant dress you're wearing. I love the orange floral on the yellow background. It looks summery and happy. Do you shop here in Bozeman?"

Dr. Bradley brushed at her bangs and cocked her head. Large gold hoops twirled beneath her ear lobes. "You said you wanted peace, Kim. That only comes after the hard work of facing your fears. Jeremiah 6 says, 'You can't heal a wound you say isn't there.'"

Across the room, the fish swam back and forth in the tank, resigned that there was no way to escape. Kim sighed deeply. "Kurt was ecstatic. It was his dream to go to Africa ever since he was about nine and an indigenous missionary spoke at his church. You should've seen him when we reached Mobutu. He was practically floating. Uzachi met us at the airport and the two were brothers from different mothers sharing the same thoughts and desires…"

Kim told all that had amazed Kurt on the trip into the bush, the tribal welcome, and the rapid growth of the church as entire families responded to him and the Word. She described the village customs and dress and individuals who comprised the warp and woof of their first eight months in Zaire as their lives were woven together.

A noise at the window broke her concentration. A sparrow latched onto the wire mesh, fluttering, twisting, and bouncing against the screen before flying away. Kim glanced at Dr. Bradley who had said very little during the long narration. The doctor was toying with a gold necklace. The fish idly circled in the aquarium. "Kurt loved everything about the people and the land, Dr. Bradley."

Dr. Bradley stirred in her well-padded metal chair. "Yes, but what did you think of Africa?"

Kim squirmed, twisted and bounced until she was at the edge of the couch. She pushed upward using both hands. Once upright she pointed to a porcelain clock on an end table next to the doctor. "Weren't you listening all this time? I said we loved everything."

"No, Kim. You said Kurt loved everything about the people and the land. You painted a vivid picture of Kurt's life among the people of the village. How did you feel?"

"We were married. We thought and felt the same."

"If you believed that when you first married, surely it didn't take you long to figure out that isn't reality. People don't lose their identity because they marry, or at least they shouldn't. They're meant to complement each other's strengths and help overcome faults."

"Since I'm the only one in this room who has been married, I think I know a little more about it." Kim's hand flew to her mouth too late. The brief surge of anger evaporated leaving only mortification. She whispered, "I'm sorry."

Dr. Bradley fingered one of the gold hoop earrings. "Why don't we break for a few minutes? You can use the restroom through the door over there, and I'll ask Angela to bring us a couple of pops, unless you prefer something else."

Kim mumbled, "Pop is fine." If she'd been offered hemlock she'd have accepted that. She rushed into the lavatory, locked the door and splashed cold water on her face to wash away tears of shame. If there were a window, she'd have found a way to crawl through and never again face Dr. Bradley.

Eventually, Kim returned to the room. Dr. Bradley was back in her usual place sipping her drink from the can. Another can sat unopened on the coffee table in front of the couch.

"I'm sorry. I was rude and unkind. I don't know why I said that."

Dr. Bradley inclined her head in acceptance. "All right. Are you ready to resume?"

"Yes." Kim picked her way to the couch. She swigged the soda pop and rotated the can several times before speaking. "I didn't like Africa. I hated the heat, the insects, the snakes, the primitive lifestyle, and the isolation, but I liked the people and I loved Kurt. I thought as long as we were together none of it mattered."

The smells and images and essence of the village in Zaire rose about her. She explained her difficulties adjusting to the culture, the language, and being so different in appearance and thought. She recalled the patience of the ladies and how Nsia had been like a little sister. She laughed as she shared the fun they'd had and how it dispelled some of the loneliness as Kurt lost himself in work.

"Nsia sounds like a very special person," Dr. Bradley said.

Kim nodded, "She was."

"I'll look forward to hearing more about her next time."

No! Oh, no! Kim pressed her hand to her chest to still sharp, quick pulses. She refrained from apologizing a final time before she trod the exit ramp and trudged across the lawn. The sturdy picnic table didn't budge as she dropped heavily onto its bench. Panic like devil drums pounded the good memories into oblivion, like a hammer drubbing hot metal into solid chain, like machine gun fire piercing—

Kim shrieked.

Jack yanked his hand from her shoulder. "It's okay, Kim. It's me."

"You startled me."

"Yeah. I didn't think you saw me waiting." He pointed to the truck sitting in plain sight not thirty feet away.

Kim forced a laugh. "I was thinking about—about the baby. He must be destined to be a gymnast, because he's sure doing cartwheels." Jack wasn't buying it, but Kim pulled herself to her feet and headed for the truck leaving him to trail behind. No need to tell him that she wasn't coming back.

Chapter Twenty-three - Jack

Jack enjoyed the trip to Indianapolis to escort Jasmine home. He met Jasmine's parents and the evening passed pleasantly as they shared a meal at Carol's house. The sun had sunk low as he stood with Carol on the curb and waved good-bye to Jasmine.

"Do you want to come in for one last cup of coffee, Jack?"

"No. I'd like to stretch my legs. How about you?"

"Love to. We've got to take advantage of these summery evenings. Soon the leaves will turn and dark will fall before supper. There's a park a couple blocks from here. I'll get Minnie."

They headed toward the park with the beagle on a lead. Jack couldn't help thinking of the difference between Carol and Karen. The quiet was uneasy so perhaps Carol was doing the same as they walked where she'd no doubt had often walked with her husband.

"Jack, do you really think Kim's improving?"

"You'd know better than I would. You two talk all the time."

"Kim tells me all the good stuff, but has posted a no trespassing sign over everything else. She seems so closed. It worries me. If you don't get the infection out, it sickens the whole body. You however see her from a third party view."

Jack considered what Jasmine would want him to say. "Jasmine was concerned that Kim was neglecting to read the Bible and pray."

"That is worrisome. What else did she say?"

"She thinks Kim should make Mitchell her boyfriend."

Carol stopped while Minnie sniffed intently at a spot on the sidewalk. "I like Mitchell."

"I hear a 'but' in your voice."

They resumed walking and passed a house with children skating up and down the driveway, perhaps the same way Kim had once done as a child.

Carol said, "Of course, I don't get a say, but it's too soon for Kim to get involved with anyone. She has a lot of unresolved issues over what happened in Zaire. You don't bounce back quickly from such trauma and loss."

Had Carol bounced back from losing her husband? Instead of asking, Jack said, "Do you know any more about what happened over there?"

Carol shook her head. "Kurt was a delightful young man, loving, caring, and 100% sold out for the Lord. After the accident, he changed. That's all I can get out of her. Is Mitch interested in Kim?"

"Yes. I haven't seen any signs of pursuit though. I think he knows to take it slow, but maybe it's a good thing he's at school."

"I was surprised Kim stayed in Free Dance."

"Whenever I'm in town, I'll look in on her. If she needs anything, I'll do what I can."

Carol squeezed his arm. "Thank you, Jack."

They walked in silence through the iron arched frame of the park. "A.J. and I used to love to walk here. I haven't been here for a long time."

"Who's A.J.?"

"My husband, of course."

"I thought his name was Andy."

"Andy, Andrew Jacob, A.J." Jack remembered his suspicions the last night at the cabin. It all was quite silly now that he knew her.

"or Sweetie-pie." She lengthened the Sweetie-pie in long, heavy syllables through clenched teeth and widened her eyes until they looked positively wild. She laughed. "If I called him that he knew he'd better be phoning the florist for a serious apology bouquet and taking the time to figure out what exactly went wrong."

"Please don't ever call me Jackie-poo."

Carol turned amused blue eyes on him and giggled. "No."

"Does it bother you to walk here with me instead of Andy?"

"No. It seems very natural."

Jack stopped and pulled her around to face him. She was so beautiful. "Yes, it does. Carol, I enjoy being with you. Between our travel schedules, I don't see how we're going to see much of each other. We could try, couldn't we?"

"Jack, I'd lik—" Carol jerked out of his hands as Minnie yelped and bolted after a rabbit, towing Carol across the park at breakneck speed. "Stop! Minnie! Stop!"

Jack raced after them, but they stayed out of his reach until the rabbit disappeared and Minnie halted to snuffle the ground. Carol wrapped the leash more tightly around her hand as she breathlessly scolded, "No girl. Don't do that again."

"No, Carol." Jack tried to snatch the leash, but the rabbit reappeared, dashing across the grass, under a parked bicycle and into brush at the park's edge. Minnie yelped, plowed over the bike, and wiggled through the small hole in the hedge. The bike crashed to the ground. With a shriek, Carol hurdled it and landed in the bushes. There was a snapping of vegetation before she staggered backwards leaves floating around her. The broken leash dangled as she braced her hands on her knees.

Jack bent over and held his sides, shaking with laughter. Carol glared at him. She straightened and placed her hands on her hips. His name sounded sharp like the report of a rifle. He laughed harder as her embarrassment gave way to angry facial contortions. Carol charged toward him and tripped on an exposed tree root. She landed face down in the dirt. A little boy in a Colts shirt stooped to look her in the face. "Lady, that was way cool. You sure can jump."

The boy's mother helped Carol to her feet, "Are you okay?"

"I'm fine." Carol turned accusingly as Jack reached her. "No thanks to you."

He shrugged and laughed again, joined by the woman and her son. Jack swiped at Carol's dirty face and took her elbow to steady her. "The important thing is you're not hurt. Come on, let's get you home."

A man with a camera sprinted up. "That was fantastic. I got the whole thing on video. It was the funniest thing I ever saw."

Carol burst into tears and raced away. Jack called to her, but she only ran faster.

"I'll give you fifty dollars for the tape," Jack said.

"Not a chance, Mister. I'm sending this in to America's Funniest Home Videos."

"Mrs. Streeter may have something to say about that."

"I'll tell you what. Here's my business card. I'll make a copy for her. When she sees it, she may have a different attitude."

Jack pocketed the card. Fetching the dog was probably the best way to make amends. He trotted down the street. Minnie's bays grew fainter as she continued her quest. After a several more yelps, Minnie quieted. He walked several blocks and turned back.

The evening was dusky as he approached Carol's house. There on the brick steps sat the beagle with tongue lolling. Carol, laughing hysterically, had both arms draped about Minnie. Jack scratched his head, wondering if he dared join in. Carol wiped her face, smearing dirt. "Don't look so stricken, Jack. I'd have laughed too."

"Good to know I'm forgiven. Here." He handed her the man's card. "The videographer asked you to call him. How about that coffee?"

"I don't think so. I'm filthy dirty. I'm calling it a night. You can drive my car back to your hotel and take the shuttle to the airport. I'll come for the car in the morning."

He took the keys she offered him. "That's generous. Thanks. Good night, Mrs. Streeter."

"Good night, Mr. Bronner."

Jack watched the smiling bedraggled woman in the rearview mirror and debated if he should go back and tell her what he was feeling. Then, she turned and went into the house.

***

Jack slouched in the second booth from the rear at Millie's Diner in Free Dance, brooding over his second cup of coffee. Life didn't wait around for you to get your feet under you. It surged on like white water rapids. He wasn't sure he could keep up with the changes much better than Kim was.

"Hey. Mind if I join you?"

Jack straightened at the greeting and wondered how he hadn't noticed the big man sooner. "Have a sit. Good to see you, Brewster. What's been keeping you busy since the rodeo?"

"Trucking. Anyway, I figured you were busy with all your company." He slipped into the seat opposite and held his hand up to the waitress to indicate he wanted coffee.

"True enough. I got to say, Brew, it's been fun having the house full. Of course, you've heard about all our comings and goings from Maggie no doubt."

"Sure did, and everybody else in Free Dance. People are saying you must really have something for that woman you pulled out of the snow to have her kids move in with you."

"It was only a summer visit. They're really nice people. That kid, Jasmine, is sure on the ball. I got the biggest kick out of her. She wants to come back next summer. I hope she does."

"Uh-huh."

"Kim is staying in Free Dance."

"You don't say."

"She took a job over at the vets. She's there now. He'd been looking for a receptionist. Do you know of anybody with a second-hand car for sale? Kim is looking."

"What does she need?"

"It'd have to be dependable enough for frequent trips to Bozeman."

"Heard Ed Wolcott had a car he wants to unload. His boy went to college and now has the idea that vehicle is beneath him. You know Ed. Keeps all his machinery top shape."

"Thanks. I'll tell her."

Brewster ordered a large beefsteak with fries, eggs, and hash browns. When the waitress left he said, "They don't make it like my Vera did, but it's still good."

Jack nodded and sipped his coffee. "After eating my own cooking for a year, it's been a real treat having Maggie at the house again."

"Is she going to stay on?"

"Nah. No need. She's just clearing stuff out of the garden. She'll leave now that Kim has found an apartment."

"What about Mitch?"

"Mitchell is finishing his last semester of seminary in Bozeman."

"That's good. And your lady friend?"

"I'll see her from time to time especially since her daughter and grandchild will be here."

Brewster's cup clinked against the saucer. "Worked out for you, huh?"

"If you're asking if I like her, I do."

"Is that what has you off your feed?"

Jack surveyed the cold hash browns and cheese omelet that still filled his plate. Surprised, he looked up at Brewster who was openly watching him. Jack motioned for the waitress and asked her to reheat his meal and bring it when Brewster got his. He waited until she topped his coffee and was gone. "How long was it after Vera died before you sorted through her clothing?"

"I didn't. It made Vera feel better to tell me to give a certain sweater to charity and another to a friend. Now, her cookbooks are the only things left. I don't need them, but I still keep them."

"I think it's time to clean the closets. The clothes might as well be where somebody can use them."

"Makes sense."

"Maybe Maggie will do it for me before she leaves. The girls stayed in the master bedroom for the summer. I suppose once they're gone, I should think about moving back into it."

"Uh-huh."

Jack studied Brewster. "How did you handle it?"

"I had to. I don't have a big place like you. There's only the one bed. The couch isn't comfortable for a big guy like me. I did take more long hauls, stayed away a lot at first."

"When does it quit hurting?"

Brewster shook his head and fiddled with his cup. "Don't know. Don't think it does. It just kind of becomes a part of you instead of being all you think about. After a while you say to yourself, 'how long have I been living like this?' cause you realize you've gotten on with your life."

The waitress delivered two hot, fresh plates of food. "Millie said she doesn't do leftovers, this one is on the house."

"Tell her thanks for me."

Brewster winked at Jack. "Well, buddy, that's one upside to being a bachelor."

As they tucked into their meals, Millie peered around the kitchen door. The bleached blonde curls of her perm bobbed as her voice filled the diner. "Jack Bronner!"

"Yes, Ma'am. The food is great."

"You don't have to tell me that. I know it is. Your second plate is free, but so's we're clear, the first plate of perfectly good food I pitched will cost you a date to the dance."

"And there's the downside of bachelorhood," Brewster said, reaching for the salt.

Chapter Twenty-four – Kim

While waiting for Dr. Bradley, Kim calmed herself by running a mental check on the things left to do for the dance and thinking of her visit with Mitch. What would he think when he saw her? The last two weeks she felt as if everything from her belly to her feet had doubled in size.

From a sitting position on the psychiatrist's couch, Kim tried unsuccessfully to lift her legs high enough past her belly to get a look. She was sure the trip over had caused them to swell like prize watermelons.

She eyed the woman moving into position across from her. Dr. Bradley wore a stunning dark purple suit with gold chains and square gold earrings. The woman had style and a definitely un-whale-like shape.

Kim's frumpy, faded blue-striped dress was going in the trash when she got home. After all, this wasn't Zaire. These thoughts, added to what she knew she had to tell, made Kim weary. She didn't waste much time with pleasantries before picking up the story. She told what her husband had done and how Nsia had found her and brought the villagers. "I don't know where he got the gun. Maybe he bought it in Mobutu or found it on the road."

She squinted, recalling what he looked like that moment. She touched her cheek. "His face was distorted, snarling and hateful, like it wasn't his at all. He aimed at our friends who'd come to help me. I thought he was going to kill us when we heard a lorry arrive. One man said, 'Soldiers.' It was like a light switch flipped. Kurt's face cleared. He said, 'don't worry my friends. I'll handle it.' He went to the window and killed all those soldiers."

"You were still chained?"

Kim raised her face to Dr. Bradley. "Yes."

"Did the villagers let you go?"

Kim went over to the fish tank and tapped the glass. The fish darted about trying to find safety. She could reach in and catch them anytime she wanted. What was the phrase? Like shooting fish in a barrel.

Dr. Bradley repeated the question. Kim shook her head and it kept moving in tiny little shakes like the tremor of someone with poor muscle control. "They were afraid. They thought Kurt was bewitched and I was cursed. Uzachi was the strong one, a real leader. And he was gone."

"How long were you chained after that?"

Of its own accord, her head continued its side-to-side negative motion. Kim pursed her lips. "I don't know. He didn't remember any of it. He acted as if we'd just arrived."

"But he didn't free you?"

"It was as if he didn't even see the chains. He seemed to think I had the flu or a cold. At first, he was kind and loving. He fed me and cared for me." She stared at her hands and whispered the shameful words. "It felt so good that I pretended everything was okay."

Dr. Bradley offered to bring her a tissue, but she was dry-eyed and refused. Kim shrugged again, throwing her hands wide apart, then clapped them together once with a note of finality. "Eventually other fighters came. The shooting went on for a long time. Only a few villagers survived. When the soldiers found me, they freed me."

"And Nsia?"

"She cared for me until I could walk. We headed to the American consulate in Mobutu."

Kim turned back to the fish and started tapping the tank. Only when Dr. Bradley crossed the room and grasped her hand did she realize she'd been hitting the glass harder and harder.

"Kim, what else happened?"

A distancing stillness passed over Kim. She looked into Dr. Bradley's eyes. "I don't have time. I've got things to do for the dance. It was a bad plan to schedule this today, but we had to pick my mom up from the airport anyway. I've got to go."

Chapter Twenty-five – Carol

When Carol arrived at the dance on Jack's arm, many of the townspeople were already in high spirits. The old barn was decorated in a traditional country theme with red-checked tablecloths, corn shocks, and scarecrows. A band, scheduled to play a variety of music, was setting up a lively square dance. From across the room Kim glowed as she moved about the barn, checking the food table, bringing more supplies for punch, and wiping a spill from the tabletop.

"I was a bit worried. Kim seemed so distant after her doctor visit," Carol said to Jack, "Perhaps she was just preoccupied with things to do. Look at her now. I think the busyness of preparing the dance was good for her."

"I think you're right. Many have mentioned what a help she's been and how much they've enjoyed working with her. Oh, excuse me for a few minutes, Carol. I have to go dance for my supper, or more accurately, my breakfast."

A round gentleman with ruddy face and salt and pepper hair moved in next to Carol. He teased. "Has Jack Bronner deserted you?"

"Let's say he had a debt to pay."

"Oh yes, Millie's free meal for a date."

"He managed to bargain it down to a dance since he already had a date for the evening. Are you Mayor Dougherty?"

"Yes and you are Kim's mother. She's been a lifesaver to take over for Marta. I've got to say, I'm breathing a sigh of relief. I was afraid Kim was going to burst with that baby before the dance."

Carol laughed. "It shouldn't be too many more days. Then, I'm sure she'll have enough to keep her hands full without any major town productions."

"Are you coming back when the baby is born?"

"I'm on vacation now. I'll stay with Kim for a month, enough time for her to get back on her feet after the baby arrives."

The mayor turned to chat with someone else as Jack returned and led Carol onto the dance floor. Jack said, "You have to keep an eye out for Mayor Dougherty or he'll have you involved in the annual Christmas Pageant."

"No, thank you. I have enough to do."

After a few dances, Carol begged for a rest. They donned jackets and left the noise and heat of the barn behind. How different this visit was from the last. Their frequent phone calls had made the quiet unstrained and companionable once again. He led her to a bench overlooking the valley.

"I'm envious. I think you have more stars than we can see in Indianapolis. Not as much light pollution to block it out."

Jack stared up at the sky. As if seeing it for the first time his gaze lingered. "It is breathtaking."

Carol huddled deeper into her jacket.

"Do you want to go inside?"

"No. I'm okay. I'm more sensitive to the cold since my ordeal. I've even worn a sweater on a hot summer day."

Jack wrapped his arm around her. "Here, snuggle close. I'll keep you warm."

Carol scooted into the crook of his arm. "You kept me warm before too. Thanks, for then and for now. You're such a gentleman."

"Will you still think me a gentleman if I kiss you?"

"It depends. Will you still think me a lady if I kiss back?"

"What makes you think I think you're a lady, now?"

Carol jostled him. "You're incorrigible. Don't think I've forgotten how you laughed at me in the park."

A chuckle rumbled from Jack's chest. "A little, bitty lady like you leaping that bike like Evil Knievel over the Grand Canyon. I'll never forget the sight. You were hopping mad when you left the park. I figured that was it for me. But, when I got back to the house and you were laughing yourself silly on the doorstep, well—"

"Well, what?"

"Well, Lady, if that wasn't the moment I fell in love with you, at least it was the moment I realized it."

Carol sucked her breath in surprise. Which was a good thing, for Jack's kiss was unhurried and complete. When he released her, she heard him whisper, "Forgive me for laughing at you?"

"Absolutely." She pulled him close for another kiss. "You know when the moment of truth was for me? It was the day I came out to the ranch and you shook my hand hello and didn't let go. I realized I didn't want you to ever let go." She shivered again.

Jack stood "Come on. Let's get back to the dance."

As they entered, Kim was standing across the room scrutinizing the crowd. She wore a strange bewildered expression. When she saw them, she gestured wildly and they hustled over. Kim squeezed Carol's arm and put her mouth close to her ear. "Mom, my water broke."

"Jack, get the car and meet us at the door," Carol said.

Jack took one look at each of them and bolted toward the door, digging in his pocket for keys. Carol helped Kim lumber toward the exit, glad no one was paying much attention. Kim paused only once to turn over the closing of the dance to Marta.

The nurses at the local health care center had her in a room within a half hour. Jack stayed until early morning. After he left to care for the horses that he hadn't yet boarded, time lost all meaning as Carol was busy coaching Kim. The new baby was born the following afternoon.

Kim's hair hung limp. Damp strands clung to her face. Carol brushed them back. "You did a terrific job. Addie-Jo is perfect, beautiful and healthy."

Kim's weak smile warmed as she nestled the baby. "After nineteen hours of labor, I was beginning to think it was an elaborate hoax."

Carol hugged both mother and baby. "What a lot of dark hair she has. The same as you had when you were born. Your brother on the other hand was bald as a cucumber."

"May I come in?" Jack stood at the door with a vase of pink rosebuds.

"Sure. What lovely roses," Kim said.

"My old science teacher is in room eight. Do you think he'll like them?"

Kim giggled. "Thanks for the flowers, Jack."

"Jasmine gave me instructions before she left. They're also from Maggie, Mitchell, and Jasmine."

"That sounds like my little cousin. What would we do without her?"

"You know, Jazz is already calling me Grampa Jack. I wouldn't mind playing Grampa to this little one, too."

"I accept before you have any chance to change your mind," Kim said sending him a sweet smile.

Jack placed the flowers on a table where they stood out against the green wall. "So can the honorary Grampa see your new little girl?"

"Meet Addie-Jo. Would you like to hold her?"

"Sure," Jack said.

Carol lifted the bundle away from Kim and situated it in his arms. "You're a natural."

Jack sat in the single chair. "I haven't held a baby since Mitchell was born. Wow, does this bring back memories. He cried every night for the first two weeks. Back then, we couldn't afford help and our family was unavailable. If Maggie hadn't offered to stay, I'm not sure Karen or I would have lasted a month. She's lovely."

Kim rested her head against the pillow. Her smile was bright even though her face was wan. Just then Maggie burst through the door. "Jack, quit hogging that baby. It's my turn."

Jack handed Addie-Jo to Maggie, making the introduction. Maggie said, "Addie-Jo is a sweet name."

"We picked names out when we were dreaming of the children we'd have. Addie for my mother-in-law Adeline, Jo for my father-in-law Joseph. Her initials are the same as my father's. We didn't think they'd see the baby much since we'd be in Africa, so we honored them that way."

"How come you got left out, Carol?"

"As long as I get to hold the baby, I don't care."

"Yep, that's the important thing and there'll always be other babies."

"Oh, no," Kim declared. "I'm never getting married again."

Carol and Jack exchanged surprised looks while Maggie crooned, "Well, this one is certainly a keeper."

A young serious-minded nurse arrived. "I'm taking the baby to the nursery so I can help Mrs. Macomb bathe. Say your good-byes." She pried Addie-Jo out of Maggie's clutches and left them to it.

"We'll see you tomorrow," Carol said.

"Okay. Thanks again for the flowers. I'll thank Mitch when I see him tomorrow and I'll call Jasmine."

In the hallway, Jack said, "Mitch must've changed his plans. He told me he couldn't come until the weekend. Have you talked with him?"

"No."

"Kim seems pretty set on staying single."

"Didn't we feel the same way when it first happened to us? Her attitude will change in time," Carol said.

"Maybe. Want to get a bite to eat?"

"I thought you'd never ask. All I've had since the party is coffee and it was thick as hot tar."

"Then that was real coffee. My Granny always said when you're done stirring the sugar, if it takes less than two seconds for the spoon to hit the side of the cup, it ain't real coffee."

"Ja-ack."

"Yes, Ma'am, but then, if I remember correctly, Granny had to shave every other day."

Carol bumped his arm with her shoulder as they walked toward a café.

Millie's Diner was filling up with the supper crowd, but they were seated without a wait. The waitress took their orders promptly and delivered tasty, hot food.

Finally, Carol pushed her empty plate away and sank back into the booth's soft cushion. "That was fantastic. I can't remember when I ate so much."

Jack leaned forward and patted his back pocket. "I carry a credit card for emergencies. Do you want dessert? I could order you another burger."

"Stop it. You're embarrassing me."

"Next time, I'll take you to this huge buffet over in Butte."

Carol was about to reply when something flickered in Jack's eyes. A woman approached calling in a sugar-sweet voice, "Jack. It's so wonderful to see you, darling."

Jack rose from his seat and the most voluptuous platinum blonde Carol had ever seen wrapped her arms around him and planted a kiss on his cheek.

Carol lowered her gaze to her empty plate but couldn't help noting the stylish woman wore a very snug dress.

"With all your traveling, I don't see enough of you these days. When are we getting together for that little talk you promised me?"

Jack's eyebrows knitted together and he drew a deep breath as he gestured toward Carol. "Have you met Carol Streeter? Her daughter Kim orchestrated the Fall Festival dance after Marta was hospitalized. Carol, meet Cherry Jacobs."

Cherry blinked remarkable purple eyes and waved a manicured hand heavy with expensive rings. "Oh, I didn't see you. I'll join you for a minute. I'm meeting a friend here, but she's late as usual." She scooted into the booth beside Jack.

Jack narrowed his eyes and hesitated before sitting. "You're welcome to join us."

"I know that darling."

"Have a seat," Carol said to the sitting woman and wondered if the comment sounded sarcastic.

"Cherry was a friend of Karen's," Jack said.

"Not only friends, dear, we were best friends. Now, I count Jack as one of my closest friends."

"How's Roy doing these days, Cherry?"

"You know Roy. He's riding rodeo."

"I'm surprised you two haven't married yet."

Cherry turned those deep violet eyes on Jack and laid a pretty bejeweled hand on his leg. Blood crept into Jack's face. Her voice was low and breathy. "Don't tease me, Jack. Roy and I keep company to fight loneliness. You know that, sweetheart. We'd never marry. At least, not each other."

Jack stood. "Excuse me a moment."

Cherry watched him walk away. "Jack and I dated before I met my first husband. I left him behind for the big city and a man with a lot of money. What a disaster. When I came back, he'd already married Karen. Jack still gets a little choked up over her. He's as faithful as the day is long. Not like my ex. So, even though there's always been a lot of passion between the two of us we bridled it for Karen's sake. You can't help who you fall in love with and he is one passionate man. The memory of his kisses still lights me on fire.

"Now that Karen's gone, we're almost ready to pick up where we left off. Karen was well liked. In a small community like Free Dance you have to be very careful. Everything you do is fodder for gossips and busybodies.

"Honey, I'm telling you this so you don't make the mistake of falling for him. He's taken. We have history. I've seen you sashaying around him. I'd hate for you to get your feelings hurt thinking the relationship can go anywhere. I swear he doesn't even see when a woman is practically falling all over him."

Jack returned to the table. Cherry rose, squeezed his arm and planted another kiss on his cheek. "I'm sorry I can't stay longer, Jack. My friend is here."

"We've finished our meal, anyway."

Cherry's unusual eyes lingered on Carol's empty platter. "So I see. Bye."

"Bye." Carol pulled a mirror from her purse and tried to apply a sense of femininity with a little lipstick. Last night Jack had said he loved her. Was she a rebound romance to be discarded for Cherry? There was definitely something between them.

Chapter Twenty-six - Carol

Carol looked up the steep stairway to Kim's apartment. The aluminum storm door yawned open in the fierce wind and smacked against the two-by-four railing. The plexi-glass window rattled in its metal frame before sweeping shut again. *Slam. Bang. Slam. Bang.* She said, "You have to get that door fixed."

"I told her. She said her husband would fix it."

"You go first so I can block your fall if this wind gusts you off the stairs. The only thing stopping this from being a hurricane is lack of warmth and water."

"Oh, Mom," Kim said with as much disgust as she could muster, but she clung to the railing with one hand and hugged Addie-Jo with the other as she struggled to the top of the steps. There she leaned against the storm door to hold it open while her mother juggled a load of baby gear and worked the key.

As soon as they stepped inside, the door thwacked shut and the wind shook the little apartment like a frustrated toddler trying to reach its toys. Carol closed the inner wooden door while Kim eased onto the couch, squirming to find a comfortable position. The room felt hollow after the whooshing of the wind in their ears.

"I'm glad to be home, sweet home."

"It's you and Addie-Jo makes the place sweet," Carol said hoping to see Kim's old sweet smile.

Slam – bang.

Addie-Jo startled, shrieked.

"It's going to be a long night if she screams every time the door bangs. Are you sure you don't want to go to a hotel, Kim?"

"No and don't do that wide-eyed look, Mom. This is my home now. We stay here."

"All right. All right. I'll get lunch."

"Good idea," Kim said between clenched teeth. She crooned to the baby, "You'll get used to it, won't you. There's nothing to fear. Besides, it isn't windy all the time, is it?"

The door continued its syncopated percussion with Addie-Jo's accompanying howls. By the time Carol set stir-fry on the table, she too wanted to scream. Kim had given up trying to quiet with words or lullabies and simply clutched the baby.

Carol studied Kim's face. It was tired, exhausted even, but a firmness in the set of her jaw indicated she intended to make this work. A new beat was added to the door and Carol scurried to answer it. "Welcome, stranger. What do you have?"

Jack entered with a whirl of wind that whipped the napkins onto the floor and tipped a lamp onto the couch. He set a metal box on the floor. "An electric drill. I saw the door was about to fly south for the winter. A couple hooks will secure it until it gets fixed properly."

Carol mouthed thank you.

Kim's protest was sharp. "You don't have to. It's fine. It's a little noisy but we'll get used to it. I don't want to be any trouble."

Jack shot a glance in Kim's direction. Carol put her lips in a tight line, opened her eyes wide, and gave a vague shrug in silent answer to his questioning gaze.

"There's no reason to get used to it," he said. "I've got all the stuff here. It'll only take a few minutes. Please let me do this for you."

"Fine. If you must, you must." Kim shifted Addie-Jo to her shoulder and patted the wailing baby's back.

Carol returned the napkins to the table, straightened the lamp, and set another plate.

Amid the whirring of the drill and the whining of the wind, Addie-Jo quieted. Kim's expression grew slack as she fell asleep with her head tilted against the back of the sofa, her face at last as peaceful as her sleeping child's.

Jack stowed the drill in its case. Carol whispered, "Thank you, so much. I was about to find a gun and shoot myself."

"So, I've saved your life twice. This hero stuff is easier than I thought."

Carol snorted. She clenched both her fists. "This is more than gloom consuming her. I'm worried."

"Don't. It doesn't help. Just keep praying. When you leave in a few weeks, I'll check in on her from time to time. If I see something needs done, I'll apply a little pressure to Dora or do it myself. She'll be fine. There's been a lot of change for Kim. Maybe she needs to feel in control."

"But, Jack, none of us are truly in control. Right now, I think she's trying to do it all herself instead of depending on God."

"If I learned anything from dealing with Mitchell it's that you have to let them do it their way. She'll only get more stubborn if you try to tell her something she's not ready to hear."

Carol rubbed both cheeks. "I know. I know. How many times have I said that very thing at grief seminars? It's so stinking hard to live it when someone you love is hurting so badly."

Jack reached over and took her hand. "She'll be fine."

She found his touch comforting. After stir-fry, Jack kissed her and slipped away. Kim continued to sleep. Carol watched over her. How long would it be before Kim would be fine?

Chapter Twenty-seven – Mitch

Mitch bounded up the steps to Kim's apartment two at a time and rapped on the metal frame. The noon sun warmed the pocket of air about the door. A few minutes passed and he rapped again. The door latch, hooked from the inside, indicated she was home. He rapped a third time with less certainty. The inner door opened a crack. Kim's blotchy face appeared. She unhooked the outer door and opened it about two inches. "I'm sleeping. Go away."

Mitch balanced an insulated container against his stomach and removed a bag. He unsealed it and pressed it toward the opening so the spicy aroma would reach her. "I brought Sicilian Stromboli and kept them hot all the way from Bozeman."

Kim sniffed. Her eyes closed halfway and her mouth worked until the stubbornness on her face melted with indecision.

"Let me in before you drool."

"Okay, but be quiet. I just got Addie-Jo to sleep."

Mitch crunched the bag shut and returned it to the heated container. He followed her inside, placed his precious cargo on the table and pulled the knapsack from his back. "Congratulations." He swept Kim into a hug. She was a stiff as a mannequin. He rocked sideways with her until she relaxed. He pushed her at arm's length and kissed her on the forehead. "You look terrific."

She ran a hand through tousled hair. "I do not. I was sleeping."

"I figured as much. You have a waffle pattern from the couch pillow on your cheek."

She rubbed her cheeks and the pale pattern turned pink against her still-tanned face. Kim brushed at a patch of baby spit dried on her sweatshirt. "I'm a mess. I'll put on a fresh shirt."

"I don't care. You look lovely as ever to me." Her face softened and Mitch tore his eyes away and busily unpacked the knapsack. He spread a blue-and-white checked plastic picnic cloth on the floor and set out bottles of root beer, apples and cannoli. "Anyway, Stromboli is messy and I forgot bibs. Better wait until after we eat."

Kim lowered herself to the floor. "This is a real feast, Mitch."

"My way of saying, 'well done little mother'. I can't wait to meet her. I hear she's gorgeous."

Kim blushed and tears threatened to spill from her beautiful brown eyes. Mitch reached for her hand and offered a prayer over the meal and a blessing for the family. He handed her one of the huge sandwiches. They laughed together as sauce and melted cheese dribbled down her shirtfront at the first bite. Kim mewed with pleasure. "This is great. Where did you find it?"

"A new food place opened a block from campus. Everyone was raving about Poppe's."

"Rightfully so and it's almost hot."

"I bribed the manager to let me borrow one of their delivery containers."

As they munched, Mitch shared tales from seminary he knew would interest or amuse her. After the last bite, she heaved a contented sigh, and wiggled around to support her herself against the rear of the sofa.

The backside of the sofa was a brighter color than the seat cushions on the front because it had not seen the light of day while shoved against the wall and hadn't suffered from constant use and abuse. He remembered the day he'd positioned it in the middle of the room with the bright side visible to visitors because she said it was less grim than the rest of her used, but free, pieces.

Kim picked at a stray thread. "So what brings you to Free Dance this weekend?"

He frowned, but he made his lips curve upward. "You and Addie-Jo, of course. I wanted to see you as soon as I could. I can't stay real long. One of my classes was cancelled this week when a professor had a death in the family. The make-up session is late this afternoon.

"So you have stuff to get from the ranch?"

"No. Besides I don't have time to go out there."

"My mom went with your dad to visit the horses. They should be back about five."

"I'll be back in Bozeman by then."

"Won't your dad be disappointed?" Her brown eyes studied him.

"I didn't come to see him. I came to see you."

A tiny mewling issued from the bedroom. Mitch brightened, "Hey, sounds like the other sleeping beauty is awake." He leapt to his feet and returned with the infant cradled in his arms, talking to her. She blinked sleepy eyes.

"Give her to me. I'll change her." Kim rose from the picnic setting.

"I know how to change a baby. You rest. I'll take care of it."

In a few moments, he returned to the living room and sat on the opposite end of the couch from Kim, who roosted like a satisfied hen with legs curled under and a softness on her face not evident when he'd first arrived. He handed over Addie-Jo. "So, were you scared?"

Kim gave a recap of the last moments of the dance that made them both laugh. She shared her observations of their parents. She gave him news from the reservation that her many youthful visitors had brought. Finally, Mitch said, "I have to go."

Disappointment rippled across Kim's face. She bent her head. "I understand. You can't miss your class."

"No. I can't." He leaned forward and stroked the baby's face. Mitch could feel the warmth of Kim's cheek near his ear.

"I've had a wonderful time. Thank you," she murmured and her breath tickled.

If he turned his head slightly his lips would meet hers. Mitch pushed off the couch and hustled to clear the mess. He tucked the tablecloth into the warming container to return to the eatery and slipped on his knapsack. "I don't know when I'll be back, but I'll come to visit when I can."

"Sure. Sure." Kim pivoted sideways on the sofa, clutching Addie-Jo. The babe whimpered and she laid Addie-Jo down on the couch. A funny sound escaped Kim. "I never did change shirts or comb my hair." She picked the baby up as if that would cover her stains.

Mitch quietly said, "That's okay. I still think you look wonderful."

Kim was watching him. He studied the floor before looking at her again. His right index finger waggled at the corner of his mouth. "Except for that gob of sauce on your face."

"Why didn't you tell me sooner?" Kim swiped at her face with one hand as she swiveled around and ran into the tiny bathroom. "Where? I don't see anything."

Mitch called good-bye. He expelled his breath hard as the door clicked shut behind him.

Chapter Twenty-eight – Carol

The next day, as mother and daughter walked downtown, Carol cast a sideways look at Kim. It was difficult to know what to say or how to say it. Any warning would be greeted as meddling. "You were in an odd mood last night after Mitch's visit."

"He's such a good friend," Kim instantly replied and related funny details of the visit.

"It's good Mitch is straightforward with you."

"Yes. Yes, he is." Kim agreed so heartily Carol was sure she was holding something back. She added, "I think Jack is straightforward, too. I think he likes you."

Carol didn't have any intentions of mentioning Cherry Jacobs, but by the time they chose a new skein of blue at the yarn shop, browsed an antique store, and headed to pick up Kim's paycheck, she was weary of the needling and ready to confide the entire meeting at the diner to Kim.

"Her eyes were this incredible shade of violet. I didn't think it was possible to have that color of eyes," she said as they entered Mullins Veterinary Clinic where the reception room was empty except for a chest-high wooden desk and a sturdy built-in wooden seat running the entire length of the opposite wall.

"She probably wears colored contacts," Kim replied.

A male voice boomed from behind the desk. "You must be talking about Cherry Jacobs and yes, she wears colored contacts."

Kim called, "What are you doing back there, Dr. Mullins?"

"Cleaning a little present Mr. Dudley left me."

"Mr. Dudley is a chow and a little high-strung, Mom."

"Ah." Carol nodded.

"Yes, he always leaves a gift whenever he comes for his shots. It never fails." Dr. Mullins straightened and the disembodied voice took the form of a man not very tall and a little thick around the midriff. A full head of white hair was layered like a thatch over a face with laugh lines and pleasant wrinkles.

"Maybe he's trying to tell you something and it's not thank you," Carol suggested.

The veterinarian chuckled as he washed his hands at a corner sink. "I see where Kim gets her sense of humor."

"Mom, ask Dr. Mullins if you want the scoop on Cherry Jacobs. He knows all the dirt on everybody in town."

Carol shook her head. "No, thank you."

"I know Jack Bronner and Cherry Jacobs dated for a few years in high school. Their love was hotter than a pepper sprout, as the song says. Then, Cherry left for college and by the next spring, she'd married some rich guy from out east. Jack took some time getting over her, but he and Karen made a great match. When Cherry came home after her divorce she moved in with them for a while. There was a lot of talk about the wisdom in that, but Karen couldn't see the bad in anybody she loved. People were watching for sparks between the old sweethearts, that's for sure. Eventually Cherry moved out and built the big old spread she has." The vet dug around in the desk drawer and handed Kim an envelope containing her paycheck.

He continued, "I personally think she still has a thing for Jack. You can feel the heat when they're together, not that it happens much. Jack's kept pretty much to himself since Karen died. Some are betting they get together now time has passed. I don't know. She hangs around with Roy Everling and she's been seeing Bodine Reynolds, the new doctor in town. He's a likely prospect, with money and all. She's a temptress. She can turn the head of any guy in town before he's even aware his neck is rotating."

"I could see that in the two minutes I met her. I felt as attractive as a wet mop."

"Feelings don't make it so. How's the baby doing, Kim?"

Kim nodded. "Fine. Dora is watching her so I could give my mom a tour of the place."

"Go ahead. Not much to see, reception, two exam rooms, a desk in a closet where I do my paper work, and the area in back for holding animals and running tests. The stable is further back on the property. Most big animal visits are made on site."

"What a lot of driving for you."

"I'm trying to find a partner to handle the site visits. These days I prefer staying in the office working with small animals."

Kim said, "Well, we'd better get going. Dora is fixing supper for us. I hope to meet Mr. Rheinhardt tonight. I've been there for four weeks and eaten with Dora nine times and have yet to meet Mr. Rheinhardt."

"Not likely you will, either."

"Why not?"

"He died in 1984."

"That can't be. Dora still sets a place at the table for him."

"I heard. He was an ornery fellow, but she loved him. Can't quite get used to the idea he's gone. I thought you knew."

"It's creepy," Kim said as if expecting her boss to laugh and say it was a joke.

Dr. Mullins shrugged. "If it brings her comfort, what's the harm?"

The door opened and a big man entered, carrying a fluffy, white cat.

"We've got to get going. Bye, Dr. Mullins."

"Yeah, you better get out of here, before I put you to work. Nice to meet you, Kim's mother."

"Carol. My name's Carol," she said, but he was already talking with his client.

They left the clinic and walked the four blocks to the bank before turning toward Dora's.

"Kim, are you going to say anything to Dora?"

"I don't know. Do you think it's healthy she does this? If I say something, do you think she'll get violent?"

Carol nearly choked. "Dora? I don't think so."

Kim grew more agitated. "I'm not going to say anything to her. Mom, you deal with grieving people. You should say something. Besides, I have to live here."

In the end, they shared a meal of wiener schnitzel and passed the food over Harry Rheinhardt's empty plate. Kim picked at her meal and as soon as Addie-Jo fussed, excused herself.

Dora clucked about how little Kim ate. Carol made excuses and accepted a double portion of weinkompott to soothe Dora's concern. Stuffed from the fruit dessert, she refused a third portion and asked for coffee.

While Dora fetched the pot, Carol wandered into the living room. The house was a two-story with three rooms on the ground floor and stairs leading up to a bedroom that was separate from Kim's apartment. The furniture was heavy and old and well taken care of with tatted doilies and potted plants and Hummel figurines. A pipe stand with five pipes and an unopened but fresh package of Cherry Blend waited beside an overstuffed chair. She returned to her seat when Dora brought the coffee.

"How did you meet your husband?"

"Harry was at Rhein-Main Air Base. I was waitress, a little thing like Kim and all alone, too. We fell in love. We married and he brought me here to live with his parents." Dora's face softened with memories.

"Do you like living here?"

"Sure thing. Mama and Papa Rheinholdt, they were good people. God bless them. They are gone now. Harry doesn't know." Dora shook her head and frowned. "Six months married then Marines sent him to Beirut. Very Bad."

"I'm sorry I didn't get to meet your husband. How long has it been since Mr. Rheinhardt was home?"

Dora wagged her head sadly, "Near nineteen year."

"Maybe he's not coming."

Anger and disbelief washed over Dora's face. "Gossip. Don't listen to that." She shook her head and resolution returned. She settled into her chair and waggled her finger. "No. No. Mrs. Streeter. He's not dead. He come pretty soon. I know. You wait and see."

Carol reached out and patted Dora's hand. "I hope so."

Carol reported the conversation to Kim and after several discussions they decided Dora wasn't a threat. They didn't raise the topic of her husband anymore and continued to enjoy her meals and her company three times a week.

The days toward the end of September brought a nip to the air that required a heavy jacket to keep warm. Carol walked companionably beside Kim as she chose diapers, baby formula, chicken, and canned peaches from the shelves. The vacation was almost over. The thought of leaving Kim and Addie-Jo made her want to cry. And Jack, of course. At the same time, she missed Trudy and Minnie and her life in Indiana.

While Kim chatted with the girl at the checkout, Carol said, "I see Jack's truck in front of the hardware store. I'm heading over to see him."

"Okay. I'll meet you back at Dora's."

Carol hurried across the street and checked her hair in the window's reflection before entering the store. A bell overhead tinkled and from the rear the unseen proprietor called "Be out in a minute."

Carol noticed Cherry Jacobs park behind Jack's vehicle and unfold herself from a bright yellow corvette. Her designer jeans and cashmere sweater made her look sleeker than ever. She pulled a plain paper bag from her car and she set it on the passenger seat of Jack's truck.

Carol moved to the right wall where rows of fishing tackle and poles hung the entire length of the store. Finding the aisle empty, Carol kept walking, the uneven wooden floor creaking at intervals beneath her as she checked each intersecting aisle for Jack.

The bell tinkled again and the same greeting came from the rear. High heels clicked along the main aisle toward the back of the store.

Carol didn't want to talk with Cherry and slowed her steps so they wouldn't meet.

"Jack, there you are, honey," Cherry said. "You left something at my house last night I don't think you meant to leave."

"What?"

Cherry lowered her voice, but Carol still heard. "Your gorgeous red silk pajamas. Yummy. I put them in your truck."

"Why'd you do that?"

"Don't worry, I was discreet. I put them in a paper bag so no one would see."

"You should've left them where they'll be used."

At Cherry's laugh, the blood rushed to Carol's head drowning out the reply. Carol wanted to be anywhere other than where she was. She hurried from the store.

Cherry and Jack, why hadn't she seen it before? Why had he called her, sent her letters, emailed her when he was traveling and taken her to dinner? Was that merely friendship? Had she misread his intentions and seen what she wanted to see? She couldn't have been mistaken about the night at the dance, his kiss, and what he said. Was it all a smokescreen to keep the gossip away from Cherry?

Carol hardly knew how she found her way to Dora's. Kim and Dora were in the kitchen near the stove when she entered. Kim cast a sharp look her way. "What's the matter?"

"I've got a headache. I'm going upstairs to lie down. Dora, I'm sorry about missing supper. Excuse me."

"I'll come with you, Mom."

"No, Kim, stay and visit. I need to rest alone."

Carol climbed the steep steps to the apartment, wrapped herself in a blanket, and clapped a couch pillow over both sides of her head as if that would keep her from hearing that terrible exchange. Still, the words rang in her head, over and over.

A heavy tread sounded on the stairs. Jack. She didn't want to talk to him. She didn't ever want to see him again. His knock rang out in the quietness of the little room. She held her breath willing him to be convinced she wasn't there. He knocked again and called. The door opened a bit and Jack stuck his head in. "Carol? Kim said I'd find you here. How are you feeling?"

"Fine."

"You don't sound fine. Is there anything I can do?" Jack came all the way into the room as Carol sat upright. He looked concerned, but she wasn't about to be played.

"Go away."

"Whoa. What's the matter?"

"What's the matter? I don't want to ever see you again, Jack Bronner. I was in the hardware store and overheard your little conversation with Cherry Jacobs. I've got to say, you had me fooled."

"What are you talking about?"

Carol mimicked Cherry's breathy sexiness and batted her eyes for effect. "I'm talking about your yummy red pajamas. The ones you left at Cherry's house last night."

"Oh."

"Yes, oh. A big oh." Carol jumped to her feet and paced a few steps. Jack stayed where he was. When he didn't say anything, she swung around to face him. He looked—disappointed.

She had expected an explanation or an excuse or an apology, but the longer he stood there the more his eyes snapped with angry fire and his facial features stiffened.

"Did you leave your pajamas at Cherry's last night?"

"Yes," Jack said.

A shrill note of frustration burst from her. "Well, then—"

Jack's lips drew into a tight line. He turned on his heel and disappeared. Carol blinked as the door slammed behind him and footsteps pounded the stairs without hesitation. With a cry of exasperation, she snatched a pillow and threw herself flat on the couch. "Cheating, lying two-faced coward."

Carol was still prone on the sofa, wrapped in a blanket, when Kim came upstairs. She positioned herself at the end of the couch holding Addie-Jo against her shoulder with one hand. She leaned over enough to lift an empty ice cream carton from the end table. The spoon clattered to the floor. "What are you doing, Mother?"

"I'm sorry I ate all the ice cream. It was gone before I realized it. I'll buy you more."

Kim patted Addie-Jo's back. "I don't care about that. The atmosphere is so tense in here it's practically a fog. What happened? Did you and Jack have a fight?"

Carol brushed at a tear from her left eye. "It wasn't really a fight. But, whatever we had is over."

"What happened?"

"Let's say Mr. Bronner isn't the person of integrity I thought he was."

Kim's eyes widened. "Mother, did he try anything with you?"

"No," Carol wailed. Why did that somehow seem worse? She would never have gotten involved with him that way while unmarried, but it hurt to think he didn't want her. "I don't want to talk about it."

Kim puffed her cheeks and huffed out the air. "I know it's no use trying to get information from you when you're like this. I'm putting Addie-Jo in her crib and going to bed. If you want to talk, I'm here."

The problem simply wasn't one to discuss with a daughter. "I'll go with you to Bozeman for your counseling appointment tomorrow. You can drop me at the airport on the way home. I'm sorry to leave even a day early, but I'm not going to have Jack take me. This way, you won't lose time from work to get me there."

Chapter Twenty-nine - Kim

Kim parked the second-hand Cavalier and passed the keys to her mother. "You can use the picnic table. It's pleasant there. Or feel free to take the car."

"I'll be here, cuddling my granddaughter."

"Suit yourself." Her mom had neatly skirted every overture to find out what had happened with Jack. Instead she had made disjointed conversation the entire drive. It didn't give Kim much to talk about to Dr. Bradley who needed to be distracted.

At their previous meeting, talking about Nsia brought back many wonderful memories of the little friend but by the end of the session, they'd nudged too close to what happened to her. Kim drew a fortifying breath. I'm doing this for my daughter, for Addie-Jo.

When the doctor rolled in dressed to the nines in a cream-on-brown polka dot knit pantsuit, Kim raved about it. She told how she'd discarded the dress she hated and replaced it with the one in cheery primary colors she was currently wearing from the second-hand store. The doctor enthused over it with what Kim deemed was genuine interest. Why couldn't Dr. Bradley just be a friend, like Tracy was to her mom? They could have so much fun.

When Kim ran out of words, Dr. Bradley said, "Tell me about the walk to Mobutu."

So Kim planted herself on the couch, purposed to stay put as she detailed the dangers, problems, sicknesses, and hunger she and Nsia endured during the long trek. "When I reached the embassy, I learned they'd been watching for me because of a photo in a newspaper. One of the rebels took a picture of me and made some kind of political statement about how foreigners should be banned from Zaire. I was there for days of medical treatment before they flew me out to the Mission Council."

The doctor moved closer. "You were saying 'we' then switched to 'I'. Didn't Nsia go to the consulate with you?"

Kim stirred. Her new top had grown uncomfortably tight. She untwisted the coil she had unwittingly formed, pushed at the wrinkles to smooth them, and wiped the sweat of her palms against her thighs. She had thought she could do this, she really did. This wasn't working after all. Coming to the doctor was supposed to make her feel better not worse. She rose and gathered up her purse, gesturing to the car where her mother sat with Addie-Jo. "I know we're in the middle of this, but I have to get my mom to the airport. I'd hate for her to miss her flight."

"Kim, you're so close. Please, stay fifteen more minutes and tell me what happened."

Hand on the door handle, Kim looked over her shoulder. Dr. Bradley leaned toward her with urgency, brow knit with intensity.

"Nsia didn't make it to Mobutu." Kim pushed through the exit and lowered her head against the bright rays of the sun as she rushed to the car.

The days passed. Kim worked at the vet's office and in the quiet moments pondered how the rest of her life wasn't working. Her fingers typed a letter for Dr. Mullins, but her mind was on the mystery of Mitch. True, his absence disappointed her at the hospital, but when he did show up he was very attentive and everything seemed great. She'd loved having her mother with her and enjoyed the luxury of sleep while Grandma cared for the baby, but she had to admit, it wasn't until Mitch came that she'd felt content. Then nothing. Six weeks of no notes, no phone calls, and no messages sent through Jack. He couldn't be found either time she went for her appointment. It was all very confusing. She'd spent endless hours trying to sort it out.

The door jingled and a blast of fresh air stirred the smell of alcohol, a constant in the small office. A woman stepped to the desk, "I'm here for my Jules."

"He's ready. I'll be right back, Mrs. Townsend." Kim went for the freshly-groomed Pekingese. She opened the cage with the label marked 'Jules', tucked the animal against her, and delivered him into the arms of his owner. Mrs. Townsend hissed as if something foul had been thrust at her. She shoved the animal back at Kim.

"This isn't my Jules. I have a dog, not a cat."

A fluffy orange tabby filled her arms. "Oh! I'm so sorry. Excuse me." She shuffled Julie the cat to a crate and returned with the Jules the dog. Mrs. Townsend ranted a few minutes longer, than left with her nose in the air. Kim sank into the receptionist's chair and let both arms dangle to the floor. Kurt had been right. She couldn't do anything properly.

Kim heard Dr. Mullins exit exam room number two. She straightened. The look on his face told her he had heard every scalding word the woman had said. "What's happening, Kim?"

"I'm sorry, Dr. Mullins. I mixed up the animals. It won't happen again."

"No, I mean what's happening with you. All this week you could barely function. It's not like you. You're usually so efficient."

Tears streamed. Kim hated to hear the whine in her voice. "I know. I know. But, since my mother left, Addie-Jo cries all the time. I'm awake with her seven or eight times a night. I can't get any sleep."

Dr. Mullins put his hand on her shoulder. "Go home. Get some rest."

"But—"

"No buts. I can take care of the rest of the patients today. Leave Addie-Jo with the sitter and get some sleep."

Kim chewed on the inside of her cheek to stem the tears. She grabbed her purse and feeling like a naughty dog, slunk home. She needed every hour she could work to pay the rent and provide for Addie-Jo. Even though he had spoken kindly, Kim was sure Dr. Mullins would fire her as soon as he found a replacement. She fell onto her bed and let blackness sweep her away.

Bang. Bang. Bang. She roused enough to think the wind had caught the door. Someone was shouting. A visitor. The idiot would wake the baby. The crib was empty. Kim focused on the clock beside the bed. In the darkened room the numbers 8:12 stood out. She'd slept for nine hours. Kim groggily staggered to the door and opened it.

"It's about time." The irate babysitter thrust out the baby carrier heavy with Addie-Jo. By the light over the landing Kim could see the woman's brows furrowed and her face tight with anger. "You left me stranded. I've never had anyone do this to me before. I was supposed to be in Butte, but I didn't know where you were. I thought you'd abandoned her."

"I'm so sorry. I didn't mean to."

"You're going to have to find somebody else. I can't put up with this."

"Please, no. I'm sorry. It won't happen again. Here." She set the carrier on the floor, scrambled for her purse and pressed twenty dollars – her grocery money for the week- into the babysitter's hand. "Give me another chance."

The woman stared at the money. "I'll give you until the end of this week."

"Thank you. I'm sorry."

The woman turned and clattered down the stairs. "Reckless. Inconsiderate Easterner."

Kim latched the door and taking the carrier with her sank onto the couch. "Well, Addie-Jo, Mommy did it this time." The baby slept peacefully with lips puckered and sucking. Kim peeled the extra blankets from her. "At least I feel better, just what the doctor ordered."

That night, Addie-Jo fussed and cried for hours. Every bit of energy Kim had gained from the day's nap sapped away. She plucked the infant from the crib. Holding her at arm's length Kim squeezed the bundle. "Shut up. Bad Baby. Bad Baby."

Addie-Jo shrieked and turned bright red as gasps wrung from her stiff little body. Kim wanted to shake the child to pieces to silence her. Carefully, she laid Addie-Jo in the crib and fled the apartment.

A cold rain drenched her. Before she was halfway down the stairs, her foot slipped. She landed on her hip and bumped the rest of the way to the concrete slab. There she huddled, wailing and shaking. What if she had hurt Addie-Jo? What if she went crazy like Kurt and she couldn't stop herself? She rocked back and forth and keened.

Dora's deadbolt clacked and turned, the door rattled open. Kim scrambled into the shadows beneath the steps and held her breath.

The beam of a flashlight played along the stairway. The door closed again and Kim exhaled with a little choke. After a while, sobbing softly, she inched her bruised body up the rain-slick stairs, closed the door, and shuffled into her bedroom. She shivered as she watched Addie-Jo sobbing in her asleep.

Kim didn't want to see Dr. Bradley anymore. She didn't want to think about those final months or the terrible secrets, but she'd do it for her baby. She wouldn't cancel any more appointments. She'd go back tomorrow, she'd go every week, every day if she had to and answer all Dr. Bradley's questions, even the hard ones.

By morning, the storm had passed and everything looked fresh. The sky was a forever blue with only a few cotton balls for clouds smearing the distant horizon. Jack drove up as she was getting in the jade green Cavalier. He ambled toward her. "Good morning, Kim. Are you headed to Bozeman?"

"Yes. It should be a good day for a drive." She tried to sound normal as though yesterday's disasters didn't weigh heavily.

"I was thinking of heading to Bozeman myself in the next couple weeks to visit a friend. I could make it today and we could go together."

"No, I'd rather go by myself." She lied, "If I'm tired I'll stay overnight, so you can quit worrying about me and Addie-Jo."

Jack chuckled. "You've got me figured out, huh?"

"I appreciate it, though."

"Since you won't let me drive you, why don't you leave your car here so I can change the brakes? I heard them squealing the other day. Take my truck."

Kim hesitated. "I've only heard it one or two times. It can wait. I can't pay for brakes right now."

"Pay me when you can. If I get desperate for the money, I'll hold Addie-Jo ransom."

She looked at the freshly washed truck and noted the interior had been vacuumed. A pine-scented air freshener dangled from the rearview mirror. She remembered the adjustable seats were so comfortable a long drive wouldn't leave her with a backache. "You convinced me. Thanks, Jack."

"Don't mention it." Jack moved the bags and the car seat to his truck and lifted Addie-Jo from Kim's arms for a quick squeeze before buckling her in. "You two take care. Drive safely. And when you see Mitchell, tell him I said hi."

She startled and blushed. She hadn't thought about seeing Mitch. Or, had she? Quickly, she said, "Okay. I will."

She was making good time. The drive was a calm one. Kim shook another stay-alert pill out of the bottle and swallowed it with a sip of cola as she buzzed along the near empty highway. In the rearview mirror she caught the cherubic sight of her sleeping child.

The little devil would sleep. She was tuckered out from her wakeful night. If anyone should be sleeping, it was mommy, not that bad baby. Instantly, shame left her feeling weak.

Kim pressed the accelerator harder and zoomed within a couple feet of a travel trailer. It swayed as she swerved into the passing lane and throttled past. A sixteen-wheeler filled the oncoming lane. Kim floored the accelerator. The imperative honk of the big truck blasted as she swerved back into her lane inches in front of the travel trailer and kept going. She couldn't get to Bozeman fast enough.

At Dr. Bradley's the receptionist's desk wasn't very large and one end was taken with a computer. Kim rested the baby carrier on the relatively empty end. "I'm so sorry. I didn't have any place to leave her."

"Don't worry, Kim. Angela will watch Addie-Jo," Dr. Bradley said.

Angela, the receptionist spoke up. "I love babies. We'll get along fine."

166

Indeed, Addie-Jo was content. Kim bit the inside of her cheek to keep from blurting if the wretched child would only be good when she was with her momma, her momma wouldn't need a shrink. "Thanks for seeing me on a Saturday."

"No problem. Come on in. How was the drive?"

Kim followed Dr. Bradley into the counseling room, hoping she hadn't caused anyone in the travel-trailer a heart attack. "It was a breeze. Addie-Jo slept the whole way. All three hours and seven minutes of it."

"Is that bad?"

Kim closed the door and swung around. "No, of course not."

"When you said it, it didn't sound like a good thing."

"I wish I could get some sleep, too, that's all."

"That's a long drive by yourself when you're tired. How did you stay awake?"

Kim took her usual position on the couch and pulled a throw pillow onto her lap for a shield. She didn't want to hear the doctor warn about taking over the counter drugs to stay awake. After all, it was only this once and it had nothing to do with why she was here. "I sing with the radio, sometimes. I think I'm beginning to get used to country western music."

Annalee Bradley chuckled and said, "I was strictly classical until I moved here. Now I'm a yee-haw gal. It gets in the blood. You look exhausted. Is Addie-Jo sleeping at night?

Tears sprang to Kim's eyes. "No. Not ever. She sleeps for the sitter, but with me she cries and cries and I can't bear it." She explained about the disasters at work, the previous night when she'd almost hurt Addie-Jo, how the overwhelming need for sleep pushed away every rational thought, and made her fears worse.

At the doctor's urging, Kim related her nightmares about Kurt and her dread of his black, disapproving presence. Tears fell fast and furious until she'd used an entire box of tissues. "I'm here because I've decided I have to do this. I have some things to tell you."

"Very wise. Kim. They're hurdles you have to jump to get better."

Kim crushed the pillow to her chest protectively as memories scampered through an exit-less maze. Where to begin? She opened her mouth and the story spilled out, all mixed up and out of order, choppy with sobs. "Kurt was sharp and impatient, jealous and suspicious. He criticized every meal I fixed, the way I dressed, or wrote a letter. He said I was stupid and ugly. Without warning, he'd push me onto the floor or grab my hair or throw water on me. He wouldn't let me sleep. He was a monster."

"All this only after he fell?"

"Yes. He broke the ham radio with the axe when he caught me trying to call for help. He punched me. I was so shocked I hardly felt the pain at first." Kim gulped. "I lost our first baby. If only I hadn't tried to radio for help."

The doctor' nodded without reproach. "Didn't anyone help you?"

"When Nsia came, I refused to see her. I said I was sick. I didn't want anyone to know. I was afraid what he might do to her." Kim wiped tears, steadied herself. "It was my fault he killed Uzachi."

The doctor straightened in her chair. "You saw Kurt kill Uzachi?"

Kim's voice dropped to a whisper. "No but they left the same time and Uzachi never came back when Kurt drove the vehicle back. He said almost as much. You see, Kurt saw us talking together and flew into a rage. I thought if he'd get help he'd be okay again. I sneaked a letter for the Mission Council to Uzachi. It was my fault." Kim fell across the couch cushions and bawled for a long time.

When the crying abated, Kim sat up and blew into a tissue. The doctor spoke for a long time. "You did what you had to do for everybody's sake. Kurt was so unstable he no longer needed a reason to be provoked. Isn't that true?"

"Yes. That's true." Kim hiccupped as she thought it through. Maybe Uzachi's death wasn't her fault. The baby's either. It sounded so reasonable now that she'd spoken it. Kim choked out another secret, "He was so horrible. I, I was glad I lost that baby."

She told how her happiness at being pregnant had changed to fear and then relief at the miscarriage. Dr. Bradley said, "That does not make you a terrible person."

Kim quietly thought about that. "I'll never hold that baby."

"No."

"But he or she is safe now."

"Yes and it's okay to be relieved and grieve at the same time."

Kim nodded as pounds of a heavy weight lifted from her heart.

Dr. Bradley leaned forward. "Kim, what happened to Nsia?"

Kim shrank as far as she could into the couch. She gauged the distance to the door and wanted to bolt. She remembered Addie-Jo and licked dry lips. "We headed toward Mobutu, walking. The roads were filled with people seeking safety. Atrocities were happening all the time, not just by military, but for personal gain. We hid as much as possible. Then, I came down with dysentery and Nsia almost dragged me to the next village.

"I didn't want to stop there. It didn't feel right, but Nsia said that was fever-talk. She had a relative there who could help us. It was a very bad place. A witch doctor had the people under his control. He was gone, but had ordered them to hold anyone who came into the village. They tied our hands with rope, but they fed us, brought fresh water, and cared for me through my fever and delirium, so we thought he might let us go when he saw we weren't a threat."

Agitated, Kim rose and moved to stand in front of Dr. Bradley. "It was my first time seeing a real witch doctor with his ugly mask with feathers and a necklace made of the bones of his enemies. He knew who we were, knew about Kurt, although I don't know how. He said we were a force come to destroy him and we had to die, just as Kurt had had to die. He was terrifying but more so was that the people did whatever he said even after they had cared for us."

Kim paced a short path, remembered images and sounds filling her like a private IMAX 3-D movie. "While the others chanted around the fire, Nsia's relative cut us loose. She sent Nsia ahead while she helped me walk. We'd just entered the jungle when we heard men chasing us. She let go of me and ran off. I hid in some bushes. From where I lay, I saw them drag Nsia into the clearing, through all of those people, right to the witch doctor. I wanted to save her, but, I couldn't, I was so sick. Nsia kept saying, 'I'm free by the blood of Christ.' She wouldn't stop. The witch doctor was furious. I watched her die slowly. Then I passed out."

"She was very courageous."

"Yes." Kim whispered, her throat tight as a noose. "Not like me, I didn't even try to move."

Dr. Bradley touched her hand. Compassionate blue eyes offered a grace Kim couldn't accept. "What could you have done?"

"I could have died with her." Kim jerked away and made a tight fist as she paced back and forth. Aren't you going to tell me I shouldn't feel that way?"

The doctor shrugged. "That'd be pointless. You do feel like that. Go on."

"In the morning the village was deserted. I crawled to the side of the road where trucks of soldiers sped by. They wouldn't stop. Later, an American journalist heading for Mobutu picked me up. He wanted to interview me about what had happened at the village, but I didn't know. I wanted him to look for Nsia's body, but he wouldn't go back. When he learned I was an American missionary, he drove me to the consulate. She was my friend, my little sister, and no one would help her. That should never have happened to Nsia. She was so sweet."

Kim went to the window and stood still. The sky was an airy ocean of blue held up by an unseen God who created the world from nothing and yet hadn't rescued a little girl when she needed him most.

The psychiatrist came alongside Kim and touched her arm. Her gaze met Kim's unflinchingly. "What are you saying, Kim, that some people should be exempt from bad things?"

"None of this should've happened." Kim wanted to scream the vulgar, venomous words that buzzed in her head, to swear and shock and make others understand how awful it had been, but even those words couldn't describe it. She rubbed her blurry eyes and gazed at the clouds.

Dr. Bradley cocked her head. "There's something else, isn't there?"

There again, the question that had to be answered in full for Addi-Jo's sake. Kim returned to the couch, pulled her knees to her chest and clasped her arms around them. She was weary beyond endurance. Her shoulders sagged. Her head dropped forward. Her words were muffled. "Just give me a minute."

Chapter Thirty - Kim

Kim stretched luxuriantly beneath a soft blanket and kept her eyes shut to savor the moment. Her fingers moved over the unfamiliar texture and found fringe. She was still on Dr. Bradley's office couch. The pale circle of sun was in the east at about ten o'clock mostly hidden by scudding clouds like black and gray buffalo stampeding across the sky. That couldn't be right. Her appointment was at eleven and she'd slept at least two hours. Frowning, she checked the clock and scrambled for her loafers. Where was Addie-Jo? Kim flung open the door to the reception area.

Wide-eyed, Addie-Jo lay on Dr. Bradley's lap. Kim sagged against the door in relief. They hadn't taken Addie-Jo away from her. Not yet, anyway.

"Good morning, Kim. Are you feeling better?"

"Yes, thank you. I can't believe I slept so long."

"I'm surprised you didn't sleep longer."

"My bladder wouldn't let me." Kim leaned over her daughter and smiled. "Hi, sweet pea, are you having fun?" Addie-Jo gurgled and kicked her feet. "You stay with the doctor a few more minutes. I'll be right back."

When Kim returned from the lavatory, she took and cradled the baby in her arms.

Dr. Bradley said, "I think Addie-Jo has trouble sleeping because you've been so tense. Perhaps it'll be better now. Secrets can torture you. They grow into godzillas in the dark."

Tears coursed and Kim's words came with a hitch of fear. "You won't tell anyone what a terrible person I am?"

"First, what you say is safe with me. Second, Kim, you don't have to prove your worth to Kurt or anyone else. You are worthwhile. Jesus Christ made you so. Another thing, you don't have to do everything on your own. Get someone to help with Addie-Jo so you can sleep."

"I can't afford it, Dr. Bradley."

"What about your mom?"

"She lives in Indiana and has her own job."

"I can't solve this problem for you. But maybe there is some friend who can take the baby a couple times a week so you can sleep. If you're rested, you'll be calmer and better able to handle those times when she is fussy."

"I'll see what I can do."

"Are you driving back today?"

"Yes. I have to work Monday, if I still have a job. How are you going to explain to the Mission Council why I had a twenty-three hour session?"

"I used the other room to see patients. The babysitting was a courtesy."

Kim's eyes misted. "Thank you."

"Before you go, tell me, how is your relationship with God?"

Kim stopped patting Addie-Jo's diapered bottom and switched to bouncing her. "I'm going to church every week. I helped Mitch with the youth this summer."

"That's not what I asked."

"I rejoiced when Kurt got better. It was a false promise. The Kurt I loved died the day he fell. It would've been better if he had died then so his name wouldn't be a bitter taste in the mouths of the people and the gospel he preached made into a joke."

"You aren't worried about the reputation of the gospel, Kim."

Kim glowered at her counselor and gnawed the inside of her cheek. "We were doing God's will!"

"What are you saying?"

"I'm saying God didn't protect us and—"

"And?"

"He betrayed me."

The chair leather creaked in protest as Annalee Bradley leaned back abruptly. "Yes. I can see your dilemma."

"We were his missionaries."

"You feel God promised that, as missionaries, your lives would be nice and neat and comfortable?"

Kim gaze flitted about the comfortable room. "No, of course not. When I went, I was ready to be a martyr—"

"Like Nsia."

Kim sucked in her breath. She met the doctor's gaze. "Kurt's accident didn't have anything to do with defending the gospel."

"Really? Are you so sure?"

"We hadn't done anything wrong and look what happened."

Dr. Bradley thumped the Bible that sat next to her on the desk. "It's all in here isn't it? You know his promises. I'll give you one. You think of another. 'In this world you will have tribulation, but I have overcome the world.' Surely some verse has nagged at you."

Kim muttered, "'Where were you when the earth was formed?'"

"Ah. Yes. How God answered Job, who had lost everything. God gave Job back far more than he lost. God loves you, Kim. He hasn't left you. He's still working out his will in your life, even if it's not the way you thought you wanted it. He's with you right this minute."

Kim curled around Addie-Jo. Tears fell. Her jaw clamped so hard it ached. She jerked. "Why? Why did it happen?"

The psychiatrist shrugged. "I don't know why. Only God knows. I don't know why this happened, either." Annalee Bradley patted the motorized wheelchair she sat in. "What I do know is God is in control and he still ministers through me when I let him." She stretched forward and snagged a tissue and offered it to Kim. With her other hand she pointed to Kim's lips.

Kim stopped the compulsive chewing and dabbed the blood. She paced and jiggled Addie-Jo who whimpered as if the rigidity of Kim's body were pricking her. Kim spun around to face the doctor and her words were stone cold hard. "I can't do that."

Chapter Thirty-one - Mitch

Mitch held the door to the pizzeria open for Jenna. As she passed, he wished he could pull the power plug on the ability to notice how great she looked, how good she smelled. Her dark plum lips were smooth and moist-looking courtesy of a tube of lipstick she used like a weapon. Ever super-friendly, she put a hand on his arm and leaned close. "There's a table back there."

At the table, Jenna popped her coat buttons open, threw her shoulders back to show the front of her black sweater to best advantage and let the coat slide onto the chair. Mitch felt heat creep up his neck. If anyone was having a problem with her friendliness, it was he. He looked away to search the dining area for his roommate. The last few weeks he'd arranged for Alan to meet them at the pizzeria so he was never alone with her. Alan made fun of him because Poppe's was always crowded.

"Alan's not here," Jenna commented. "Do you think we should send a search party? I'm surprised we could pick a table on our own."

"Very funny. Ha. Ha."

"Seriously, Mitch. I'm beginning to wonder if you are a couple."

Mitch noticed a girl who looked like Kim near the door. She was looking over the crowd. Aloud he said, "A couple of what?"

"A couple, as in Mitch and Alan. You can't seem to go anywhere without him."

Mitch scrunched his face. "You're talking crazy. Excuse me, a minute." He pushed through the lunch crowd and shot toward the door. The girl rushed to exit. "Kim? Kim, it is you. What are you doing, here?"

"I was in Bozeman and your dad said to say hi. I thought if you were hungry, maybe we could catch a bite for lunch, but, I see you're busy."

"No. No. I'm not busy. How'd you find me?"

"Your roommate. He said to tell you to bring him back food."

Mitch laughed. "Sounds like Alan, always looking for a handout."

Kim's brown eyes searched his face then darted toward the table. Jenna wore a vexed expression. "You are busy. I only stopped to say hi. It was a dumb idea."

Mitch wished Jenna was anywhere than where she was. He pulled Addie-Jo's car seat from Kim's grip and despite her protests, herded her deeper into the pizza parlor. "No. It's a great idea. Come on in. Kim, this is Jenna. A student I tutor. Jenna, this is Kim and this," his voice softened as he pulled the blanket to uncover her face, "is Addie-Jo."

Jenna's face smoothed into a smile as fake as the loser's congratulations in a beauty contest. "It's so nice to meet you. Your brother has only nice things to say about you."

"Mitch isn't my brother."

"Really? I must have misunderstood. We were standing here the night his dad called to say the baby was born and I was certain he told my friend you were his sister. Oh, now I remember. He said you were a close family friend, like a sister."

"He did?" Kim's face crumpled a bit. Strain and weariness showed around her eyes.

Jenna continued, "Mitch makes a great friend."

Kim's voice held a tight, unnatural quality. "He certainly does. He's a wonderful friend."

Mitch knew the situation was getting out of control. "Jenna, tell Kim about what we studied today."

Kim rose. "Mitch, I can't stay, after all. I've got to get going."

"I thought we were going to have lunch together."

"I planned to, but got a late start and now I've got to keep going or I'll get back to Free Dance too late. I've got so much to do tonight and I have to be to work early in the morning to clean the dog cages and the surgery. I only stopped because your father sent his greetings."

"Come on, Kim. Have a bite to eat, and then go. You won't have to stay late."

Clutching Addie-Jo's carrier, Kim edged toward the door, bumping into people on her way. "No. No. I have to get going. It's been nice to meet you, Jenna."

"Have a safe trip," Jenna said with more than her usual perkiness.

Mitch stared after Kim and then cast a look at the enticing co-ed. "Jenna?"

"Yes, Mitch?"

"I can't tutor you anymore."

"But," she protested. Mitch didn't stay to listen. He plowed through the crowd.

Chapter Thirty-two - Kim

Kim hurried from Poppe's Pizza. It had been a terrible idea to come. Of course he had a young and beautiful girlfriend. Now she knew how her mother felt about Cherry Jacobs. It was like comparing a ripe peach to a pile of seaweed.

Logic told her she couldn't trust a word of what Jenna said but her emotional ship was sinking faster than the Titanic, dragging logic with it, leaving her iceberg-cold and very, very tired. She was a widow seeking company of a bright, young college man. "I'm such a pathetic loser."

"Kim! Kim!"

At Mitch's call she raced to buckle the baby in and slide into the driver's seat. She fumbled in the diaper bag for keys and dumped the contents onto the seat in a desperate attempt to find them. She checked her pockets, the ignition, and reached to feel under Addie-Jo.

Mitch splashed straight through puddles, soaking his shoes and pants. Kim hit the lock button as he reached the truck.

"Kim, open the door."

She stared at him through the rain-and-snow-smattered window. Mitch bent and retrieved her keys from the pavement. He shook the slush from them and wiggled them at her. She unlocked the door. He grabbed the door with both hands, pulled it wide and wedged himself in.

"Hey, Mitch, you looked like a maniac chasing after me"

"I can't let you go this soon. I'm so glad to see you." His eager face changed to concern. "You're crying. What's the matter? What's happened?"

"Nothing's happened," she lied. "It's a mother's moment. I couldn't find the keys." She gestured with her hand to convince him tears were normal.

"Come on, stay. There's a very nice little upscale Italian place where the high-carb pasta is fantastic and guaranteed to lift the blood sugar. Plus, they have this wonderful dessert they call a Neapolitan. It has your name written all over it."

When a giggle caught her, Mitch smirked. She knew as he knew that she was going to say yes. "Come on. It's a perfect place for a handsome man to take a beautiful woman."

They were words she longed to hear, yet fear rose like the Rocky Mountains bursting from the molten earth. The laughter froze in her throat.

Mitch's eyes closed and his head bowed. He lifted his head until they were face-to-face. He smiled charmingly. "It is the quintessential place for a handsome friend, *moi*, to take his most beautiful lady friend out for a catch-up-on-all-the-news-from-home-dinner. I'm so homesick for you all. Come on. It's about three blocks."

At these words, Kim pushed fear deep into the recesses of her heart and a tiny bubble of hope surfaced. Addie-Jo let out a little squeak.

"See? Addie-Jo says, 'Yes, Mommy, go for it.'"

Kim nodded and could feel her entire face lift into smiles. She gathered baby paraphernalia and re-stuffed the bag as Mitch unbuckled Addie-Jo's carrier. He set up a steady stream of talk about the wonders of the menu intended to prevent her from changing her mind. As they headed down the street, she interrupted, "What about Jenna?"

"Tonight was our last session. Frankly, I'm very relieved to be done with it. I never felt very comfortable around her."

"Really?"

"Don't get me wrong. She's nice enough but I could never relax around her. Do you know what I mean?" A happy feeling spread through Kim. She tucked her hand around his arm. He grinned and said, "It's so good to see you."

Mitch hadn't exaggerated about the pasta or the dessert. Relaxed and content, Kim let the spoon clatter onto the plate. "I'm stuffed."

"You ought to be. Are you on the once-a-month eating plan?"

"I should be gaining weight. Dora feeds me lots of heavy German food three times a week. She's a wonderful cook."

"Good because you still look thin as a New York model. You're sure everything is okay? Did the drive tire you?"

"Addie-Jo doesn't always sleep at night and that drains me. I miss my mom. Did you know my mom and your dad had a tiff?"

"No. I haven't talked with anybody from home for a few weeks, Dad's usually on the trap line about this time. What was it about?"

"She won't tell me." Kim cupped her hands around the base of the glass bowl of the centerpiece. A candle flickered within. She related the events of that day to Mitch. "Your dad hasn't mentioned it either and I've been too chicken to ask. As far as I'm concerned, he acts like nothing has happened, fixing the brakes on my car and letting me drive his truck here. Whatever it was must have been pretty bad. Do you think she caught Cherry Jacobs and your dad kissing? Dr. Mullins says they had a hot romance when they were in high school."

"Not a chance. Dad says Cherry is the kind of woman you must always be on guard around. She takes liberties with friendship. Did they yell and scream?"

"No. Not at all, I'd have heard from Dora's."

"If Dad thinks he's right about something, he doesn't have any problem stating the facts and on occasion enjoys a loud discussion. If he thinks he's been wronged, he'll get real quiet. His face squinces."

"Squinces?"

"Yeah. His face gets real tight and his eyes become slits. If that's the case you're mom is obviously in the wrong."

"What?"

181

"At least from my dad's point of view," Mitch hastened to add.

Kim contemplated this as she played with the candle. "Hmm. What should we do?"

"Stay out of it. It's their business. They'll figure it out."

She pretended to scowl as she reached for her coat and he helped her slip it on. She adjusted Addie-Jo's blanket. "You're always telling me to butt out. Is that how you handle your problems? You let things take care of themselves?"

"No. I handle my problems, but this is their problem."

"I hope they get it solved before Thanksgiving."

"Yeah. Definitely before Christmas; I want us all to be one big happy family and get lots of big gifts."

She couldn't help but laugh. This rascal was the Mitch she knew and loved.

He zipped his jacket and faced her. "That's more like it. When you relax, your eyes sparkle."

Her pulse went staccato. Was he going to pull her close? She wanted him to. She wanted to lay her head on his chest and listen to his strong and steady heartbeat. Panic stirred. What if he did?

"How in the world did you get food in your hair? I'll fix it." He plucked at her head and shook his hand over her plate. She didn't see anything, but when he used both hands to smooth her hair it felt wonderful.

Chapter Thirty-three – Jack

Snowfall had been spotty rendering snowmobiles useless so Jack packed the horses with trapping gear and left in the faint light before dawn. The trees and grass and shrubs were coated with heavy frost and the ground was frozen hard as he picked his way up the mountain to the place he trapped and hunted with Myron each November.

Jack swayed back and forth in rhythm with his horse along the steep narrow path. The whiff of wood smoke teased as he approached the camp. With it another scent made his stomach rumble. Myron held an iron skillet over the fire with one hand and sipped from a cup with the other. He set the coffee down, and used a fork to flip a thick slice of bacon in the pan. Jack hailed the camp.

Myron looked up. "I see your timing is good – the food's about ready."

"Good to see you, too, Myron. Been here long?"

"Two days."

"I had some business to finish before I left. Is the coffee hot? I could sure use some." Jack secured the horses and stepped toward the fire. A curl of steam rose into the chill air as Myron poured coffee. Jack settled on a log and stretched his legs toward the fire. "How's the river looking?"

"It's up several of feet. That old pine fell over at the narrow bend. The beavers have been working it. I caught a thirty-five pound-er, a marten, and two muskrat yesterday." Myron shared more information on the area he had explored. When breakfast was over, he said, "We'd better get to it, unless you intend to lounge all day around camp."

"At least let me finish my coffee," Jack replied. He gulped it down and stood. The two men gathered equipment and set off to do a day's work along the river.

The evening light was fading and the cold mountain air was settling upon them before they had a chance to talk again. Jack poked at the fire into a blaze and warmed his hands. "How are things going with you and that Pince Nez gal? What was her name? Rosie? That was getting pretty serious."

Myron shook his head. "We're not seeing each other anymore. She started dating a teacher in the same school she taught."

"Sorry it didn't work out."

"I could never give her much time. My job was always getting in the way. She didn't fancy moving to West Yellowstone and I didn't want to leave the power plant for another engineering job."

"Seeing anyone else?"

"Dated a few times. Nobody special. I've been putting in extra hours at work and finally got the bonus I told you about."

"Congratulations. Is it enough for that big power boat?"

"I decided against the boat. I'm thinking of building a house."

The fire cast wavering shadows across the wide, handsome face of the well-built Indian. His dark eyes were serious. "After Rosie, I realized I'm ready to settle down. It's time to stop horsing around and thinking only about myself. The available girls keep getting younger and sillier. If I don't watch out, my aunt will arrange to marry me to some reservation widow with a long history and a face like a beaver."

Jack broke a smile. "Well, don't rush it, God's timing, my friend, God's timing."

Myron took another bite of jerky. "Yeah. All I'm saying is I'm ready."

Far beyond the crackling of the fire, a coyote howled into the night. A series of yips responded.

"I got rid of Karen's clothes and moved back into our old bedroom."

Myron chewed thoughtfully. "Good for you. Anyone in particular prompt that?"

Jack looked sharply at his friend but Myron wore his poker face. What did it matter? Jack had nothing to hide and never had tried to hide anything from Myron. Even though Myron often knew what was going on in the width of lower Montana, he wasn't one to betray confidences.

"Carol, of course."

"You know, I never did get the whole story, just the general release version."

Jack took his time telling Myron about Carol, from details of the rescue to feelings he'd experienced over the summer but hadn't shared with anyone else. He talked about Kim's uncertain spiritual health, the new baby, Mitchell's improvement, and finished with how he missed Carol.

"Long-distance relationships are difficult. Look at Rosie and me," Myron said.

"Until now, it's been good. It gave me time and space to heal. You're right though, about time and relationships. I'm wanting more."

"I can't see you leaving the family ranch. Will she move here?"

"It's a pretty good bet. She misses Kim and the baby. Her schedule has slowed. When she does, I'm thinking about ranching again, nothing big, a few cattle, horses, maybe teach more trapping clinics at the ranch and travel less. I left Karen alone too much. I don't want to make the same mistake again. Carol is talking about writing fiction. I think I'll hire Maggie back and maybe our friend Morgan, if he wants to come, so she could be free to write."

"This is what Carol wants?"

Jack shrugged. "I don't know. I haven't talked with her yet. We had an argument and we haven't spoken in a while."

Myron bent his head back and howled with laughter. Jack's face burned. His friend continued to hoot and Jack, feeling foolish, joined him. Myron finally settled down and the two gazed into the snapping fire. "So what did you argue about?"

"Cherry Jacobs."

Myron shook his head. "Trouble follows that woman like a dog scenting steak."

"Cherry is Cherry, always causing trouble and leaving me with damage control. This time it wasn't even on purpose. What really upset me was Carol jumped to a negative conclusion. A relationship isn't much if it isn't built on trust."

"Maybe she was hurt before."

"Maybe, but if I hadn't proved what kind of a man I was after all the time we were confined in that secluded cabin last winter, I don't know what else I can do to prove it."

Jack related the whole event and added, "Maybe by now she's thinking more rationally. She's the type who has to analyze everything from top-to-bottom, not like Karen whose temper flashed hot but cooled quickly. This is Carol's problem, not mine, and she'll have to work out on her own."

"How long has it been?"

"Five weeks." Jack tossed another log in the fire pit and stared glumly as it caught fire and brightened the campsite. The wind picked up and the tent swelled and exhaled with the currents, sounding like a flag flapping on a mast.

Myron propped one elbow on his knees and leaned forward to pour another cup of coffee from the pot at the edge of the coals. "Remember the time you jumped on that stake and I carried you back to safety? That was right after my mother left. It was the first time my father said he was proud of me."

"You never told me that."

"He said two are better than one, if one falls the other can help him up. He also said the mountains are beautiful, exciting, and dangerous. You have to be on guard to survive, but they're nothing compared to relationships. Relationships call for going the extra mile."

Jack met his friend's gaze and nodded. He would go to Carol.

Chapter Thirty-four – Carol

Carol hunched over in her home office with her back to the computer and stared at the piles of unanswered mail that demanded attention like piglets rooting for their mother.

Daunted once again by their sheer number, she swiveled around and clicked on to her email account hoping against hope it would be easier to tackle. The in-box recorded 1982 unopened emails, fifty-four more than yesterday. None of them from Jack. She clicked one open. "Dear Mrs. Streeter, thank you for your book. It made such a difference in my life. My boyfriend—"

Why doesn't Jack call? Or e-mail? If I was wrong about the situation, he should explain. Carol went over every moment of their time together until she arrived at the same heart-crushing tidbit of information that had spelled their separation. She sipped hot blueberry tea from a mug he'd bought her and miserably concluded again that his failure to explain was an admission of guilt. The doorbell chimed, interrupting the swirling cloud of dark thoughts.

A slender woman wearing sunglasses, hair combed to cover her face, in a pretty sweater far too thin for the winter temperatures stood on the porch. Her voice was a soft southern drawl. "Mrs. Streeter, I'm sorry to bother you, but I don't have anywhere else to go."

"Cynthia Faulkinroy? What a surprise. Come on in. You'll catch your death of cold out there. Where's your coat? Where's Peter?"

With a furtive backward glance into the street, Cynthia stepped into the foyer. Carol peeked out too. Fat snowflakes floated to the ground like late season cherry-blossoms on a windless day. No one and nothing else was out there, not even a car. She closed the door and hustled Cynthia into the living room.

"I'm sorry to bother you, ma'am," Cynthia repeated sitting on the edge of the couch.

"Nonsense. I'm pleased you've come. Call me Carol. What can I do for you?"

Tears filled Cynthia's eyes and she clutched an already shredded tissue as she blurted, "Peter treats me awful. At first he talked mean just once in a while when he was angry with me. Now, I don't know what to do. It's getting worse."

"You poor thing." Carol moved beside her and put an arm about the younger woman's shaking shoulders. Carol raised her hand to snatch the afghan at the back of the couch. Cynthia cried out and ducked. Carol froze. "I'm sorry. I only wanted the blanket. You're shivering." Carol reached again for the afghan and draped it over the woman. "What happened?"

Cynthia removed her expensive sunglasses to reveal the reddish-blue marring her left cheek and eye.

Carol sucked in her breath. "Peter did that?"

The former beauty queen nodded and sobbed. "This morning."

A fresh understanding of Kim trickled in as she recalled a similar reaction. She listened to the story and did her best to comfort. Sometime later, Carol left Cynthia asleep in Kim's old bedroom and returned to her office.

She no longer thought of the workload, but the broken lives the piles of mail represented. It staggered her. A.J. had faults for sure, but this… She was certain she'd never have to deal with this with Jack either. Jack was kind and thoughtful, through and through.

An abrupt shadow crossed her desk. Carol gave a shout and spun around.

"Carol, what are you yelling about? You nearly scared the skin off me," Trudy scolded.

"You startled me."

Trudy spread her arms toward the piles of correspondence. "I thought you could use some help with the mail. Not that I don't have

188

enough of my own at the office, but I'm taking pity on you. I noticed the other day when I was here you didn't seem to be thinking of anything but Jack."

"I'm not thinking about Jack."

Trudy waggled her finger. "Thou shalt not lie."

Carol stomped over and collapsed into her chair. Folding her arms over her head, she dropped it onto her knees and whined, "Oh, I am thinking about him. I don't want to, but I can't get him out of my head. I can't believe he'd do this."

"Maybe because he didn't."

"I heard him."

"So you keep telling me."

"If it isn't true, why isn't he calling me to explain what happened?"

Trudy shook her head and stared out the window to where the flower garden lay covered in snow. "Have you even given him an inkling you would listen?"

"Do you think that's it?"

Trudy rapped Carol tenderly on the head. "Hello? What have I been saying for six weeks?"

"Should I call him?"

"Are you ready to remove your judge's robe and let the jury go?"

Carol flinched. "Ouch. You're tough."

"That's 'cuz I'm your best friend and I luv ya."

"Thanks, Trudy."

"Don't mention it." Trudy held the phone out. "Call him."

Carol stared at it. "What if he won't talk to me?"

"He'll talk to you. He might make you wait five weeks for an answer, but he'll talk to you."

She gasped. "Do you think he'd do that?"

"I know I would, but Jack's different. He's a gentleman. If he doesn't return your call, you can always go out there for Christmas

189

and fall on your knees in abject humility and beg his forgiveness. Now, call."

Carol punched in Jack's home phone and disconnected when it rang. Trudy stood over her pointing at the phone with a serious I-mean-business face. Carol re-dialed. She twisted her lips in frustration as a voice on Jack's phone recited, "Leave a message after the beep."

She gulped. "Jack, this is Carol."

Trudy motioned with her palm to keep talking. "I'll try you again, later. Bye." She replaced the phone with both hands. "Argh! I feel like I'm thirteen."

"You're acting like you're thirteen." Trudy lifted her head as a faint bump sounded from somewhere in the house.

Carol held up her hand to silence Trudy. "Sh. I heard something,"

"I heard it too. So what? Minnie sounds like an elephant when she gets off your bed."

"Minnie is outside. Cynthia is here."

Trudy squinted at Carol. "Cynthia Faulkinroy?"

"Yes. She needed someplace safe." Carol tiptoed down the hallway to the pink-and-white room that had once been Kim's. She peered around the corner past the mirrored vanity that held a porcelain doll, a music box with a ballerina, and a blue ribbon from the county fair.

A perfect athletic body towered over the bed where Cynthia slept with one arm dangling over the edge. Her discolored swollen eye contrasting against the white bedspread, was a reproach that Carol hoped would wake Peter from his self-centeredness.

Peter poked his wife's arm and spoke low. "Get up. Get in the car."

Cynthia jerked awake with a cry. Eyes wide, she scooted from him until she was against the wall and drew the blanket around her as if she hoped it were a magical cape of invisibility.

"Be quiet," he ordered. "You're always embarrassing me but this is the worst. How could you go to Carol of all people with our private life? The woman can't be trusted."

190

Carol ordered her heart to be bold and made her voice sound steady. "Hello, Peter. I didn't expect to see you here."

Peter turned a scowl on her. "I didn't expect to find my wife here but she's so stupid she used my credit card to pay the cab."

"You don't let me have any money," Cynthia whined.

Trudy rounded the corner. With a puzzled frown she turned an assessing eye to the state of Cynthia's face and to Peter's angry stance. Her eyes widened in understanding.

"You don't have to go, Cynthia. You can stay here," Carol said.

Cynthia's gaze flicked between Carol and Peter. She shook her head and pushed aside the comforter. Her accent thickened. "I don't want to cause you trouble."

Peter poked Cynthia again. "It's too late for that. Hurry and put your shoes on."

Cynthia complied. She slipped a dainty foot into a stylish black pump, but her eyes were lifted toward the women in an all too obvious plea.

"Leave her alone, Peter," Trudy ordered, moving closer. "You need professional help. You're sick."

"You always did act like you're better than others, Trudy." He clasped Cynthia by the arm and dragged her toward the door still carrying one shoe.

Carol blocked the way. He pushed her hard against the wall. Pain shot along her scalp. Her vision blurred momentarily.

A fierce gargling erupted as Trudy turned sideways, her foot flashing upward. She caught Peter in the center of the chest. His breath expelled in a short burst and there was the sound of bone cracking. He crumpled to the floor with a thud. Cynthia, emitting short little shrieks like an intruder alert, stumbled and fell on him. He yelped and shoved the former beauty queen away. She scrambled to the other side of the room.

Before Peter could move again, Trudy dropped to the floor beside him and rested the weight of her elbow on his neck. His eyes bulged with the effort to suck air and his hands and feet flopped without finding purchase.

Carol straightened herself and rubbed her bruised head and shoulder. "Wow, Trudy that was amazing. I didn't know you could do that."

"Carol?"

"Yes?"

"Do you think you could lend a hand or something?"

Carol squatted. "Sure, what can I do?"

"Call 9-1-1. Sheesh. Do I have to do everything myself?"

Peter bucked and Cynthia edged closer saying, "This isn't good. Oh dear. What's going to happen?"

"It'll be okay, Cynthia." Carol knelt over Peter, her words clear and crisp with uncharacteristic ferocity. "Peter, you have many fine qualities. Get some help for your anger issues or, or I'll press charges for attempted murder when you left me on that mountain. I was caught in an avalanche and nearly died. I gave a statement in Montana to the local sheriff after I was rescued. The report is on file. Do you understand me?"

Peter tried to wave his arms. Beads of perspiration dotted his face.

"I said do you understand me?"

Trudy made a *tsk-ing* sound. "Carol. He can't talk. I'm barely letting him breath."

"Oh. Blink twice if you agree."

Peter quickly blinked twice.

"Good. I'm glad that's settled. Oh, and don't even think of firing Trudy. Understood?"

Peter tried to buck, then blinked twice again.

Carol stood and cocked her head as she looked down. "You know Trudy. You're right. I should get things straightened out with Jack. Since my publicist has been refusing to book conferences for me I happen to be free. I'm going to fly out there and see him."

"Good for you, Carol, that's great. Now will you call 9-1-1?"

"Oh, sure. Um, maybe you should let up a little. He's a little whitish-blue about the lips."

Chapter Thirty-five – Carol

At the half-size stove in Kim's apartment, Carol tested the temperature of the bottle of milk. She lifted her grandchild from the carrier on the table and popped the bottle into Addie-Jo's mouth. As casually as possible she said, "Have you seen Jack?"

Kim pulled fabric taut over the ironing board and pressed the iron over the back of a blue dress. It sizzled and spit with steam. "I wondered when you'd get around to asking. He's on the trap line. He said he'd be back by tomorrow."

Carol sank with Addie-Jo into a hard-backed chair. Of course, he hadn't returned the calls because he hadn't gotten them yet.

Kim laughed. "What a big sigh of relief."

"I guess I'm not fooling anybody, am I?"

"No mother. You've got it bad. It's actually kind of fun to watch, except you've been in such misery and you've put Jack through the wringer."

"What did he say?"

"He didn't say anything. I can see it. Admit it, Mom. You care for him. I know you didn't come out here on the spur of the moment only to see Addie-Jo and me."

"I've behaved badly and it's time I clear up this problem."

Kim kissed her mother on the cheek. "Come on, the St. Stanislaus women's guild is having a Thanksgiving fundraiser for needy families. We'll have lunch there."

The gymnasium at the school hosted the big event and a large crowd was spending their Saturday browsing the re-sale items, playing bingo, and filling their plates with chicken and noodles.

Carol caught sight of Kim's landlady. Her round, happy face was red with exertion.

"Dora, What are you doing working in the kitchen?"

"I make noodles. Make big money for needy. Ja," she stated with pride.

"But I thought you were Lutheran."

Dora waved her hand briskly in the air. "No matter. I help."

"You're a good woman. I can see your noodles are popular. We'd better get in line, before they sell out."

"Ja. Go. Eat."

Carol and Kim found a place at the end of one of the long tables. It was a strategic position, for at least half of Free Dance stopped to greet Kim and Addie-Jo. During a lull in the company, Kim pointed out a corner of the gym where racks of clothes were displayed. "I want to take a look through Threads when we're done eating."

Carol nodded toward the far corner. "There's Cherry Jacobs. I wouldn't have expected her to shop for clothes here."

"Cherry Jacobs is in charge of the clothing drive. She does a terrific job of finding new and like-new duds. People come from surrounding towns to scout out the clothes. I hear she donates from her own wardrobe, so every woman around wants a Cherry Jacobs."

"It's a good way to recycle, though I hate to admit anything good about her."

"Yes. Of course, I'm sure she claims a healthy tax deduction and buys more new clothes. Next to the dinner, Cherry brings in the most money. This year she's vowed to top the dinner proceeds. She started months ago."

Dora appeared at their table. She carried a bag from Threads. Her face flushed with excitement. "Look what I find." She drew a large pair of men's red silk pajamas from the bag.

Kim's mouth opened in surprise. Carol said, "Who are those for, Dora?"

"Mr. Rheinhardt. Who'd you think? The milkman?" Dora laughed heartily at her own joke, then dropped to a whisper. "He come home very soon. Any day now. Ja."

Kim's face stiffened in an effort keep the smile in place. "Great."

"It has been so long." Tears rimmed the green-gray eyes as she folded her find with loving care and returned them to the bag. Dora cooed and chucked Addie-Jo under the chin. Addie-Jo waved her arms, her whole body squirming with delight.

When Dora had gone, Kim said, "That was uncomfortable. I think she's getting worse. Are you listening to me? What's the matter? You're as red as a beet."

Carol put both hands to her cheeks and whispered, "Those were Jack's pajamas."

Kim squinted hard. "How do you know?"

"Cherry brought them to him at the hardware store. She said he'd left them at her house by mistake. He said to leave them where they'd be used. I thought—"

"Mother."

Carol put her hand over her mouth. "I didn't even give him a chance to explain."

"Well, you'll make it right tomorrow when you see him."

"I'm so embarrassed."

"You should be. But, you've come all this way to talk to him. Don't let pride stop you."

From the kitchen, a shriek pierced the loud drone of noise in the busy gym. A string of German followed. Chairs scraped the floor as people stood craning for a view. Carol and Kim moved around until they saw Dora in a deep embrace with a tall, gangly man. A swell of whispers and shouts raced toward them like a surfer on a wave, "He's back. Harry Rheinhardt is home."

Chapter Thirty-six – Jack

Through the window of the fur shed, Jack watched an unfamiliar car snake up the long bumpy road. Maybe a rental car? Carol. He shucked his blood-and-fat-smeared rubber apron and scrubbed his hands with soap using a small brush. He shook his head. Would this comedy of errors, never end? Carol couldn't have picked a worse time to come.

Cherry Jacobs remained near the door with the sleeve of her jacket pressed to her nose. "Honestly, honey. I don't know how you stand the smell. Anyway, I couldn't wait to tell you the news and I had to do it in person. I know there's always been this unspoken thing between us, left over from our youth. While it may be hard to move on, you have to admit our lifestyles are simply too different for us to have ever made a good match."

The sedan made the last curve and Jack knew the exact moment Carol caught sight of Cherry's bright red Chevy Blazer. The car skidded to a halt and bounced on its shocks. Cherry droned on, "Don't look so stricken, Jack. It was bound to happen sometime. I swear you're taking this almost as hard as Roy."

The car resumed its slow crawl forward into the yard and Jack exhaled.

"Well, to come to the point, Bodine proposed and I accepted."

Jack swung toward her. "Cherry. I'm thrilled for you. Bodine is a great guy."

"And don't forget rich. He'll be able to keep me in the manner to which I've become accustomed," Cherry batted her eyes in a flirtatious way Jack knew was only half-teasing.

The smile he gave her was genuine but he stayed near the ugly heap of bloody carcasses. "I would never hold you back from true happiness. Congratulations."

"Do you mean it, Jack?"

"Absolutely."

"Oh, Jack. You're the best." Cherry rushed forward and wrapped her arms around him as Carol came through the door.

Jack returned the embrace with a bear hug yet hastily lifted one hand to motion his visitor in. He shouted, "Carol, you're just in time to congratulate Cherry on her engagement to Bodine."

The pained expression evaporated from Carol's face. "Cherry how wonderful for you."

Cherry Jacobs released Jack and her look was shrewd as she shrugged. "I'm sure it's as wonderful for you as it is for me, Coral."

"Carol," Carol said.

"Anyway, take good care of him. I'm going to be far too busy with my husband to worry about an old friend."

She laid a manicured hand on Jack's chest. "One thing, we'll be a married in June and I hoped you could construct an archway for a garden wedding, darling."

"I could. Consider it my wedding gift."

Cherry moved to the door. "I really don't know how you stand it in here. It stinks."

A moment after the door shut the Blazer roared to life. Cherry gunned the motor and spun the wheels in a dramatic exit. The vehicle careened away.

Jack took both Carol's hands in his. They felt warm, soft. "Hi, lady, you're a sight for sore eyes."

"I tried calling. I was upset and forgot you'd be gone."

"I figured that. I left a message for you a little while ago."

Carol's cheeks reddened. "Oh, Jack, I'm sorry. I should've realized there was a reasonable explanation."

"I gave Cherry my pajamas for the clothing drive."

"I know. Yesterday Dora bought them for her husband."

"Is that so?"

"I think I learned something about myself. It wasn't you I doubted. It was me. I know I don't compare in looks to Cherry. I was jealous of her." Carol hung her head.

"You're kidding, right?" Jack was amazed.

She whispered, "Will you forgive me?"

She was staring at his lips. Maybe she wanted to kiss as much as he did. Jack pulled her closer. "I already did. I should never have let the silence go on so long."

"I'll never be so foolish again, I promise."

"I promise to never use pajamas again."

He cut her laugh off with a kiss. When they broke apart, he said, "This will have the gossip mills going."

Carol said, "Between Cherry's engagement and Dora's husband returning, the gossip mills have plenty to keep them busy."

"Harry returned?"

"He made quite a stir with his arrival at the fundraiser. I have to say Kim was worried when Dora told us he was coming home any day now. We thought she bought your red pajamas for a ghost."

"Harry was listed as Missing in Action, Presumed Dead in Beirut in 1984 just before the American forces pulled out. I think most accepted he was dead. Dora never did. Come on. Let's go to the kitchen. I'll make coffee." He led her by the hand towards the door.

"I hope I've learned from her about having faith in God and believing in my man."

Jack reached past Carol to darken the lights. He took the opportunity to kiss her on the cheek. "I'm counting on it. I never want to be without you again."

Chapter Thirty-seven – Kim

Kim straightened the black sweater-dress, which had looked sophisticated in the mirror of the apartment, but was nothing special in comparison to the skirt-and-sweater set Dr. Bradley wore in warm shades of brown. She wouldn't even be thinking about fashion if she were still in the backwaters along the Congo.

The psychiatrist, as always, was professional, yet comfortable and at ease. She had Cherry Jacob's flair for style, Maggie's indomitable spirit and common sense, and her mother's experience and intuition. Her voice was congested and a bit raspy as she said, "You've come a long way, Kim."

"I have my baby to think about."

"With that in mind, why don't you make the final decision?"

"What do you mean?"

"Your healing will never be fully complete until you surrender to God."

"I've done pretty well so far on my own."

"This is the last session the Mission Council originally agreed to pay. Do you plan to continue?

"Yes, but I can only afford to come once a month." How did Dr. Bradley always look so pulled together? Of course she didn't have a kid or a husband, and she probably paid others to keep her house. It wasn't fair.

The doctor wheeled to her desk and picked up a folder. She jotted something inside it and said, "Good. I think monthly sessions will give you a chance to work through the steps and choices we've laid out while still giving you an anchor."

Dr. Bradley pulled a sheet from the folder and brought it to Kim. "I have convinced them it's important for you to continue. It's highly unusual, but due to the severity of your loss, they've allotted you an extra year of monthly appointments before they review the case again."

Stunned, Kim forgot about clothes. "You mean they're going to pay for me to keep seeing you?"

"Once a month for the next twelve months."

She glossed over how the death of Kurt, her first baby, Nsia, Uzachi and others could be neatly packaged as 'severity of loss.' Kim snatched tissues and blotted at a steady flow of relieved tears. "That means so much to me. I'll send them a thank you."

"Good idea and you might consider sending a little thank-you to the One who is looking out for you." Kim shrugged. She accepted the paper Dr. Bradley offered her. "This is for a physical. Take it to your physician; it has all the billing information on it. I'll need the report from your GP before you come next time."

The doctor sneezed into a tissue and wiped her nose. She pulled another tissue from the box and apologized as she dabbed puffy eyes. "This cold medicine is wearing off. I think I'm going to call it a day and go home. Merry Christmas, Kim. You've made strides, but don't be fooled. There's a lot of work up ahead. It's better not to walk that road alone."

"I hope you feel better. Merry Christmas." Kim pulled on her coat and exited into the white coldness before Dr. Bradley could suck her into a spiritual discussion. At the curb a puff of exhaust was swept away from the Cavalier's tailpipe in a gust of wind. Marta, who had come to Bozeman with her for holiday shopping, sat in the passenger seat. Kim inhaled deeply of the cold air. She was glad for friends and family and the doctor, but none of them could ever fully understand. Kim exhaled. "No one understands. I am alone."

Chapter Thirty-eight – Mitch

Mitch stood in his father's living room and viewed the landscape glistening in the setting sun. Carol stood beside him. She said, "The snow on the trees looks like someone dusted them with powdered sugar and the rolling hills remind me of mounds of white frosting."

"Very poetic. To me it simply looks like home."

Carol nudged him and nodded toward the room. "That's a good word. This all looks very homey."

Multi-colored strings of Christmas tree lights glowed brighter as the sun tucked behind the mountains. The fireplace crackled and snapped. The buzz of conversation had died to a hum. Jack and Harry Rheinhardt studied a chessboard. Dora occupied the recliner. Her wuffling snore indicated a nap was in progress. Kim, with the sweetness of a Madonna, sat at one end of the sofa feeding a bottle to Addie-Jo. Forrest Mullins and Maggie argued good-naturedly over cards since they were losing to Brewster and the tall, gawky ranch hand, Morgan.

"This is Christmas as I always knew it—with lots of friends," Mitch said.

"It's been years since Christmas felt this magical, since before my husband died. The only thing that would make it better is if my son were with us instead of a continent away," Carol said.

"And my mom."

Carol blushed. "Yes, of course. I'm sorry. That was a thoughtless remark."

"No. It's okay. Pastor Jim said adulthood is accepting the bittersweet. Appreciating what you have and not forgetting, but not focusing on what you don't have any longer. I sure didn't feel that way the last couple of years and I was miserable. This year I'm focusing on what I have. The turkey was wonderful, thanks to the efforts of Maggie. What everyone else brought made the meal a real feast. Do you know what I ate last Christmas? Part of a bean burrito off someone else's plate."

Carol raised her eyebrows. "It does lend perspective."

"I was touched when Dad read about the Savior's birth with the same clear, strong voice of authority I remember from childhood. Jesus is the hinge pin."

"True. And made more real for today by Harry - injured in the explosion, held hostage by the Amal in Beirut, sustained all those years by faith, and then miraculously released."

"Exactly. So see, I miss Mom, but I'm glad you're here Carol. This has been a good Christmas. Sharing it with you makes it even better."

"Thank you." Carol dabbed a tear and moved away from him to sit beside Kim.

When the dispute over cards was settled, Dr. Mullins asked, "What are your plans after graduation, Mitchell?"

Mitch stepped away from the window. "I have the most fantastic job offer. I answered an ad for a grant posted on the board at school. Ledbetter's, a pharmaceutical company, is willing to foot the whole bill during a one year mission opportunity in Boston, Massachusetts."

"I didn't know they did stuff like that," Maggie said.

"Apparently the grant is part of a philanthropic effort they've had for years. It's not well known, but very generous."

Dr. Mullins' lower lip stuck out in a meditative pout. "Why Boston?"

"It was one on a list of churches asking Ledbetter's for help. There were other places, but this one leapt right out at me. I applied and got the grant."

Harry shook Mitch's hand. Jack said, "Congratulations. What exactly will you be doing?"

"I'll work primarily with church youth and I can use this as research for my thesis whenever I go on to get my Phd."

202

"I'm real proud of you, son." Others echoed his sentiment. "When do you leave?"

"I report the week after graduation. Since I have to find a place to stay, I'm heading out the day after commencement."

Carol said, "That's great. It sounds right up your alley."

The heartfelt approval was gratifying. Then Kim spoke. Her tone was hard as flint. "What about the reservation youth? Are you going to leave them stranded?"

In astonishment that echoed his own, everyone's gaze shifted to Kim. Her face was red, her jaw clenched, and her eyes flashed. Some of his joy faded. "I helped them last year. I made it clear it was only temporary. I never intended to stay. Pastor Ralph knows that. He's made other plans."

"Oh, I really don't care what you do." Kim swept out of the room.

Carol made to follow, but Mitch motioned her to stay. He found Kim, stony-faced, stiffly perched on the edge of the bed in the den, Addie-Jo balanced over her shoulder. She refused to look at him and began a rhythmic tom-tom on the baby's back. He leaned against the doorframe to give her space. "Kim? Why are you upset?"

"I'm not upset. I really don't care."

"You're strung tighter than a high-powered hunting bow."

"Why didn't you tell me? You could've at least said something when Marta and I were with you for dinner last week instead of springing it on me like this."

"I only found out yesterday. I didn't say anything before because I didn't think there was any chance I'd get it."

"But you did. So go."

Opening piano chords of "Silent Night" wafted in as the group in the living room sang along. In the gathering blue of dusk, past the frost flowers growing on the outer windowpane, it was snowing again. What should he do? She didn't want to be apart from him. Mitch went on bended knee before her. "Kim?"

Kim hid her face against Addie-Jo. Her sobs were muffled.

Mitch bit back his proposal. God help me, he thought, that was a close one. He put his arms around her and rocked her. The sobs grew into full-fledged weeping.

Kim quieted at the third verse of "It Came Upon a Midnight Clear". She said, "I'm sorry. It's Christmas, and, and—" She pushed him away gently and snuffled.

Mitch didn't press her to explain. Like a big brother, he helped her to her feet and kissed the top of her head. "Let's go sing carols."

"You go. I'll put Addie-Jo to bed first."

At the doorway Mitch glanced back. Kim's face was sorrowful. She bent and positioned Addie-Jo on the bed, tracing the baby's features with a single finger.

When he joined the others around the piano he said, "She's okay. She's putting the baby down" Wordlessly, Morgan put a hand on his shoulder. The caroling continued through a series of hymns.

Kim appeared as they belted out "Jingle Bells." Her eyes were still pink from crying. She even smiled when Maggie ran her fingers from one end of the piano to the other for a finale and called out, "Hey, how about some eggnog?"

A murmur of assent went around the group. Jack held up his hand. "Wait a minute. I have something to say. You are dear friends and I'm grateful you chose to spend Christmas at the ranch. This year I have much to be celebrate—my friends, Brewster, Maggie, and Morgan who always stand by me. Harry's return. Mitchell's homecoming."

"Even though I can be a pain in the neck at times?"

"Even though." His dad chuckled. "I'm also grateful for new blessings I couldn't have imagined a year ago such as Kim and my honorary grandchildren, Addie-Jo and Jasmine, and of course for Carol." He threaded his fingers through Carol's and drew her close to his side.

Carol's cheeks colored as she looked up at him. Jack stalled a few seconds as he held her gaze. "I'm kind of taking a chance here in front of our friends."

"No guts, no glory," Harry called.

Jack nodded. "Right. Okay then. Carol, will you marry me?"

Both Carol's hands flew to her mouth. Her eyes sparkled like sapphires as her shoulders hunched and she gave a prolonged squeak of excitement. She flung her arms around his neck. "Yes. Oh, yes."

Jack, with a smile as big as the state itself, crushed her to him as cheers arose.

This was one of those bittersweet moments, Mitch thought. "Kiss. Kiss," he chanted after only the slightest hesitation and the group joined in.

"I have to make the presentation first." Jack plucked a round, red ornament from the tree and handed it to Carol.

Carol wrapped the string around her finger so the ball sat on top. "What a bauble."

"You could've done better, Jack," said Maggie.

"Cheap, cheap," Forrest Mullins said.

Brewster spoke in a stage whisper to Morgan, "I once got one of those in a giant-size box of Cracker Jacks."

"This group is a bunch of hecklers." Jack eased the ornament from Carol's hands and opened it to reveal a ring. He plucked it out and presented it with a flourish. Carol's smile was dazzling as she slipped it onto her finger.

The friends cheered again. Jack kissed her. Maggie played, "Where Does Love Begin," as the friends pressed forward to congratulate the new couple.

Mitch said, "Hey, Maggie, isn't that song a little dated?"

"More appropriate than 'What's Love Got to do With It?' How big of a non-church repertoire do you think I have, boy?"

Kim had stood stiffly next to him through the goings-on. Now she approached their parents and her words were warm. "I'm glad for you, Mom. Jack's a great guy. Jack, you're getting the best lady in the world. Now Addie-Jo will have a grandpa who really is her grandpa." Mitch clapped his dad on the back and planted a kiss on Carol's cheek.

Hours later while the Bronner men waved to their departing guests, Mitch said, "You surprised everyone."

"Really? I thought everybody in Free Dance knew. It surprised me when she said yes."

"Aw, come on, Dad. You wouldn't have asked in front of us if you thought she'd say no."

Jack drew a deep breath and looked into the star-studded sky. "True. True. We talked about marriage, yet, somehow, it still surprised me."

Mitch's grin faded. "Kim is struggling."

"She did seem upset you were going to Boston."

"One moment I think she cares for me. The next she pushes me away." Mitch shook his head and stared at the snow accumulating on the porch steps.

"Tread carefully, son. Kim's very confused right now, terribly hurt and angry at God."

Mitch stuffed his hands in his pockets. "I know, Dad. I know. I feel God wants me in Boston, yet I hate to leave her."

"Perhaps God wants Kim to turn to him instead of you or anybody else."

Mitch remembered the rough feel of the pig's snout against his mouth. He wiped his hand over his lips. "Yep. Been there. Done that. Did the rehab."

Chapter Thirty-nine - Kim

The Christmas party drew to an end and Kim climbed into the back of Dr. Mullins's Suburban. Addie-Jo sat between her and her mom. Brewster and Morgan, in separate vehicles headed to Free Dance while Harry and Dora climbed into the middle seats and Maggie buckled herself in beside the veterinarian. Before long the chatty group broke out in singing. Kim didn't feel like singing. She didn't feel like talking. She certainly didn't feel joyful.

She hoped she appeared to the others as silent and as still as the softly falling snow, but inside, thoughts raged like a blizzard sweeping down the mountainside. She needed to get her balance, to catch her breath. What was the point of staying in sleepy, slow-moving Free Dance if everybody changed? She wanted to scream, "Stop!"

Mom and Jack. Why couldn't she be excited? She'd wanted them to get together. It was a perfect match that they'd made happen on their own. They hadn't needed her. Now, Jack would no longer do all those little projects she never asked him to do but which made her life more bearable. Instead, he'd spend his time flying to Indiana to see her mother.

Mom would be consumed with Jack and wedding plans and would never have time to visit. People always said nothing would change, but romance changed everything. They'd have each other and she would have no one. Everyone else, including that despicable Cherry Jacobs, had someone.

Dora had her Harry. The invitations to dinner would stop because they wouldn't want a fifth wheel like her. Maybe they'd ask her to leave her little apartment. Where would she and Addie-Jo go in the dead of winter?

Addie-Jo shifted in her car seat and Kim patted the baby in a silent promise to always be there even if no one else in the whole world cared. Her eyes burned. It was a painful world and she couldn't shield Addie-Jo no matter how much she wanted to. Then, one day, Addie-Jo too would grow up, find a guy, and leave her high and dry without a second thought.

Mitch certainly couldn't wait to leave for Boston. He was leaving even if she didn't want him to. He was probably glad he didn't have to check on "poor Kim" anymore. The closeness they'd shared in the summer was ministry-related, nothing more. What difference did it make if he went to Boston, Massachusetts or Timbuktu, Africa?

She recalled Kurt's face the day they disembarked in Africa. He'd spread his arms like a bird and spun in joyous wonderment. He was as radiant as Moses fresh from the mountain of God. He'd exclaimed that God was good. He hadn't known what would happen. Kim covered her heart with her hand to gentle the pain. Kurt was gone. She was alone in a frozen wasteland. She sobbed, "Let them all leave. See if I care."

"What did you say, Kim?"

She glanced at her mother. The "Silent Night" duet hushed as they waited to hear her reply. She mumbled a lie, "There's an African carol about leaving to see Jesus, but I can't remember it."

"Too bad." Dora resumed singing in German with Harry.

Carol reached past Addie-Jo and patted her hand, a motherly gesture, prompted by the happiness of a recent engagement. Kim's feelings seemed so intense that it was surprising the others didn't feel them too. She was alone. Too softly to be heard she said, "I'll show them. I don't need any of them, especially Mitch."

Chapter Forty - Kim

Kim wrinkled her nose. The place smelled like a locker room. Blinding flashes from a big silver ball on the ceiling twirled over a few females in front of a juke box. A smoky haze, thick as fog, hovered overhead.

Like birds on a fence, several men perched on stools the length of the bar. They hunched over drinks, undisturbed by her arrival. Other men, playing pool or cards went on point like a pack of birddogs. Under their scrutiny, Kim plopped onto the nearest vacant stool and tried to be unnoticed. She fanned her face. Why was she here?

A dark-eyed, square-jawed man with a bored expression moved directly in front of her. "What'll you have?"

Kim chewed her lip. What did people order when they were upset and needed comfort? "A hot toddy," she squeaked.

The bored expression morphed into amusement. He moved a toothpick from one side of his mouth to the other.

On her left, a grizzled old man snorted. Kim wasn't sure if this last reaction was in response to her since he continued to gaze into his shot glass as if it held his fortune.

She swallowed hard. Her throat was as dry as any cowboy on the range. "Just joking. A beer."

"What kind?"

"Diet, please."

The bartender smirked. The man on her left wheezed again although his eyes never left the amber liquid in his glass. They were both definitely laughing at her.

"Do you have I.D.?"

Kim rummaged in her purse and produced her driver's license and passport. She slid them to him. The bartender chose the passport and flipped it open. He examined it and slid it back. "I'm not the border patrol. I only need to check your age."

Kim whipped the passport and her license off the counter and stuffed them into her purse. She'd been stateside almost a year. Why was she still carrying a passport?

The old man was shaking his head as the bartender placed a glass and an icy cold brown bottle in front of her. Someone hollered, "Hank." He lifted a hand to signal he'd be along in a moment.

"Thanks." She noticed the word LITE in broad print across the front. That's what she should've said instead of diet. Kim poured, watching foam fill the glass to the brim. Hank pulled the toothpick from his mouth and watched too.

Kim nodded to him and took a healthy swig. She spit the nasty fluid back into the glass. "Eww," she sputtered.

Hank guffawed. "You are wet behind the ears," He said, moving away.

The grizzled man beside her pounded his fist on the bar and cackled. He turned to look at her. Bleary-eyed, disheveled, he didn't look too healthy, but she wasn't scared. She said, "How do you drink this?"

The old man scratched his bearded jaw. "I never touch the stuff."

"You don't?"

He belted back the last of the fluid in his glass and slid off the barstool. "Taste's as tame as diet pop. Better skedaddle while you can, missy. The coyotes are circling."

"What do you mean?"

Hank set a pop on the bar in front of her. "Here, it's diet."

"Good floor show, Hank. You should hire her permanent. I haven't laughed so hard in years." The old man nodded toward Kim as he dug money out of his billfold and tossed it on the counter. He shuffled toward the door.

Kim sipped the soda pop. It tasted too sweet after the bitter beer.

Hank chewed his toothpick. "You're new around here. Are you hustling business?"

Why would she drum up business for a veterinarian in a bar? Was he asking her if she was looking for a job? For the third time in as many minutes, heated embarrassment rushed through her as she understood. "Oh. No. Nothing like that."

Hank removed his toothpick, probably so he wouldn't swallow it as he engaged in a deep belly laugh. His tone was kind, "You've been watching too many TV reruns. This isn't an establishment where you make friends and everybody knows your name. You might want to try Millie's Diner or Zandra's Hairstyles. You don't belong here."

Kim stared into smoky space. The man's words rang true. She didn't belong here. She belonged home with Addie-Jo. Suddenly, she was more sure of herself than she had been when she walked in and nodded agreement. She opened her purse. "What do I owe you?"

Hank shook his head. "Eddie paid for your drinks. He's right. You better scoot. The coyotes are circling."

A man in a black Stetson lowered himself into the seat vacated by the old man Eddie. He leaned toward her and breathed beer in her direction. "Well, now, if I said you had a beautiful body, would you hold it against me?"

"The lady is leaving," Hank said.

"Hey, you're not going after you were giving me the come-on. I saw you eyeing me from across the room." The man snatched the sleeve of her jacket. Kim cried out and shrank from him.

"Well, I ain't going to hurt you," he said.

Hank spoke low, menacingly, "Let her go."

Bolstered by Hank's tone, Kim straightened and forced two regular breaths. She slid the full glass of brew toward the cowboy. "I have to go, but no hard feelings. Here's a beer for you."

The cowboy let Kim slip away through a cloud of smoke. He grabbed the beer she'd rejected and saluted Hank. "Well, all right, then. She's a real lady."

Chapter Forty-one – Hank

Hank found the ticking clock to be as annoying as a leaky faucet. The room before him was clean and neat since he always made sure it was ready for company. Even so, he knew the truth. It was an empty house. Even his sister Brenda and her family didn't make it over much since his niece was in second grade and his nephews in kindergarten. There was simply too much to do to keep her family going without having to visit a bachelor brother.

Hank slouched deeper into the overstuffed chair. His long legs stretched before him to the blue throw rug. In his right hand was a glass of beer, in his left hand, a pop. He alternated sips.

He'd make them last fifteen more minutes and then he would go to work. It wasn't his dream job, but the long hours at the Lone Star Saloon kept him occupied and sober since he never drank on the job. Ironic.

Hank tilted his head and screwed his lips together. He refused to get into self-analysis for his mind was a dangerous place. Besides, thinking about the past wouldn't give him a better start in life nor bring back the men who died fighting beside him. No, he wasn't going to go there, not to either place.

The floor under the trimmed tree boughs held no presents for it was Brenda's turn to have Christmas this year. He had put up a real tree anyway and decorated it with hope and the same decorations he had bought the first year he returned to Free Dance. This year the twinkling lights and the colored bulbs, shabby silvery tinsel and bright gold star only seemed to emphasize the fact that no one was there to share it with him.

Hank swirled the pale yellow liquid with the thin topping of foam and swore softly. It was getting so that the present wasn't any more agreeable than the past. He drained each glass and added them to the others stacked into the shape of a Christmas tree. It was a game he played every year, a game with a purpose. The shape would be finished tomorrow night—New Year's Eve. He always had the shape finished by then, but never earlier. It kept him from solitary bingeing during the loneliest week of the year. New Year's Day he'd clean it all away when he packed the Christmas decorations.

He lifted his sheepskin jacket and Stetson from the hook by the back door, doffed them and left the dark house. Falling snow had laid a fluffy quarter-inch carpet onto his shoveled sidewalk. Hank brushed snow off his truck, but it kept coming down thick and soft so that the distant mountains appeared only as gray shadows. All around softly colored lights of the Montana town brightened the snowy twilight. It was the pits when the best part of the day was leaving instead of coming home.

Chapter Forty-two – Kim

Kim grunted as she maneuvered the shopping cart around a pile of cabbages. It never failed. She either got the squeaky cart or the wheel that locked. The left rear wheel had been locking ever since aisle two.

"I forgot the flour for Dora, oh, nuts." There was no way she could push the broken cart all the way through the store again, but Addie-Jo was sleeping peacefully in the bottom of the cart and she wasn't sure about leaving the baby even for a few minutes. What should she do? She frowned with concentration. These days every decision felt like a major event.

"Hello."

Kim yelped and leaped backward into a pile of potatoes, toppling one of the bags onto the floor.

"Whoa. I didn't mean to startle you," a man said.

She reached for the sack and resettled it on the stack. "Sorry. I was lost in thought."

"I noticed. You're the diet beer lady, aren't you?"

Kim bit her lip and twisted her neck scarf. The memory of her disastrous adventure was one she wanted to forget. Yet the bartender who had witnessed it all, including how she had spit the foul-tasting brew back in the glass was standing in front of her. His gray eyes sparkled with mischief and his crows-feet crinkled as his mouth twitched. "The cowboy sends his regards for the beer you left him."

"Oh."

Hank burst into deep rumbling laughter. "Yep. He enjoyed his beer right down to the last drop."

Right there between the cabbages and the potatoes, Kim held her sides and quaked until she laughed out loud. Hysteria edged and receded leaving her exhausted, but relieved. She wiped her eyes. "You didn't tell him I spit in it?"

"Naw. He got what he deserved. He's such a blowhard. Full of himself, as my grammaw used to say. My name's Hank Barlow."

"Kim Macomb."

"It's nice to formally meet you, Kim. Can I help you with your cart? Take mine. It doesn't stick or squeak."

"Thanks. But, I have to go back to get some flour."

Hank commandeered control of her cart and Kim had nothing to do but follow him to the baking aisle, since Addie-Jo was still in the basket.

"How did you ever find your way to Free Dance, Kim Macomb?

"I came to visit for the summer at the ranch of some friends. Do you know the Bronners?"

"Sort of."

"I liked it well enough to stay."

"I took you for a big city woman. What about this hole-in-the-wall place attracts you?"

"The pace is slow. The people are friendly. I feel at home. It's a nice place to raise Addie-Jo."

"You sold me. Your daughter doesn't look very old."

"Three months."

"And where is her daddy?"

The question, as always, broadsided Kim. She resented having to explain, resented being reminded. "My husband died when we were on the mission field."

"That's why you had a passport. How'd he die?"

"You certainly are nosy." Kim stooped to claim a five-pound bag of name-brand flour.

"I can be when something interests me."

"Revolutionaries."

This evidently surprised Hank because as he regarded her, he pulled a toothpick from his front shirt pocket and chewed on it.

She blurted, "I'm here because I'm having some trouble adjusting after watching his torture and death."

Pain and a faraway look surfaced and disappeared. Hank grunted. "I was in Desert Storm. A bomb blew. Lost three of my friends and a local girl I was sweet on. They didn't all die at once. It's hard. You're glad it's not you. You wish it could've been you. You wish it was the enemy. You wish it wasn't anybody. You wish everything could be like it was before. It's all so senseless."

Hank rattled the cantankerous cart to the end of the aisle. Kim gazed after the man who in a few sentences encapsulated her feelings. She followed him. He rounded the corner and headed for the checkout. "It's New Year's Eve. Do you want to go to the square-dance with me tonight?"

Kim nibbled on her lip and tugged her scarf. The invitation felt casual as if they'd been meeting off and on at the grocers for years. Yet she knew nothing about this man who had summed her up so easily. "Sure, if I can get a babysitter."

Chapter Forty-three – Mitch

Mitch kicked the snow from his boots with three sharp raps against the storm door. He blew on his fingers and imagined how pleased Kim would be. The three of them would go out to eat and then come back to the apartment to play Scrabble or watch a video and ring in the New Year. It would be a real nice evening at home.

Anticipation melted as the door opened to reveal a handsome man in a red western-style shirt with pearl buttons and a pair of new black jeans. "Yeah?"

Mitch felt his brow furrow. "I'm looking for Kim."

"Come on in." The man stepped back, allowing the door to open completely and called out, "Kim, someone's here."

"I'm Mitch Bronner."

"Yeah, I know who you are. You were three years ahead of me in high school. I'm Hank Barlow. I don't expect you to remember me. All you seniors acted like freshman were trash. Kim mentioned she was friends with you." He shook Mitch's hand in a grip just shy of painful. Kim came through the bedroom door with her head bent and her arm reaching behind her neck to finish closing the zipper of a red gingham dress. She put both hands on her waist and pushed toward her hips as if to rearrange its contents. She flounced the gingham, puffy from under-netting. "This dress of your sister's is so tight I can barely breathe."

Hank whistled softly. "You're stunning. Brenda never looked like that."

"Thank you." The comment seemed to fluster and please Kim. She looked up. "Mitch. I thought you were the babysitter. What are you doing here?"

"I came by to surprise you for New Year's."

"You should've asked me ahead of time. I've got plans."

"I noticed. Where are you going?"

"To the square dance. I was busy birthing a baby at the last one and didn't get to dance. Hank's sister lent me her competition dress. Isn't it pretty?"

"I didn't know you wanted to dance. I'd have been happy to take you."

"Yeah, well, you didn't ask me, Hank did. I'm going to go have some fun." Her tone was somewhere between rebellion and reproach.

Mitch stifled an angry retort. He kissed her on the cheek. "You'll knock 'em dead. I'll wait here until the sitter shows. You two go on ahead."

Kim's defiance drained from her face and tears threatened to spill. She hugged him. "Thanks, Mitch. I've been looking forward to this all afternoon. Addie-Jo should sleep for another hour then she'll want to eat. I've got milk in the 'frig. Warm the bottle in a pan of water on the stove. Put a test drop on your wrist, in case it's too hot. Diapers are on the dresser. Ali should be here any minute. I've told her all this but you may have to repeat it. Oh, and—"

"Kim, I know how to take care of Addie-Jo. Go on, have fun."

A look of rebuke passed over her face and tears welled again. "I'll get my coat," she mumbled and headed into her bedroom. When she reappeared, her face was stony. Her nose tilted upward and her chin set. "I'm ready."

Hank glowered at Mitch as he escorted Kim out the door. Mitch shook his head. Sometimes he didn't think even Kim knew what she wanted.

The clock on the stove read 4:10 when the sound of footsteps mounting the stairs woke him. He threw off the blanket and rose stiffly. The heavier set retreated and Kim tiptoed into the apartment. "What are you still doing here? Where's Ali?"

"The church was having a teen doings and the Buerger boy asked her to go. I told her to go ahead, I'd watch Addie-Jo."

"You had no right to do that. I'm her mother. I left here thinking Ali was in charge."

"It's not like I appeared out of the blue and dismissed her. I was here before you left."

"You had no right and if Ali can't deal with me directly then she isn't capable of watching my child."

Mitch's voice rose to match the increasing volume of Kim's. "Don't take it out on Ali. She's knows we're close friends. She knew Addie-Jo was safe. No one expected you to come sneaking in at four in the morning."

"I don't have to sneak. This is my place. And you weren't supposed to be here."

"I wanted to be with you."

"Well, you should've called ahead."

"I guess I should've."

"Yes, you should have."

They glared at each other. Mitch snatched his jacket off the couch. None of this was going the way he planned. The words slipped out before he could think. "I love you, Kim."

Kim made a noise he could only describe as a dangerous growl. He ducked in time to avoid a half-full glass of pop. With a sharp crash and tinkle, liquid sprayed him. Addie-Jo shrieked.

"Now look what you've done. You woke the baby." Kim headed into the bedroom.

"I woke the baby? You're one mixed up woman, Kim. I'm leaving."

Kim returned joggling Addie-Jo. The baby's face puckered and tears flowed. Kim's face looked the same but she spat out. "Go ahead and go. I'm not stopping you."

Mitch plunked his hat onto his head and opened the door.

"And I don't need your pity." Kim bounced Addie-Jo on her hip.

Mitch slammed the door shut, yet still heard her. "I don't need you. I'm not a princess, you know. I don't need anyone."

Chapter Forty-four - Hank

Hank grinned with great satisfaction as Mitch stormed down the steps from Kim's apartment and stomped to his vehicle. It hadn't escaped his notice that sparks were practically flying between Kim and Mitch Bronner. He'd noticed, but he'd never been one to hold back when he saw something he wanted. It helped his claim since Kim was fragile in a way he was familiar with and Bronner wasn't.

Bronner's old red truck disappeared around the corner. Hank started his own engine and drove home. He passed a few revelers in the downtown area and a pair of snowmobiles zooming along the darkened residential streets.

The holiday lights along the front roof of his home winked cheerily as he pulled into the drive. It had been a great evening. Kim was terrific. Smart. Funny. Sensitive. Beautiful. Scared stiff. She needed someone strong and gentle to treat her good and take care her and be a father to that sweet baby girl, too. Finally, finally, something was going his way.

Hank woke alert and ready for action before nine the next morning. He packed and stored the Christmas decorations, washed the glasses of his Christmas tree tower, and paced the kitchen tile waiting for an appropriate time to call on Kim. How long would a three-month-old let a momma sleep on a holiday morning? Not long, he was sure, but he certainly didn't want to be the one to wake her if they were sleeping.

Willie Nelson sang the words, "you were always on my mind" as Hank scrambled two eggs with sausage and made a stack of toast. He washed breakfast down with a pot of coffee while reading the previous day's newspaper. There was an interesting article about some guy who was making money on the West coast with a series of specialty coffee shops. He skimmed it twice and tossed the paper aside.

Light spilled through the window and brightened the table where his coffee mug sat. Hank took it as an omen and reached for his coat and hat. A dusting of snow had fallen since he'd come home, but he didn't bother to clear his walk. He did sweep Kim's steps with an old broom he found propped in the corner behind the door. Addie-Jo wailed and then quieted. Finished with sweeping, he rapped a staccato beat of seven raps.

Kim answered the door wearing a pair of blue sweats. Her hair was disheveled. The previous night's eye makeup looked more like war paint with the fierce scowl she wore. "If you think—"

"Hi."

Her eyes blinked rapidly and her mouth parted in surprise. The scowl faded, replaced by confusion. "Hank. Oh, hi. I thought it was someone else. What's up? Did you forget something?"

"No. I came by to see you."

She bit her lip gently and then her face broke into a welcoming smile. "Oh, well come on in."

Silently he chalked one up for himself on the mental Hank vs. Bronner scoreboard.

"I hoped I wouldn't wake you. Did you get much sleep?"

"About three hours. I had trouble getting to sleep," She glanced at him with caution, "because of Addie-Jo."

"I figured as much," he said, although he figured it was because she was angry with Bronner. They stood inside the door and he didn't remove his coat. Everything with Kim had to be timed perfectly or she'd shy away.

"Look, Hank, I haven't showered or put make-up on or eaten or anything, yet."

"I can take the hint. I'll go. I came by to invite you to Brenda's today for a get-together. Brenda and Bo, the niece and nephews, good food, football and conversation, maybe some cards, you and Addie-Jo. It'll be a pleasant day. It's kind of a family tradition. Brenda said she'd like to meet you. It's loose, so there's no time pressure. We show up whenever we show up."

"I don't know. I was thinking I'd sleep most of the day."

"Great. Naps are almost mandatory. A side benefit is you'll have somebody to watch Addie-Jo while you do nap."

Her eyes sparkled when she laughed and she became the most beautiful woman he'd ever seen. "Okay, you convinced me. Where does she live?"

"I'll pick you up. Would one o'clock be good?"

"I can drive. If Addie-Jo gets fussy I can leave without bothering you."

"No bother. Anytime you want to go home, I'll take you." He put his Stetson on and made a quick exit before Kim could have second thoughts. As he drove away he glanced up hopefully and waved. She still stood with the inner door ajar.

Chapter Forty-five – Kim

Kim felt warmed by Brenda's welcome. "I'm glad you came. As a big sister, I'm always interested in my brother's business. Did the dress work last night?"

"Oh yes, it was beautiful. I didn't bring it because I'll get it cleaned first. I did bring some chips and salsa."

"Wow. I didn't expect that. Great."

Did she mean great about cleaning the dress or bringing food? Kim didn't have time to sort it out as Brenda was pointing to the children bouncing all around Hank. "...Bobby and Leann and that's my husband, Bo."

A fair-haired man with a hint of a beer belly sprawled on one of two couches that formed a "V" in front of the TV. A football game was in progress. When Brenda said his name he cranked his thick neck around, lifted his hand in a sloppy wave and called, "Hello Hank. Hello Hank's friend, drinks are in the fridge, help yourself."

"We're informal here. I hope you don't mind," Brenda said in a soft-spoken voice. She nabbed one of the boys, either Bobby or the boy whose name she didn't catch. Brenda said in a firm but quiet voice. "Settle down, you'll knock the baby out of Uncle Hank's hand."

"I want to see," the child wailed.

Hank set the baby carrier on the faux-wood floor and pulled the cover back. The tow-headed children crowded around as the newcomers removed coats and hats and stored them in a closet by the door. "Can I hold her?" the seven-year-old girl asked.

"Maybe later, it's my turn now. Go play and don't pester your Uncle. He's got company," Brenda said. The boys dashed off arguing over who'd get the video game controls while the LeAnn hung around watching the baby. Brenda lifted Addie-Jo out of the carrier and made lilting sounds and smiled broadly. Addie-Jo lit up like an open-for-business sign, cooing and waving her arms and kicking her legs.

"She certainly likes you," Kim said, thinking she liked Brenda very much, too.

Hank went into the kitchen and returned a moment later with a beer and a diet cola. Brenda sat next to her husband and LeAnn perched on the couch arm. Hank and Kim settled on the second couch. The televised roar of the crowd rose to a frenzied level and Bo bellowed in agitation, pounding the couch arm with his fist.

Kim jumped, yelping. Bo pointed his finger at her and said, "I see you're a die-hard fan. About time Hank dated someone who likes football. Right LeAnn?"

"Right, Daddy." LeAnn nodded and her straight blonde hair brushed back and forth.

Brenda elbowed him and he sat back. "What?"

Kim blinked tears as she lowered herself to the couch. "Go team," she stammered.

The weight of Hank's arm bore down on her shoulders. He nudged her closer. She leaned her head against his chest and heard his steady heartbeat. She curled her legs under her and recalled what it felt like to feel safe.

The afternoon passed pleasantly. Between the end of the football game and the start of a family movie Hank lifted her face to his and sneaked a kiss. It surprised her, but it surprised her even more that she liked it. The memory of it stayed as she lie in her bed alone that night and was stronger and more stirring than memories of Kurt before he fell and more potent with pleasure than the hope and frustration Mitch evoked. She woke the next morning remembering that kiss.

When she got to work, Kim listened to the messages on Dr. Mullins answering machine. She sipped coffee and rolled her eyes to hear Julius had a stomachache, again, and would be in about ten o'clock. "Keep your Godiva chocolates where the dog can't get them, lady," Kim said to no one as she deleted the message. She added Julius' name to the schedule as the machine beeped.

"Kim, I'm sorry about our argument. I came by New Year's Day, but missed you. I'm about to leave for Boston. I didn't want to go without talking to you. I'm sorry I missed you again. Anyway, I've got to go they're boarding. Bye."

He was really gone. She snatched a tissue from the box on her desk and dabbed runaway tears. Kim hit the delete button and the next message played.

"Hey, Kim, It's Hank. Yesterday was fun. Everybody liked you. The first day back after a holiday is always exhausting, I hope you have a good day. You get off at five and I don't start work until six tonight. Do you want to catch a quick bite to eat? I'll call later."

Hank. He asked her to dinner instead of assuming she'd go. He didn't examine her like a bug in Biology class. He didn't tiptoe around her as if she would shatter. Most importantly, he understood her. She could be who she was and not explain. Her emotions rose and fell throughout the morning and lunch.

Kim blew her nose and answered the ringing phone. "Mullins Veterinary Clinic."

"Kim, it's Mitch. How are you?"

Kim clutched the phone with both hands. Hope stirred. "Where are you?"

"Boston. Wait until you hear about the trip out. There was this—"

"Look, you can't call me here. You're going to get me fired."

The phone went quiet for a moment. "That's not true, Kim."

"You didn't even ask if you could call me here."

"Oh-kay. I'd like to talk with you. Can I call you?

Kim screwed her face up in resolution. "I don't like to take personal calls here."

"You don't have a phone at home. How are we going to talk?"

"What is there to talk about? You're a thousand miles away. I've got to go."

225

"Kim—"

She hung up and slumped into the chair. The tile floor looked cold and the waiting room, like her life, was empty. Not completely empty. Hank was nice and easy to be with. He was from Free Dance and he was never leaving. It didn't hurt that he was a good kisser, too.

***

For the first time in a long time, Kim wasn't wrenched from sleep by an insistent demand for food, a dry diaper, or consolation. The soft sucking noises of "milk dreams" issued from Addie-Jo's crib. Kim lay perfectly still with eyes shut, unwilling to do anything to disturb the moment.

The comforting weight of the quilt, the smoothness of the sheets against her bare skin, the softness of the feather pillow cradling her head felt as secure as if she were in a cocoon.

A pretty memory flitted like a butterfly—curling with the cat in a patch of sunshine on pink carpet in her bedroom. It was only a fragment but she had been perfectly happy.

Others came. Christmas when she was eleven and the house was full of company and contentment, fishing with her dad, making cookies with her mom, and her wedding dance with Kurt, his eyes so tender with love that her heart squeezed—

"You're having happy thoughts." The bed bounced.

Kim's eyes flew open. "Hank."

The toothpick moved from one side of his mouth to the other. "Here I thought I was the reason you're smiling so pretty; instead you'd completely forgotten I was here."

"No, no, I was kind of dreaming. You know that place where you're half awake and half asleep and everything feels so safe and good." Kim tucked the quilt modestly about her.

"I'll take your word for it."

Her lips trembled with emotion. "I can't remember the last time I woke on my own. Thank you."

He lay beside her on top of the covers. "What were you thinking?"

Kim told him about the childhood memories. When he didn't speak, she added, "And then, I was remembering Kurt."

"Tell me about him."

"You don't want to hear about him." Kim tried to rise, but Hank pinned her beneath the blankets and kissed her forehead with great tenderness. He whispered in her ear. "Yes, I do. Tell me about your husband. It couldn't have been all bad for you to smile like that."

She bucked against Hank's hold. "Let me up. Now!" He released her immediately.

She stood, wrapping the sheet around her body. "It wasn't all bad. It was very, very good. We were so much in love and everything was new to us both. Kurt lived every moment in a big way. He wasn't just happy he was joyful. He didn't just run he raced to win. I felt like I was flying when I was with him. I adored him. He was everything to me. Until he fell."

Sorrow tethered to a megaton of bad memories crashed upon her. Kim bustled to the bathroom. She returned clothed in a maroon sweatshirt and sweatpants. She brushed her hair angrily. "I thought we weren't going to get into this. We said we'd accept each other the way we are."

"Would it help to hear about my past?"

"I can't handle your demons. Mine almost overwhelm me."

"Yours do overwhelm you."

Kim stopped brushing. She opened her mouth to say she was more than a conqueror in Christ and she'd get through the grief and the pain. Then she remembered she'd walked away from God. She'd walked away and kept walking until she'd ended in Hank's bed, well, technically, her bed, Hank's arms. At any rate, the point was, God had disappointed her first.

"Calm down, Kim. We don't have to talk about this. I get it. You adored your husband. He was everything to you. Things went sour. It's not what you wanted. It's not what he wanted. It happened. Nobody's to blame."

God is to blame. Kim didn't say it aloud. She let Hank draw her to his bare chest. She hooked her fingers into belt loops at the back of his jeans and let his arms shelter her as they swayed. After a time, the tension melted away.

Chapter Forty-six - Carol

Carol recognized the sharp little tick as a sign of irritation, even over the phone line. Her desk chair squeaked as she straightened. In the yard outside the office window, oblivious to the tension, Minnie snuffled as she followed a rabbit trail in the late snow. Carol gripped her mug of coffee, but didn't sip. "What's the matter, Jack?"

Jack clicked his tongue against his teeth again and silence followed, but Carol did not believe for one second that they had lost connection. The vibes were as strong as sirens.

"Let me get this straight. You picked out the wedding invitations, the cake, the flowers, the songs, and the menu. You hired a caterer, a band, and the minister. Did you buy the rings and choose the best man, too?"

Carol bit her lip. This wouldn't be the time to tell him she had reserved a set of rings at Goldberg's and had tried but couldn't reach Mitch. She was glad that line had been busy.

"I'm not some twenty-year-old who can only think about the wedding night. I thought we'd discuss and plan our wedding together. Planning is part of the pleasure, don't you think?"

Carol chewed on the end of her pen as she watched a cardinal fluff its brilliant plumage against the snow-filled wind. She had indeed spent many pleasurable hours planning the perfect wedding. A.J. had always been happy to let her do so. She'd prided herself on her ability. "It never occurred to me you might have suggestions, Jack. If there's something special you want on the menu or a certain song, I'll add them."

There was another long silence. Carol thought he was about to list some songs or name a food when she heard that unmistakable tick. "Not an add-on. I want to be part of the decisions."

"But I've already got everything done. Traditionally it is the bride's role."

"Traditionally, it's the bride's family's role, but we're doing this ourselves."

"Are you saying you want me to scrap everything and start over?" A seed of panic blossomed in Carol's stomach.

"I asked you before when you wanted to get together to plan."

"I thought you were being polite."

"I'm going to fly in tomorrow night with my friend, Joe. He thinks he's found another small plane to buy. I can give you a call when I get there. Will you be free?"

"Sure. Tomorrow. Come to dinner. I love you."

"And I love you."

"... and you'll love what I've done," she said. She disconnected the call. Would he like what she'd done? What did she know about him anyway? He might want a traditional Indian wedding officiated by his friend Myron Yellowtail who was descended from a medicine man. Or maybe he'd prefer to go to Las Vegas and get married by Elvis like Trudy suggested. She shuddered. Why hadn't she asked him about this? What kind of man planned his own wedding? Didn't he trust her?

The next evening, Carol inhaled the scent of sugar cookies rising from candles. The dinner table was set with her mother's china and silver. The rhubarb pie was well browned and tart. Everything was ready except for her emotions. The thought of discussing wedding plans with Jack created "what ifs" that hounded her with ever more outlandish fears.

"Stop it," Trudy ordered as she came out the kitchen.

Carol jumped. "Stop what?"

"Stop sighing."

"I didn't."

"You did. I could hear you all the way in the kitchen. Jack is not going to have you exchange vows while skiing Skeleton Run. You are not going to skydive to your reception. You are not going to be married naked in front of the White House."

Carol made a face. "Don't exaggerate. I never thought he would."

"Well, your other fears are equally outlandish." Trudy squeezed both of Carol's shoulders to reassure her. "It'll be fine. Everything is ready and looks great. It's a good thing he wants to be a part of the plans. It shows he's interested in making a life with you."

"I keep thinking about how controlling Peter was. Cynthia couldn't even pick out her own clothes."

"Jack is not Peter."

"I know."

"He's not Andy, either. He's Jack."

"He's not Andy. He's Jack."

Trudy hugged Carol. "You sound like you're cramming for an exam. Be yourself and let him be himself."

"I was myself. That's why I made all those plans. Now he wants to change everything. Trudy, I'm not sure I'm ready to remarry." The doorbell rang. Carol hissed, "He's here. How do I look?"

Trudy squirmed into her coat and patted Carol's shoulder. "You look fine. This dark blue lace is terrific on you. Now get a grip. You're acting like a teenybopper." Trudy followed Carol to the front door and greeted the new arrival. "Hi Jack."

"Hi, Trudy. Are you joining us for dinner?"

"No, I'm leaving. Now, remember, Carol. Jack is too dignified to wear an Elvis costume and skydive at his own wedding, so you scratch that off the list, and that whole Washington gig, a definite no-go."

Carol pushed her friend firmly out the door, "Good-bye, Trudy."

Jack raised his eyebrows. "A skydiving Elvis?"

"Trudy's sick idea of a joke." Carol closed the door.

Jack gathered her into his arms for a kiss. "You look wonderful."

"I hoped you'd like my dress. I'm a little nervous and thought something new would help bolster my courage."

"It works for me."

At the appreciation in his eyes and the tenderness on his face, Carol sank against him. Jack was Jack, big, comforting, and kind. She was being silly.

"I like to think you missed me, but can I get out of my coat?"

"Sure. We're almost ready to eat. I'll throw the steaks in the broiler."

"Great. I'll wash my hands." He reentered the dining room as Carol placed salads on the table. "It smells good in here, makes me hungrier than I already was. Sugar cookies are one of my favorites."

"Actually that's the candles. We're having rhubarb pie for dessert."

"Um."

Carol shot him a look. "Don't you like rhubarb pie?"

He looked apologetic. "No. I don't."

Carol blinked a few times and swallowed hard as she went into the kitchen. "Oh, well, we probably won't have room anyway. We're having steaks. I know you like those, and mashed potatoes and asparagus."

"Sounds good. Shall we pray?"

Carol's agitation eased. This was what she loved about Jack. The sense of oneness they had when they prayed. Afterward, she smiled at him as she picked up her fork. "Have you seen, Kim?"

An indefinable something passed over his face. "I saw her and Addie-Jo in the grocery a couple days ago. I asked them to lunch, but they had other plans. She looked well."

Carol munched lettuce and tomato. "I was wondering because the last few times that I've called her, either the doctor needs her or she's in a rush and doesn't want to talk. All I know is something happened New Year's Eve between her and Mitchell and they haven't patched up their problems. Maybe Kim is avoiding us because she feels we're all pressuring her to make the first move to reconcile. What do you think?"

"I'm sure she has her reasons."

His guarded attitude and the words waved red flags. "Like what?" Jack took so long to answer Carol starting talking. "If you know something, you should tell me. She is my daughter. I have a right to know."

"She's grown. If she wants to tell you, she will."

"Tell me what?"

Tink. Jack's fork settled on his plate. "It's not like it's a secret, even if she isn't talking about it. She's been keeping company with one of the local bartenders. Dora has thought of confronting her, but is afraid she'll simply move in with him. We hope it'll blow over."

"Live with him. Are you saying Kim has a man living with her?"

"He has his own place, but he spends the night."

"Kim wouldn't. She'd never be a hypocrite. She couldn't do that and then go to church as usual."

"She's not been going to church."

Carol stared at her half-eaten salad through a blur of tears. She couldn't work out if she was grieved and angry at Jack or Kim or the nameless suitor. Maybe all three. She could think of no reason for Jack to lie and it sure explained the problem with Mitch.

Jack reached across the table to cover her hand with his. "None of us can live her life for her. We can't smooth everything over, either, not even you. All we can do is pray and love her. She's got lots of people praying for her, Carol. She knows right from wrong. She's going to be fine. It might take a little time."

Carol pressed the linen napkin to her eyes and blotted the tears. "Do you know the guy?"

"Hank's a good enough sort, a local. He tends bar at the Lone Star Saloon."

"Not a high recommendation in my book."

"He treats her and Addie-Jo right."

"So did Mitch."

Jack laid his bunched napkin beside his plate. "Yes, he did. The way I see it, Kim loves Mitchell as much as he loves her. Right now she doesn't know what to do about it. Maybe she's afraid of becoming emotionally invested, then losing him like she lost Kurt."

Carol couldn't argue with his assessment. Jack's gaze darted past her the same moment the alarm blared. Smoke roiled out of the kitchen, carrying the smell of charred meat. "The steaks!" She waved her way into the kitchen. Carol groped the counter for potholders and threw open the broiler. Flames shot upward. She yanked the pan out and howled as the holders slipped, burning a finger. The pan dropped onto the stove, splattering grease as it knocked the pot of mashed potatoes into a nearby roll of paper towels which rocked and toppled into the broiler pan, and flared.

Jack reached from behind and lifted the roll of paper towels into the sink. He banged open several cupboards before finding the carton of salt. He doused everything with salt, until the last flicker was gone.

Carol coughed. She flung the back door open. Smoke poured into the cold air. She shook her burned hand and brushed despairingly at the grease splatters on her new dress, "Look at this mess."

Jack flipped on the oven exhaust to help clear the air. He wrapped ice in a fresh towel, wet it, and pressed it to the burn. The alarm silenced but her ears rang in the sudden quiet.

"Oh, Jack. Our special dinner."

Jack pulled her close. Carol clutched at him and blubbered until she was cried out. "Maybe things will get better for Kim when I'm closer."

He agreed without conviction. "Come on. I'll help you clean the kitchen."

Calmness in crisis and the comfortable way they worked together were two more items on the growing list of things she liked about Jack. Once a pizza arrived and they were situated on the couch, Jack pointed to the planning book. "Okay, Lady. Show me what you've got."

"No, not yet, let's talk first. Other than the calendar date, I never asked you if you had something in mind for the wedding. Now I want to know."

Jack searched her face. "First of all, I don't mind having the wedding here. However, I think we should also have a reception in Free Dance."

Carol hadn't even considered this but realized most of the Montana folks wouldn't travel east for the wedding. "That makes sense. Okay."

"Second, it seems to me since we both had big church weddings the first time around, perhaps a small wedding of close family and friends would do."

Carol turned her head from him to look out the window. Darkness had fallen and she couldn't see anything except reflections of the room. "I know second weddings are traditionally small, but I'm moving to Free Dance and won't often be back. It would be like a going away party. Plus, I have a lot of friends, business associates, as well as all of Andy's family that I'm still close to and want to introduce to you. I'll cash in a bond. I can pay for it."

"The cost isn't the issue, although it did seem like an extravagance. I can see your point, however."

"I really want to do this."

"All right."

"Really?"

"Really."

A ton weight of worry fell from her shoulders. "The only thing is I don't think I have time to plan two parties."

"You won't have to. Maggie and several other old friends want to organize it. All you have to do is arrive on my arm and look beautiful. The wedding is July third. I thought we'd fly the next day to New Orleans. We'll spend a few days recuperating from the hubbub, then fly to Greece. We'll return to Free Dance mid-August. They want to have the reception the following weekend."

"That I think I can do." She had gotten worked up over nothing. Now, if she could only do something about Kim.

Chapter Forty-seven – Kim

"You're looking alert and well-rested," Dr. Bradley said. She wheeled into her customary spot and adjusted the navy blue sweater that was almost identical to the one Kim wore in powder blue.

Kim settled back with confidence. Even her chin-length dark hair looked as stylish today as the doctor's. "I took your advice and found extra childcare. It really helps. The new sitter, Brenda has three children of her own and Addie-Jo loves being there."

Dr. Bradley smiled and her cute nose wrinkled. "I knew you could do it. Are you sleeping better?"

Kim nodded. She did feel better now that she was sleeping through most nights. Hank never seemed to mind the sleep he lost getting up with Addie-Jo, he didn't seem to need as much sleep as she did. It really was all working out.

"I went to the New Year's Eve square dance. My new friend, Brenda, lent me one of her outfits with the bouncy crinoline underneath. I looked good and I had fun."

"That's terrific, Kim."

"Yeah," she said and glanced at the fish swimming placidly in the tank. Now that Dr. Bradley knew about what happened to Nsia, she felt ready to go into more detail about their fateful trip—if the psychiatrist brought it up again. It was good to get things out in the open. Secrets really weren't healthy.

***

"Come on, Kim. You haven't had a day off for a long time," Hank said as he kissed her neck. "Brenda said she'd be happy to keep the baby and you know how Addie-Jo loves the kids."

"We've never been apart for that long. I don't know if I can leave her." Kim turned her head to look past the couch into the bedroom where her daughter was sleeping.

"It's one night. Thirty hours at the most. Think about it. We'll shop the big mall and buy you a dress for your mother's wedding and try it out at dinner in a fancy restaurant, just the two of us. We'll get you a swimsuit and spend the night lounging in the hot tub at a hotel and eat room service, sleep in late, and do absolutely nothing."

"Absolutely nothing," Kim murmured the enticing words. She could hardly imagine what that would be like. Hank had stopped talking and was kissing her hand and her arm. It suddenly seemed very important to go. Irresistible. "Okay. Just the one night."

His gray eyes grew smoky as he beamed with pleasure. "It'll be wonderful. You'll see."

It was wonderful. He shopped with her instead of just dropping her at the mall. The dress she picked was a flowing affair of burgundy. After Hank's spontaneous, "You're beautiful", she had felt as grand as a princess. The restaurant was classy, the meal delicious. They lingered and laughed behind their hands over the fussy maitre'd. Late that night they sneaked past the closed sign and soaked in the hot tub and swam in the pool. The dark room shimmered romantically with blue underwater lighting. Everything was so perfect she almost told Hank she loved him.

They slept until noon. She slipped quickly into her clothes while Hank tipped the maid to look the other way as they left hours after checkout. Giggling like teenagers, he held her hand and hurried her down the back steps to his truck.

They stopped for burgers and fries and milkshakes at an out-of-the-way ice cream parlor. Hank played "She Don't Know She's Beautiful" on the jukebox and mouthed the words to her.

When it was time to leave, he helped her into her coat and kissed her. The kiss topped the whole outing off like a cherry finishes off a chocolate sundae. It was like a vacation/summer camp/

honeymoon all rolled into one day of pleasure. She forgot she was a surviving widow and a mother. She was simply a young woman having fun. What could go wrong?

Chapter Forty-eight – Hank

Hank smiled, filled with deep satisfaction over the success of the weekend. Kim looked unworried, gorgeous and her brown eyes sparkled. She slid next to him and threw both arms around his neck, pressing her lips against his cheek again and again. She wasn't wearing her seatbelt, but her spontaneous affection and closeness was worth any fine he might have to pay.

Hank backed out of the parking space at Barney's Old Ice Cream Emporium. A smiling woman driver in a handicap-equipped van raised a hand in greeting and pulled into the spot he'd vacated. Hank nodded and waved back. Today the whole world was his friend.

Kim glanced up. Instantly, her easy demeanor disappeared like the soft muscle of a clam hiding in its shell. She bit her lip and forced a smile. "It was a really wonderful day, but I'm tired. I think I'll sleep now." She stretched across the bench seat with her head on his leg and pretended to nap, but her torso rose with suppressed sobs and the tears she couldn't catch dampened the leg of his jeans.

Like the summit mist parting to reveal the mountain peaks of late spring, Hank knew two things. The woman was Kim's doctor and Kim hadn't mentioned him to her. She must be ashamed of him. Ashamed she needed him. Maybe she didn't want anyone to know she was dating someone from the wrong side of town. Although she never mentioned him, maybe she still wanted Mitch.

Hank let her pretend to sleep all the way to Free Dance. He didn't speak because her betrayal struck so profoundly that no amount of lies or reasoning could excuse it. He feared she'd see his weakness.

They picked up Addie-Jo and installed her safely in her own bed in the tiny apartment above Dora's. They stood side by side peering into the crib. Kim's face still blotched from her crying.

"I better get to work," he said. He kissed her on the head.

Kim clutched him and kissed him fiercely, a passion he suspected was driven by her need for his forgiveness. The knowledge cut even deeper into the wound of betrayal, yet he stayed, his own need for her sharp. He stayed and started his shift late because what else could you do when you loved someone who was shattered like glass?

Chapter Forty-nine – Mitch

Unable to sleep longer, Mitch rose early enough to watch the sunrise, but none could be seen on the third of July. A soft rain trickled down the window of the Indianapolis hotel. Today he'd see Kim.

The months since New Year's eve had sped by in every way except one. When it came to Kim everything seemed stuck. The few conversations with his dad had been distinctly unproductive and Carol was only a little more informative for Kim seemed to be avoiding her, too. Mitch prayed and read the Bible and strained to hear God's direction regarding her.

As the time of Jack and Carol's wedding approached, rain hammered the church. Lightening flickered over the stained glass while incessant booming drowned out the soloist.

Wearing soggy street clothes, Mitch and Myron strode up the side aisle. They passed pews of equally damp wet well-dressed guests fidgeting in semi-darkness of a power outage. Near the apse, a multitude of candles sucked air, leaving the sanctuary hot and close.

Jack opened the carved oak door of the groomsman's room and greeted them with nervous effusiveness. "Thank God you're finally here. This weather is causing all kinds of problems. Thanks for risking life and limb, Myron."

"That's truer than you know. Lightening hit the plane as we landed. Knocked the electrical system out, but nobody was hurt. I hear things aren't going well here." Myron said. "Mitchell said the minister was hospitalized."

"The update is kidney stones. It's just one more thing on top of Carol's poison ivy."

"How is she doing?"

"The poison ivy is really bad. The prescription made her swell like a balloon. She could barely fit into her dress."

Myron bowed his head. His hand covered his mouth. Mitch bowed his head too, but the prayer he expected didn't come. A quick glance revealed the Native American's big shoulders were heaving with suppressed laughter. Myron snorted, "It'd be tragic if it weren't so funny."

Jack said, "She promised me she'd make it down the aisle even if she had to wear her bathrobe." They broke into wild laughter.

One of Carol's many in-laws popped his head into the room. "Trudy sent me over to tell you the women are ready. How's it going here? Having a good time, I see. Still planning on marrying Catastrophe Carol?"

Jack grimaced. "We're ready. Mitchell and Myron are changing now."

The man had barely left when the door reopened. An ancient minister with a bright red nose and a bad hairpiece said, "Quite a day we're having. Are you sure you want to go through with this, young man?"

"Reverend White, this is my best man, Myron Yellowtail."

The minister didn't shake hands. "Good. We'll start in five minutes."

When the minister left, Jack said, "I'm going to punch the next person who suggests I call off the wedding."

Myron buttoned his jacket and adjusted his tie. "Don't do it. You'll mess yourself up. You're looking pretty good for once. I'm the best man. I'll handle it."

"Come on, Dad, let's pray." Mitch raised his voice to be heard over the storm rattling the windows. When he finished Jack said, "I'm proud of you, son."

"I'm proud of you, too, Dad. You picked a good woman. "I bet you're glad now I urged you to call her."

Jack clapped him on the shoulder and herded him out the door. "Yes Mitchell. Of course. You get all the credit."

Mitch slipped through the heavy door and took a direct path to the front row. Kim perched on the pew opposite, more beautiful than ever in soft burgundy. Addie-Jo sat on a small, white blanket at her feet. Had Kim looked the other way when she saw he was staring at her? In the flickering candlelight, he couldn't be sure.

He fastened his eyes on the cross above the altar. He glanced sideways. Like a promise, she was looking at him with such longing it told him everything he wanted to know. When he was done in Boston, he'd go back to Free Dance and marry Kim. He'd be a daddy to Addie-Jo. He settled back contentedly.

The minister moved into place with slow, shuffling steps, Jack and Myron positioned themselves at the bottom of the steps. Piano trills played while Trudy in a gold lace gown headed up the flower-strewn aisle. The opening chords of the bridal march resonated as Carol approached in a creamy dress with hem embroidered in gold and burgundy. She carried a cascading bouquet of yellow, red, and cream and looked like a fairy flower queen from a story his mother read him before he was old enough to object to such things. His Dad's eyes were only on her. Jack stepped forward to escort her to the altar as the last notes of the music faded.

Coughs and rustling of fabric prompted Reverend White to raise his hands to still the congregation. "Today we're here to witness the marriage of Jack Brandon Bronner and Carol Renae Streeter. Jack and Carol have written their own vows. I don't normally go for this kind of thing, but since I'm only standing in for the regular minister and he's allowed it, my hands are tied."

Jack lifted the worn Bible, opened it, and laid it on the table. "Carol, I promise to the best of my ability to obey God as instructed in his Holy Word. After God, you'll be most important to me. I pledge to love and cherish and protect you. I'll always be true to you."

Trudy wiped her eyes and pressed a fresh handkerchief into Carol's palm. Jack drew a breath and continued, "Despite snow, wind, fire, or flood I pledge to rescue you as many times as it takes, until death parts us."

Carol's squeal was muffled by the hanky.

Someone mumbled, "That's a full time job." Mitch sought a distraction to keep from laughing aloud. The baby's big eyes fastened on him. He smiled and waved. She smiled back. He extended his hand and wiggled his fingers. Addie-Jo popped onto all fours. He gathered loose flower petals from the floor and let them flutter through his fingers. Addie-Jo crawled toward him, but Kim didn't notice as at that very moment Hank was slipping into the pew next to her. Hank's jeans and plaid shirt were drenched. He ran a hand through dripping hair and smiled at Kim. She stiffened. Kim's terse whispered, "— doing here?" reached Mitch and his heart skipped with joy. He scooped Addie-Jo into his arms.

Kim turned from Hank. She frowned, looking around for Addie-Jo. She gestured for Mitch to send her back. Mitch pointed at Kim and then the altar. She motioned again, but he pretended not to see and cuddled the baby as Carol draped her bouquet on top of the open Bible.

She said, "Jack, from this day on I promise to bring the sweet fragrance and beauty of a godly wife to our marriage. Following God's word, I will respect and honor and be faithful to you. I promise to laugh often, share my thoughts and plans, and not jump to conclusions until the day death parts us."

After that red pajama debacle, the vow was appropriate. What vow would he give to Kim? What was something that she would know would be just for her?

Addie-Jo straightened her legs and slid from his lap to the floor where she played with the tassels on his dress shoes. Mitch loosened his tie to breathe easier in the hot, stuffy room. The faces of the entire wedding party glistened in the candlelight. Trudy, blinking fast, swayed and fell in a heap.

Carol fanned Trudy with the bouquet. Jack and Myron helped her sit up. Mitch strode forward, carrying Addie-Jo, to see if he could help.

"This is most irregular," the minister said, glaring at him with displeasure. Mitch bit back a retort.

Myron called for a bottle of water. Kim produced one from the diaper bag and hurried to him. He gave it to Trudy while Jack brought a chair and Hank and Myron lifted her into it. After a few moments she said, "I'm okay now. Let's go on."

Anticipating Kim was about to take Addie-Jo, Mitch returned to his seat. He heard her quick huff when she realized what he'd done.

"Everyone take your places. The congregation will cease tittering," said Reverend White. "Let's continue."

Myron fished the bride's ring from his breast pocket. Jack slid the ring on Carol's finger. It stuck at the knuckle. Carol pushed her hand into the ring. "Ow." She reversed her efforts. The ring released and arced through the air, ricocheting off Jack's wrist as he reached for it. It bounced off the floor with a *ping* and disappeared. Carol lifted her hands in helpless supplication while the groom and best man squatted to search.

Kim and Hank were in deep discussion, but all other eyes were glued on the wedding party. Mitch left Addie Jo on the floor. He moved about in the hopes of catching a glint of the ring.

Trudy said, "What's Addie-Jo got in her mouth?"

Chapter Fifty - Mitch

The wedding party rushed to the baby. Addie-Jo stuffed another flower petal into an already full mouth. Mitch swabbed her mouth with his finger, pulling out rose petals, but no ring. "Ow. She bit me."

Kim huffed. "Don't be a baby, Mitch, she doesn't have any teeth."

He held his index finger for her to see. "That's a tooth mark."

Kim explored Addie-Jo's gums with a finger. "Her first tooth and I didn't even know it." She snatched her daughter from him and stomped back to her pew.

Myron gave a triumphant cry and wielded the wedding ring high. A collective sigh arose throughout the church. Carol eased it on her little finger.

Lightening flashed. A boom shook the stained glass windows followed by a crack, a creak and a metallic crunch. A voice from the back of the church called out, "Man, I hope that wasn't the limo." The guests tittered again. With obvious disapproval Reverend White clapped his hands. Once again they found their places. When Carol scratched her thigh, Trudy rolled her eyes and Myron struggled so hard to keep his face neutral that Mitch stifled a laugh and prayed that nothing else would happen.

The communion chalice slipped from Carol's swollen fingers, but Jack caught it with only a few drops spilling onto the table. They smiled and knelt for the final blessing.

"Help Me" in black magic marker was written across the bottom of Jack's shoes. Mitch sank lower in the pew. He wished he hadn't marked them. Perhaps they weren't visible in the dusky room.

Swelling laughter dispelled that hope. Soon the entire church throbbed with it.

The minister intoned, "Everyone rise. Please welcome Mr. and Mrs. Bronner."

The organist pumped the recessional and guests broke into enthusiastic whistles, stomps, and applause, which almost covered the sound of shattering glass from some deep recess of the church.

Chapter Fifty-one – Carol

Carol took her place beside Jack in the reception line. She was relieved that with all that had gone wrong, a party spirit prevailed. No one seemed to care that they were damp and held hostage by the storm. If anything they hugged her harder and were more gracious. Guests lingered in the foyer or slipped into groups in the pews to socialize. Perhaps even Kim and Mitch had mended their quarrel. They stood in the receiving line next to each other, Mitch holding Addie-Jo.

"Carol, Jack," Trudy said. Carol tensed at the look on her friend's face. What now? She cringed at Trudy's whispered news.

Jack called for attention. Everyone quieted until only the constant hiss of the pouring rain was heard. "Folks, there's been a change of plans. Due to downed power lines the police have closed the roads in the downtown area where the reception is. The good news is the caterer is willing to come to us. So, Reverend White, if we could use the friendship hall in the basement, we'll be all set."

"Oh, dear," he replied. "That will never do. The basement is flooded and a window was knocked out."

Carol was suddenly aware of an intense itching along her waist. She wrung her hands as groans of dismay arose.

"Trudy said, "We can use Peter's office."

Peter shot Tracy a scalding glance, but Cynthia dug her elbow into his side. Her southern drawl lost none of its charm as she loudly announced, "What a wonderful idea. My husband, Peter Faulkinroy, of Faulkinroy Publicists is thrilled to host the reception."

Carol sucked in her breath and scratched her arm. Peter didn't look at her, but turned his charm on the group. "I checked my phone messages moments ago and the answering machine was on, so we'll have electricity."

A cheer of approval arose. Trudy gave directions. "You can't miss it. There's a huge banner with New Home of Faulkinroy Publicists on the building."

Peter said, "We are running a promotion with Hawaiian shirts, shorts, and muumuus. I'll gift them to anyone wanting dry clothes."

"Yahoo!" Mitch said. Addie-Jo squealed as he lifted her high overhead. Clapping drowned out the rain. The festive mood grew giddy.

Carol threaded her way through the crowed to Peter and hugged him, kissed his cheek, and whispered. "If I hadn't forgiven you before, I forgive you now."

Peter's handsome face clouded over, then the scowl smoothed away. "I shouldn't have left you like that. I didn't mean you any harm. I wanted to scare you. To punish you."

Cynthia beamed at her husband. "Peter is wonderfully generous. The therapist said we're making real progress. We plan to renew our vows on our next wedding anniversary."

Carol squeezed Cynthia. "I wish you all the best."

"You're the bride. That's my line," Cynthia drawled.

Carol congratulated Peter and gave him another hug and whispered, "Of course, what I said about pressing charges still stands."

The patter of rain ceased. A steady *peck, peck, peck* grew into a thunderous roar. Carol squeezed her eyes shut. It couldn't be. Myron pushed open the large arched door of the church. Jack gripped her hand as they peered at hail coating the concrete steps like non-pariels on a tiered cake. The warmth of Myron's hand covered most of her shoulder. "Congratulations. All you're missing is a volcanic eruption."

"Or an earthquake," Mitch added.

Carol swatted her new stepson. "Bite your tongue."

Trudy squeezed past Mitch and touched Carol's elbow, leaning close to her ear. "I'm going ahead with Peter and Cynthia to get everybody settled."

"Thanks, Trudy. What would I ever do without you?"

"Honestly, Carol. I can't imagine. Myron, would you like to ride over with me?"

Myron smiled. "Sure. This party needs all the help it can get."

Trudy batted her eyes at him, at least Carol thought she had. Then Trudy threaded her arm through Myron's and the two dashed into the hail and splashed through ankle-deep water to Peter's truck. Like a grand finale to a magic act, the hail ended and the clouds parted to expose a dazzlingly golden sun.

Carol led the cheer. She and Jack watched from the top of the church steps as guests streamed out of the building and waded to their cars. Many of the vehicles wouldn't start or stalled in the flooded street. People, who didn't even know each other, carpooled to Peter's office as if they had been friends for years.

Kim looked over the chaos and then up at the sky. "At least the rain stopped," she said without sounding too happy.

"I think the entire storm has passed," Carol replied.

An SUV halted in front of them and Mitch piled out the back. He ran up the steps. "Your ship awaits, milady." He scooped Kim and Addie-Jo into his arms and carried them to the waiting car. Mitch situated Kim with Jasmine's family. He started to close the door, leaned in, pulled out and leaned in again before finally shutting the door.

"The cargo is secure Captain," he called to Jasmine's dad.

Carol leaned against Jack. "I think he's enjoying this."

"He does seem to be in a particularly good mood," Jack replied.

Mitch slogged to them while the SUV wheeled onto the road. "Do you need a ride?"

"No. We're okay. The driver said a huge tree missed the limo and its engine started without trouble. We'll be right behind you," Jack said.

251

Carol pointed to a little old woman with a slight dowager's hump testing her way down the steps. "The minister has to stay and tend to the storm damage so the organist, Mrs. Eaton needs a ride."

"Done." Mitch introduced himself and lifted the tiny frame of the elderly organist into his arms to ford the floodwaters. As he passed, he winked at Carol. "Now, Mrs. Eaton, I'm holding on to you real tight, but I don't want you getting any ideas."

With Mrs. Eaton smiling widely from the passenger seat, Mitch powered the sedan to a crawl and the wake washed behind them, leaving the parking lot empty. Seconds later, their driver emerged from the side of the church. "I'm sorry. The engine died. I can't get it restarted."

"We're going to miss our own reception," Carol said.

They turned simultaneously as a deep voice said "I've got room in my truck."

Jack said, "You're Hank Barlow. Best tight end receiver the school ever had. Thanks for the offer. We appreciate it. Carol, I don't think you've met Hank, yet."

"I'm so glad you could make it after all, Hank." Hank frowned briefly and then broke into a smile Carol catalogued as cordial. She liked his firm handshake, but got the feeling she'd said something wrong. "It's nice to finally meet you."

"Yes, Ma'am."

They navigated streets littered with tree limbs and leaves, but no further obstacles barred the way. Carol pointed. "It's the gray building in the next block."

"They said to look for a sign. I don't see one," Hank said.

"The wind must have taken it. Oh, it's hanging funny. Look, they've left a parking space for us right in front."

Hank eased the vehicle to a stop. Beyond Myron and Trudy, who held the doors open, the lobby was filled with people in brightly colored Hawaiian shirts. Carol bubbled with happiness as Jack handed her out of the cab. She smoothed her hair and dress, brushed wrinkles from Jack's coat and straightened his tie. "You look very handsome, Jack."

"You are beautiful, Mrs. Bronner." He offered his arm.

"It was nice meeting you both. Congratulations," Hank said.

Carol looked into Hank's gray eyes. "Aren't you coming in?"

"No Ma'am. I'm not expected."

"You have to," Carol said.

"We insist," Jack said.

Something behind them caught and held Hank's attention. Carol turned to see Mitch helping Mrs. Eaton into the building. To the side stood Kim, her face flushed. With a determined nod he said, "Okay. Thanks."

"Good." Jack said. He applied a slight pressure to Carol's arm and led her across the sidewalk, Hank following. A tremendous ripping rent the air. Gallons of water smacked over them. Jack bellowed. Hank swore. Carol staggered and gasped. Tiny rivulets made their way down her back and between her breasts, her legs. "Trudy," Carol screamed at the same time Jack hollered, "Mitchell."

Myron yelled, "Look out."

Her head snapped as Hank jerked her and Jack backward. Peter's banner flopped in front of them its ropes lashing like whips about the sidewalk. Jack's embrace steadied her. Through wet clumps of hair, she peered at the guests staring back in stunned silence. Myron boomed with the voice of a circus ringmaster, "Ladies and Gentlemen, Mr. and Mrs. Jack Bronner."

Carol laughed and sobbed at the same time, a sense of hysteria tickling her brain. Everyone surged around them, talking at once.

Diners from a nearby restaurant poured onto the sidewalk to gape at the broken ropes, the ripped sign, and tell each other how they had seen the whole thing. A numbness took hold of Carol. Trudy and Kim each took an arm and led her into the building.

Chapter Fifty-two – Jack

Jack watched her go and wiped excess water from his eyes and face, suddenly aware of the heaviness of the sodden tuxedo. The usually unflappable Myron appeared shaken. "Are you okay, Jack?"

"I think this day is one for the records. I hope it's over."

Hank Barlow interjected. "What else could happen?"

Jack rubbed his sore neck. "I don't even care to think about it, but those tiki torches worry me."

Myron and Hank shouted, "Put out those tiki torches." They pushed through the throng to make sure it was done.

Jack followed slowly, feeling as if he'd swum the English Channel. In the foyer Mitchell held Addie-Jo. The child lunged at Jack and gave him a sloppy open-mouthed baby kiss.

"Thank you. Sweet Thing, that makes everything better. I'd take you, but Grampa Jack is all wet."

Mitchell thrust her at Jack, "a little damp won't hurt anything." Addie-Jo wrapped her arms around his neck and gave him a big squeeze.

"Uh-oh. We've done it, now." Jack pointed to where his wet burgundy tie had bled onto Addie-Jo's white dress.

Mitchell blew his breathe out. "Kim's going to kill me."

"Excuse me. I couldn't help but hear. Gentlemen, let me help." Cynthia Faulkinroy reached for the child. "I say we find the tiniest Hawaiian garb possible and accidentally lose the dress. Come on, little girl. I believe we have a mini muumuu for you. Now, you men better get yourselves changed. The party is waiting for the bride and groom. This will be our little secret."

They thanked her. Mitchell threw an arm around Jack's shoulders. "Come on Dad. Trudy saved a bright red shirt for you, unless you'd prefer to be truly Hawaiian with bare chest and grass skirt."

"No thanks. It'd probably catch on fire."

Mitchell grinned. "Or fall around your ankles during the wedding dance."

"That'd be about the only way left to shock this crowd."

The lovely Cynthia glanced over her shoulder and giggled. "You boys are so naughty."

Chapter Fifty-three – Carol

Upstairs, Carol's jangled nerves settled as the others fussed over her. Kim snugged her into a purple muumuu. Trudy brushed her hair straight back and held it in place with a crown made from a lei and a wire coat hanger Jasmine made. The two stepped back to survey their handiwork. "You look lovely."

"I feel funny."

"This whole day is funny. You couldn't make a movie about this, no one would believe it," Trudy said.

Jasmine pinning a flower behind her ear said, "I think it's romantic." Kim started it and pretty soon they were all giggling into their hands and hugging each other.

When Carol and Trudy emerged from Peter's office, a waiter paused to offer them hors d'oeuvres. Carol bit into the treat and whirled toward her best friend. "Why are they serving lobster?"

"It's another blessing. A party cancelled on the caterer so we got upgraded to crab balls, lobster tails, kiwi tropical salad – appropriate, I thought—and champagne."

"Trudy, I can't afford real champagne," Carol hissed. "I don't want champagne."

"No sweat. The caterer charged the other party full price for canceling at the last minute. The couple had a big brouhaha at the altar. At least that didn't happen to you. Plus a bunch of conventioneers stranded by the weather paid her double to serve your original menu to them. This is what Bert the chimney sweep would call a fortuitous circumstance. Look."

Carol surveyed the room of friends and family who stood about laughing, eating, and talking. It was all working out well, even if it didn't go according to plan, even if there weren't any tables or a wedding cake.

"Well, okay to everything but the champagne."

"I'll take care of it," Trudy said and glided away.

The orchestra moved from the overture of *South Pacific* to the opening chords of "Some Enchanted Evening." Jack waved and headed for her from across the room, but every few feet he was stopped and congratulated. Carol was about to go to him when the glow she felt suddenly faded. "Wait a minute. I don't know these people and where did the orchestra come from?"

Peter appeared at her side. "Several of the restaurant patrons came over to investigate the little incident outside and stayed. The orchestra was for the cancelled wedding. They helped the caterer and I paid them to stay and play."

"I'm so sorry, Peter. I had no idea this would get so out control."

"Well, I'm not sorry. I've made two business deals already."

Jack finally reached her and spoke pleasantly to Peter before sweeping Carol away. She threw her head back as Jack whirled her around the makeshift dance floor. "This is wonderful," she declared. "It's all so perfectly imperfect."

Chapter Fifty-four – Mitch

Mitch entered the office where Kim was changing Addie-Jo's diaper with Jasmine's help. He softly closed the door.

Jasmine said, "Hi, Mitch. Good to see you. I've missed you. Isn't this quite the wedding?"

"Yes, but my dad and Carol seem happy, despite the setbacks." He hugged Jasmine. "It's good to see you, too, Jazz. Um, Kim, I'd like to talk with you."

Kim's beautiful eyes met his and for the first time since Christmas, she didn't seem angry, only sad. "I got your cards and letters."

"I figured you did since they didn't come back."

Jasmine hefted Addie-Jo to her shoulder. "You two talk. I'll take her into the other room and put her to sleep." The door clicked shut.

"You kissed me in the SUV right in front of Jasmine and her family," Kim said.

"Twice and you didn't resist."

Mitch expected her to say she'd been shocked, instead she said, "Why?"

Mitch gathered Kim's hands in his. "I've missed you. I could hardly believe it when I saw you today. I realized how stupid I was to let this argument come between us. I should've kept calling you until you did talk to me or even flown home to get your attention. I'm sorry."

"I'm sorry, too." Her lips parted as if to say more, but she didn't.

Mitch kissed her and with only minor hesitation, she kissed back. It was sweeter than he could've imagined. "Kim, I've been attracted to you from the first. When I got to know you, I realized it wasn't infatuation. I loved you. You were hurting so badly, I didn't feel I should say anything. Then, after Christmas, you were mad at me all the time."

"I didn't want you to go away."

They kissed again. "Then why are you dating Hank?"

Kim looked as if she were going to cry. "He understands me."

"I lost someone, too. Not a spouse, but I grieved."

"He's seen things, lived through things in the war. He understands."

"God understands you better than I can, better than Hank, even. God will heal you, if you let him. I love you and you love me. You do love me, don't you, Kim?"

Kim nodded and Mitch kissed her again. "There's no rush. We can take it as you're comfortable. I believe in long engagements. Will you marry me?"

Kim shook her head. Frustration welled, but he waited as she floundered for the right words. "I can't. I've messed up, Mitch. I've been doing stuff."

"Doing stuff? You mean you have a drug habit?"

"No. No. I mean with Hank."

"Hank doesn't know God. Where can your relationship with him go?"

"It's complicated." Tears splashed out of her closed eyelids as she whispered. "I've messed up everything. I'm sorry."

"Well, Kim, is your good friend Mitch congratulating us?" They turned toward the deep voice. Hank stood unsteadily inside the door. He spread his legs to gain firmer footing and raised a champagne bottle in the air.

Kim caught her breath. "What?"

"I found the pregnancy test in the trash when I was picking up after that pest of a raccoon you were feeding in the spring."

From the desperation on Kim's face, Mitch had no choice but to believe it was true. He closed his eyes, "I see." He released her and shuffled toward the door, stopping in front of his adversary. "Do you love her, Hank?"

"I'm here, aren't I? I drove all the way here when she didn't even invite me. Yes, I love her."

Mitch punched him in the stomach. Hank doubled over, clutching his gut. The bottle thumped to the carpet and rocked on its bottom. Mitch bent over Hank. He hissed as he pointed at Kim. "It's not love when you take advantage."

Kim wailed. Her hands covered her nose and mouth. Her eyes pleaded with him as he backed out the door.

Chapter Fifty-five — Hank

Hank straightened with a grunt. He went to Kim. She shook off his touch. He tried again. She turned away, sobbing harder. Not knowing what else to do, Hank left and found his way through the party to a quiet spot. He slid onto the floor. Nearby the orchestra players were taking a break. One of them indicated the bottle Hank carried and asked, "You celebrating all on your own?"

"Should be, but I'm not. It's a crying shame." Hank rested the bottle on one knee and hung his head. The man pulled a fifth of whiskey from an inner pocket. He broke the seal and offered it. "Leave the bubbly to the partygoers. Here's a drink to mourn a crying shame."

"No thanks, that stuff is mean."

"Life can be mean."

"Well, now, if that ain't a fact." Hank accepted the bottle and belted back a burning swig.

***

Hank groped for the steering wheel and pulled himself upright. His head contained a huge clapping gong and an entire Marine brass section blowing for all they were worth. He pressed his temples, but the noise didn't stop.

Outside his truck the bright summer morning was filled with balloons, flying flags, hundreds of people, and numerous vehicles blocking his way out of the parking lot. A fire truck and a police car passed with lights flashing and sirens blaring. A band marched by playing a jazzy version of "Layla". Everywhere he looked Hoosiers were turning their Fourth of July into serious fun.

He unlocked and pushed open the door. Hot, rank air rushed out of the cab. The foul taste of whiskey was still on his parched tongue. It was revolting mixed with the super sweet smell of cotton candy from a nearby vendor.

One leg was tingling and uncooperative from his cramped sleeping position, he stood, staggered and hopped, hanging on to the door for balance. Nearby, a voice of thunder said, "Well, Buddy, I'm glad you're alive. I've been rapping for five minutes trying to rouse you. A couple more hours in this heat and you'd probably be dead."

"That'd be an improvement," Hank said thickly. He looked up into the face of a police officer. "Oh, uh, thanks for waking me, officer. I drove straight through from Montana yesterday. I'm wiped."

"Right. Can I see some identification?"

Hank fumbled for his billfold. The officer looked it over and said, "I'm going to have to take you in for public intoxication."

Hank sighed. The sounds of the marching band faded, replaced by a calliope. Several clowns performed antics and the crowd laughed. Feeling returned to his leg and Hank was able to stand without pain. "I'm not intoxicated. I'm hung over. And I was in my private vehicle all night, not in public."

"Keep talking. I'm adding loitering and trespassing to the list. This is a restricted parking zone. No overnight vehicles."

Worry filled Hank. "Come on."

"Life is mean."

"Yeah," Hank groaned. "That's what started this whole thing." Where was Kim?

"Hands behind your back, Buddy."

A soft southern drawl said, "Officer, this man was a guest at a wedding reception last night that my husband and I hosted. He had permission to be in our parking lot."

Hank and the officer both looked over at the beautiful blonde with not a hair out of place. Her engaging smile was emphasized with pink lipstick. She was dressed in white and despite the heat looked as cool and refreshing as a Popsicle. She offered her driver's license. "I'm Cynthia Faulkinroy. I apologize for my woeful neglect of one of our guests. I can assure you, he didn't drink and drive. We'd have been back sooner, but we were stuck in traffic. My husband is waiting in the car a few blocks away. We'll be back for the truck after the parade."

"Okay, Mrs. Faulkinroy," the policeman said, handing back her license. "May I suggest that in the future you keep your guests in a hotel?"

"Thank you, officer," she said sweetly. "We'll certainly do that."

Hank grabbed an overnight bag from the truck. Cynthia led him away. "Thanks, Ma'am."

"Don't mention it. The cleaning ladies called this morning to tell us you were here. We thought we'd better check on you. Where can we take you?"

"Do you know where Kim Macomb is staying?"

"I believe she is at her mother's house. Peter and I can drop you there. If you need a ride back here to get your truck, give us a call." She wrote a number on a piece of paper and handed it to him. "And you might make cleaning up a priority. No girl wants to receive a suitor in your condition."

The nod he gave felt like someone slapped the back of his head with a blackjack. He blinked. "Yes, ma'am."

Kim wasn't thrilled to see him, but she let him into the house and he supposed he should be grateful for that much. He took Cynthia's advice and felt much better after he showered and shaved. He poured himself a cup of coffee and gulped half of it down before following Addie-Jo's screams and finding both his girls in a bedroom.

Kim looked strained and exhausted, her pretty face lined and hard. Gently he brushed a kiss on her forehead and took the baby. In a few minutes the child quieted and fell asleep with catching sobs and tiny hiccups.

"I'm a terrible mother."

"You're a good mother. Yesterday was a big day. She's overexcited, that's all. By this afternoon or tonight at the latest, she'll be her regular sunny self." He laid Addie-Jo in a portable crib.

"I hate the thought of flying with her alone."

"Cancel your flight and drive home with me."

"How can you stand me, Hank?"

"You're my girl, Kim. You're both my girls." He placed his palm on Kim's belly. "Maybe three girls. I'm outnumbered and like it."

She nodded with resignation. He bit back any words that asked for a commitment. Instead he guided her into another bedroom, covered her up and watched over her as she soundlessly cried herself to sleep. She was at war. He was familiar with internal battles. Maybe he'd lost the skirmish, but he was going to win the war. He was going to win the fight for her.

Chapter Fifty-six – Kim

Kim awoke rested and comfy as the first fingers of morning poked through the curtains of her little apartment. She stretched to every corner of the bed. Alone. She sighed into the peacefulness and checked the crib. Empty. She peered into the living room. Hank sprawled on the couch with Addie-Jo asleep on his chest. It was a tender picture.

She would've expected someone with Hank's disadvantaged background to be harsh and rough. He wasn't. He was kind and patient. If Brenda couldn't watch Addie-Jo, he did. Here in the pre-dawn hours he'd again care for the child so Kim could sleep and sleep and sleep.

She was grateful and at the same time relieved that his job kept him out of the apartment most evenings. She strained against her dependence on him as the days passed in a blur of child care, work, and the physical demands of her changing body.

Secretly, desperately, she wished the problem to be purged from her. She buried this last straw of faithlessness deep, hoping Hank couldn't read her mind. Most of the time, she ignored the problem and simply clung to the shipwreck of her life, waiting to be rescued. Not dealing with it worked pretty well, except on the drives to Bozeman when the truth nagged for attention.

After she'd been seen with Hank in Bozeman, she'd admitted to the doctor that she'd been dating and Hank often cared for Addie-Jo. It'd been hard, but starting over with another doctor would've been worse. She had to keep going for Addie-Jo's sake, as long as she could.

How long could she hide this pregnancy? How long would the Mission Council allow her to see Dr. Bradley? When would the

Mission Council withdraw funds? When she needed them most would they toss her out? Weren't her husband, her health, and her fatherless child sufficient sacrifices? These thoughts skipped like stones across the surface before sinking into the hopeless quagmire of her situation. She sighed again more heavily. Why can't I love him? Despite all his efforts, Hank was not Mitch.

Kim missed Mitch terribly. No one talked about him and she refused to ask. There were no more long letters from Mitch and she didn't often let herself read the old ones hidden in her underwear drawer. Now that he knew about her, he didn't want her anymore. She had to let him go. She should quit driving by the college after counseling sessions, stop eating where they'd eaten, and stop thinking about him and be thankful Hank hadn't left her too. Maybe they'd all be better off if she left them, but now there was a fourth person to think about. Life kept getting more complicated.

Kim rose and pulled on jeans and a faded shirt and slipped into cowboy boots.

Hank's voice was gruff with sleep. He smiled up at her, "Morning. Where're you headed?"

"Dr. Mullins let me take a few more hours cleaning the pens and stables and feeding the animals on Sundays. I can take Addie-Jo with me."

"She's sleeping. No need to disturb her."

"You don't mind?"

"We're fine. You don't have to do this, Kim. I make enough money to care for all of us."

"Don't start, Hank. I don't want to argue today."

Hank's face tightened then he forced a smile. He grabbed her hand as she headed for the door. "Got a kiss for me?"

How sweet it'd be to be part of the family picture Hank and Addie-Jo made. Life had fallen into a routine that was comfortable even if it wasn't the life she wanted. She should make an effort. Kim bent and swept his lips with her own. At the door she put on her jacket and dug keys out of the pocket. She smiled. "Bye and thanks for taking care of Addie-Jo."

Chapter Fifty-seven - Hank

Hank stared at the closed door and wished he could open Kim like a surgeon doing a heart transplant and remove all the pain and grief. She was losing ground, the pregnancy twisting the good thing they'd had. At least, he'd thought they'd had the start of a good thing until he'd seen her with Mitch. This was a rabbit trail with no favorable end and Hank left off from following it.

It stung to know he didn't measure up no matter how good he was to her. He fended off another onslaught of bleak thoughts. It was a full-time job staying positive when Kim's dark moods oozed into every corner of their life.

He turned on the radio. The channel was set to golden oldies where The Carpenters sang, "rainy days and Mondays always get me down—"

"—and Sundays," Hank said. He silenced the depressing song with a snap of his wrist.

Addie-Jo stirred, her mouth curving happily. Hank stroked the dark fluff of hair. "You deserve better than this. Don't worry. Your momma is going to get better. She's fighting awfully hard right now. It's time we made a tactical change. We need help."

An hour later, Hank lifted Addie-Jo from the car seat and carried her into the church. Hank intended to slip unseen into the back pew while the singing was in full force, but he'd misjudged the timing. People were walking about shaking hands, being social.

Maggie said, "It's great to see you, Hank Barlow. Where's Kim?"

"She had to work."

"Here, I'll take Addie-Jo to the nursery." Maggie took the baby and walked down a hallway while other people pressed in to welcome him. When everyone settled into seats, he sank into the last row, wiped his brow with a crisp handkerchief, and muttered, "So much for anonymity."

Cyrus Higgins, a beefy Afro-American Hank knew for a fact had done time for armed robbery strode to a tall stool in the middle of the stage with his guitar and plucked a tune. A young, very petite blonde held the microphone. She gave Cyrus a nervous nod. Cyrus strummed, stopped. Cyrus reached over and took the microphone.

"You all know me and you know my history. This song is special because I was in prison. Worse, I was in a spiritual prison of my own sinful making. Through the grace of God I've been set free. I was an angry, bitter man and I did some evil things. That ugliness is behind me, replaced with hope and peace. Jessie, tell them what this song means to you."

Jessie's pretty face flushed bright red. She looked as if she wished she were anywhere than where she was. Her hands trembled as she took the microphone. She stammered. "I've been a part of this church since I was born. I've won Bible memory contests and been baptized and went to summer camps. I thought I was pretty well set with God. Then, Jesus showed me I was doing it all to look good, not because I loved Him. He set me free from my self-centeredness. I'm forgiven and whole." Cyrus nodded. He strummed and Jessie's shyness disappeared as they sang "He Set Me Free."

Hank slipped from the pew and out the sanctuary door, but their stories and the song went with him.

The next Sunday he waited until the singing was finished before finding a place in the last pew. The minister was speaking about the Apostle Peter's denial of Jesus and later acceptance by the resurrected Christ.

Hank understood why Kim struggled so hard with her own failings and fears. She was caught smack between the cock's crow and the resurrected Jesus. Kim was a friend of God who struggled. She needed this Jesus, who would take her back in the same way he had Peter, Jessie, and Cyrus.

It was different for Hank. He'd always fallen short. It was one of the things that had driven him, a poor boy from the bad side of town, to believe the Army slogan "Be all you can be". Two tours of duty and the body count in a bloody foreign war had crushed the boyhood dreams of heroism. Only a drinking problem and a trail of regrets remained. The Army had been a poor substitute for the family life he'd imagined he'd have one day, and an even poorer substitute for God. He was a nothing who had nothing, not even God.

Bronner was right. He couldn't help Kim. Religion was for people like Peter the Apostle, like Kim and Cyrus who came from good church families, messed up for a while, and went back to God. No wonder Kim was cranky. She wanted to go back and felt stuck on the wrong side of the fence with him.

"Hank."

Surprised, Hank noticed the church had emptied. "Hey, Cyrus, how's it going, man?"

"Good. I got a job wrangling for the McCleary's. The pay's pretty good, and I get to be outside. I love those wide, open spaces. How're you doing, Hank?"

"I'm still over at the Lone Star. I'm thinking about finding something more respectable. Do you know anyone who is hiring?"

Cyrus tapped his temple. "I've got an idea which might interest you. You want to get a bite to eat and we'll discuss it?"

Hank suspected Cyrus wanted to talk about God and edged toward the door. He threw a thumb toward it. "I've got to get Addie-Jo from the nursery. Kim's waiting for me at the clinic."

"We'll do it another time."

Driving to get Kim, Hank decided he wouldn't attend any more services. He'd be extra kind and maybe Kim would forget all that God stuff. This was his little family. He wasn't going to give them up.

The following Saturday, Hank stepped out of the convenience store as an old blue truck stopped at the fuel pumps. He pocketed his wallet and sauntered over. The smell of petrol wafted through the hot air when Myron lifted the latch on the pump.

"Well, if it isn't Mr. and Mrs. Bronner. Welcome home. How was the trip?"

"Hi Hank. It's was great," Jack said.

Carol stretched her arms out and gave an intentional shiver to convey her enthusiasm. "Greece was wonderful. Where are the girls?"

"Kim's at work and Addie-Jo spent the night with my sister, Brenda. I was headed over there to get her. Kim didn't mention you'd be in today."

"She doesn't know we're back early," Carol said. "I can't wait to see them."

"Kim has a meeting with Marta after work and won't be home until late. Why don't you come to lunch at my place tomorrow after church? I've got some prime steaks."

"Sounds wonderful," Carol said and Jack nodded approval.

"Myron, you're welcome to come, too," Hank said.

"Thanks, no. I'm running up to the airport tomorrow to get Trudy. We'll get back too late to join you." He hung up the nozzle and capped the tank. After a few more exchanges the trio piled into the vehicle.

"Until tomorrow," Hank called watching dry dirt along the road's edge swirl behind the truck. He wasn't sure Kim would be happy with the plans. Better to surprise her than give her time to worry about the shock in store for Jack and Carol.

At church the next morning the pastor spoke of how Saul the Christian persecutor became Paul the Apostle after meeting the resurrected Christ on the Damascus road. Hank summed up the sermon as Pompous Do-gooder Becomes Humble Do-gooder and Hank didn't fit either category. Why did he keep coming back to hear how he'd never measure up?

Hank slipped out while the Bronners were greeting friends and drove to the animal clinic. Kim exited the office and waved. Her face was free of tension and her posture relaxed. Caring for the animals was good for her. He returned the gesture and chuckled. She looked like a cowgirl doll with dark hair tousled into a ponytail and a red calico dress brushing the tops of her boots.

Kim slung her purse over her shoulder, swiveling to lock the office door. The dress caught under the purse and defined the baby belly she still tried to hide as if their relationship were sordid. She climbed in and tickled Addie-Jo, "Momma's here. I've got your bug." Addie-Jo giggled and squirmed and put a finger out to tickle Kim back.

"You're beautiful," Hank said.

"Oh, yeah. I smell like horse and Mrs. McPherson's Pomeranian vomited on me."

"I didn't notice. I only saw you smiling. Oh, by the way, we're not going to Brenda's today. I've got dinner ready at my house–grilled steaks and potatoes."

"Great. I'm starved." Kim chattered about the particulars of her morning.

Hank let out his breath slowly. So far, so good. As they parked in front of his house, Jack and Carol pulled in behind them. "Kim, I've got a surprise. Your Mom is coming to dinner."

She looked where he pointed, squealed and pushed open the door so fast he didn't have time to blink. She sprinted forward and grabbed her mother in a fierce bear hug. "Mom, I missed you so much."

Carol wrapped arms around her daughter and squeezed. Astonishment crossed Carol's face. Hank winced and rubbed his chin and dug in his breast pocket for a new toothpick. Hank quickly moved toward them with Addie-Jo. Carol latched hold and swung her around. The child squealed. Without warning, Addie-Jo dove towards her mother. Laughing, Kim caught the baby. When she saw Jack staring at her belly, the happy face turned into a scowl. "Hank, how could you do this do me? I'm filthy and look awful. You should've warned me. I'm going in to shower." She charged up the concrete sidewalk into the house.

This time Hank stared at the distant mountain not wanting to meet their gaze. "That went better than I imagined. Come on in. I'll get the steaks started."

Chapter Fifty-eight – Carol

Hank's house was unfussy and comfortable, but Carol was far more interested in her daughter than the decor. "Grampa Jack, can you take Addie-Jo? I'll visit with Kim."

Hank said, "There's a bag of maternity clothes on the bed my sister sent. Kim can wear something out of there."

Carol nodded and wandered in the direction he'd indicated. She found the door of the bathroom situated at the end of the hall between two bedrooms. She entered the bedroom on the right where a paper grocery sack sat on the inspection-ready bed. The room, in rusts and browns was clean and neat with the lived-in feeling that happens when a space fits the personality of its creator.

One by one, she lifted maternity clothes out of the sack. Each was pretty and clean. She chose a blue cotton dress with capped sleeves and a square yoke and knocked at the bathroom door. "Kim, it's Mom. May I come in?"

"No! Uh, don't bother. I'm almost done. I'm sorry I was so filthy. I've been cleaning the stalls and feeding the animals. I don't have anything here to wear so I'll have to borrow one of Hank's shirts. Maybe you can grab me one from his closet. Men. They don't think of these things."

"Hank did. Here's a dress his sister sent for you. It's a little wrinkled, but I'd love you no matter what. I'll lay it on the counter."

"Oh. Okay. Thanks." The sound of running water stopped and Kim peeked around the curtain. Carol extended a towel, which Kim accepted with one hand from her hiding place.

"How far along are you, Kim?"

"Dr. Bradley says I'm coming along pretty well in the sessions. Would you mind waiting outside for me. It's such a small bathroom."

"Sure. No problem." Carol closed the door gently and stood in the hall, thinking. From there she heard Hank ask, "Do you want a beer, Jack?"

Chapter Fifty-nine – Hank

Hank winced at his mistake and quickly added, "Uh, probably not." He handed Jack a cola instead. Jack thanked him and he led the way into the yard, with its unobstructed view of the mountains, one of the reasons he'd bought this particular house. A stone fence enclosed a grassy area, a shade tree, and a table covered with a cheap plastic print that he'd set with dinner plates, turned upside down to keep from getting dirty. He pointed to a baby seat attached to table. "You can put Addie-Jo there, if you want."

"I prefer holding her a bit." Jack settled onto the long bench at the table and bounced her on his knee. "This is a nice little house you have here."

Hank plucked potatoes out of the glowing coals and tossed them into a lidded crockery bowl to keep warm. He revived the fire, laid the steaks on the grill. "I bought it when I came back from service. I hoped to start a family someday."

"And now you have."

Hank paused and looked at the older man. "It's not quite the way I imagined it."

"I suppose not."

Carol came out the back door. Kim followed, her thick, damp hair hanging loose. She looked almost like a teenager in a blousy, blue dress. Her eyes were red-rimmed, but otherwise calm.

"Great timing. The steaks are medium rare. Except for Kim's. She likes hers well done ever since she—" Hank broke off at the ugly look Kim shot him.

Carol pretended not to notice. They settled around the table and waited awkwardly. Hank said, "Um, Jack, you want to say something over the food?"

"I'd be honored. God, thank you for bringing us home safely, caring for our loved ones, and also for this food Hank's prepared. Give us grateful hearts. Amen."

Hank echoed Carol's Amen, but Kim looked like a wary dog ready to snarl. She shook herself, reached for the pickles and asked about the trip. Tension around the table eased as she got caught up in vacation tales.

Afterward, Carol cradled Addie-Jo in her arms. "I missed her so much. She's gotten so big."

Kim stirred a packet of sugar into a glass of iced tea. "Is that why you're home early?"

Jack chuckled. He popped open another can of pop. "Nah, your mom felt an urgent need to be back here. She said you needed her. I'll give more credence to her intuitions from now on."

"You could've called."

"And you'd have said everything was fine and we'd have still come home early," Jack swigged the pop.

"Well, I am fine."

Hank coughed. "No, you're not, Kim. This pregnancy has hit you hard."

Kim caught her breath. She glared as if he'd used foul language in front of her mother. "Shut up."

Hank glared back. "Come on, Kim. Everybody in Free Dance can see you're pregnant. You're the only one pretending it isn't so."

"Liar." Kim threw her tea and caught him full in the face. He swore and jumped to his feet. Jack and Carol looked stunned.

Kim's eyes were wild. Wailing, she rushed into the house. The screen door slapped shut. Clattering rolled from the kitchen.

Hank dropped his head, lifted it and hollered. "You can't take my truck. I've got the keys."

Kim shrieked. An inside door slammed. Silence.

Hank wiped his face and clothes with his hands. "I don't know what to do anymore. Everything sets her off."

Carol placed her granddaughter in Jack's arms. "She was pretty emotional when she was pregnant with Addie-Jo, too. Don't take it personally."

"My sister said the same thing, but I think it's more than that."

"I'll see if I can calm her."

Hank tugged his shirt off and used the hose to rinse the sugary fluid from his head and torso and shirt while he composed himself. The valve squealed as he closed the flow and straightened.

Jack was watching. "Are you planning to marry her?"

"Kim won't discuss it."

"Yet she stays with you. She must love you."

Hank wrung the shirt more tightly than necessary. "No. She needs me to help with Addie-Jo. She won't quit work and let me support her. When she isn't working she's sleeping or crying."

Jack said, "What're you going to do?"

That was the question that had dogged the chaos of his entire life. Hank shrugged. "Play the hand 'til all the cards are on the table." He sat heavily next to Jack and leaned against the table. The clouds cast shadows on the mountains. A few bees found the remains of dinner, but he didn't rise to clear the dishes. At least Jack wasn't offering useless platitudes. It lessened the embarrassment.

"It was a pleasant surprise to see you in church, Hank. When did you start going?"

"A few weeks ago. I went looking for answers to our problem, but I've learned it's no use."

"Why? Don't you believe in God?"

"Oh, I believe there's a God. I believe he takes good people to heaven. The pastor preached on Peter, and Paul, and those two brothers who were fighting over who was the most important. I'll never be like any of them. I was raised all wrong. We never went to church."

"Christ came to save whoever believes in him, not just church people. Jesus spent a lot of time with outcasts and sinners."

"I didn't hear that."

"There was a woman caught in adultery, and another who'd had several husbands and was living with another man, also thieves, murderers, and even people who were hated by the Jews such as Samaritans and tax collectors."

Hank pushed hope down. There had to be a catch. "Don't I have to do something? You church people are always doing good."

"To show God's love not to buy our way to heaven. The most religious person on earth couldn't do enough, so Jesus did on the cross what we couldn't do for ourselves. He made peace between us and God for anyone who accepts him."

"It seems too easy," Hank said, still waiting for the catch.

"It cost Jesus everything. God knew we couldn't do it our own. God is holy and just, but God's love is also most gentle. Whenever we ask his forgiveness, he extends it. Even believers often fail. When we do, we can ask forgiveness and he helps us start over again."

Hank rubbed his chin and studied the path of a bird as it flew out of the tree. "Kim knows this?"

"Yes."

"Then why did she come to me instead of God?"

Jack squeezed the aluminum pop can until it crinkled flat. "I don't know."

Hank moved the toothpick from one side of his mouth to the other and gazed into the distance. How could he help the woman he loved if she ignored the answer to the problem?

Chapter Sixty – Carol

Carol rapped on the bedroom door then entered without waiting for a reply. Kim stood sideways in front of a full-length mirror. Her left hand resting on top of her bulging baby bump, her right hand held the fabric tight beneath the bump. Her eyes were anguished. "I'm going to have another baby. What am I going to do? I can't even handle Addie-Jo. I'm falling apart."

Carol sat on the bed and pulled Kim to her. She nestled her daughter's head onto her shoulder as they used to do back home in Indiana. She stroked Kim's hair. "It feels like it, honey, but you're not. It's what is. You'll handle it, with God's help."

Kim stiffened. "Like he "helped" me with Kurt?"

"Kim, sweetie, you have to let go of Kurt. What you had was good, but it's over. Your life is different. You have to live it where you are today."

"You don't understand."

"No? Then tell me."

Kim flounced off the bed and held the door open. "I've got to clear the dishes. It's the least I can do for Hank after he did the cooking. I'm glad you and Jack had a nice time. I'm glad you're home. I'll come by and see you this week."

"I guess that's good-bye and good-night." Carol rose from the bed and touched her daughter's arm. She went through the kitchen into the yard where the guys were deep in discussion. "Hank, thanks for lunch. It was delicious. Jack, it's time we go."

Jack's eyebrows shot toward his hairline, but Hank nodded with resigned understanding. "Glad to have you here. I enjoyed talking with you, Jack."

They each kissed the baby good-bye and Jack handed her to Hank. Stiff as a statue, Kim watched from the screen door as they drove away.

Carol shared the conversation she'd had with Kim, and Jack highlighted the theological discussion with Hank. She said, "I'm as sympathetic for Hank as I'm empathetic with my daughter's grief. I've never seen her act like that. Until Kim shares and releases the pain, the situation will only get worse."

"I know. It doesn't look good," Jack said.

At the ranch, Carol settled in a rocker on the porch in the thickening darkness. Twin lights bobbed up the lane. Myron bringing Trudy. She couldn't wait to see her friend and talk over the fiasco with Kim.

The car halted and Trudy forged from the vehicle and up the steps with open arms. "Carol. How was everything? I want to hear all the details. Was Greece the best?"

"Fantastic. Let's go in the house. I need to talk with you about Kim before the guys get back. Myron, Jack's in the workshop."

Without a word, Myron headed toward the outbuildings with his customary ambling gait.

Carol opened the screen door and let her friend enter first. "I'm so glad you're here. However did you know we'd be coming home today?"

Trudy gave her a look Carol couldn't interpret. "Piece of cake. You know I have impeccable timing."

Chapter Sixty-one - Kim

Days later Kim extricated herself from her car and traipsed to the barn. She cleaned cages and gave fresh food and water to each animal. Wet with sweat, curls formed at her nape, along her forehead and ears as she mucked out the stable. She brushed the two horses and for a little while was too busy to gnaw on her troubles. She finished and stood back.

Each night that week after work she'd fallen on the couch in a daze, relieved that more and more Addie-Jo preferred Hank. It felt wrong to give up, but she had no energy for outrage. She was worthless. They'd all be better off without her.

Kim put the brushes away. The sweet grassy smell of the bales mingled with dust and horse odor. Mewling came from a corner of the barn where straw was stacked as high as her head. Kim climbed behind the bales and squatted to peer into the shadowy corner of a crate. Two squirming wet balls were near a calico cat struggling to birth another.

"You're in trouble, poor thing. Dr. Mullins is away, but I'll help you," Kim reached into the crate. The momma cat snarled and slashed her. "Ow." Kim sucked her fingers and sat on her haunches.

The cat panted, labored, weakened, lie still. Kim scooped up the cat. She shrieked as claws slashed her face and arms and ripped the dress. Kim held tightly, but the mama didn't relent. Kim returned her to the box. When the mama and kittens died, hopeless helplessness made her ache. With a dirty, bloody hand Kim slicked back flyaway hair tickling her cheeks and whispered. "If only you'd let me help."

If only you'd let me help. The voice filled her heart. The longing behind those words were underscored with such deep love, that tears came. Every way that she'd ignored God since leaving Zaire flooded back. She'd been too self-absorbed, too angry with him for taking Kurt to see his hand reaching out to her through the people around her. Look where that had gotten her. She scratched and bit everyone who came close, everyone who loved her. She put her head in her hands and wept. "God? I'm sorry. I'm dying here without you. Help me."

Love and peace, a sense of being forgiven infused her.

"Thank you, Jesus. I'll never turn away again." Kim wiped tears of joy, not caring that she was streaking mud. "I have to tell somebody." She gathered up the still-warm bodies of the felines and scrambled over the bales. She stuffed an empty bucket with straw and gently placed them in it. She'd bury them later. Now, she had to go. She had to tell somebody. She had to tell everybody what God had done for her.

Kim burst through the sanctuary doors, and focused on the stoop-shouldered reverend in the midst of his sermon. She stopped, suddenly shy. Pastor Swanson Frazier halted mid-sentence. His gentle eyes searched hers. He stepped from the pulpit and extended his hands. Kim straightened with determination. The old rubber stable boots flopped and squeaked with each step. A buzz of whispering followed her. She grasped his hands like a lifeline. He lowered his head and listened as she whispered. He said, "You don't have to do it this way, Kim."

Aloud she replied, "Yes, I do. I need to tell all of you and I only have courage to say it once. I want to be clear what God has done."

He helped her mount the steps then moved to one side of the platform. All eyes were on her. She bit her lip and brushed at her filthy, ripped dress. She squared her shoulders, licked her lips. "Most of you know me even though I've only been here a year. I came after I lost my husband on the mission field. Many bad things happened to me there." Her voice cracked. She swallowed. "You went out of your way to make me feel at home, like family. Thank you."

A few nodded. Others spoke encouragingly. Kim chewed her lip to maintain composure and held up a palm to quiet them. "I clean the cages and stalls on Sundays for Dr. Mullins. Today I tried to help a momma cat with a difficult birth. She wouldn't let me." Kim pointed at the bright red scratches blazing across her hands and cheek and held her sullied dress out as if to curtsy. "The kitties and the momma died. I was so sad. Then, I realized God was sad too. I needed his help, but I've been fighting him just like that momma cat fought me."

A sob escaped. Kim pursed her lips and swallowed hard. She blinked several times. "You see, I was so angry with God I refused his comfort and looked for it where I had no business looking." Her voice failed. After several tries, she turned sideways and displayed the fullness of her belly. "Today I asked him and God forgave me. I beg your forgiveness, too." Tears streamed unrestrained.

The big black man named Cyrus slipped behind her and picked up a guitar. A very beautiful blonde Kim knew as Jessie gave her a hug before joining Cyrus. Humming as he strummed, Jessie broke into song. "What can take away my sins? Nothing but the blood of Jesus..."

Pastor Frazier helped Kim step down. As she retraced steps down the aisle, hands reached out to pat her, voices spoke kind words. Most, but not all of the faces were sympathetic. Kim looked past a grim-faced woman to Jack's encouraging smile. Tearfully, her mother wrapped her close. A man rose to his full height and sidled into the aisle.

"Hank? What're you doing here?"

"Learning more about our Savior."

Kim leaned into the security of his protective arms. She'd never, ever forget his support in this most humbling moment of her life.

"Come on, Kim, I'll take you home."

The next day, Kim walked through the office door, circled the sunny room a few times without the usual conversational exchange with Dr. Bradley. She flitted to the couch and alighted on the very edge.

Dr. Bradley's pretty face was interested, her eyes alert. She leaned forward as if knowing the moment she'd been prodding toward all these months was about to be revealed.

Kim expelled the long deep breath she'd been holding for what felt like years. "I got right with God."

"Good. That's the most important thing. He's here with you now to help you. He was there during your ordeal, too."

Kim locked eyes with Dr. Bradley. "I'm pregnant again."

"Yes. About six months along, I'd say."

Hank was right. Everybody knew. "I'm not married."

Dr. Bradley nodded and sat back, unruffled and non-judgmental.

Kim rocked back and forth in short, jerky movements. She forced the words through tight lips knotted as if to keep the words from spilling out. "Soon after he killed the men in the jeep, the real Kurt completely disappeared. I was pregnant with Addie-Jo and we both would've died if Nsia hadn't brought food and water whenever she could sneak in. Then the rebels came."

Kim bowed her head. Her hair fell forward covering her face. Suddenly she could bear it no longer. She lifted her head with obstinate daring. Her cheeks felt on fire. Fiercely she whispered, "I saw what they did to him with their bullets and machetes. I cheered them on. I laughed out loud. I'd have done what they did, if they'd given me the chance. Once he'd been my world, but I hated him. He'd hurt me and I wanted him to pay."

Chapter Sixty-two - Kim

With her dark thoughts in the light, Kim felt a thousand pounds lighter. Having asked for forgiveness, she could again focus outward. As the days passed, she noticed others and reached out to them. They reached back with many acts of kindness, accepting her. They accepted Hank too, who was around as much as she'd allow.

The night of the annual fall dance, Kim lost count of how many people patted her big belly while recalling the previous year's delivery and asking if birthing classes followed line-dancing. She laughed good-naturedly.

October passed on a turtle's back, although each day raced past like a hare, ending almost before it began filled with work, home, Addie-Jo, as well as lessons and activities prescribed by Dr. Bradley as a Biblical guide to healthy recovery. She missed Hank's comforting presence at night. While Mitch was lost to her, Hank still wanted her, still waited for her to say they could be a family. She might have given in, but Addie-Jo was sleeping most nights, which meant she slept too. She wished she could store sleep like a rechargeable battery against the time the new baby would demand her attention.

Kim held the apartment door open. Carol said, "I don't know when I've been in such good shape, between carrying Addie-Jo and going up these stairs. I'm praying you don't birth on them some snowy night."

"I'm not ready to move," Kim replied, "and I don't want to live at the ranch."

Carol gave a little shrug. She placed a favorite stuffed toy on the floor by Addie-Jo. "Where are you going to put the baby?"

"The new baby will take the crib and Addie-Jo will sleep with me." Kim poured hot water in two cups for tea and set the pot on the stove. "I'll grant this baby elephant drains me and I have to rest midway up and practically take oxygen but compared to last time, mother, I'm as light as air."

Carol dunked the teabag up and down in the cup. "I've noticed. Less mood swings, too."

"Whenever the past pesters me, I stop to see if I'm trying to do things in my own strength, nurturing resentments, or letting Satan talk me into accepting guilt and shame Jesus already washed from me."

"I'm proud of you Kim. You're really coming through it all."

Kim spooned sugar into her tea. "I'll always have to work at it day by day. Doctor Bradley says if I reach the point I think I can handle it instead of trusting God, I'll relapse."

"Same as everyone else on the planet. How long will you keep seeing her?"

"The Mission Council will pay for visits through the end of the year. I may keep going. We'll see. Who knows what will happen after this baby is born?"

"Right, Kim. Only God."

Mitch's face came to mind, tugging at her heart. Kim took a sip. "Right, Mom. Only God."

***

Kim loved Andrew Barlow Macomb without reservation. He was a big boy with dark fuzz, pudgy cheeks, and a strong grip. His daddy was thrilled beyond measure. It pleased and amused her how Hank hung around her hospital room as any proud papa, boasting about his boy. She was wrong to refuse to marry him.

From Grampa Jack's arms, Addie-Jo dove for the brightly colored Mylar balloon hovering like a guardian angel over two stuffed bears and a fuzzy crocodile. Jack caught her and stepped away. Next, she grabbed for the bouquet of fragrant roses, saying "Smell."

"She's restless. A certain little girl is getting hungry," Grandpa Jack said.

"We'd better head to the ranch," Carol added. "Say good-bye to mommy."

From Grandpa's arms, Addie-Jo's warm little arms circled Kim's neck. A kiss landed damply on her cheek. A warm spot grew in her heart as baby brother and Hank got the same treatment. When the door closed behind them, Kim leaned into the soft pillow and smiled contentedly at Hank.

He kissed her cheek and they held hands in the comfortable way parents do and talked about the baby. She rolled the bottom lip between her teeth to work up the nerve to say, "Hank, I'll marry you." The door opened. Her heart quickened. Mitch?

Wearing big smiles, Harry and Dora Rheinhardt bustled forward.

Kim covered her disappointment with a hearty greeting. Hank tipped his head back and stared at something on the ceiling. Fear nudged her. Did he know she longed to see Mitch? Strained to hear his voice? If Hank did, he hid it with boisterous bragging and determined laughter. Kim prayed silently, "Lord, I don't know what to do. If I need to let him go, please take these feelings or help me hold on if you want me to wait for him."

Christmas Day Kim did her best. She chatted with Trudy about Indiana friends. She asked questions when Myron talked about the technological advances he'd seen at an engineering trade show and when Jack talked about his trap line. She helped Maggie and her Mom in the kitchen and never mentioned Mitch although she thought about him constantly.

A knock at the front door brought a flurry of greetings. Kim hefted Andy to her shoulder and rounded the corner to see if her prayer for Mitch had been answered. A blast of cold, fresh air hit her as Kurt's parents entered. She blurted, "What are you doing here?"

Disapproval washed over Carol's face and Kim tempered her chagrin and tried again, stammering, "What a wonderful surprise. Mother Macomb, Father Macomb, I didn't know you were coming."

"We couldn't resist," her former mother-in-law said.

Kurt's father added, "Forgive us. She packed the bags, and presented me with the tickets this morning. She said she was coming with or without me. Here we are. We didn't even stop at the hotel yet. She wanted to drive straight to Addie-Jo."

As if on cue, Addie-Jo tottered around the corner holding onto the wall. Grandmother Macomb swept her up and smothered her with kisses. "Here's our namesake."

Addie-Jo's protest didn't bother either grandparent. They chuckled and unloaded colorful packages, which, at Kim's urging, Addie-Jo opened.

It took thirty minutes before the newcomers had shed coats and noticed anyone other than their grandchild. Mrs. Macomb hugged Kim, "You look so much better than at the funeral. I hate that you live so far away, but Montana has obviously agreed with you."

"I like it here, but it's been rough. I'm still sorting things out."

Mrs. Macomb chucked Andrew under the chin. "Who's this little one?"

Kim drew a fortifying breath. "This is my son, Andrew Barlow Macomb."

Mrs. Macomb frowned. "But this can't be Kurt's baby."

"No. He's five weeks old. I wouldn't have wanted to shock you like this, but I didn't know you were coming. Let me introduce you to the baby's father, Hank Barlow." She waved toward an empty spot where Hank had been sitting.

"Kim, you're a married woman!"

Immediately Hank's reassuring hands rested on her shoulders. In a calm voice he said, "She's not married. She's a widow."

"Mother," Mr. Macomb put his big hand his wife's forearm. He shook his head to restrain words that might accompany her scathing look.

Kim blinked back tears. "Admittedly, I lost my way for a while. I'm better now."

"We both are," Hank said. He was such a good man, a loyal man. She sent him a look of gratitude.

The heat of Mrs. Macomb's glance slowly chilled. She turned away, leaving Kim feeling like something unpleasant on the bottom of a shoe.

Mrs. Macomb fawned over Addie-Jo, but spoke with clipped phrases as little as possible to Kim. Hank and the new baby were ignored. Mr. Macomb talked with everyone while keeping an eye on his wife who, like a bee, hovered among the guests seeking gossip nectar to strengthen her sting. Frustrated at every attempt she indicated she wanted to leave after two non-festive hours.

At the door, Kim coached Addie-Jo to wave good-bye. The older couple returned the wave and called to the child. As the car navigated the turn-around between the snowbanks, Kurt's mother sent her a contemptuous sneer. Kim reached for Hank. He took her in his arms and she rested her head near his heart.

Chapter Sixty-three – Mitch

On New Year's Day, Mitch stomped the snow from his boots and entered the ranch house. He removed his outer gear and still hadn't heard a sound. Good smells of Christmas lingered in the empty kitchen. He nabbed a few cookies and went into the living room. Gentle, playful nudging produced eye-flutters as beautiful Kim roused from a nap. She wiped her eyes with the palms of her hands, smearing her makeup. She scrambled into a sitting position on the couch and sent him a big smile. "Mitch. When did you get in?"

Reservations disappeared. He grinned. "A few minutes ago."

"I didn't think you were coming back until February."

"I got the congregation interested in helping the Indian reservation this year. I'll finish my internship here. They sent me ahead to ready things for the group to do a building project."

"That's great. Then back to Boston?"

"No. They've already hired someone else. I put my resume in all over and no word yet."

"I can't understand that."

"It's okay, I'm waiting on God. How're you doing? You look great."

Kim pushed her lush dark hair behind her ears. "I look like a raccoon. I'm not getting much sleep these days. Whenever Addie-Jo's not awake, Andy is." There was no whining in her voice and she ended with a laugh. "The other day, I almost fell asleep climbing the apartment stairs."

Mitch cocked his head. Didn't they live at Hank's place? Hadn't Hank and Kim married quietly? Conversations with his Dad and Carol mentioned activities and events, like the baby's arrival but admittedly he'd been in a funk at the turn of events last July and had never asked after more than her health, thinking she was a closed chapter in his life. "You're radiant. Motherhood agrees with you."

"Motherhood is going to be the death of me. It's not an accident babies are born cute. I think that was part of God's plan so they'd survive the first couple years."

"Well, where is the new baby? Where's Addie-Jo?"

"Since the house is quiet, they must still be napping. I hope you don't mind, your old room is a nursery. You can peek in on them if you want. I'm staying right here." She patted the couch pillows still bearing the imprint of her body. "If I get anywhere near my son he'll wake. He's very proprietary."

Mitch understood completely. He was fighting the urge to gather Kim into his arms and profess his love even considering how badly it went the last time. When she yawned, he said. "I'll let you get back to sleep."

The grandfather clock gave a steady tock-tock-tock as Mitch left the room. He stole a last look and, for a moment thought Kim gazed after him with a face filled with longing. His heart jolted. Then she heaved a big sigh and snuggled into the couch. She craved sleep, not him. Maybe he wasn't ready to be home. With Kim here, maybe he never would be.

In his old bedroom a whiff of baby powder mixed with fabric softener greeted him. The light was faint and lingered over Addie-Jo who sprawled on his bed like a miniature fairy princess awaiting a kiss. Mitch tucked the blanket around her. He'd missed playing daddy to her. Now she was well on her way out of babyhood.

A crib, nestled against the wall, held only a stack of clean, folded baby clothes. In the shadows, Hank occupied a rocker, the same wide-seated, hand-carved rocker Mitch's great-grandfather had made. Propped on his chest was a baby boy with dark hair and plump cheeks. A tiny thumb rested against pink lips.

"I wondered how long it would be before you showed, Bronner."

Despite the quietness of the spoken words, the air crackled with hostility. The baby stirred in his father's arms.

"Hello to you, too, Hank."

The baby squeezed his eyes tightly and complained. Hank patted the tiny back and rocked until the child resettled.

Mitch kept his tone conciliatory. "You've got a handsome boy there."

"Yeah. I've got two great kids."

Addie-Jo stretched, yawned, and crawled to the edge of the bed. Mitch greeted her. She shied away, but relaxed as her eyes fell on Hank. She stretched both hands toward him. It was like being stabbed in the heart, but Mitch swung her onto Hank's lap. She snuggled against Hank and hooked her hand around her brother's leg. Big brown eyes like her mother's gazed curiously at him. Mitch patted her cheek. "I've got to find the folks yet. See you, later."

Chapter Sixty-four – Hank

That evening, chairs scraped as the family settled around the long ranch dining table. From his usual seat beside Kim, Hank kept close watch to see if she acted differently with Mitch present.

The savory smell of beef stew rose from a steaming iron pot Jack placed at one end of the table. Carol entered from the kitchen with a platter of hot biscuits stacked high. Heads bowed in prayer. Hank took two biscuits and passed the plate to Kim, adding his own silent prayer of gratitude that Jack and Carol still treated him as one of the family, despite Mitch's presence.

Jack said, "This is the best, to have a full table and be surrounded by family. Mitchell, it's great to have you home. What are your plans for the new year?"

Mitch explained about the end of his internship and answered questions about the building project. He crunched a pickle. "My ordination is May 17th. Keep the date open."

"I'll be available," Carol said. "I won't be taking any more speaking engagements. I've two conferences I need to attend, but then my interests are here at the ranch with Jack."

"Carol promised to run a four-day trap-line with me."

"Venturing into the mountains after your traumatic experience? It must be love." Mitch pointed his spoon at her in a Golden-boy way.

Carol smiled back, charmed. "Your father promises to keep me from freezing. Personally, I suspect he's planning on putting me back in the snow bank because I've changed his life a little too much."

Jack patted his wife's hand. "All good changes every one."

A gnawing ache that food wouldn't fill clawed Hank's stomach. Jack and Carol had the kind of relationship he wanted. Why couldn't Kim look at him that way instead of at Mitch, although to her credit she tried to hide it?

Carol continued, "Also, I hope to be able to help Kim as a babysitter."

Kim's fork clanged against her plate. "Mom, are you sure?"

"Are you kidding? I've been waiting for this since Addie-Jo was born."

Kim licked her lips and raised her napkin to dab tears. "Well, I may need you a lot. Annalee, I mean, Dr. Bradley, wants me to go for my degree in psychology. If I do well and graduate, she's offered me a job. I can room with her and get a babysitter in Bozeman, but I didn't feel it was the right thing. I didn't see how I'd pay for it. If you'd keep Addie-Jo during the week, well it'd be an answer to prayer."

Amid a chorus of supportive voices, Hank kept a poker face. He resumed eating, but no longer tasted the stew. She hadn't told him. Was he being quietly dismissed now his services were no longer needed? He wouldn't be dismissed. The bright excitement receded a bit from Kim's face as her eyes met his. Sheepishly she lowered her head.

Like an fox watches a mouse, Mitch pounced. "You don't look too happy, Hank. Don't you think Kim should finish her degree?"

The room crackled with tension as Hank and Mitch eyeballed each other. Hank said, "On the contrary, if she has the drive and desire to get it done, now would be a good time, especially with her mother willing to care for our kids. I'm starting a new venture, too. It'll demand a lot of my time so I won't be able to watch our kids as much as I have in the past."

He put a hand on the back of Kim's chair. "The plans aren't firm, so we don't want it to be common knowledge, but we've found a building and a backer. Cyrus and I want to offer teens a safe place to interact. We're opening a Christian coffee shop in Free Dance. He and Jessie will offer live musical entertainment and I'll lead Bible studies. We'll have cyber hook-up among other things."

Carol stammered, "When did this all happen? I hadn't heard a word."

"Cyrus and I have been talking about it for months. So far, I've only mentioned it to Kim, since it affects her." Kim blushed and he continued, "I've wanted to get out of the bar since before Andrew was born. Cyrus doesn't want to be tied to a place by himself, since he likes being a cowboy. This combines both our dreams. By the time Kim has completed school, the business will be established and won't demand so much of my time."

Kim's napkin was knotted and twisted in her lap, She was working to hide her surprise and yes, agitation that she didn't know his plans had progressed this far. Good. Maybe she felt she had some claim to him and his confidences.

Meanwhile, Mitch was nodding approval. His eyes held a glimmer of admiration. Could Bronner's concern for Kim and the children be more than romantic rivalry? Maybe promoting solidarity would stop him from pursuing Kim. Hank put his arm around Kim and drew her into a sideways hug. "Things are happening for both of us."

Kim said, "Hank wants to help others understand God meets us each wherever we're at, whatever we've done."

At the end of the table Jack looked around approvingly. "It sounds as if my life is the only one which will stay the same, although I guess with two babies around, I'll have plenty of changing to do."

Chapter Sixty-five - Hank

The push broom slid from its resting place against the wall and smacked the floor echoing throughout the emptiness of the large room. Hank retrieved it and leaned on it as he stared through the dust-filled air. The place didn't look like much, but it would when he was done.

He wrestled the full trash barrel out the door and set it on top of the dirty heap of late March snow that lined the street. The blast of cold air was a wake-up call that he also needed to quit wrestling inside. It wasn't ever going to work out between him and Kim.

He'd made trips to visit her at school. He'd stayed at the ranch on weekends to be near her and the kids, yet the connection they'd shared, built on mutual neediness, dissolved in the force of life much as a flooding spring river eroded the snow banks in its path. Hank drew the toothpick from his mouth and flicked it into the trash bin. Trying to force a relationship wasn't healthy for either of them.

He missed Kim, yet even more, he missed the idea of having his own family. For the sake of a family, he had been prepared to love Kim even when she didn't return that love. If he were completely honest, he'd known since their first date she was in love with Bronner. He'd tried to take what wasn't his. The man would always be first in her heart unless he married someone else, which wasn't likely since he was crazy about Kim even if the fool refused to press his advantage.

Hank returned to the store. Mitch's keep-it-cool, let-Kim-make-the-first-move scheme was working even though it went against the grain of Hank's being and what he'd learned about women in general. "Maybe I'm the fool. There never was anything general about Kim," he said to the empty room.

Kim was getting healthy and going on with her life. Perhaps he'd have a chance at happiness if he'd let go of keeping something he never had. What they'd shared was over and had been long before Andy was born.

For a moment an image like an angel shimmered in the blinding reflection of sun on the snow then advanced toward him through the door. "Why are you looking at me like that, Hank?"

"Oh, Jessie. I didn't know who it was for a moment. The glare blinded me."

She moved deeper into the room. Jessie wore ripped and faded blue jeans and an oversized sweatshirt. Her hair was pulled back into a tight braid. "I came to help. I can clean with the best of them. Tell me what you want me to do."

"Do you do windows?"

"I do windows but you better get this dust out of here first or it won't do any good. First things first. How in the world can you work without music?"

He snorted with gentle amusement. "I don't know. What was I thinking?" He resumed sweeping. Jessie started a CD and carried a second broom to the other side of a room that no longer felt empty. They worked side-by-side until the room gleamed.

Much later, Jessie wrung the rag she'd used to wash the inside of the windows and sat back on her heels. "Well that about does it. Are you going to paint tomorrow?"

"If I can figure out what color I want. Cyrus wasn't much help. I know what I want it to feel like, but I don't know what colors will make it happen."

"What do you want it to feel like?"

"Why don't we go get a burger and I'll tell you all about it?"

"Won't Kim mind?" Long dark lashes framed pale blue eyes that were intent and frank.

Hank looked at his boots, shook his head, and with complete honesty said, "No. Kim's heart belongs to Mitch Bronner and always has. He loves her too. They'll work it out someday. We share a kid and I love Addie-Jo like my own so I help Kim as much as I can, but there is nothing between us anymore. I'm good with that."

In the sparkle of Jessie's blue eyes Hank felt new hope rise.

"Then, let's go eat." Jessie dried her hands on her pants, and twisted her neck to get the kinks out. Her braid swished back and forth. They donned coats and walked to Millie's Diner.

Hank explained how he imagined kids welcomed into an upbeat, teen-friendly place where they'd hear the Truth in a relevant way. Jessie had amazing, workable ideas. After supper they had pie, then more coffee. He told her about his past and about Kim. "I'll always value friendship with Kim. She's a courageous woman and doesn't give up. She keeps working the steps to healing that Dr. Bradley taught. I still have a long way to go to overcome all the effects of what I've lived through, but somehow it no longer feels as if the deck is stacked against me. Knowing what Kim's been through I know there's help for me too. For the first time in my life, I'm certain of God's interest and his help. I haven't had a drink in seven months."

Jessie went a little teary. "That's good," she said. "God is at work in all our lives." As she filled in the details of her story, Hank found they were so different and so alike. She didn't carry all the baggage he did, yet she still understood grace.

Chapter Sixty-six - Kim

In the marvelous warmth of a bright mid-May day temperatures neared mid-sixty. The park near campus was packed with sun-hungry people. Kim stuck her hands deeper into her jacket pockets and closed her eyes with the effort to remember the list of symptoms for bi-polar disorder. She could feel Mitch's presence as she recited them. She chewed gently on her inner cheek. "Did I miss any?"

"No. You got them all."

Mitch lay on the blanket on his side, his Stetson nearby. Every time she looked at him, he was watching her. She uncrossed her legs and batted him playfully. "How would you know? You're supposed to look at the book, not me."

"Kim, I've had enough."

"Okay. Let's finish this section then take a break."

"No. I mean I've had enough of playing big brother."

His face was serious and solemn. Kim fought tears she didn't want to show and bit her lip. "Oh, I see. Are you going away again, Mitch? I'm sorry. That's not fair. I can't expect you to stay around here to help me forever. You're a wonderful minister. Some church somewhere is going to be blessed to get you. Where are you going?"

He bolted upright and grasped both her arms. "Don't pretend you don't understand me. I've loved you since we first met, but you needed time to grieve and then that New Year's you already had Hank."

"It was only our first date."

"But not your last. You wouldn't talk to me at all. When you got pregnant, I thought you'd marry Hank, so I bowed out... Then I thought you needed to concentrate on your school without distraction so I've waited."

His words warmed her and the ball of fear unwound. She studied his face. "You distract me, Mitch, whether you're here or not. I can barely think of anything else, but you."

A strand of hair caught in her eyelashes. She swiped at it and Mitch helped smooth it back. He held her head in his hands. "I need to hear it straight out."

"I love you, Mitch."

His kiss ended further comments until he pulled away. "Will you marry me?"

"Yes."

Mitch leaped to his feet, pulling her with him. He shouted. "We're getting married."

Nearby students took a break from their studies to clap and cheer. Someone yelled, "Way to go."

Kim hunched her shoulders with joy and laughed. "It's definitely the way to go."

Epilogue – Kim

Kim leaned out the upstairs bedroom window of the ranch house and looked over the last minute wedding preparations that were underway. The smell of roasting hog wafted into the late summer air from an open spit. Her mouth watered as she imagined the taste of the sweet and spicy marinade.

Life was like that – sweet and spicy. You didn't get to pick just one, but took it altogether and, with God, it turned out. Not what she'd imagined, but it was good anyway.

Below, Carol was testing the tautness of the lines on the cake tent. She pushed down on the cake table to make sure it was secure as two deliverymen carried in a three-tiered cake.

Kim giggled. It couldn't be any more secure. Beneath the golden-yellow tablecloth, the base was eight-inch concrete blocks stacked to table height and covered with a heavy sheet of plywood.

Carol followed the deliverymen out of the cake tent and zipped the netting shut. She moved to where Jack was arranging chairs for the guests. He held up his hand to stop her questions and his voice floated upwards. "Everything here is secure. Each chair has been sat on personally by Myron or me. You don't have to worry about them collapsing on some little old lady. We also laid plywood sheeting underneath the runway so the bride won't trip or sink into the ground. Of course, there isn't much chance it could happen, the ground is as hard as rock. And Cherry's men did a good job installing the archway. I checked it twice, it's not going anywhere."

"She was very nice to let us use it, even if it meant she had to be here, too," Carol said.

"You know Cherry. She has to be part of everything."

"Do you think the weather will hold?"

"It's dark to the northeast, but it's not going to come this way. Take a look at the white mesh draping and boughs of flowers."

"They look wonderful, Jack."

"Notice despite the breeze they're staying in place? They've been nailed, glued, and wired. Nothing is going anywhere until we forcibly remove it."

Carol hooted, "So that's what the racket was early this morning. Trudy thought you men were ridding us of a skunk invasion."

Jack gathered Carol in his arms. "Pay no attention to her. Everything is going to be fine. No disasters allowed."

"Well, that's it then. Everything is done that can be done."

"Hey you two love birds," Kim called down to them. "You did a great job. It's going to be as perfect as Trudy planned. A piece of cake. And just in time, too. I see guests coming up the road."

Carol startled. "Oh. I've got to get plates on the cake table."

"Grab somebody and have them do it, Mom. Delegate."

"Right," Carol said and returned her daughter's smile.

Jack called up, "How are you doing up there?"

Behind Kim, almost-four-year-old Addie-Jo dashed out of the bathroom. "Mo-om. I'm all wet."

Kim called, "Got to go. Your granddaughter has a mini-crisis." She pulled her head in and tucked her pink flowered kimono about her. She herded Addie-Jo back into the bathroom. "I told you not to play in the water. We'll blow-dry your hair, and re-curl it, but we won't have time to dry your dress."

"But it's wet," Addie-Jo whined.

"It's August. It'll dry on its own and don't you dare lie on the ground or pet an animal or eat anything until I tell you," Kim spoke over the whir of the hair dryer. "There. Now go watch a video with your brother while I put my dress on. Oh, see who's knocking at the door."

Kim headed toward her garment spread out on the bed while Addie-Jo flung the door open.

"Sweetheart, you look beautiful," Jack said. Addie-Jo giggled and spun around. Jasmine followed him into the room as he faced Kim and Trudy and added, "Ladies, everybody is here and the groom and I are about to get in place."

"Thanks," they chorused. Jack left and Trudy, determination etching her face, said, "Kim, we have a problem. Andy won't give up his holster and pistols."

Andy stood with his feet wide apart, his hands on his hips and an equally stubborn frown on his chubby face. A cowboy hat sat back on his head. A black belt with two holsters hung over his tiny white tuxedo.

"Don't worry. Ten minutes is like a year to a three-year-old. He'll be playing with something else by then. Come here, Trudy, and let me fix your lipstick. You smudged it."

"I'll do it." Jasmine said. "You still have to dress,"

Kim picked up her dress. "Where's Addie-Jo?"

Jasmine said, "I think she went out after Jack."

"No," Kim groaned. She tightened the kimono belt about her as she nodded toward her son. "Don't let the cowpoke out of your sight, Jasmine. I'll round up the renegade." She padded to the ground level, calling and searching the rooms. Through the window she spotted Addie-Jo ducking under the netting of the cake tent. She dashed out the back door and pushed past Cherry Jacobs, making apologies.

"Kim, darling, your outfit, how avant-garde. I love it," Cherry enthused.

"Excuse me, I'm chasing my oldest. Talk to you later."

Inside the cake tent, Addie-Jo stood in front of the cake. She turned when she heard her name and gave Kim a big smile. "Isn't the cake pretty?"

"Addie-Jo, did you taste the cake?"

"No mama. You said not to." Addie-Jo looked offended as Kim checked her fingers and dusted a little dirt. There was no evidence of icing.

"I also said watch a video with your brother."

"I forgot."

"Come on. It's time to start. You need your basket of flowers and I still have to put my dress on." Kim hurried Addie-Jo to the bedroom and turned her over to Jasmine.

The opening chords of Cyrus's song floated through the open window. Trudy rushed over, "That's the final song before the wedding march. Kim, let me zip you. Hurry. Hurry. Hurry. This is it."

Kim nabbed three baskets of flowers and pressed one into Trudy's hand. "You're gorgeous, Trudy."

Trudy beamed and hugged her. "You are too. You're like the daughter I've never had."

Kim hugged her back. "And you. You're special. Thanks for —"

"Stop this mushy stuff. You'll make me cry and ruin my make-up."

They laughed and together descended the stairs and emerged into bright sunlight. Carol was waiting for them. She gave her best friend a hug. "Everything is according to plan down here."

Trudy nodded. "Great. Thanks, Carol."

Carol beamed. "What a great day this is." She turned away quickly and signaled the musicians. They started a new song and Carol picked up a bouquet and walked up the aisle.

"Okay, Addie-Jo. Do it just as we practiced. Follow Grandma down the aisle," Kim said, handing a basket to her daughter and starting her down the aisle.

Mitch appeared. "You're stunning, Mrs. Bronner, especially in red."

"You dress pretty well yourself, Reverend. Shouldn't you be up front?"

He pressed a quick kiss on her ear. "I'd rather stay back here and kiss you, but I do have a wedding to perform. Here's a souvenir of the day." He placed six tiny pebbles into her hand.

"What's this?"

"Addie-Jo's cake decorations. I found them in along the bottom of the cake. It's a good thing your Mom sent me in there with the plates."

Addie-Jo was almost to the front of the short aisle. She was taking a long time dropping each petal and if she didn't like where it fell, she stooped and adjusted it, unaware of the amused reaction of the guests. She reached the front and Matron of Honor Carol motioned her granddaughter to stand beside her. The child took her place and with a slight lisp called to Andrew. "Okay, now, brother. It's your turn."

Andy no longer wore the black holster and cowboy hat, but still clutched a pistol in his hand. Every step he pretended, with soft spitting sounds, to shoot the rose petals his sister dropped.

At the third row, he lingered to chat with his daddy and his new step mom, Jessie. Laughter deepened as Grandpa Jack retrieved him and guided him into position.

"I told you they were too young," Kim hissed.

"Oh, pooh. They're adorable," Trudy whispered back. "Our turn."

The music changed and everybody stood for the bridal entry. Trudy minced down the aisle escorted by Kim. Her smile couldn't be any wider. Her eyes stayed locked on the groom, Myron, who stood tall and proud next to Jack.

Mitch stepped forward, greeted the guests, and said, "Who gives this woman to this man?"

Kim replied, "Her church family and friends do."

Myron's dark eyes glowed. He gently claimed Trudy, and led her beneath the archway. Kim settled into a chair in the front row to watch her husband perform his first wedding for this woman who was her mother's best friend and like a second mother to her.

The service progressed. As Myron said his vows, buzzing from a low-flying aircraft momentarily drowned out his words. The plane gained altitude and circled wide. Andy squatted then rolled onto his back and aimed his gun into the sky. "Pow. Pow. Pow."

Not quite in reaching distance of him, Kim hissed, "Andy, stop it."

He pointed his pistol upward and replied in a stage whisper, "I'm shooting birds."

Reverend Mitch said, "You may kiss the bride."

Myron complied. Everyone clapped. When they broke apart he gave a broad smile to his wife and pointed skyward. Fast-falling dark spots blossomed into colorful parachutes. Five jumpers landed nearby and shucked gear to reveal jet-black hair and white jumps suits with sequins. "Trudy, your day is complete. Elvis has arrived."

Trudy clapped and shrieked, "It's too wonderful."

The droning overhead increased as the plane dipped and dove trailing white smoke, skywriting C-O-N-G-R-A-T-U-L-A-T-I-O-N-S! Mitch drew the couple's attention to it. "Kim and I wanted to do something special for you, too. Look."

Trudy, Myron, and all the guests stared into the blue canopy of space where a brisk wind quickly distorted the fluffy white letters until it read, "O RATS!"

The End

A Word from the Author

I hope no one will endure such experiences, but if you do, I pray that you find relief and release in the very real person of Jesus Christ. If you wish to find out more about a relationship with him, please contact me.

www.marymarieallen.com

or

wordgirl_mary.allen@yahoo.com